SHADOWS ON THE HEART

ELIZABETH OLDHAM

Edited by Katie Zdybel, Sophia Dembling and Cheryl Andrichuk
Cover Design by Imran Khaliq

Library and Archives Canada Cataloguing in Publication

Oldham, Elizabeth, author
Shadows on the heart / Elizabeth Oldham.

ISBN 978-1-7388226-2-1 (paperback)
ISBN 978-1-7388226-3-8 (ebook)

Published by Doppia Press
PO Box 143
Castlegar, BC V0G 1X0

ONE

Lita

THE WARNING BELL SOUNDED. Ten seconds left.

Lita launched a frenzy of punches and elbows onto the woman below her, sweat stinging her eyes and blood from her broken nose filling her mouthguard. Her opponent curled up, arms around her head, and the referee moved in and stopped the fight.

Lita released her hold and collapsed onto the mat on her back gulping for air. Kroker and Cap appeared above her, smiling.

Her coach, Kroker, squatted next to Lita. His blue eyes sparkled. "Great job gaining guard. You reversed quickly, didn't give her time to get set up. Kicked her ass, in fact."

"Nice ground and pound, Wildcat." Cap, her sparring partner, threw her a towel.

Kroker pulled her to her feet, and she greeted her opponent with a hug and a handshake. The ref called them to the center of the cage to announce the winner, and as he lifted her hand in victory, a familiar *whoop!* made her search the crowd.

"Way to go, Lita!" Felix stood on top of his seat four rows deep from the circular chain-link cage. He whooped again and swung a bandana in the air above his head. His broad face shone, his smile surrounded by a finely trimmed moustache and goatee, curly hair cut tightly on the sides and gelled on top in an organized swoop.

Her eyes slid to his right and met Oscar's, who grinned, brown eyes dancing. A year older than Lita, jet black hair, and tiny wrinkle lines on the outside corners of his eyes, he looked perpetually happy. He whistled and yelled through cupped hands.

Lita exited the cage with Kroker and Cap. Kroker had two more fighters on the card, so he left after a hug and a clap on the back. Cap followed him, and Lita headed to the locker room to shower and change. After months of training and a severely restricted diet, she wanted pizza and beer.

Plus it was her birthday, and Lita celebrated her birthday like other people celebrated getting fired. Every stinking year she drank to oblivion and blacked out at the end of the night. She hated the day.

She showered and dressed, then sat on the wooden locker room bench, took out her phone and punched in a number, ignoring the pain in her nose. A man answered.

"Hola, chica! ¿Cómo te fue? ¡Feliz cumpleaños!" Cars and children sounded in the background.

"Hola, Papá!" Lita pictured her dad in his tiny yard in Hermosillo, surrounded by her stepmother's flowers and herbs, grandchildren running around. "I kicked her ass. She ate my fists until she curled up into a ball."

"That's my girl. How about you? You sound plugged up. Shoot—hang on." Her dad covered the phone, and a rushing noise filled her ears, all but filtering out the sound of heavy coughing. His voice, when it returned, sounded tired. "Damn cold. I've been fighting it for a couple of weeks. Feels like a cactus lodged in my throat."

"Tell Rosa to give you some of her tea." Her stepmother foisted herbal teas on friends and family like a pusher.

"Hah! She's been filling me up with all sorts of stuff. No bug survives her bitter brews."

Lita laughed and filled him in on the fight. They said good-byes, and she hopped up, wincing gingerly, then grabbed her gym bag and held the ice pack to her nose as she left the locker room. She wouldn't see Kroker and Cap again until she went back to the gym in Tucson.

"Lita!" Felix waved his arm at the entrance with a broad, happy smile. Married to her best friend, Karmen, he was eternally cheerful, a kindergarten teacher with an endless supply of patience and good nature. "Great fight, Lita! A finish on the ground! Karmen says congrats. How's your nose?"

She lifted the ice pack, and Felix whistled. It felt like her face had been slammed by a two-by-four and her nose lit on fire.

"It's seen better days," she said, shifting the bag slung over her shoulder. "I'm starving and need a beer. Where's Oscar?"

"He's outside. Where do you want to go?"

"Pizza and beer." Pizza wasn't on Lita's training menu, so she hadn't eaten it for weeks.

They found Oscar near Felix's truck. He tamped his cigarette out and tossed the butt into a garbage can before wrapping Lita in a big hug. "Congrats, Lita. Wildcat triumphs again!"

Lita felt wired, full of adrenaline. It would take hours to get her sense of equilibrium back, to let go of the tension from days and weeks of discipline and training.

"Happy birthday." His voice was a low murmur.

"Thanks." She dropped her shoulders and relaxed. Even with her broken nose, Oscar's spicy cologne warmed her like sunshine. Embracing him felt comfortable, like hugging her pop, though her dad was shaped like a barrel and only inches taller than her, while Oscar looked more like a long-distance runner, lean and narrow from the hips to the shoulders. Her head fell below his chin.

She squeezed him and stepped back. He shot her a crooked

smile, one of her biggest supporters since they'd met a decade ago after she'd rented a room from his mom.

She felt a flash of guilt—she shouldn't have slept with him last week. Neither of them needed that confusion. She chalked the moment of weakness up to the intensity of the fight prep, fatigue, and anxiety about the fight. She couldn't even blame alcohol, having been dry for the last month of training. If only he weren't so damned easy to be with.

"Okay, let's find some food." Lita threw her bag into the back of Felix's Silverado.

SHE SAT BACK from her plate, stomach full, and sighed contentedly. Two empty pizza pans lay on the table with an empty pitcher of beer, and a second pitcher half-full. At nine p.m., the pizza parlor was dead. Most tables sat empty, though the kitchen seemed to be hopping. Take-out orders, Lita guessed. The fight adrenaline had completely left her, and the combination of beer and exhaustion made her lightheaded. Her shoulders sagged, and she lay her head on the back of the vinyl booth.

"What's next, Lita?" Oscar's sonorous voice roused her. "You taking a break?"

She sat up and swished the beer in her mug, then finished it. "A couple of weeks. Can't spar with a broken nose. But no longer than a month. I'll definitely have time to get those struts changed on your car." A mechanic, Lita worked with Felix's father-in-law and kept her friends' cars in working condition.

"What's the longest you've ever stayed out of the cage?" Felix filled her glass with the pitcher.

Lita thought, then shook her head, igniting a burning pain in her swollen nose. "Shit, I don't know. Maybe a month? I don't feel right if I'm not moving." She didn't have the words to explain how fighting had given her an anchor, had kept her moored in the wake of the rough waters of her life. "And speaking of moving, looks like you guys have stopped drinking. I've got a long tradition of drunken birthdays to uphold."

"I'm driving." Felix said quickly. "You're going to have to get shitfaced with Oscar if you're looking for a drinking buddy."

Oscar slid his mug over to Lita. "I'm your man, Lita. Fill me up."

Lita reached for the pitcher but stopped when her phone vibrated on the table. She didn't recognize the number.

"Hello?" She balanced the phone and picked up the pitcher to fill Oscar's glass. Beer sloshed out as she poured.

"Am I speaking to Lita Bravo?" A man's voice crackled through the poor connection.

"Yeah, I'm Lita." Lita set the pitcher down and lifted her mug in a toast to Oscar.

"My name is Officer Ron Gibbons, and I'm with the San Leandro Police Department in California. I'm calling about Jacob McGovern. I understand he's your brother?"

Lita set the beer down. Warning bells rang in her head. Her mouth suddenly felt dry, and she found it hard to swallow.

"Yeah, Jake's my brother."

"I have some difficult news."

Sweat broke out on her forehead. Oscar drank from his beer. Felix jiggled his leg under the table. They watched her.

The man continued. "Your brother and his wife, Amy, were killed in a car crash last night."

Lita sucked in her breath . "No," she said.

"I'm sorry to tell you."

Not Jake. Not him. On her birthday.

"Your nieces and nephew are at their home in the care of a neighbor, a Mrs. Sandy Wells. You're identified as their legal guardian."

Her brother's face appeared in her mind, his sandy hair and smile, his laugh. How long had it been since she'd seen him?

This wasn't happening. She leaned back against the booth. "Legal guardian? There's no one else?"

"Your mother Evie Long...."

"She shouldn't be taking care of kids." Lita fought to control her voice. Her mother's name brought a wave of unwelcome emotion.

"That's clear and why I've called you."

Lita gripped the phone as he continued to speak. A roar of white noise filled her head. She hadn't seen Jake in more than twelve years. Hadn't even met his kids. While he'd kept in contact with Christmas cards and the occasional phone call, she'd hardly made an effort.

The officer paused, waiting for a response.

"I'm sorry. What did you say?"

"When can you arrive in California?"

Shit.

"Two days."

He rattled off the name and phone number of the neighbor and told her to contact his department when she arrived. "I'm sorry, Ms. Bravo. I know this can't be easy."

"Okay,. Thank you."

She moved the phone from her ear and stared at it in her hand. The last time she'd seen Jake, Amy had been pregnant with their oldest. Jade must be eleven or twelve by now.

"What was that about?" Felix watched her intently.

Oscar touched her hand, still holding the beer mug. "You okay?" he asked.

Lita swallowed. Her eyes burned. She stared at the full mug, then picked it up and chugged it in one long gulp. She started to speak, but the words wouldn't come.

Jake. Dead.

"My brother." Lita choked the words out. Could there have been a mistake? She didn't want to believe it, didn't want any part of this. He couldn't be gone like this. Why the fuck hadn't she been to see him?

Her voice shook. "He died last night. I've got to go to California to pick up his three children."

TWO

Jade

THE HOUSE FELT TOO QUIET. Last night Jade's parents had gone to the city for dinner, and she'd babysat four-year-old Jersey and her six-year-old brother, Jupiter. She'd tried to get them to bed on time, but they'd argued and stayed up way too late. Not wanting to wake them this morning, she tiptoed past their closed bedroom door.

Her parents' bedroom door, however, sat wide open, their bed tidily made. Jade puzzled over this. Her mom usually stripped the bed first thing on Saturdays, laundry day.

"Mom?" She whispered as she proceeded down the hall and into the kitchen. "Dad?"

The house remained quiet.

In the family room, two big bowls lay upturned on the carpet; popcorn littered the floor. An empty two-liter bottle of root beer hung over the edge of the coffee table. She'd been too tired to pick up last night, so she did it now, gathering the bowls as well.

She pulled back the curtains. No car in the driveway. *Where are Mom and Dad?*

Maybe they went to La Crêperie, her mom's favorite breakfast place for their caramelized banana crepes. But Jade couldn't imagine she'd go without the family.

She carried the bowls and bottle into the kitchen and set them on the counter for her mom to wash later. She pulled a box of Honey Nut Cheerios out of the cupboard and shook it, looked inside, and frowned at two lone Cheerios. *Jupiter.* Who else would empty a box and put it back?

A knock sounded like the crack of a baseball bat on the front door, and her hand jerked, letting the box go and sending it flying across the table. She rushed to the front window and hid behind the curtains to peer out.

A police car sat at the curb. Two uniformed officers, a man and a woman, stood on the porch with a woman dressed in black pants and a teal, button-up blouse. The man looked up and down the street, studying the neighborhood, his hands on his leather belt. Like him, the woman officer looked weighed down by her belt and its tools: a gun, billy club, and handcuffs. The non-uniformed woman, a navy messenger bag slung over her shoulder, looked at the window. Jade shrank back, veiled by the curtains.

Why are they here? Her pulse beat wildly, but she remained motionless, willing her mom or dad to come home.

The second knock sounded louder and more insistent.

"Mom? Dad?" Jade yelled out. She didn't care now if she woke Jersey or Jupiter. She wanted someone else to be awake. Her eyes darted to the open door of her parents' room. Where were they? They always left notes when they weren't going to be home.

The male officer left the porch to walk around the front of the house and saw Jade in the window. He made eye contact and pointed at the front door. Jade nodded dumbly. Her stomach roiled as she turned the knob.

The woman officer offered Jade a thin smile. She shifted her weight, her belt creaking. The man stood stiffly, and the woman in plain clothes gave Jade a syrupy smile, too sweet for a stranger. They scanned the living room behind her. At least Jade had picked up the mess.

"Good morning," the woman officer said. "I'm Officer Lyons. This is Officer Giles. We're with the San Leandro Police Department. This is Ms. Richardson with the California Department of Family Services. What's your name?"

"I'm Jade." Her heart pounded, her palms felt clammy. Police didn't visit people for the fun of it.

A door slammed in the hallway, and the officers tensed. Jupiter ran out shirtless with his arms wide like an airplane, curly blonde hair flying behind him. "I'm the Blue Angels!" he yelled. He swooped in a circle behind Jade, then stopped suddenly when he noticed the police at the door. He stared. "Why are you here?"

The officers looked at each other. The plainclothes woman spoke. "Jade, may we come in?"

"My parents aren't home." Her guts started a slow churn. If she let them in, something bad would happen.

Jupiter marched to the door. "Do you have guns?"

The officers smiled at him.

"Are there any adults here, Jade?" Ms. Richardson's eyes searched hers.

Maybe they thought she shouldn't be in charge. "Yes, Nana. But I'm twelve. I passed the Red Cross babysitting training last year." She grabbed her brother's shoulder and pulled him back to her. "This is Jupiter."

"I'm six." Jupiter folded his arms and stared at the officers.

A second door slammed, and Jersey, also shirtless, hurtled down the hallway. Her favorite purple tutu swirled around her chubby hips, and she waved a sparkling wand with silver ribbons streaming from it. Her eyes widened at the officers, and she stopped, grabbed Jade's hand and tugged it.

"Why are they here?" she asked in a loud whisper.

Jade scowled at her sister. "Shh."

Officer Lyons spoke to Jade. "Can we speak with your nana?"

Her parents had always told Jade to let Nana sleep as long as she needed in the mornings, otherwise her sleep pattern became unpredictable. "She's sleeping."

The officers exchanged another glance. "Can you wake her? We'd like to speak with her."

"Go get Nana," Jade whispered, and Jupiter and Jersey scampered down the hall.

Should she let them in? They were police officers. They'd asked to come in. They were strangers, but they were the police. *Where are Mom and Dad?* She wished they'd leave.

"Jade, we'd like to talk with your nana inside the house."

Reluctantly, Jade stepped aside, and the officers entered.

Jupiter returned to the living room. "Nana's coming," he said before he flipped on the TV. He picked up a lone piece of popcorn from the carpet and stuck it in his mouth.

Jersey ran into the room and jumped on the couch. She swung her wand towards the hallway as Nana appeared. "Ta-da!" she sang.

Nana didn't look like she was having what Jade's mom called "a good day." Loose strands of long gray hair, braided down her back, whirled like a storm cloud around a saggy face creased with sleep. The neck of her nightgown hung loosely, exposing a white, bony shoulder. She shrugged herself into a bathrobe and tugged the strap into a knot.

"Nana," Jade said. "These police officers want to talk with you."

Nana's blue eyes lifted to Jade, then widened at the police officers standing behind her. Her head drew back, and she straightened, her body rigid.

"Did you find her? Is she alive?"

What is Nana talking about?

Nana's eyes darted around the room. "Where is she?"

"Nana." Jade began, but Nana ignored her, attention fixed on the officers who looked confused.

Nana pleaded. "The other officer told me you'd bring her home." Her eyes glazed over, lost their focus. She shuddered. "He wasn't nice."

"Ma'am, can you sit down?" Officer Lyons stepped towards Nana, her hand outstretched to take Nana by the arm.

Nana backed away. "No." She looked irritated like she did when Jade's mom tried to make her take a bath.

"She has dementia," Jade said.

Ms. Richardson swung her head to Jade. "Dementia?"

Jade nodded. Officer Giles frowned. Nana's voice sounded shrill in the room.

"If you haven't found her then leave me alone." Nana said. "I told that other officer the same thing, but he kept coming back." She rubbed the sides of her arms, the robe slipping down her shoulder.

"Nana." Jade wished her dad were here. Nana usually listened to him. "They need to talk to you."

"No." Nana shook her head. She backed up to the wall and slid towards the hallway. "I will not hear it." She scurried into the bathroom.

"Jade," Ms. Richardson said. "Is there another adult we can call?"

The morning had spun out of control. Jade felt her legs start to tremble, and she lowered herself to the couch next to Jersey. "My friend Ophie's mom." She recited the phone number, grabbed Jersey onto her lap like a shield, and waited.

THREE

Lita

THE TRUCK BACKFIRED as she pulled up to the curb. She hadn't had time to fix the exhaust valve leak, like so many other things that got postponed when training for a fight. She wouldn't have normally brought the pale yellow 1977 Ford Crew Cab with a camper shell on a fifteen hour drive, but she'd need to bring the kids back with her, something that the Hornet, her motorcycle, couldn't do.

Wiped out by the two-day drive and dreading what awaited, she rested her head and hands on the steering wheel then lifted her gaze and stared blankly at her brother's house. A low green picket fence surrounding a rock garden took up the small front yard, overseen by a large picture window. A paved stone walkway led to a small porch. The stucco had a faded ivory tinge, though it might have been yellow at one point, and a green bird feeder filled with sunflower seeds hung in front of the window.

She took a deep breath, climbed out of the truck and dragged herself up the porch steps. She raised her hand to knock but paused, heart pounding, will faltering. Before she could change her mind, a little boy yanked the door open, curly blond hair sticking up in all directions.

He glared at her fiercely, blue eyes defiant. "Go away," he shouted. "Get out of here!" He threw a piece of bread at her, then slammed the door.

Lita swallowed and ran her hand through her hair. *Fuck.*

A slight, pale woman with a blonde ponytail and a weak smile opened the door. Her eyes widened, and her eyebrows shot up in alarm at Lita's face.

"Oh, wow. Are you okay? Your nose! Sorry, are you Lita?" the woman asked. "I'm Sandy Wells. My daughter Ophie is friends with Jade.

"Yeah, I'm Lita," she croaked, her mouth suddenly dry. "I'm okay. Broke my nose in a match two days ago. An amateur fight. Mixed martial arts."

"Oh, ok." Sandy didn't sound sure. "I didn't realize you'd arrived until I heard the door slam. I'm glad you made it."

Sandy opened the door wider and motioned Lita in. Her smile faltered beneath pinched eyes and a worried brow. She wore a pair of black leggings with a deep heather crewneck sweatshirt that fell to mid-thigh. Her hands fluttered as she spoke. "I'm sorry that we're meeting under such awful circumstances. Jade told me that you live in Arizona. Was the drive okay?"

"Yeah, it was fine."

The smell of ground beef and Italian spices greeted her, and her stomach growled despite its turmoil. The boy was nowhere to be seen. A tattered armchair sat next to a stained wood coffee table, and two pink-and-green neon beanbag chairs lay in front of a dark TV, a row of family photos lining the wall behind it. Jake and Amy with the kids at a pumpkin patch. The family at the beach, windblown hair covering shiny faces. A school picture of a girl with brown hair and brown eyes.

Holy shit, she looks just like Jake.

From behind the couch, a chubby, curly-haired blonde girl stood up quickly, then dropped out of sight. The little boy lifted his head, gave Lita a blazing look, and disappeared.

"I haven't seen much of Arizona, except for the Grand Canyon. Is that near you?" Sandy turned her head and called out, "Jade? Jade, your aunt is here."

Lita's stomach twisted at the prospect of seeing Jake's lookalike. "Bisbee's in the south, far from the Grand Canyon."

"Near the border?"

"Yeah, five miles. I've been there twelve years. Jake used to be stationed at Fort Huachuca in Sierra Vista. He and Amy had just gotten married when I last saw him. She was pregnant, and they were moving to California after his discharge."

She couldn't stop rambling. Lita had thought about nothing on the drive but Jake and her family and their losses, and now those thoughts were pouring out of her mouth to this stranger. "I never made it out here to see him. I'm not so good at keeping in touch. I barely see my dad, and we're only six hours from each other."

Sandy tilted her head at Lita. "Jake's dad is still alive?"

"Different dads," Lita replied.

A door shut in the hallway, and two girls appeared, the first tall and brown-haired with Jake's face, the other blonde and shorter.

Lita hesitated, a tennis ball stuck in her throat. She swallowed. "Hi Jade, I'm your Auntie Lita, your dad's sister."

Jade stared at Lita silently, her eyes swollen and red-rimmed. Lita would have guessed her age as fifteen or sixteen rather than twelve. Tall—about five foot ten—her body was both gawky and curvy. *Like Laurel.* She and her friend both wore blue shorts and shirts, almost matching. Jade had Jake's dusty brown hair which she wore shoulder-length with bangs, and she studied Lita with his brown eyes.

Lita didn't want to look into those eyes, those sorrowful eyes. She knew no words of comfort, only bleak apologies for life, which could be so fucked up.

"I'm sorry Jade. I'm sorry that we're meeting like this. And I'm sorry about your mom and dad."

The corners of Jade's mouth trembled slightly. She swallowed and blinked rapidly but didn't speak, and Lita didn't blame her. What was there to say? Jade clutched her friend's hand, her knuckles white with pressure.

The boy and girl sidled out from behind the couch to stand next to their older sister. The boy glowered, his eyes narrow and sharp, and the little girl stood solemnly on one foot with the other positioned against her shin.

Sandy reached out and brushed Jade's hair out of her eyes with a tenderness foreign to Lita. "Jade's been incredibly strong and helpful."

Jade looked shrunken and lost; her grief hit Lita like a roundhouse kick.

Sandy laid her palm down on the boy's head. "You met Jupiter at the door. And this is Jersey. She's been very brave."

Jersey shook her head and whined. "Why is her face black and blue? And she's dirty."

"She's not dirty, stupid. Those are tattoos!" Jupiter practically screamed at his sister who swung her head and moved to slap him.

"I'm not stupid!"

Whoa. Lita stepped back.

Sandy moved between the kids quickly. "Jupiter, remember your inside voice. Jersey, no hitting." She touched Lita's arm. "It's horrible about your brother and Amy. A tragedy."

Lita tensed at Sandy's touch and pulled her arm away. "Thank you," she said thickly. "Jake was a good man. He had his shit together."

She crouched into a squat in front of the kids even though her thighs burned from the fight two days ago. Was it really only two days ago? She'd rather face a beating than this.

"I'm your Auntie Lita." What more to say? Their naked grief made her hesitate. "I wish we'd met before. Your dad told me all about you. He loved you very much."

Sandy seemed to be waiting for her to do something, and

the kids stared at her, waiting. For what? She'd never prepared for this. She didn't know what came next.

Her stomach growled again, and she welcomed the normalcy of hunger. She stood and glanced around the room, remembering the food she'd smelled when she'd entered the house.

"I'm pretty hungry after the drive. Is there any food?"

Sandy's face flashed relief. "Oh, yes, lasagna. Come into the kitchen and sit down. I'll fix up plates." She went into the kitchen.

Behind a closed door a toilet flushed. The bathroom door opened, and a tall woman with long ashen hair walked out, head down, fiddling with a loose piece of fabric on a long, rustling skirt. She lifted her head and met Lita's eyes.

Lita's head recoiled like she'd been slammed by an uppercut. She took one staggering step backwards. "What the fuck?" Lita whispered.

No.

She stared in disbelief. Brown hair turned salt-and-pepper, blue eyes faded and framed by wrinkles, her body with a slight stoop, a gentle curve to her shoulders that never used to be there. The once-taut dancer, though still thin, sagged. But it was, sure as shit, her mom, wearing a purple, gauzy, layered skirt and a white peasant blouse. A thick braid cascaded over her left shoulder.

Evie's gaze moved from Lita to the children, then to the kitchen where dishes clattered, then back to Lita again. She finally stepped forward, her hand outstretched.

"I'm Evie."

Lita backed up, staring at the hand like a bloody stump instead of five long, manicured fingers.

"I know who you are." A laugh burbled up, a crazed laugh that she cut off before it erupted. It wasn't funny. She couldn't do this. She backed out the front door.

She marched to her truck and slammed her fist down on the

hood, then put her hands on her head and rocked back and forth. *You're tougher than this.* She paced around the truck. *You're tougher than her.*

Eighteen years. She hadn't seen her mom in eighteen years. Her mom didn't recognize her. Why was she here?

The front door opened, and Sandy approached Lita warily. "Are you okay? The kids said Evie disturbed you. She's harmless, really. Dementia is such a challenging disease. Has it been a while since you've seen her?"

Lita stopped pacing and looked at the house. Four children and Evie stared at her from the large picture window. She turned her back on them to face Sandy, who was peering at her cautiously.

"Shit, I'm sorry." Her hands shook as she ran them over her hair. "I don't know how much you know about my family, but we're a bit messed up. I haven't seen my mom in almost twenty years, didn't know she was here. She has dementia?" That explained why she didn't recognize Lita.

"Oh, that makes sense." Sandy sounded unsure. "She's been living with your brother for about two years."

Sandy was being kind. It didn't make sense to most people. But their family had more twists and turns than a corkscrew, and Jake had understood. He'd understood so completely that he'd neglected to tell Lita about Evie moving in with him. Could she still do this? *Fuck.* She needed to talk to Karmen. Or Oscar. Or her dad. *Shit.*

A river of anger rushed through Lita's head, and she felt herself pulled into its currents. She needed to get a grip, and that wouldn't happen here on the sidewalk with an audience.

"Listen, Sandy, I gotta take a drive and think this out. Make a few calls. I'll be back soon."

Sandy looked shocked. "You're leaving?" Her voice rose.

Lita would regret going in there without clearing her head. "Yeah, I'll be back within an hour. I promise."

She escaped into the truck, leaving Sandy aghast at the curb.

She tore through a drab neighborhood of houses, strip malls, and business parks, her thoughts shooting around in her head like fireworks. She gripped the steering wheel to steady herself.

She didn't belong in California. The cement freeways and rows of homes bore down on her, pressed in on her. She drove west towards the water, pulled into the empty lot of a regional park where she could breathe. She called Karmen who answered on the second ring.

"Lita!" What's going on? Are you in California yet? "

"I'm taking a walk. In San Leandro."

"Are you with your nieces and nephew?"

"No, there's a friend staying with them. But Karmen, my mom's there."

"Your mom? Oh my god, Lita."

"She tried to introduce herself to me. I didn't know what to say, so I left."

"What do you mean?"

"She stuck her hand out and introduced herself. I ran out the door."

"Lita! You ran away from those babies?"

Shame filled Lita. But she pictured her mom's outstretched hand, and her anger rose. She latched onto it gratefully. "They're not babies, Karmen. They're children."

"Motherless children! Fatherless children! You walked out on them! What are you thinking?"

Her shame roared back. "I didn't think, Karmen. I reacted." She paced in the lot and ran a hand across her brow then gazed at the water where a dozen birds rose and fell on the swells of the bay in the darkening light. "She didn't know me."

"What are you talking about?" Karmen questioned.

"She's got dementia. She's been living with Jake for two years."

"He didn't mention it?"

"Evie was an out-of-bounds topic. I made that clear a long time ago."

"Oh, sugar. You've got work to do."

"What do you mean?"

"Well, you've got to make amends with your mom. Sounds like she needs someone to take care of her, too."

Anger surged hot in Lita's chest. "I'm not taking care of her."

"Where is she going to go?"

"I don't care. It's not my problem."

"Okay, okay. What about the kids?"

"I barely met them. The oldest, Jade, looks exactly like Jake. The other two are blonde like Amy and my sister Laurel. It's awful, Karmen. I don't know how to act, how to talk to them. Jade stared at me like I was speaking a different language."

"Lita, go back to those kids. They need you."

"Karmen, I don't know how to do this. I'm no good with kids. I don't understand them."

"Kids need love and attention, Lita. They need to know that they're safe. You running out doesn't help. They lost their mom and dad. Grow up! Face your mom and be there for those kids. If your mom doesn't know who you are, doesn't that mean that there's no baggage between you?"

"I can't forget, Karmen."

How could she? Moving from dingy apartment to dingy apartment. Drinking and parties. Evie bringing men home from the bars. Some of the men had been nice. Most had ignored her completely. But not all of them. Evie hadn't kept her safe.

"Lita, you're bigger than her. Don't desert those children because you hate your mama. They lost theirs! Get back to that house and take care of those kids. They need you."

The fireball in her chest flamed out. "You're right, Karmen. Jake never mentioned that she lived with him, and I wasn't ready. Now I know what to expect. I'll adapt. Like a fight."

"Don't you go throwing your mama into an arm bar."

"Since when do you use fighting terms? Don't worry. Defense only here. No attack."

Watching the water soothed her ragged nerves. She *was* bigger than her mom. And she was tough, a fighter. She knew the fear of being all alone at a young age, and she didn't want Jake's kids to feel that. She'd do what was right. Despite Evie. But she needed help.

"Karmen, do you think you can come out here?"

"Oh, man. I used up my leave going to Hawaii last month. But you can do this, Lita. You don't need me."

"What about Felix? I'm going to need help packing and moving everything. Beds and toys and who knows what else." Felix was like a child-whisperer. Kids loved him. "Can you ask Felix? I'll ask Oscar, too."

"That's a great idea. He doesn't have to go back until the week after next. And he's driving me crazy with his handyman projects. He's taken my laundry room apart, and I haven't been able to use my dryer for three weeks!"

"I'll take him off your hands then. Thanks." Lita hung up as the dark slowly crept over the water in front of her. She'd over-reacted. She'd rushed off like she always did, half-cocked and ready for a fight. *Shit.* If only this were something she could fight her way out of.

FOUR

Evie

PHILLIP APPEARS ONE DAY, dusty hair hanging over hazel eyes that lock on to hers when they pair up for a waltzing pas de deux. His smile ignites a low flare in her stomach below her navel, a pilot light that surges into flame when his hand touches her. She stumbles, uncharacteristically. He steadies her, and she tingles from head to toe. Color rises in her cheeks, and his eyes gaze at hers solidly, unwavering in their intensity and unlike any other boy in her studio.

She doesn't tell Daddy about him. Enrolled in ballet as a tot by her mother in an attempt to channel her constant motion, Daddy has never approved. At fourteen, she overheard him talking to the pastor at their church: "I don't like the physicality. Or the outfits. But I guess it's better than softball. It keeps her focused, too. Evie's like a dog in a ballpark. She'll chase anything that catches her eye."

A tall man, Daddy dominates by size alone, but his body is dwarfed by his righteousness. He knows the Bible, and it rules their home. He rules their home. Evie's mom urges her to stay in her place, firmly behind the men of the world. Evie doesn't argue with Daddy.

"Be careful," said Pastor Dan, a man with carefully sculpted dark hair and a body that reminded Evie of a walrus. "Physical dedication can develop self-control, but it can also lead her away from God. In 1 Timothy, Chapter 4, verse 8, God says 'while bodily training is of some value, godliness is of value in every way, as it holds promise for the present life and also for the life to come.' Don't forsake her godliness for dance, Ed."

Daddy sees good and evil, with nothing in between. Their home has Bible verses painted in fancy script on the walls. In the family room, royal blue lettering on eggshell walls: *I can do all this through him who gives me strength.* Philippians 4:13. In the hallway, purple script: *So I say, walk by the Spirit, and you will not gratify the desires of the flesh.* Galatians 5:16.

As a little girl, Evie appreciated the purpose and guidance of these verses, but now, at sixteen, they feel like threats—particularly the one painted in green in the kitchen: *Wives, submit to your own husbands, as to the Lord.* Ephesians 5:22. She already knows that men run things, but are they the same as God, the beacon of safety, security, and righteousness?

Dance captures Evie's soul in a way that God never has. The energy that runs through her body when she dances surprises her, and she wonders if other dancers feel this same passion. The very essence of her being is so wrapped up in pirouettes and jetés that she spends more time in the dance studio than at school. She devotes herself to dance with little room for God, capturing leading roles in the studio's productions. Tall and willowy, she pairs with older dancers, men who lift and catch her fluidly, who guide her promenades. She thinks nothing of these men, only as tools to enhance her dance, like pointe shoes, tights, or hair bun nets.

When Phillip holds his hands up to hers for their first pas de deux, everything changes. She spends every free moment with him. She loves him fiercely, and he reveres her, promises a life together without limits, without the harsh judgements of her father or the confining box of church.

She sees a future with Phillip, a house full of children. When she becomes pregnant, Phillip arrives on a Saturday morning and holds her hand as they face her parents, who sit on the pastel-blue couch in the living room beneath the script painted in teal: *My salvation and my honor depend on God; he is my mighty rock, my refuge.* Psalm 62:7. Her father is stony-faced, his cheekbones sharp, his eyes piercing. He doesn't usually sit and listen; his body is coiled like a spring. The sharp point of his gaze pierces her bubble of happiness.

Phillip's hair is wet; he's come from a shower after an overnight shift stocking shelves at the Market Basket, clean and groomed to meet her parents on these new terms. Forbidden from dating, Evie has told them nothing of him other than that he is her dance partner. But for Evie, dance is life.

She takes a breath for courage. Phillip's hand gives her strength. "Daddy." She chokes on her words. "I, uh…. Phillip and I…."

She swallows and reminds herself: *Pregnancy is a gift from God.*

Her mother's eyes are pinched, her hands clenched together in her lap, white knuckles straining. Evie's father sits on the edge of the couch, Bible in hand to smack down the devil.

She forces each word out. "Phillip and I love each other. I'm going to have a baby, and we want to get married."

Her mother covers her face with her hands. Her father straightens and stands in one fluid motion, grabs her by the shoulders, and squeezes hard. She cries out, and he shakes her, his face inches from hers, ablaze with anger. He raises his hand, and Phillip breaks Ed's grip and steps between them.

"Don't touch her." His voice is strong, his back straight.

"Daddy, it's a blessing." Her voice shakes. This isn't what she imagined. A sob escapes. In a tiny voice, she appeals to her father. "You said all things come from God. This is God's will."

"Don't talk of God, Evie. You've forsaken Him." He speaks through gritted teeth.

She feels unmoored, adrift on a raft in a choppy sea. She's

her daddy's girl, obedient and respectful. "Daddy," she whispers. "We love each other. Heart and soul."

"Your soul is forfeit." His eyes blaze, and he clenches and unclenches his jaw before speaking again. "You're seventeen. You're unmarried. Defiled. You've cursed yourself in God's eyes, and disgraced our family."

Evie's body feels numb. When she looks at her father, at his full six foot three height rigid with anger, she wonders for the first time if God truly cares. If so, how could this have gone so wrong?

Phillip wraps his arm around her shoulders, and she shrinks into his embrace. He stands tall beside her. "Mr. Jameson, Evie and I are going to be married. I love her."

Her father looks at Phillip in the same way that he'd look at dog mess on the floor, his lip curling. "Then do it. She's yours. She's no longer our daughter."

Evie's ears ring, and her face burns. "Daddy," she says, her voice cracking. She releases her arm from Phillip's waist and steps towards him cautiously.

Her father turns his back and folds his arms across his chest. "Get out of our house," he says coldly over his shoulder. "Gather what you need and leave. You are dead to us."

Evie stares at his back. She wants to grab his arm and turn him around. She's his little girl. How can this be happening? Where is God's love in all of this?

"Mom?"

Evie moans when her mom refuses to look at her.

"Fifteen minutes." Her dad marches across the living room and opens the front door beneath the verse in yellow: *For it is by grace you have been saved, through faith—and this is not from yourselves, it is the gift of God*—Ephesians 2:8. "This door will not open to you again. Once you pass through here, do not return."

"NANA!"

The voice startles Evie. The girl, brown haired and stormy-faced, stands hands on hips, surrounded by packing boxes and suitcases. Evie blinks. The girl is familiar.

"What?" Evie asks.

The girl's frown deepens. "Auntie Lita went to the airport to pick up her friends to help pack boxes and move us. But I don't want them in my room. I don't want them here at all. I don't want to move. Why can't we stay here?"

Evie wants to rid the girl's face of its sadness. "It's okay, sweetie. Moving's not a bad thing. We get fresh starts in new places."

The girl's voice breaks. "All of my friends are here. And this is where Mom and Dad are."

Evie ponders this. "I didn't want to leave my mom and dad either. But sometimes we aren't given a choice." She wants to say more about this, make a connection. But she stops, mouth open, mind empty.

The girl slumps her shoulders and falls to her knees, her shoulder leaning against the bed where Evie sits. "Nana, you're going to stay with us, aren't you? Auntie Lita can't make you go away, can she?"

Evie isn't certain. A fog drifts over her certainty about anything, obscuring meanings. This girl, for example. Evie's heart lifts when she sees her, but her mind can't tell her why. She struggles daily to connect what her body feels with what her mind hides from her, experiencing moments of clarity and total obscurity. Shadows on her heart. She feels ten steps behind.

"I'd like to stay with you," Evie says.

The girl's tone shifts. "Auntie Lita doesn't know anything about us." Her voice breaks on the last word, and she rests her forehead on the bed. "She's taking us to Arizona without a choice, but I'll make her want to send me back to California."

"Who?" Did the girl say Lita?

"Auntie Lita." The girl's long sigh tells Evie she's lost something critical again. "Your daughter."

"Lita? My daughter?" Evie's life is proof that God has cursed her. She's lost so much, including her little girl. "You saw Lita?"

The girl sighs again, and her head drops back down onto the bed. *A bit dramatic.* She approves. Drama makes life interesting.

"Ugh. Nana, She's here."

"What? Where?" Evie stands quickly, looking around the room.

"No, not here, here. In California."

Evie steps towards the door. "I'll go find her."

"Nana, she's at the airport."

Evie's irritation grows. "I'm going to check." The girl follows, sighing deeply as Evie walks into the hallway. Ignoring the photos that line the hall, she marches into the living room. Empty. She proceeds into the kitchen, also empty.

Odd. Everyone has disappeared.

"She's gone," she says to the girl.

"No, Nana. She's at the airport."

"Lita's missing. I've got to call the police officer. He gave me his number." She shivers despite the heat. She wishes she could avoid the officer's daily visits—she's thought about refusing to answer the door—but no one else is helping her.

Outside the kitchen window the swoop of two humming-birds by a hanging glass feeder catches her attention. "Where's the woman?"

The girl narrows her eyes. "Which woman?"

"The one who watches these birds. She lives here." Evie studies the girl and remembers. "Your mother. Where is she?"

The girl's eyes shoot to the hummingbird feeder. Evie looks again. The birds are gone, and tears are rolling down the girl's cheeks. Evie's heart hurts at the pain in her eyes, and she steps forward, her arms open. "Come here."

The girl wraps her arms around Evie's waist and shakes silently. Evie's own cheeks dampen with tears. She has no idea why but also no time to think about it, because the front door opens and a little boy runs into the house, followed by a little girl. The children begin circling them, clamoring for attention. The older girl releases Evie and wipes her face with the back of her arm.

"Jade! Look!" The little girl holds her hand out, a sparkling gold rock on her palm. "Oscar gave it to me."

The boy hops around the two of them, holding his own rock up for inspection. "Mine's calcite!"

"I'm getting out of here," Evie says. The little ones tire her. She walks through the living room and out the wide-open front door. A reedy, dark-haired man smokes a cigarette at the bottom of the driveway. Lean and sharply dressed in a pair of jeans and a button-down shirt, he flashes a grin, and his eyes sparkle. Evie moves towards him but is stopped by a hand on her shoulder.

"Watch out, Evie. Felix is backing up the U-Haul." The hand belongs to a small, tattooed woman who directs the truck with her other hand.

"He can't park here." Evie's never seen the vehicle before.

The woman dismisses her. "Don't worry about it."

"You don't live here."

"You're right. I don't live here." The woman removes her hand from Evie's shoulder, and the U-Haul stops at the top of the driveway. The driver exits the truck and tosses the keys to her. "I'm here to pack up this house."

Pack up the house? Why? The man at the bottom of the driveway tamps his cigarette against the curb and straightens.

She approaches him. He holds the butt in his left hand and smiles.

"I'm Oscar." He offers his free hand with a smile and an open face. Evie's braid has loosened so that strands of hair have fallen into her eyes. She pats her hair down with one hand and shakes his hand with the other.

"I'm Evie," she says. He smells of spicy cologne, his hands smooth but tough. Leathery. "Are you from around here?"

He shakes his head. "No, I'm here to help Lita. Felix and I flew in from Arizona."

"I like your smile," she says.

He reddens slightly, and his smiled broadens. "Thanks. It doesn't cost anything to smile."

Evie agrees. She's dismayed when he drops her hand. He watches the tattooed woman walk up the porch steps and into the house. "Is she yours?"

He looks startled. "She doesn't belong to anyone," he says.

"Your eyes follow her." Evie observes.

The man's mouth twists, and his eyes dart to Evie's, then back to the front door. "She's why I'm here. Felix and I came to help her. She's a friend of ours," he murmurs.

"I see." Evie watches the second man, who stomps his feet on the welcome mat and walks into the house. "Every woman needs a man. Even if she doesn't know it."

He laughs loudly, and Evie isn't sure of the joke.

"You smell good," she tells him.

He puffs his chest out and beams. "That's good to hear." He holds his arm out to her. "Let's go inside."

She slides her hand into the crook of his elbow, and they walk up the driveway together, Evie smiling inside. A good man makes a woman stronger.

FIVE

Jade

JADE GRIMACED at the sound of the blender. *Mom is being way too loud.* Then the past few days rushed back to her, and she moaned. *Mom.*

Mom was gone. She had an aunt now. A strange aunt who'd turned the house into a foreign place. Auntie Lita barely cooked anything, but the kitchen looked wrecked all the same, the sink filled with dishes, the counter littered with half-empty cartons and drinking glasses. Her aunt's friends had taken over the living room with their luggage and their smiles, smiles that hurt Jade. How could they smile at her like that?

Felix, the stocky one with the goatee, had a friendly face and an infectious laugh. Jupiter, captivated, had been shadowing him since they'd arrived yesterday. Oscar was quieter, not as outgoing but still friendly. But while Felix's attention focused on her brother and sister, Oscar's eyes followed Auntie Lita everywhere.

She remembered the last time her dad had spoken about Auntie Lita. He was watching a mixed martial arts fight on TV while she sat in front of the couch and worked on a puzzle.

"Your aunt's a fighter like these guys, Jade—mixed martial

arts. I watched her fight once, right before you were born, and it blew me away." He sounded proud.

"How come we've never met her?" Jade asked.

"She's not a huge California fan—too much traffic and too many people."

"But doesn't she miss you and Nana?"

"That's a big question with a long answer." Her dad patted his legs, inviting her onto his lap.

She hesitated—she was getting too big after all—but climbed up anyway. He smelled like Old Spice—a familiar, comforting scent.

"You remember that my dad and brother—your Grandpa Phillip and Uncle Randy—died when I was thirteen?"

Jade nodded.

"We lived in Mexico at the time, and Nana brought us back to California the next year. Quite a culture shock. She'd never held a job before, and none of us fit into life or schools here."

He jiggled his leg, and Jade giggled and put her head on his shoulder. "We had a rough time adjusting, my sisters especially. Nana struggled too. I wanted a different life, so I joined the army when I turned eighteen. Laurel left shortly after me, and Lita decided to go live with her dad."

Jade frowned. "What? What do you mean?" That didn't make sense. "Wasn't Grandpa Phillip her dad?"

"Auntie Lita has a different dad in Mexico. And she never came back to California, never saw Nana again."

"What?" Jade was amazed at this news. "Why does she have a different dad? How could she not see her mom? I'd never leave Mom."

Jade couldn't imagine a life without her mother's hugs, or her banana pancakes, or her bright, tinkling laugh.

"Questions for another day, sweetie. Maybe we'll take a trip out there next summer. Your mom and I met at Fort Huachuca, near where Auntie Lita lives. It'd be fun to visit the old stomping grounds."

They never took that trip. Shortly after that conversation, Nana started showing signs of trouble. Her phone got disconnected because she hadn't paid the bill. Then, on Thanksgiving, she arrived shivering and coatless, accompanied by a neighbor who'd seen her run the car up the curb and into the juniper bushes in front of his house. She moved into Jade's room that week.

IN THE KITCHEN Oscar washed dishes and Felix flipped pancakes.

"Good morning, Jade." Felix said. He spoke with a smile.

"Good morning," she said gruffly.

Oscar gave her a shy grin. "Morning, Jade," he said.

Jade didn't smile back. Their presence meant the end of her life in California.

Auntie Lita was alone in the backyard with a cup of coffee, gazing at the roses that Jade's mom had tended and adored. Her aunt looked tiny from this angle, and Jade could hardly believe she was related to her dad. Like Jade, her dad had been tall and fair-skinned with straight brown hair and brown eyes. But Auntie Lita couldn't be more than five feet tall, and her short hair—the part that wasn't dyed in a red skunk stripe—looked almost black. From neck to toe, tattoos decorated her body, taut with muscles in droopy basketball shorts and a T-shirt. How could her dad have forgotten to mention the tattoos?

Her aunt approached the glass hummingbird feeder sparkling in the sunshine outside the kitchen window. She reached her hand up to turn it, the colorful purple-and-gold patterns swirling around the orb.

Jade ran out the back door. "Don't touch that!" she cried.

Auntie Lita whipped her hand away and whirled around in surprise. "Whoa! Sorry, just admiring it. It's beautiful."

"It's my mom's, and it's fragile" Jade didn't want Auntie Lita to touch it. Her aunt didn't take care of things—the mess in the kitchen a prime example, her yellow truck with its rust spots and cracked windshield, another.

"What are you going to do with my mom's things?" The words rushed out of her. She'd never cared about her mom's knickknacks and wall hangings, but now they mattered. If she didn't keep it all, would she lose her mom completely?

"We'll pack up everything you want to keep. Maybe it's a good idea to take this down now so we don't forget it."

Jade didn't want to think about packing, and she wouldn't help with any of it. "I'm not packing. I'm going to Ophie's today."

A frown flashed on Auntie Lita's face then quickly disappeared. "Uh… oh. Well, I was hoping you could stay home to watch your brother and sister. I'm meeting with the lawyer, and I'm not sure Felix and Oscar are ready to be solo with the dynamic duo. What do you think?"

Jade looked at Oscar in the window, head down as he scrubbed a dish in the sink. He'd immediately gained her brother's and sister's trust with the gems he'd given them. And he'd given Jade a piece of turquoise, something called Bisbee Blue found only in one specific corner of Arizona. He'd pointed out rust-like spots amidst the distinct blue/lavender veins running through the stone, and she'd begrudgingly admitted it was amazing.

Felix and Oscar seemed better suited to handling kids than her aunt. What kind of person fights in a cage?

"I'm going to Ophie's. I'm not a built-in babysitter." Jade surprised herself. But she wouldn't make anything easy for Auntie Lita. She wanted to stay in California, to live with Ophie's family.

"Alright then. The boys it is." Auntie Lita scanned the backyard, her eyes moving across the dry lawn and the toys scattered across it. "See anything else out here that you want to keep? Tomorrow I'll take away whatever's not packed. We'll leave the day after.

Take away their stuff? The day after tomorrow? Her parents had barely been gone a week.

Jade stood on tiptoes and removed the birdfeeder from its hook. "I'll pack this."

She cradled it carefully in her hands and walked into the kitchen, to the sink where Oscar moved aside and dried his hands. He watched her empty the nectar from the feeder and wash its glass bowl with hot water.

"That's a pretty feeder," Oscar said in his low voice. "Looks like handblown glass. Have you ever seen anyone blow glass?"

She shook her head.

"I have a friend in Bisbee who's a glass blower. The process is intense. He does a lot of beautiful work, but I've never seen him do anything like this. This marbling is crazy." He peered at the piece as Jade carefully dried it with a dish towel. "If you're ever interested, I can take you to his studio."

"Oh… yeah, maybe." Jade excused herself and carried the feeder into her bedroom, not wanting to risk it getting knocked over in the kitchen. She looped the nylon cord over the corner of her mirror where it hovered like a speckled moon above the circle of ceramic fairies.

Auntie Lita appeared in her bedroom doorway. "Hey, kiddo," she said. "I know you're going to your friend's, but can you pack your travel bag first? Oscar and Felix are going to pack what's left today. It's a two-day drive to Bisbee, and you'll need a change of clothes and a toothbrush."

"I don't want them to pack my room."

Her aunt studied her. "Someone has to do it. And unless you get it done before you head to Ophie's, they will." She stepped into the room and scanned it, her eyes falling on the empty boxes at the foot of the beds. "Your grandma's no help. Is there anything that you don't want to keep?"

Though she had several sets of clothes that had become too small, she wouldn't throw them away on her aunt's orders. "I want to keep it all," she said. "I don't want them to touch my room."

Auntie Lita started to argue but instead grimaced. "Jade, I need some help here. The guys won't know what's yours and what's your Nana's."

"Nana's almost six feet tall! We have separate dressers! How could they not know?" Jade's voice rose hysterically. "I don't want them touching anything of mine."

"So you'll do it all yourself? When?"

Jade felt a twinge of satisfaction at her aunt's annoyance. "Tonight. After I get back from Ophie's."

Auntie Lita's mouth twisted and she sighed. "Jade, please pack your travel bag, and we'll get the rest done for you."

"No! I'm not packing right now. And don't touch anything!" If she resisted long enough, maybe her aunt would change her mind and let her stay in California.

"Well, at least eat breakfast before you go. Felix made a stack of pancakes."

"I'm not hungry," Jade said. She turned off the light and left Auntie Lita alone in the room then marched out the front door headed to Ophie's.

SIX

Lita

———

THE OFFICE HAD dark paneling and burgundy furniture. A leather armchair and loveseat faced an imposing desk. Credentials and degrees hung on the wall behind it, books filled floor-to-ceiling shelves on either side. Lita had only seen this type of office in the movies. The tall ceilings made her feel smaller than usual. She cracked her knuckles as the lawyer looked over the papers in front of him.

She'd brought all the documents she'd found in a box in Jake's closet—birth certificates, passports, tax paperwork—but the lawyer had focused primarily on Jake's and Amy's wills, and a document giving Jake power of attorney over Evie's affairs.

Mr. Donavan had a body like lumpy mashed potatoes and long white hair in a ponytail. His suit coat hung askew on round shoulders. His tie was loosened and his collar unbuttoned. He'd greeted Lita politely, blue eyes widening at the faded bruises on her face.

"You've been identified as sole custodian of the children in both wills." He straightened the papers on his desk and folded his hands on top of the stack. "It's straightforward, as there are no other close family members except your mother, Evie Long."

Lita's stomach plummeted like a boat between swells. She'd

hoped he'd have found someone else, that there'd been a mistake and she'd been misidentified as an appropriate guardian.

"Amy didn't have any family?" She managed to speak despite a lump in her throat.

"No, her parents are both gone, and she was an only child." He flipped to the next sheet of paper and looked up. "Both your brother and sister-in-law had significant life insurance policies, which you'll be able to access, and which should assist you in caring for the children."

Lita should feel relieved. Adding the kids to her household on a shop mechanic's salary, good as it was, would have been tough. But money was not her primary concern.

"What about Evie?"

"You'll receive a transfer of power of attorney for your mother which could become more complicated if you take her out of California."

Lita fidgeted. She didn't want to be saddled with her mom. Her leg bounced nervously, and she picked at a loose thread on her shorts. "Yeah, well, I can't stay in California. Is there anywhere else she can go? What are the options?"

The lawyer's meaty brow rose above his bushy eyebrows. "Nothing that you'd want for your mother. She's unable to live independently, so the only option is to place her in a care home. Senior Services will become involved if she's abandoned, but it's not an immediate process. She'd be a ward of the state, which I wouldn't encourage. There's not enough funding to take care of everyone who needs help. That said, if you're willing to wait for your brother's house to sell, you should have a chunk of cash to invest in her care at that point."

Lita liked the sound of that, though it meant Evie would be with her in the short term. "Alrighty, let's get the house listed and put her on a care home wait list. What do I have to do?"

. . .

FROM THE TRUCK in the lawyer's parking lot, Lita called her dad.

"Hola mija."

"Hey Pop." Lita felt nervous. It had been years since she'd spoken to her dad about Evie. She tried to keep the quake out of her voice. "I need some advice."

"Que paso chica?"

Lita told him about Jake's death and meeting his children, then filled him in about Evie. "She's completely out of it, doesn't know me. And the lawyer says if I don't take her, she'll go into state custody. So I'm taking her to Bisbee until I sell Jake's house.

"But you know what, Pop? I can't bear to look at her. I don't want to be around her. She didn't take care of me, so why do I have to take care of her?" Her voice broke, and she cursed herself for sounding weak. Karmen had told her to grow up, but she felt like a child around her mom. Why was that?

Her dad didn't say anything and she thought maybe the connection had been lost. She was about to speak when his voice croaked over the line.

"Chica." He paused. "Listen." He paused again. "It doesn't matter if she knows you or not. She's your mother."

Lita felt her anxiety spike. "But Pop...."

"Your mom loves you."

"How can you say that?"

"Your mama got lost. I think she's always been lost. Now tell me again why you're in California."

"Because Jake's kids are orphans. I'm all they've got."

"Because you're their family. They need to be with family." He paused then let out a dry, hacking cough.

Family? "Okay, I get it."

She did, but she didn't like it. She also didn't like the sound of her dad's cough. "Pop, are you still sick?"

"Yeah, you're hearing the tail end of this cold. There's a piece of it hanging out, that's all."

"Take a few days off then," she said, knowing he wouldn't.

"Believe me, Rosa's been saying the same thing. But I can't sit at home, chica. I can't sit still that long."

Lita understood. She preferred motion, couldn't sit still to read a book.

"Alright but take care of yourself. And tell Rosa and everyone hi. I have no idea when I'll be back out there." Not with all of this going on. She couldn't imagine how she'd make it to work each day with four dependent people in her household. She'd think about that when it came time. "Te amo, Papá."

"Te amo, Mija."

SHE RETURNED to half-filled boxes scattered across the living room floor and no one in sight. Following the sound of laughter to the backyard, she found Evie on a lawn chair with Jersey on her lap, sitting next to Oscar and smiling, watching Felix and Jupiter with horseshoes in their hands. Evie looked so old.

Felix stood far back against the wall of the house and tossed his horseshoe which landed short of the stake. Jupiter lined himself up with Oscar's lawn chair, much closer to the stake, and threw his last one. It fell on top of Felix's.

"I won!" Jupiter shot his arms into the air and ran to the pit to inspect the horseshoes.

Felix grinned at Lita. "Hey, Wildcat," he said. "We're taking a break from packing. Jupiter requested horseshoes, and Jersey requested a dance party."

"Her name's Auntie Lita." Returning from the pit, Jupiter eyed Felix. "And I beat you!"

"Winning isn't everything. And Wildcat is your aunt's fighting name." Felix crouched slightly as he talked to Jupiter. "People can have more than one name, you know. That's why your name is Super Juper."

"Super Juper?" Jupiter's face lit up. "How did I get that name?"

"Because it fits." Oscar chimed in. "Except I'd call you Super Duper Juper."

Jupiter's eyes sparkled. He opened his mouth to speak but instead his face turned red and crumpled, and he looked down. His breath hitched in tiny gasps, his shoulders quaking.

Felix looked at Lita in alarm, then put his arm around the little boy. "Hey, hey, Jupiter. Why are you crying, buddy? Did I say something wrong? I'm sorry, chico. It's okay."

Lita felt inept. She had no idea how to handle a crying boy.

Felix lifted Jupiter's chin with a finger and stared into his eyes. "What's wrong, buddy?"

Jupiter's mouth was a jagged gash in a puffy face. He spoke haltingly. "I want… to tell… Daddy… about… my nickname." He squeezed his eyes shut as his face buckled. He rubbed tears off his cheeks and lifted wounded eyes. Lita's heart broke at his naked grief. "But… I can't."

Jersey's lip trembled, and she also began to cry. "I want Mommy. Is Mommy coming back?"

Evie wrapped her arms around the little girl. "She'll be home soon, sweetie. She's probably running errands."

Jupiter sobbed. "She's not! She's not running errands! She's with Daddy, and they're dead!" His voice turned into a wail. "I want my Daddy."

Lita ached for her niece and nephew and ached for her brother and Amy. She watched uselessly as Felix hugged Jupiter and Jersey buried her face in her Nana's neck and bawled. Lita had no tools for this. She couldn't wrestle or strike her way out. She only hoped she didn't make it worse.

JADE ARRIVED home after dinner and marched through the living room and straight to her bedroom without a word.

Evie's head swiveled from the front door to the hallway

where Jade had disappeared, her eyes wide, her mouth agape. "Where did she come from?"

"She was at a friend's house. She's...." A crash and a scream interrupted Lita.

She ran to Jade's bedroom where Jade knelt, red-faced, shards of colored glass from the shattered feeder on the carpet around her.

Jade shrieked louder when she saw Lita. Her shoulders shook and tears streaked down her face as she held up the pieces. "It's broken!" Her voice, shrill and unhinged, filled the house.

Lita sensed the rest of the household behind her. "Jade, I'm sorry..." she began.

Jade screamed again, a piercing sound that hurt Lita's ears. "You made me do this!" Her whole body shook with deep, gulping gasps.

Lita moved towards her slowly, hands open as if approaching a wounded animal. "Jade, I'm sorry. We can find another one."

"No! We can't!" She stared at the pieces of colorful glass and picked them up, dropping shards into the palm of her hand. She lifted her eyes, and the pain in them made Lita want to retreat. Jade's voice dropped to a whimper. "It was her favorite."

She let the glass pieces tumble onto the carpet and sobbed, her face a red, blotchy mess. She curled into a ball on the floor and covered her face with her hands.

Lita knelt beside her cautiously and softly touched her shoulder. Jade shrieked and scrambled out of reach. "Get away!" She wrapped her arms around her knees and rocked back and forth as she gulped and sobbed. "Don't TOUCH me. I DON'T EVEN KNOW YOU!"

AN HOUR LATER, with the little ones in bed, Evie and Jade in their room, and Felix on the phone with Karmen in the backyard, Lita sat on the couch with Oscar in the living room, exhausted.

"I feel like I just finished a five-round fight. Is it always going to be like this?" she wondered aloud.

Oscar's lips thinned into a sympathetic grimace, and he gave his head a quick shake. "Nah, Lita. These are early days. It'll get better."

Lita had experienced enough loss in her life to doubt that. "I hope so. And thanks for coming out to help."

"We're your family too, Lita." His face softened as his eyes met hers. "I'm always on your side."

"I don't know what I'd do without you guys," she said honestly. The days before they'd arrived had been brutal. The kids' sorrow never ended, rolled from one day into the next, and Evie's presence threw a wrench into it all. "They're so lost."

Oscar reached his hand over and massaged the back of her neck. "Death turns the world into a threat. You need to make them feel safe."

"The world is a threat, Oscar." She tilted her head forward as his fingers released some of her tension. "No getting around it."

"It doesn't have to be. Your brother did a good job of protecting them. Why not you?"

"Yeah, Jake did normal better than any of us. I don't know where he got it." She laughed a dry, humorless laugh. "Evie didn't exactly set us up for a normal life. When I started kindergarten in California, I had no idea how to sit still, stand in line, or walk instead of run. I couldn't figure out how all these kids knew what to do. I still don't understand how everyone knows what's right all the time."

"They don't. They just act like it." Oscar ran his fingers down the back of Lita's skull where it met her spine. Her nerve ends tingled, and she shivered. "Everyone's figuring it out as they go along, just like you."

"They sure as hell seem confident."

"When you enter the cage for a fight, do you act scared?"

"Hell no," Lita scoffed. "I cast the evil eye and throw a few practice punches."

"Exactly. Everyone does it in their own way. We all fake it. But eventually it'll feel right. You'll grow into it." Lita groaned, and Oscar removed his hand from her neck and wrapped his arm around her shoulders, bringing her in for a hug. "It's overwhelming now. But you'll find your way. I have complete faith in you."

"You're the only one." She murmured into his chest. "Jade certainly doesn't." The weight of her niece's sorrow pressed in on her again. She closed her eyes and took a deep breath. "But I hear you. Fake it until I make it."

"Something like that," Oscar replied. "And remember, we're here to help."

"Yep, saving my ass. I'd be lost without you guys."

SEVEN

Evie
———

THEY MARRY AT THE COURTHOUSE, her and Phillip. Married! She's a married woman!

Mrs. Phillip McGovern. They move to Mexico. Born to missionary parents in Chihuahua, Phillip speaks Spanish fluently and has always wanted to go back. "I want a simple life," he tells her.

Simple or not, she wants any life with Phillip. She's a wife, soon to be a mother. She can teach dance. She'll learn to cook. She'll bake Phillip's favorite treats. Maybe she can teach English. Everyone wants to know English, don't they?

Perdido, a small village one hundred miles north of Hermosillo on the Sea of Cortés, in the Sonoran Desert, becomes their home. By the time they move into the small, cement-brick house with a slanting metal roof that's hot as a griddle in the dry summer heat, she's eight months pregnant, swollen and heavy like a water-soaked stuffie. Though the house has no running water, a pump tap on the property draws cold, clear water from deep in the ground.

People typically don't rent here, Phillip tells her. He found this place through his parents' missionary friends, a rarely used respite home with the basics: two rooms, scant but tidy furniture, and a small kitchen perfectly adequate for her limited cooking skills. He uses their van as a delivery vehicle, contracting himself out as a driver to bring supplies and special orders from Hermosillo to their little village, occasionally taking a neighbor to the city for a medical appointment.

She decorates the walls with pages from magazines. Phillip brings home an ancient sewing machine, and she begins to sew. Hours formerly occupied by pirouettes and pliés are now filled with cotton and chiffon, light fabrics for the desert heat. She picks out patterns from catalogues and sews baby clothes and T-shirts, curtains, and long, flowing skirts.

Local women bring over food and introduce themselves. Though her Spanish is rudimentary, their interest and kindness touch her. They share baby clothes and food. Stories, too, most of which fly past her in a jumble of Spanish.

She marvels at her new life. Her house. Her husband. And when Jake opens his little blue eyes for the first time, her heart swells with a love so strong she cries. It happens again when Laurel arrives two years later, and Randy after another three years. She sends announcements to her mother and father but receives no response. No matter, she loves her children, her husband, and their little house with the view of the sea at the end of the road.

Then Phillip tells her he must travel farther and longer to keep up with the expenses of their growing family. "We're barely making ends meet, but I've got a line on a new contract which can change things up for us."

"We have everything we need," she protests, nursing Randy on the rattan couch while Laurel naps and Jake silently pages through picture books. "What are we missing? What don't we have?"

Phillip can't sit still. He paces around the room. "Why should we tread water when we could be swimming, Evie? I don't want to survive. I want to thrive! I've made connections with guys who need drivers to cross the border. The pay's much better than I've been getting on these supply and taxi runs."

The border? This doesn't sound good to her. "It's at least a six-hour drive!" Panic rises. "No. I don't like it, Phillip."

She's never spent time alone, certainly not at night. With his current schedule, Phillip returns home every night. "You can't leave us all alone!" Surely he knows she needs him.

But Phillip has a plan. "This'll change everything, Evie," he promises. "It's a new market. We'll be able to get ahead. No more counting change to buy groceries. No more hand-me-downs for our kids or relying on kindness from neighbors."

Evie likes the community she's built with her neighbors. Though not a seamless part of the fabric here, they fit in fine, don't they? She thinks of the women with whom she meets in the park most afternoons, her friends. She doesn't need new things. Doesn't want them. Not if it means Phillip leaving.

"Don't do this. We don't need money. I can't bear the thought of staying here without you. Who are these people, anyways? They aren't friends of ours."

"No, Evie, they're businessmen. And they need someone who can cross the border." He tucks a long strand of her hair behind her ear and kisses her nose. "That's me. We'll be able to build our own house with this money. Big enough for our three kids, or more!"

They argue, though she knows the decision is his. He's the man, after all. She doesn't want a bigger house. But he won't budge. He's decided, and it's done.

When he drives away the next week for his first trip, she can't bring herself to watch him go and huddles on the couch in the living room, stifling sobs so not to disturb the kids. Jake wakes her, patting her shoulder. She rubs her face and stares blankly at him.

"Breakfast, Mommy. I want breakfast."

. . .

EVIE DOESN'T RECOGNIZE ANYTHING. A Mexican flag hangs from thumbtacks on the plain white wall across from her. A small closet faces her bed, surrounded by boxes, open and unopened. On the floor, a familiar girl, mouth gaping and arm flung over her brow, lies with her legs tangled in sheets on an air mattress, her pillow on the floor.

A small nightstand holds a lamp and a framed photo. Evie picks up the photo and studies it. A studio portrait, a man and woman on a royal blue loveseat surrounded by seven children, all with dark hair, dark eyes, and bright smiles. Something in the man's eyes touches her. Soft, friendly.

Is she in Mexico? It would explain the flag. Where have all these boxes come from? Did she pack them? Are they hers? Her heart pounds. When did she get here?

She leaves the bedroom, closing the door quietly so not to wake the girl. The short, dim hallway leads to a main room where a small figure lies on a couch bed near the front door. The early morning light—is it morning?—barely allows her to see. Nothing feels right.

Where am I? She glances at the figure again, hoping for a hint, but it lies shrouded in sheets and shadows. Pulling the curtains to peer outside, she sees a beat-up yellow truck with a camper parked on a cement pad next to a motorcycle. The truck looks familiar.

A set of hooks near the door holds a collection of keys. She lifts off several but isn't sure which one she needs. She pulls aside the curtain again, uncertain where to go or what to do.

"Good morning, Evie."

The voice startles her, and she drops the keys. A tattooed woman pushes up to her elbow on the couch bed, her short, dark hair sticking up awkwardly in front and flat on the right side of her head. Her eyes look puffy and tired.

"What are you doing up so early?" she asks.

"I'm looking for my keys." Evie studies the keys on the floor.

"You don't have keys," the woman says.

"Of course I do."

The woman glances at her phone, lets out a large breath, then swings her legs over the side of the bed and rubs her face. "Fuck me. It's a quarter to five in the morning, Evie. I thought you'd sleep longer after we got in so late. That drive from California is a beast. You don't always get up this early, do you? Goddamn. Let me make up this bed and get coffee going."

Evie peers outside again. Daylight has begun creeping over the land. The road stretches away from the house. *Follow me*, it seems to say.

"Where does the road go?" She drops her hand from the curtain. The woman is folding up the bed and moving quickly.

"Downhill goes to town," she says as she pushes the cushions back in place. "Turn left, and you continue up the valley and end up in the mountains. Nothing there except cacti and javelinas."

"Javelinas?"

The woman walks into the kitchen, picks up the coffee carafe and rinses it at the sink. Evie doesn't recognize the tiny house. "Wild boars. They run in packs around here, and it's best to avoid them. They're unpredictable."

The woman continues. "I've got to register the kids for school today. It starts next Tuesday, and apparently, I'm way behind schedule." She pours water into the tank, adds coffee to the filter and flips it on, then yawns and heads back into the living room. "And I need a shower. Wake myself up a bit. Do you want the TV on?"

Evie shakes her head. "No." She doesn't care about TV. The people move and talk too fast. She wants something that feels familiar. Nothing here does. "I'm going home."

The woman sighs and looks down the hall wistfully. "This is your home, for now. There's nowhere else to go," she says.

Evie is shocked. Is this true? She looks around the small living room with the TV in one corner, the couch across from it, and boxes everywhere. Confusion, like a breeze, flutters around her. "Who are you?"

The woman's face darkens, and she shoots a look down the hallway, then sits heavily on the couch. "I'm Lita," she says. "And, normally, I'd be jumping in the shower right now."

What are the chances? "My daughter's named Lita," she says.

"Yeah. That's me." The woman's voice sounds flat and tired.

Evie stares at her. "My Lita's a little girl."

"Nope. She's not. I'm Lita."

Evie never argues with people who make no sense, and she won't start now. This tattooed woman isn't her quiet little girl with soft brown eyes like caramel and milk chocolate.

"Lita used to dance with me," she tells the woman, hoping this will settle it. This hard woman isn't a dancer. "She loved to dance."

The woman stretches her arms across the back of the couch, eyeing Evie and nodding slowly, crossing her legs and leaning back into the cushions. "Like I do."

Evie narrows her eyes. "You dance?"

"You gave dance lessons to the kids in Perdido. Going to dance lessons with you is one of my first memories." The woman smiles, and it lights up her face. "I remember the day Laurel hid your music. When you started the tape player, Metallica came blasting out, and we warmed up to heavy metal."

Evie isn't sure what to say. Can it be true? Images whirl in her mind. A house by the water, a fishing boat, and children, lots of children. She sees a silver-haired woman holding a baby next to a young man with dark hair. A stage. A white church by the sea with a large wooden cross.

The tattooed woman's criss-crossed leg bounces. Evie opens her mouth but can't find any words. The images float loose, like clouds. If she could connect them, perhaps something would make sense. This woman. This house. The sudden desire to take this woman's hand and apologize. Nothing is clear.

"Why do you have so many tattoos?" she demands.

"Chrissakes, Evie. Again?" The woman's legs bounces. "Some tell stories. Some I like."

Evie doesn't have any tattoos, only stretch marks, which she supposes tell stories in their own way. "What kind of stories?"

The woman holds out her forearm and points to a motorcycle. "This is my first bike. A 1991 Honda XR250L. I got it when I was fifteen in Perdido. I worked it off in Eduardo's shop." She lifts her leg and twists to reveal her calf. Evie follows her fingers to the outline of a pair of shoes.

"Pointe shoes!" Evie immediately warms to this woman. "Do you dance ballet?"

"Nope, not a chance. That's your tattoo. I've got a tattoo for everyone in both my families. Spread out, of course. Can't have them all together." She slides the tank top strap off her right shoulder and twists to indicate a tattoo on the back of it. "See this bull? That's Pop. Stubborn as shit and strong."

"Who's your dad?" Evie is fascinated. She always thought tattoos were for criminals.

The woman meets Evie's eyes and pauses. "Jose," she says. "You knew him once."

Evie can't remember all the people she's known. She's forgotten most, actually. Nothing sticks in her head anymore, memories or their meanings.

"Who else? Any sisters or brothers?" Evie is drawn to this tiny woman.

The woman lifts her shorts to reveal her upper thigh and points to a tattoo of a small bucket with a tiny shovel and rake, the type used at the beach. "That's Randy. I don't remember much about him, but I do remember he loved the beach." She shifts again and turns her left calf with an image of a cat's face towards Evie. "I got this for Laurel. She loved animals, especially the cat we had for a while."

"Laurel," Evie repeats. She stares at the cat in wonder. She remembers a cat. And Laurel, her second-born, her little party girl who makes life so bright. "She always wears dresses. She refuses to wear pants."

Something bothers Evie, niggling around her thoughts, a sadness, a grief circling like water in a drain, a vortex of emotion she doesn't understand.

"Laurel," she murmurs. Then, louder, "Where is Laurel?" She can't remember when she's last seen her.

The woman sticks her arm out and flips it over, pointing to a date inked in shaky black script on her inner wrist: January 18, 2004. "When Jake called to tell me Laurel had died, I didn't know what else to do. I put the date on my wrist." She points to a second date below it: August 2, 1993. "Later I added the date when Phillip and Randy died."

Evie's mouth has gone dry. She doesn't like these stories. "What are you talking about?"

The woman flips the waistband of her shorts down and points to a tattoo on her hip: a woman's face with black, skull-like makeup surrounded by red roses. "La Calavera Catrina, the Lady of the Dead," she says. "I added La Catrina later. To keep Laurel company. I didn't like the idea of Laurel being alone, you know? She always had so many friends. I didn't want her to be alone."

Laurel dead? Phillip and Randy? Evie feels anxious, troubled. She wants to start again, without the dates or the Lady of the Dead. She recognizes an image on the woman's thigh and latches onto it gratefully.

"The bridge!"

"The Golden Gate. Got this one in Tucson after Jake moved back to California." The woman pushes herself up off the couch, then twists her torso side to side and stretches her arms overhead. When she stops stretching she looks Evie in the eye. "You'll stay here while I shower? I don't want to find my truck gone when I get out."

Evie purses her lips and frowns. "Why would I take your truck? I'm not going anywhere."

"Let's keep it that way." The woman turns on the TV and hands Evie the remote. "I know you said you didn't want to watch TV, but there might be something on."

"Who said I didn't want to watch TV?" Evie doesn't understand this woman and her strange ideas. She sits down on the couch and watches cartoons as the woman disappears down the hallway.

EIGHT

Jade

JADE JUST WANTED TIME ALONE. The two-day drive from California in Auntie Lita's old truck had been filled with her brother and sister bickering, Nana questioning, and Auntie Lita barking at all of them like a drill sergeant. She wanted her aunt to get in the truck with Jersey and Jupiter and leave for school already.

Arms folded across her purple ruffled shirt, she tried to ignore the sour, stale-body smell coming from the battered green couch beneath her. She'd chosen the purple shirt because purple meant "I am royalty, leave me alone." The ruffles around the scoop neck were pretty, though a little girlish.

Fake wood paneling in the living room kept the house dark despite the morning sunshine blazing around the edges of the curtained picture window above her. She turned on her knees, opened the curtains and winced at the brightness then returned to sit with her arms crossed and feet on the scratched-up coffee table.

"Hey, Jade, can you keep those curtains closed?" Auntie Lita stood on the threshold into the kitchen. "The sun really turns this place into an oven."

"It's called daylight, Auntie Lita. You know, sunshine?" She sank deeper into the faded green couch. "I'm not a vampire."

Her aunt knew nothing. She'd slapped down bowls of cereal in front of Jersey and Jupiter like a surly waitress and now was trying to herd them outside so she could drive them into town and register them for school. But she couldn't get them to listen to her. Jade had no desire to see the school and had told her aunt so last night. She hadn't wanted to leave California and didn't want to go to this new school. But Auntie Lita kept asking her, over and over.

"You sure you don't want to see it? Take a look before you start tomorrow?"

"No, I don't." And she really didn't. She didn't care about school in this stupid town. She wished she were back home with Ophie and Lily and Annie getting ready for their first day as seventh-graders together.

"Okay, suit yourself." Her aunt stopped at the front door, keys in hand, then walked to the coffee table and dropped a twenty dollar bill on it. "It'll be easier to get through registration without Nana, so she's yours for the morning. If you want to explore downtown, take this. And make sure you go down the canyon, not up. Oscar's jewelry shop is near Main Street, if you want to stop by."

Jade made a noise to acknowledge her but didn't look up, though she could feel Auntie Lita's eyes boring into her. Her aunt sighed and finally got Jupiter and Jersey out the front door. When the truck started, Jade's shoulders relaxed, and she lay her head back on the couch. Auntie Lita stressed her out with her constant movement, always tense, jumpy.

Nana walked out of the bathroom and into the living room. "Where'd the woman go?" She peered out the window as the truck backed away. Though she'd rather be alone, Jade preferred Nana to Jupiter or Jersey.

The newly fallen silence of the house soothed Jade, despite

Nana disrupting it. With only two bedrooms, a small kitchen, bath, and living room, the house was too small for five people to move around without bumping into each other, rubbing elbows, and hearing each other's farts and whispers.

"Auntie Lita took Jupiter and Jersey to register for school."

Nana continued staring out the window. "Where does that road go?"

"It goes to town, Nana. Do you want to walk into town with me? I'm bored here."

Nana's face lit up. "Yes! Can we get some wine?"

"Uh, no. I'm too young to drink."

Nana's eyes narrowed at Jade. "Says who?"

"Duh. It's against the law."

Nana whirled one hand in the air. "What are we waiting for?"

Jade got off the couch and pocketed the bill Auntie Lita had tossed on the table. She put on sandals and made sure Nana changed out of her slippers then took Nana's hand as they left the house. The road felt empty. Barely paved, they followed a thin line of cracked and broken asphalt, winding past dusty houses and dry yards, walking about fifteen minutes in the sun before they reached a block of buildings announcing they were downtown.

The sun blazed down on everything, and Jade felt like a wilted flower in this heat. But Nana's hand felt like ice.

They reached a yarn shop, and Nana stopped to admire a bright pink knit headband in the window. A cement retaining wall with graffiti and no trespassing signs crowded the left side of the road, and a tall red-brick building overshadowed it on the right. They wound slowly through jewelry shops and art galleries, coffee shops and restaurants. Some of the buildings were boarded up and graffitied while others sported fresh paint and sparkling windows. The brown mountains held an ochre tinge and stretched away from them in all directions. Sweat trickled down the back of Jade's neck, where her hair lay flat and sticky.

Down the block, The Queen Beanery, an artsy café with chalk art and a sandwich board of specials on the sidewalk looked like a good place to hide from the sun. She pointed it out to Nana. As they approached the entrance, a group of teenagers emerged, laughing and jostling each other. A tall boy in blue jeans and a faded green T-shirt pushed his friend into a girl who shrieked and pushed back. Another boy slammed his shoulder into the tall boy, sending him directly into Nana's path.

As he stumbled into her, Nana gave a small cry and clutched Jade's arm. Jade gripped her and glowered at the boy, who held his hands up in an apology.

"Hey, sorry, didn't see you." He flashed a broad smile, and Jade's heart did a somersault. As tall as Nana, with shaggy brown hair under a navy ball cap, his eyes were a deep brown, and he looked about fifteen. Jade took in his rather large mouth with full lips and straight white teeth. Dreamy cute.

Nana regained her balance and scowled at him as the other kids gathered. "Where are your parents?"

Oh god. Please Nana, don't say anything embarrassing.

"Uh. My parents?" The boy's eyes met Jade's, and she suddenly wished she'd worn a different shirt. She didn't want to be dressed like a little girl.

"Do they know you're out here roughhousing?" Nana's voice grew louder. One of the kids snickered, and they all stared at Jade and Nana: four boys and three girls, all teenagers. One girl, with pink hair and a pierced lip clung to a dark-haired boy. She leaned in to whisper something to him. He glanced at Nana and smirked.

The boy who'd knocked into them tilted his head sideways at Nana, then glanced at his friends with a smile and bowed towards Nana.

"Apologies, madam. I did not mean to interfere with your walking path."

Another snicker, and Jade wanted to disappear. Nana's voice softened.

"Nothing good comes from too much freedom."

What does that mean?

"Nana, let's go into the café." She tugged on Nana's arm and tried to lead her around the group.

Nana resisted and instead pointed at the tall boy. "Who are you?"

Jade rolled her eyes at the group. She didn't want to prolong this encounter, though she couldn't help but sneak glances at the boy who'd stumbled into them.

"I'm Logan," the boy said. He looked at Jade as he spoke. Jade's heart pounded like a bass drum. "You guys visiting Bisbee?"

Nana opened her mouth but didn't say anything. Simply stood there, slack jawed, looking at the kids and then at the shops with a puzzled expression.

"No," Jade said softly. "We just moved here."

"Really?" Logan aimed his wide grin at her. "You starting school tomorrow?"

Jade nodded.

"We're going, Logan." One of the girls tugged his arm as the group started walking away. He frowned and shook her off.

"My party beckons." He bowed again, deeply, and tipped his ballcap to Nana and Jade. "It's been my pleasure, ladies."

One of the girls snorted. Jade wished they'd hurry up and leave.

Logan suddenly locked eyes with Jade. "What's your name?"

His eyes might have been the softest brown eyes she'd ever seen. She wanted them to stay locked onto hers forever.

"I'm Jade." Her voice had suddenly become a whisper.

"Well, Jade, maybe I'll see you again." He spun around and jogged to his friends, already half a block away.

"Look!" Nana was pointing at something, but Jade couldn't

stop watching Logan. He reached his friends and jumped on the shoulders of one of the boys in the group. The boy folded, and Logan slid off him sideways, laughing and landing on his feet. He shoved his friend playfully, turned and waved at Jade, then ran around the corner and out of sight.

NINE

Lita

LITA SHRUGGED her jacket off and hung it on the hook in the shop. She hadn't taken a two-week break from work since she'd started working here twelve years ago. She was happy to get back to doing something she knew, something she was good at.

She stepped into her coveralls and up to the tiny wood desk in the office where the day's repair schedule sat: a lube and oil change for a 2015 Honda CRV, a brake job on a 1998 Ford 150, and a new head gasket on a 2010 Subaru Outback. She liked working on the older models, before the engines got computerized.

The Ford sat in the shop, but the other vehicles hadn't arrived yet. Neither had Ronaldo nor anyone else. Lita liked to arrive before the others, getting time to absorb the silence of the shop and the familiar smell of motor oil and metal. With two garage stalls, it kept three mechanics busy. Though they primarily served locals, they'd get the occasional tourist needing repairs on a flat tire or a busted air conditioner. No one wanted to drive through Arizona without air conditioning.

Lita started coffee and was removing the Ford's front wheels when Scott entered, followed by Ronaldo.

"Hey Scott," Lita nodded at him.

He grunted amiably, then muttered, "Sorry about your brother, Lita." He'd moved to Bisbee five years ago after twelve years as a mechanic in the army, including two tours in the Gulf. With blonde hair, blue eyes, and standing over six feet tall, he stuck out from the rest of the crew. Scott kept conversation to a minimum, which Lita appreciated.

Karmen's dad, Ronaldo, on the other hand, could never stay quiet.

"Mamacita!" He burst into the garage with a big smile and arms wide open. Lita allowed him to wrap his thick arms around her shoulders and hug her for a moment before he pulled back to look at her. "Getting used to being a mother?" His eyes twinkled.

She'd never met anyone as fatherly as Ronaldo. He may have been the biological father of eight, with Karmen the oldest, but he'd mentored dozens of others, Lita included. He'd coached soccer for nearly twenty years, and his flatbed truck was a mainstay in the town's annual Founder's Day parade that wound down the canyon in June. Ronaldo laughed hard and forgave easily.

"Parenting's one long ground and pound, Ronaldo." Lita said. "Blow after blow, and all I can do is try to defend. Those kids strike hard—especially my oldest niece."

Ronaldo laughed and tousled Lita's hair with his broad hand. She ducked her head and scowled. He treated her like a child, but not as much as Karmen's mom, Marieta, who clucked and fussed over Lita, trying to fatten up her lean frame and soften her hard edges.

"You'll get used to it, Lita. No one's prepared for parenting. Right, Scott?"

Scott, who had two boys in elementary school, grunted again. "Your life's over until they're out of the house. You got, what, a decade?"

"Ugh, Scott. Jersey's four."

Scott whistled. "Let me know if you want to get the boys together to play. Angie's always keen on play dates."

"Thanks, Scott. I'm still trying to figure all of this out."

"Don't forget: Raising children takes a village. You can't go it on your own." He laughed wryly. "I never knew how important a good babysitter was."

She got back to the Ford's front end, her mind whirling. It'd been a mad rush this morning, running the kids to three different schools. Jersey had entered a full-day preschool with a daycare where Jupiter would go after school. Jade hadn't said a word to her.

Lita hadn't known what to do with Evie. She'd left her sleeping at the house and hoped she wouldn't disappear or hurt herself. She'd check on her at lunch.

Lita removed the mounting bolts and the brake pads on the left tire, then began to remove the old rotor. Usually working on vehicles soothed her. Each job had a clear beginning and end. People dropped off their broken cars, and Lita returned them fixed. But today she felt on edge, thanks to Evie.

SHE'D BEEN fourteen and drunk when Laurel burst into her room with a ripe blast of body odor and the attitude of a matron in a boarding school.

"Out of bed." Laurel commanded.

"Fuck you," she replied.

Lita didn't know what day it was, hadn't known her sister was back from Southern California where she'd been living.

Lita's head reeled when Laurel ripped the blanket off her body. She protested and clamped her eyes together. "You're not in charge. Leave me alone." She curled up in the cold air.

Laurel dragged Lita's arm, pulling her off the bed and onto the floor. "You gotta get out of here."

"What the hell?" Lita's head hurt. It spun. She couldn't focus. Cold from the floor seeped into her hips. She placed her forehead on her knees and closed her eyes. Her head throbbed; her stomach didn't feel good.

Laurel crouched on the floor, her breath reeking of cigarettes and unbrushed teeth. Lita gagged and opened her eyes. Her sister hadn't washed in weeks. Open sores lay around her mouth; her skin looked sallow.

"Mom can't take care of you, Lita. You need to leave."

Lita's head pounded, so she closed her eyes again.

Laurel slapped her lightly on the cheeks. Lita frowned and groaned. "Knock it off." She tried to raise her head, but it felt so heavy she let it drop. She kept her eyes closed and spoke into her knees. "What are you doing here?"

"Are you drunk?" Laurel shook her shoulders. "Lita, this place is a mess. Mom's a mess. You're going to wind up in Family Services if you stay here."

"News flash, Laurel: I don't have anywhere to go." Lita opened her eyes and had a thought. "Can I live with you?"

Laurel shook her head adamantly. "No. Definitely not." She scratched at her face and looked blankly around the room. "I'm here to get something. But you've got to leave."

Laurel had the nerve to show up after abandoning her and acted surprised everything had fallen apart. "Fuck you."

"Oh no, you don't." Laurel grabbed Lita's hands and crouched in front of her. "Listen, Lita. One thing I've learned since I left home is you can't rely on anyone. You have to take care of yourself. And that means getting out of here. You're not safe."

"No shit," Lita mumbled. She put her head back down on her knees and tried to keep the room from spinning.

Laurel sighed and shook Lita's backpack empty. "You need a couple of changes of clothes. Toiletries. ID."

Laurel meant it. Despite her thudding head, Lita tried to focus on her sister. Was she right? Did she need to leave? Hope licked at Lita like a flame reaching for a curtain.

"Where am I supposed to go? How come I can't come with you?"

Laurel gave a short, hollow laugh. She handed the empty backpack to Lita. "It's not safe where I am either. But you need to get out before you get stuck in foster care. Go to your dad's."

"My dad's?" This roused her. She hadn't seen her dad since they'd left Perdido ten years earlier. In fact, she remembered him less than she remembered her abuela's soft lap and sugar cookies. "Why do I have to leave?"

"Do you honestly want to stay here? I'm surprised you haven't been taken away yet, Lita. How long has it been since you went to school?"

Lita frowned. "I don't know."

"Well, they're due here anytime then. Believe me. I've got friends who went through the system, and you don't want to be in it. Get up and get dressed." She walked to the doorway, and Lita saw a figure lurking there she hadn't noticed before. A young man, early twenties—Laurel's age—with dark eyes, bad teeth, and a vacant stare. He looked at Laurel intensely while she spoke to him.

"I'll go into my mom's room. You go through the rest of the apartment." He nodded slowly and disappeared from view. Laurel turned to Lita. "You're not going to want to be here when Mom wakes up."

Laurel disappeared, and Lita got dressed quickly. She grabbed a change of clothes and threw them into her backpack. She got her toothbrush from the bathroom but wasn't sure what type of ID she had. She didn't drive yet.

She stepped into the hall as Laurel came out of their mom's room holding a handful of cash and some papers. She counted out three hundred dollars and gave Lita half, putting the rest in her own pocket. Then she handed Lita her birth certificate and proof of US citizenship.

"What's Mama going to live on?" Her mom's monthly benefits didn't always reach the end of the month.

"She'll survive. She always does." Laurel's friend met her in the small living room. The pack on his back looked stuffed. Lita wondered what he could have found worth taking.. "Come with us. We'll take you to the depot and get you on a bus. Anywhere is better than here."

Lita's tongue felt thick and heavy. Her head thudded dully. She followed her sister to the front door, then suddenly stopped. She ran back to Evie's room and entered hesitantly. "Mama," she said. "I'm leaving."

The smell of alcohol triggered queasiness in her belly and a sharp pain in her head. Her mom lay alone, long and lumpy in the dark under an array of tattered blankets, the smell of alcohol and sleeping bodies infused into the fabric of the room. Her mom's breathing rattled in a light snore. Lita felt a sudden despair, and her breath hitched. She wanted to cry. She wanted to scream.

Her mom faced the wall. Lita tiptoed between the wall and the bed to see her, half-hoping she'd rouse and hug her, tell her she couldn't leave, tell her things were going to change. But her mom slumbered on.

"Why can't you stop drinking?" she whispered. Evie's breath caught, and she groaned. Lita hated her mom and her beautiful long legs that moved too fast for Lita to keep up. She hated her wild laugh that made others stop and stare. She hated her balle-rina arms that used to wrap around Lita when she was a little girl.

A framed photo sat on the bedside table. Evie's favorite, it had been there for years, a postcard-sized photo with six figures posing in front of a large beach umbrella. Evie and Phillip stood in the center. Lita, dark-haired and tiny, lay with her eyes closed in Evie's arms. Randy, blonde, maybe four years old, sat on Phillip's shoulders with an ecstatic, excited grin. Laurel and Jake stood on either side of their parents, Laurel beaming mischievously at the unseen cameraman, and Jake standing straight and rigid with a smile full of clenched teeth. They looked so happy. She barely recognized them.

She took the photo out of the frame and slipped it into her back pocket, pushing the twinge of guilt away with righteous anger. Her mom didn't deserve pity. She'd failed Lita. She'd failed them all. Her vision blurred.

She cried as she left the house but shrugged off the consoling arm Laurel threw across her shoulders. She wiped her eyes and remembered what one of Evie's violent ex-husbands had taught her. Fight, don't cry.

LITA COULDN'T GET the old rotor free, and she pounded on it until the caliper broke loose. When it finally fell with a loud clang, she fought the urge to keep smacking the metal.

Laurel had died the following year. Her mom hadn't even called to tell Lita. Jake had done it.

Lita didn't go back for Laurel's funeral. Instead, she inked the date on her wrist, stole a bottle of tequila from her uncle, and puked in her abuela's flower bed.

Like mother, like daughter, she'd thought grimly.

And now the roles had reversed. She'd be a better caregiver than her mom. She'd keep Evie safe until she could send her back to California.

"Hey Lita, where you at with the Ford?" Ronaldo's voice nearly made her drop the wrench. He held a clipboard and stood behind her left shoulder. "Mercy Jackson wants to bring in her Escape, and I told her we'd be able to take a look before lunch. Can you fit it in?"

"Yeah, I got another hour here, but I should be able to get to it. What's the problem?"

He glanced at the clipboard. "A clunking sound when she brakes."

Lita nodded. Most likely bearings or brakes. "Yeah, I should be able to get to it, at least diagnose it."

She wondered if Evie were awake yet. Sometimes she slept late, and other times, she got up way too early. This morning she'd slept through the school prep and the rush to get the kids where they needed to be. Lita had been happy not to have to deal with Evie, but now she wondered if she should check on her.

"I'm going to take off and check on Evie at lunch, make sure she's up and functioning. It shouldn't take long." She tightened a bolt and glanced at the clock.

"Do what you need to do, Lita. But I warn you, Hector's gunning for your job, pestering me to let him do more than sweep and oil changes. I had a hard time keeping him out of your bay while you were gone." Ronaldo's eyes sparkled.

Ronaldo had encouraged his kids to find their own career paths, and his youngest son Hector, currently finishing his last year in high school, was the only one who'd chosen to work in the garage. He showed up after lunch each day, and Lita marveled at his ability to hand her tools before she'd asked for them.

Lita laughed. "Give him the Honda," she said. "He should be able to do the oil change before I start on the Subaru."

Ronaldo gave her a thumbs up then turned back to the tiny cement cube of an office. As Lita worked on the second rotor, she thought about the photo she'd taken from Evie's bedside years ago. She hadn't looked at it in years but kept it, wrinkled and folded, in a Bible Abuela had given her when Laurel had died. It lay in her nightstand drawer, next to her bed, where Evie now slept. Maybe she should return it. Would Evie even recognize anyone in it?

TEN

Jade

DESOLATION. INTRODUCED TODAY AS A "NEW" vocabulary word, one she'd already learned two years ago. Endless *desolation*.

This school sucked. Jade slumped in her seat next to the window and stared out at the pale brown mountains stretching away from the school. She'd been forced to move to a place with rattlesnakes, scorpions, and packs of wild pigs called javelinas which she'd never known existed.

What did anyone do here to entertain themselves? No malls, no bowling alleys, no movie theaters, nothing. This school was tiny—nothing compared to her school in California. And no one had spoken to her yet, but she didn't care. She didn't need friends.

She sighed and doodled circles in her notebook. Or, no, not circles but black holes to suck everything around them into oblivion.

"Jade?"

Jade jolted.

"Will join us please?" Her teacher stood by the door, the students lined up and waiting, staring at Jade. Her face flamed as she realized she sat alone in the rows of seats. She kept her head down, ignoring the stares, and made her way to the line.

"Where you from?"

A short girl turned around as Jade joined the end of the line. She had ragged, limp blonde hair and a big gap between two front teeth that jutted out. Her hair looked unwashed. She wore a T-shirt with a Monster Energy drink logo, and jeggings two sizes too small, stretched saggy in the back and rising well above her ankles although she was short as a garden gnome.

"California," Jade replied with as much venom as she could muster. She didn't want to talk to this girl. Or anyone.

"I've got an aunt in California." The girl beamed at Jade.

Jade ignored her.

"She lives in San Diego."

"Whoopee."

"I've been there twice."

So what?

"She has a swimming pool." The girl hopped around, couldn't stand still.

Who cares?

"Lots of people have pools in California." Jade used her snottiest voice, the one she usually reserved for Jersey.

"I'm Brooklyn." The girl smiled. "I have a dog that can do tricks."

Jade stopped herself from rolling her eyes. This girl must not have any friends. The line started to move, and the students filed out of the classroom, jostling and whispering and laughing. She and gap-toothed girl seemed to be the only two without a group of friends. She'd become a loser in this loser town already, talking to the only other loser in her class. And the day had barely begun.

"Where are we going?"

"Assembly," Brooklyn told her. "We have an all-school assembly on the first day of school. And the first Monday of every month."

"For what?" They didn't have a lot of assemblies at her school in California—usually only for class elections or special awards ceremonies. Her old school was so large they'd staggered attendance to make sure the gym didn't exceed capacity—probably not an issue here.

"This one kicks off our Founder's Day parade." Brooklyn beamed.

"Founder's Day parade? When's that"

Like the flip of a switch, Brooklyn became animated. She talked quickly, paying no attention to anything or anyone around her, gesturing wildly as they walked. She even spat a little, and Jade was slightly disgusted. She looked around for a way out of the conversation.

No luck.

"We plan it all year. There are class competitions and costume competitions, and it finishes with a parade on Founder's Day, in June. It's part of our seventh-grade project. Each group designs their own float and everything!" Brooklyn's eyes shone.

Jade hated parades. She'd gone to a Disneyland parade with her parents when she was nine, and her feet had hurt from standing and waiting. Too small to see over the crowd and too big to sit on her parents' shoulders, when the parade had finally started, she'd only been able to see lights and the heads of Disney characters waving from the moving vehicles, all behind a wall of visitor's backs and butts.

"No thanks," she said curtly.

"It's a lot of fun! The whole town comes out for the parade, and they vote on the floats! Have you ever built a float before? You'll never believe how many decorations go on it. All the parents help, too. Your dad could drive one of the floats!" Brooklyn grinned widely, showing her beaver teeth.

Jade cut her off. "My dad's dead. My mom, too. Parades are stupid."

Brooklyn snapped her mouth shut and stared at Jade. She spoke quietly. "My mom's dead too. I live with my dad." She looked sadly at Jade. "I hated it here at first. But working on the

Founder's Day Parade gave me the first good thing to do at this stupid school."

She turned her back on Jade and walked single file behind the girl in front of her. Jade stood still, last in line, and watched Brooklyn and the rest of the students march away. She felt mean and dumb.

The assembly took nearly an hour, and the students were raucous, with lots of whooping, hollering, and clapping. The teachers encouraged the students to make as much noise as they could.

Jade wanted to leave. The whistles and whoops and the cheers of all these losers made her angry. School wasn't supposed to be this way. It was supposed to be orderly, predictable. Teachers were supposed to be professional and calm, not dressed in costumes and whipping their students into a frenzy.

When the assembly finished and they were back in the class-room, Jade sat blankly while the teacher ran the class through a writing assignment. She didn't pay any attention to either the teacher or the assignment, staring out the window at the dry, rolling hills.

At lunchtime, she left. She didn't know where to go, but once off school grounds, she kept walking. The school faced a cemetery in an industrial area with dusty cement buildings that looked plopped down in the middle of a scrub- brush desert. She reached a junction leading back to Bisbee's downtown and turned the opposite way.

She'd never left school without permission before. Had never pleaded sick to avoid it. Had never cut a class.

No one tried to stop her. She walked through a small neigh-borhood of houses and passed by the empty playground of Jupiter's elementary school. Some of the houses seemed new, and the neighborhood looked more familiar to her than the crowded, dusty, cement or clapboard houses in downtown Bisbee.

An ache started in her chest and swelled into a prickly ball. Who knew a little thing like the type of houses could make her miss her parents?

WHEN SHE REACHED a tired little park on the edge of the neighborhood, with nothing in it but parched grass and a few benches, Jade sat down. There weren't any trees to speak of. What's the point of a park with no shade?

Her stomach growled. She'd left before lunch and hadn't brought it with her. But she'd rather be hungry than in school, a relief to be out of there. Hardly anyone had spoken to her aside from that weirdo Brooklyn.

She felt a pang of guilt. Brooklyn had been friendly, and Jade had been rude. But Brooklyn was so geeky.

Jade didn't want to be a geek at this new school like the old Jade. This new Jade felt older than her years, older than her peers. The old Jade color-coordinated her clothes with her friends. The new Jade didn't have any friends. The old Jade enjoyed school and got good grades. The new Jade didn't care.

Being this new Jade would be easy. Auntie Lita, who hadn't graduated from high school, certainly didn't care about attendance or grades.

My parents cared.

Her mom and dad would never have brought her to this desolate wasteland. The prickly ball in her chest rose and emerged as a sob. She hated it here. She hated her new school and her new house and the new room she shared with Nana.

How had her dad thought Auntie Lita could take care of them? She couldn't make a frozen pizza without setting off the fire alarm. She had no patience. Everything she said or did carried a rough edge.

Jade longed for her mom's warm, soft cuddle, her arms holding Jade in a hug. Though she'd grown taller than her mom, she'd always had a place on her mom's lap.

Auntie Lita had no soft edges; she was tough and razor sharp. Sitting on her lap would be like sitting on a cactus.

Jade cried until she felt emptied out. She shuddered with a last sob and sat stiffly on the bench. She didn't know what to do now or where to go.

"I saw you leave school."

Jade jerked upright and saw Brooklyn behind her. Standing next to the flagpole in the middle of the dry grass, she smiled at Jade. Red-faced and sweaty, her too-small jeggings climbed up her shin as she put one foot on top of the other.

"I live a few blocks away from here. Do you want to go there? My dad's at work."

Jade considered her options. Other than going back to the school, she didn't have any. She took a deep breath and wiped her eyes. She nodded and followed Brooklyn.

ELEVEN

Evie

THE CRUSHED ROCK of the road pokes Evie's feet through her slippers. She clutches her purse and shuffles past a small brown clapboard house with peeling paint and a yard full of yellowed weeds and dirt. A small dog barks in the window. She ambles past a solid cement-blockhouse with a wraparound porch and luscious garden in a fenced backyard. Nothing's familiar. She tightens the sash of her robe and keeps walking.

The sun beams down on her, and a trickle of sweat runs down the back of her neck where her braid lies thick and heavy. Normally she basks in the warmth of the sun's rays, but it's oppressive this morning. The sheer fabric of her nightgown clings to her legs. Sweat rolls down her forehead. Should she turn around? Where would she go? She can't stay here. She doesn't know where *here* is.

Passing a few more desolate-looking houses, she reaches a cheery yellow house with sunflowers as tall as the roof. A woman waters the garden with a hose and stares at Evie as she shuffles by. Evie waves, and the woman waves back tentatively, then puts the hose down and waves again, walking briskly out to the road.

"Good morning!" The woman has a pleasant voice.

"Good morning," Evie stops, grateful for the pause.

The woman's blonde hair is pulled back into a high ponytail. Evie doesn't wear ponytails much. She prefers dancer's buns and braids, both of which keep stray hairs from floating into her face. Ponytails are more appropriate for children. This woman, not a child, looks like an athlete, outfitted in running shoes, shorts, and tight tank top.

No tattoos. Evie doesn't know why she thinks this.

"Can I help you?" The woman eyes Evie curiously.

Evie hopes so. "I can't find my car."

"Oh." The woman's mouth forms a circle. Her eyes dart up and down the road, then return to Evie with a question. She surprises Evie by asking, "Would you like to come in for a glass of water or a cup of tea? It's hot out, and it might be good to take a break."

Evie agrees. "Do you have any wine?"

The woman's eyebrows shoot up higher, and she laughs. "My day will be short if I start drinking at ten a.m. I wouldn't be able to get anything done!"

Evie ponders this, and the woman laughs. "I've got black or herbal tea, or ice water. Or juice, if you'd like to get out of the sun for a minute."

Evie nods. She *would* like to take a minute. Her back drips with sweat, and her feet feel tender. The car can wait. She follows the woman from a side porch into a kitchen and looks around. Colorful paintings and large framed black-and-white photos of landscapes and people adorn the pleasant room. None of the photos feature the woman. Evie sees no evidence of a husband or children.

"It's my passion," the woman says, watching Evie eye the artwork. "I dabble in all mediums—photography, watercolors, oils. I do sculptures, too, usually granite. I couldn't pick any art form to specialize in, so I do it all."

"You're busy." Evie likes this sunny woman and this sunny kitchen.

The woman pulls out a chair and motions to sit. Evie does

so heavily, and her throbbing feet rejoice. Her nightgown clings to her breasts, and she plucks at the front of it to pull it away.

"Busy enough." She holds her hand out to Evie, and Evie shakes. "I'm Jodi."

"Evie." So pleasant and agreeable, a welcome change of pace from the folks she's been with recently. *Where are they? Do they have my car?*

"I don't think I've seen you before. Are you new to town? What kind of tea would you like? I've got herbal, black, Earl Grey…." Jodi reaches into a cupboard for a tall glass, fills it with water, and sets it before Evie. She fills an electric kettle with water, plugs it in and turns it on. "My wife and I have been in this house for five years. We lived in Tucson before. Came here on a lark one day and decided Bisbee was the place for us. We haven't been disappointed. It suits us perfectly. Do you take sugar or cream?"

The water cools Evie's throat. "No sugar, please. Milk, if you've got it."

"Sure thing," Jodi speaks cheerfully. "Are you visiting family? You walked down from the upper canyon, and there aren't a lot of properties past mine. Who are you staying with?"

Evie thinks. Where has she come from? *Lita.* The name pops into her head, but it can't be. Something isn't right. "I live in Mexico. Perdido."

"Oh, fascinating. I'm not familiar with Perdido. How long have you been there?"

An uneasy feeling tugs at Evie. Something has changed. The words are wrong. She's left the sea and her little house. "I tried to go back home."

"Where's home?" Jodi asks. She pulls two tea bags out of a box and puts them into white mugs she's set on the counter.

Evie gulps water. She's thirsty. "Somewhere near here," she says, waving her hand in the air. She frowns and twirls her water glass. She has more to say, but words elude her. They feel out of reach, on a high shelf out of sight. An image flashes in her mind. "My father," she says suddenly. "He wouldn't see me. Or the kids."

"Oh, Evie, I'm so sorry." The water kettle clicks off, and Jodi fills the mugs. "Families can be difficult, can't they? I've had friends cut off from their families because they've loved the wrong person."

Her words fit Evie like an old sweater. "Yes! Phillip…." She straightens and beams. A warmth spreads throughout her body, dashed cold by a vision of her father. "Daddy won't see me again. Cursed by God, he says. I tried to see him when I came back. He took one look at Lita and told me I'd burn in hell for eternity." Her voice softens and trails away.

"That must have been hard." Jodi murmurs softly.

Evie stares at the water glass, frowning, trying to remember what's important about all of this. "I made so many mistakes."

"Don't we all, Evie? Life is full of mistakes. I approach them like steps to overcome. Every day is a climb, but with one step at a time, it's easier."

It sounds slow and painful, and Evie has never moved slowly, drawn to action like a magnet to metal. Dance keeps her moving. She's always loved dancing. The only other thing she's loved more than dancing was Phillip. And her children. What has changed?

She gasps suddenly. "I lost them. They're gone." She lifts her eyes to meet Jodi's, and her voice drops to a whisper. "God did curse me."

Jodi puts her hand on top of Evie's, its warmth soothing. "Evie, this may not be a popular view, but I don't believe in God. I certainly don't believe in a God that exists solely to punish us. What kind of faith relies on fear? And who hasn't made mistakes in their lives? I don't know a single person who hasn't. It's not possible. They don't exist."

"No God?" Evie ponders this. She likes this woman and her happy energy and colorful house, like a relaxing afternoon in Perdido, post-nap, when she'd gather in the park or at the beach with other mothers to let the kids run wild. But those days are gone. And her kids gone, too. As if a cold wind has entered the kitchen, Evie shivers. "I've lost everything I've loved."

"Loss sticks with us, doesn't it? I still feel the pain of my mom's death two years ago. She went quickly, thankfully. Cancer. Damned cancer." She splashes a bit of milk into one of the mugs and slides it to Evie. "Are you living with someone in Bisbee? Or visiting?"

"Bisbee?" It sounds familiar. "Yes, I've been visiting. But it's time to go home."

"Where's home now?"

Evie turns the rainbow heart mug around on the table and dunks the tea bag up and down. *Where?* Where is home? How can she forget something so important?

Jake. She remembers. And his family. "California. The Bay Area. I live with my son."

"I love the Bay Area. You're visiting Bisbee, then?"

This has started to feel like an interrogation, and Evie isn't sure which answers are needed. She pushes her irritation away and focuses on the woman's open face. "I'm a dancer."

"Oh, you're an artist too! Bisbee's kind of an artist haven, I'd say. Not as many performing arts, but lots of artists around here. I'm sure you've visited some of the galleries."

Has she? Evie can't remember. Where is Jake? She blows on her tea and nods slowly. She should find her car and get home soon. But it's cool in this kitchen, and she doesn't feel the need to leave. Not yet. She sips her tea.

Outside, the whine of a small engine grows louder. A yellow motorcycle flashes past the house.

"Hey!" Evie straightens and stands as it zips quickly past the house. It disappears and the sound fades.

"Do you know Lita?" Jodi is glancing from Evie to the window and back.

Evie is sitting back down and reaching for her tea but her

hand jerks at the question and she nearly spills it. "Lita? My daughter Lita?"

"Huh." Jodi sets her cup down on the table and peers out the window. "You know, I think she might head back down here pretty quickly. I'm going outside to see if I can catch her before she scoots past."

Evie stands, too. "I should get going. My car must be down the road. Thank you for the tea."

"You're quite welcome, Evie, I've enjoyed our visit." The buzzing whine of the engine sounds from up the canyon, and Jodi dashes out the door waving her arms. The yellow motorcycle slows and stops in front of the gate.

The driver removes her helmet. *I know her.* Short dark hair, red stripe on top, tattoos, and a wiry, taut stature. Evie walks towards them. The tattooed woman speaks animatedly with Jodi. Her eyes float to Evie on the porch, and her brow furrows.

I know her. Evie smiles at the familiar face on this confusing morning and approaches the two women at the gate. "Good morning! I didn't know you lived here!"

The tattooed woman grimaces and shakes her head, not in a good mood apparently. "Shit, Evie. I'm sorry. I'm an idiot. I thought you'd stay put until lunch. Did you find the cereal and coffee I left out for you?"

What is she talking about? Evie had woken up without a problem, thank you very much. "Don't worry about me. I'll be on my way as soon as I find my car. Have you seen it?"

The tattooed woman speaks to Jodi, ignoring Evie completely. "Evie moved here with my nieces and nephew. We've had a rough couple of weeks." She nods her head towards the road, then glances at Evie with her lips clamped together in a tight line. She blows air out of her cheeks in an exasperated sigh. "It's the first week of school, but I don't have a plan for Evie yet."

What's this? Evie stands taller and tries to butt into the conversation. "Plan for who?" she demands. "Have you seen my car?"

"I was outside watering the garden when she appeared," Jodi says. "We had a nice talk over tea. Your mom says she's a dancer."

Evie looks from one woman to the other. "Whose mom? Can you help me find my car?" She steps towards the gate, but her nightgown clings to her legs like a wet sheet. She looks down irritated. "Where are my clothes?"

The tattooed woman's eyes drop to Evie's slippers and her face falls. "Fuck!"

This woman's foul mouth bothers Evie. "Stop cursing," she says.

The woman ignores her and turns to Jodi. "It was all I could do to get the kids ready for school this morning. I obviously didn't think this all through." Her cell phone rings. She glances down and frowns, gets off her bike and walks slightly away from the gate before putting the phone to her ear.

Jodi takes Evie's arm and smiles at her. "You and I have got to visit again. I really enjoyed our talk."

"Fuck!" The biker stares at the phone as if it's bitten her.

Evie ignores her and smiles back at Jodi. The sun beams down on her, more comforting than hot, a kiss of warmth on her face. "A pleasure. I don't come out this way very often. Maybe I'll look you up when I do." How pleasant Jodi seems, unlike the prickly woman cursing into her phone.

"Wonderful." The woman nods agreeably. "I don't think you left anything in the kitchen. Do you have your purse?"

Evie looks at her empty hands. Before she can reply, the tattooed woman returns, face stormy. She takes a deep breath, then speaks. "We gotta get back to the house and get you dressed, Evie. Jade walked out of school at lunch and didn't come back."

TWELVE

Lita

JODI WENT into the house to retrieve Evie's purse, and Lita paced in the yard. What a fucking nightmare. She'd panicked at the empty house. Thank god her mom had walked down the canyon towards Bisbee instead of heading up into the dry brush. What if she'd fallen or gotten lost?

Evie looked at the motorcycle suspiciously. "We're taking this?" She approached the bike and gathered her nightgown in her hands, and Lita realized Evie couldn't ride the bike in a nightgown.

Jodi, returning with Evie's purse, noticed too. "Evie, how about I drive you back to the house in my car? I've got to run some errands in town, and I might as well get started now. It's a quick drive." Jodi ran back into the house and returned with a set of keys, unlocking a silver Honda CRV parked parallel to the fence.

Lita's chest tightened. Why was this woman being so helpful? They'd never met before.

"Um, thanks." Her voice husky, she cleared her throat. "I'll call Marieta Ramos to see if she can come by and keep Evie company. I don't want to take her to the school with me."

Jodi studied Lita, then spoke carefully. "You may think this is weird, Lita…."

What could be weird with this woman? Honestly. She seemed so normal. Jodi and her wife, Elise, were avid trail runners who competed in the annual Bisbee 1000, a four-and-a-half mile race up and down the stairways climbing throughout the city. Lita waited for Jodi to tell her how royally she'd screwed up, how she couldn't take care of a hamster much less three kids and a senior with the mind of a toddler.

Jodi smiled at both of them. "Evie, would you be interested in accompanying me on my errands around town? Now that I know where you belong, I can enjoy your stories a bit more. You've had a fascinating life."

Lita grunted. Jodi had no idea.

The offer was too good to be true. Lita didn't want Evie tagging along, but she also didn't want to ask Karmen's mom to drop everything to help. Marieta did bookkeeping from home and had flexibility, but not always time. Lita studied Jodi. Except for the flip-flops on her feet, her neighbor looked ready to take off on a long run; she didn't look like someone out to victimize a vulnerable senior. And Evie seemed to like her.

"I can call Marieta."

"That'll take time, and I can help now. I'm going to be out and about for an hour or so, and Evie might want to see a bit of the town, if she hasn't toured it already." She looked at Evie. "Evie, do you want to cruise the town a bit with me this afternoon? Maybe we'll have time to visit a gallery or two."

Evie, who had been peering down the canyon road, turned to Lita. "Do you need me this afternoon?"

Lita refrained from rolling her eyes. "I think I can handle it." She turned to Jodi. "Are you sure about this? You're in for some entertainment."

Jodi looked at Evie, then smiled at Lita. "I've been missing my own mom quite a bit recently. This'll be fun."

Lita lifted her eyebrows. "We have different ideas of fun."

Jodi laughed. "Nothing can be worse than the bookkeeping I'd planned for this afternoon. Books, ugh." She tilted her head and looked at Lita with a wry smile. "How about Evie and I follow you to your place, where she can change? I'm heading down to Safeway and the hardware store, and we might grab a bite and visit a gallery or two."

Lita frowned, and Jodi touched her arm lightly. "I'm ready to help. It's what good neighbors are for."

Good neighbors? Neighbors usually called the cops due to loud music or too many cars blocking the street.

"Okay," Lita said finally. She turned to Evie. "Jodi's giving you a ride home, and I'll meet you there. She'd like to spend the afternoon with you. Are you good with that?"

"I'd much rather ride in this"—Evie pointed at the silver CRV—"than that little thing"—she pointed at the motorcycle. "I rode those when younger. But always with a good-looking man on the front."

At the house, Evie changed, then left with Jodi. Lita got on her bike and drove down the canyon wondering if she'd done the right thing. She considered where to look for Jade. The middle school sat three miles down the highway, and she thought it unlikely Jade would climb up the hill to come back home.

When she reached the highway, she pulled a sudden right instead of turning left towards the school, drove past the Old Miner Saloon, and swung into a small, clean alley behind a side street off Bisbee's main drag. She parked the bike in the alley and went through a solid white fire door leading into the back room of a small jewelry shop where Oscar leaned over a worktable with a magnifying lamp perched on his forehead and a brilliant blue gemstone in his hand. Beyond the workroom Rikki, a lithe young woman with blonde hair and a sunburnt nose was polishing the glass counters.

Oscar looked up and greeted Lita with a wide grin, his dark

hair flattened by the headlamp above his ears. He flipped the light off. "A pleasant surprise."

Lita's face flushed. Rikki's presence in the other room, a new hire to help with the crush of summer tourists, irritated her. His business had grown steadily since he'd opened it three years ago, and until this past summer he'd functioned alone as jeweler, janitor, and shopkeeper. He needed the help, but Lita found herself annoyed by Rikki's efficiency, her pleasant smile, and her attention to Oscar.

She pushed her irritation away. She didn't hold any claim on him, which made the fact she'd slept with him last month a real bummer. But she could count on him.

"What's up, Lita?"

"Jade's missing." Lita erupted like a kettle boiling over, pacing around the small space and holding her fists tight to her body so she didn't punch the wall. "She left school after lunch and hasn't returned. And Evie took a walk in her nightgown and slippers and ended up at a neighbor's having tea. The neighbor offered to spend the afternoon with her because she obviously realizes *I can't handle a fucking thing.*"

Rikki's head swung up to look at them in the back room. Lita wanted to hit something but stopped herself. She swallowed a scream.

Oscar's smile faltered. "Whoa." He removed his headlamp and placed it on the counter with the piece of turquoise he'd been holding.

Lita felt herself growing angry. Why did she feel so emotional? So incompetent?

"Fuck me, Oscar, I am not cut out for this."

"Easy, Lita. Tell me again what's happening."

Lita stopped pacing and shot Rikki a glance. Rikki quickly dropped her eyes and busied herself at the front counter. Lita fought to ignore her.

"Jade's missing from school. She went AWOL at lunch. And Evie walked away from the house this morning while I was at the shop. She's with a neighbor, so good for now. But I need to find something for her to do when I'm at work. And I need to find Jade. Where do you think she'd go? Where the hell am I supposed to look?"

He came around the counter and put his hands on her shoulders. "First of all, Lita, close your eyes. Take a few deep breaths. Slow down."

His soothing tone had the opposite effect. It ratcheted up the feeling that she was too high-strung for parenthood. Shouldn't she be able to stay calm without him? She fought the urge to headbutt him and forced herself to close her eyes. His hands felt like restraints on her shoulders, so she grabbed them and simply held them. They stopped hers from trembling. She took one deep breath, then another.

"Okay," she said, her panic starting to recede. She looked at the time. "It's one-thirty. The school called me twenty minutes ago. Let's start there." She squeezed Oscar's hands and smiled at him, her face close to his. She felt more grounded now, more clearheaded, and a bit embarrassed she'd interrupted his workday in a panic. "Do you have time to help?"

"Of course I do." He freed his hands from hers and wrapped his arms around her shoulders in a tight hug. "I'm on your team. You know that."

"Yeah, I do. Thanks." She squeezed him once and stepped out of his embrace. "We need to get moving. Maybe the school will have a clue as to where she's gone."

Her phone buzzed, and she frowned at the screen. "Hello?"

"Is this Lita Bravo? I'm Cynthia Shields, the principal of Bisbee Elementary, calling about Jupiter."

"What can I do for you?"

"We're very happy to have Jupiter join us this year, and Jupiter seems very happy to be here."

She'd met the principal, who was warm and welcoming when she'd registered the kids last week. Jupiter had liked her. Why was she calling?

"Good to hear." She waited for the other shoe to drop.

"But we've had a little incident with language."

Here we go. Lita braced herself. "What kind of incident?"

"I'm not sure I want to repeat it, but Jupiter got into an argument with another boy and called him a…'fuckturd.'"

"A fuckturd?" Her laugh sounded like a bark. "Hah! He didn't get that one from me."

"Yes, well, it's not important where he learned it, but it is important he keep that type of language out of school."

Lita stopped laughing. "Yeah, it's something we'll work on. We're all going through a big transition here."

"Yes, I realize. And I don't want to make things more difficult…."

Lita rolled her eyes at Oscar who watched expectantly. "It'd be hard to make things more difficult than they are now, so don't worry. In fact, I'm going to the middle school to deal with an issue related to my niece. What else?"

"No, well, and I realize this is only the first day of school, but we may need to troubleshoot this further if it continues to be an issue. I've asked Jupiter's teacher Felix—Mr. Segura—to help Jupiter remember to moderate his language. Kindergarten can be tough when kids are learning the difference between family norms and those outside their homes."

"Okay, sounds good." She looked at her watch. *Where could Jade be?* "I really gotta go now. We'll work on the language."

She ended the call and shook her head. "Jupiter's lighting up the schoolyard with curse words. And I'm at a loss here, Oscar. I'm out of my weight class." Lita stared at her phone as if it had bitten her. "Holy hell, I've barely got control of my own life, and now I'm in charge of four others."

"Okay, okay. Let's focus on facts. Evie's with a neighbor?" Oscar's calm tone soothed Lita's fried nerves and helped her settle. In the cage, Kroker had taught Lita to center herself and attack with purpose. She wished she could do the same in everyday life, finding it easier to be in a fighting state than anything else. Fighting was her center.

"Yeah, Jodi. About half a mile down the canyon. She stopped Evie from walking downtown in her pajamas. Now they're running errands together." Lita's eyebrows pinched together in a scowl, and she let loose out an exasperated sigh like a growl.

"Hey, hey." Oscar opened a drawer and picked up a set of keys. "First things first: Evie's taken care of. So don't worry about her. And when do you need to pick up the kids from daycare?"

Lita frowned. "Anytime between three-thirty and five. Jupiter takes a bus to Jersey's daycare, and I pick them up together." She'd thought it would be so easy, getting the kids off to school and going about her workday as normal. Was it always going to be like this?

"Well, we've got some time. It's only one-thirty, so let's figure out where Jade would go."

"We should organize a search party." Lita started pacing again.

"Slow down. We haven't looked yet."

"Yeah, you're right. I guess we head to the school."

Oscar nodded. "A good start. Let's take my car."

Lita hesitated. The bike was so much faster. But of course she couldn't take the bike if she'd be picking up the kids. "Okay, where are you parked?"

Oscar told Rikki he'd be back before closing, and they walked to a parking lot a block away and climbed into Oscar's white Ford Focus with a large dent in the back bumper.

"Shit!" Lita exclaimed suddenly. "Car seats. We'll need car seats for Jersey and Jupiter."

Oscar nodded and angled the car up the canyon towards Lita's. Lita pointed out Jodi's house. "That's where I found Evie. She walked down here in her slippers."

Oscar studied the house as they passed it. "I know Jodi. I've met her at a Chamber of Commerce Showcase. She's a pretty famous artist in these parts."

"Yeah? I'd never talked to her before today. Apparently Evie ambled by, and Jodi flagged her down." Lita's panic came back like a flying knee to the chest. "What if she'd gone up the canyon, Oscar? She could have died."

Oscar gave his head a shake but didn't look at her. "She didn't, Lita. Give yourself a break. You're going to make mistakes. We all do."

Lita ignored him and sat back . "Holy hell."

His voice held a flash of irritation. "Lita, you're a fighter. One of the strongest people I know. Cut out the pity party and put yourself in those kids' shoes."

"Damn, Oscar, do you think I haven't? Jade hates me, Jupiter doesn't listen to me, and Jersey won't look at me. And what the hell do you know about raising kids?"

"Give them time."

Lita's voice rose, filling the tiny car. "I'm trying, Oscar." How couldn't he see this? She didn't like the way her voice was rising towards hysteria. "And why do I have to be responsible for Evie?"

"She's your mom, and there's no one else." His voice was low and gentle. "I'd have given anything to be with my mom, no matter if her mind was gone or not."

Lita winced. "Oscar, your mom loved you. She cared for you. My mom spent my childhood drunk and negligent."

Oscar's face hardened. He kept his eyes on the winding canyon road. "But now she's a vulnerable adult, and you're her caregiver."

"Temporarily. Until Jake's home in California sells. Then she's going back there and into a care home."

Oscar set his jaw. "Yeah, I know. I'm guessing you haven't told the kids."

"No." Lita sighed. "I'll tell them when we get to there. No sense in making things more difficult now."

"Maybe you should put her in a care home here."

"I don't want Evie in my life. The sooner she's gone, the better."

"What about the kids? She's part of their lives." Oscar pulled the car into the short driveway and parked.

"Why don't you get it? It hurts to be around her, Oscar. Jake was big enough to reconcile with Evie, but not me. She never wanted me. Besides, she belongs in California. The kids will get used to it."

Oscar turned off the engine and sat, hands on the steering wheel, staring straight ahead. Lita unbuckled her seat belt and pushed open the door.

"Why are you being so cold, Lita?"

Lita stopped, her hand on the door, one foot on the driveway. "What?"

"I mean, I get your mom neglected you. I get it. You've gone through a lot. But you're one of the strongest people I know, and you're acting scared. What are you scared of?"

"Scared?" Lita's temper flared. "You want to know scared? Try sleeping in a house every night not knowing if you're safe. Or crossing the border at fourteen without speaking the language."

Lita stopped to take a deep breath. When she'd crossed the border alone, she'd asked about a bus to Hermosillo and had attracted a small crowd. A young man—also from California, he said—had offered her a safe place to stay the night until the bus left in the morning.

"You know what my mom's family legacy is, Oscar? Never trust anyone. Not the person you love the most, not the people who offer to help you, not the priest in your fucking church. That's what I learned from my mom."

She'd never told anyone. She didn't get on the bus the next day. The young man and his friends had kept her locked in a room, stripped her of her money, her clothing, her belongings. She'd waited days for an opportunity to escape and, finally finding one, she'd run to a café and stumbled through the back door where a heavyset man with thick jowls and a massive belly lifted his bushy eyebrows in surprise, crossed himself with a quick prayer, then wrapped a tablecloth around her and called his wife. By afternoon Lita had made contact with her abuela, and after an overnight bus trip, she'd arrived in Hermosillo wounded and wary.

"I don't expect you to understand any of this, Oscar. My mom and your mom are not the same. There are a lot of bad people in this world, and my mom opened the door and invited them in."

"Lita, c'mon. She's still your mom."

"How can you pretend the past doesn't exist? My mom never wanted me. I don't want her either. I don't owe her anything."

"It's compassion, Lita. It's not about debts. She's not the woman you grew up with."

"What the hell do you know, Oscar?" She hissed like a battle-scarred cat. "Every day for the past two weeks I've woken up and wished I could rewind my life. I didn't ask for any of this, and I'm trying my best."

"Are you, Lita? Because I've seen you prepare for fights. Watching tapes of your opponents, following a strict diet, going to the gym six days a week to get ready. You devote yourself to fighting, and it shows. You win. You've got to do the same thing with parenting. And I'm including your mother. Because she's like a child. And right now you don't have a ground game. You need to find it."

What he said made sense. She truly didn't have a clue. But she also didn't want to be lectured. "Okay, Oscar. I get it. I'm a loser. I should accept Evie haunting me for the rest of my life." She stepped out of the car and leaned over the open door. "I can do that. But I'll figure it out by myself. You can go back to work."

Oscar's knuckles whitened as he gripped the steering wheel. "Lita, you asked for my help."

"Yeah, well sorry. I'll handle this on my own. Don't worry about me."

"You've got a small army of people willing to help you. But you'd rather struggle solo." Oscar's voice shook.

Her anger rose up in a cyclone, whirling and twisting. "Goddammit, Oscar. I haven't been able to think of anything but the kids since this happened. My life has been completely derailed, and I'm trying to get it back on track. And no shit, I haven't had time to prepare. Because this isn't a fight. It's a tragedy."

Oscar shook his head. He wouldn't meet her eyes but stared out the windshield at the house, tapping his fingers on the steering wheel. "Which makes it important to ask for help. I'm here to help, Lita."

"Which you've already said." Despite his words, Lita was on her own. No one else could handle this for her, and Oscar certainly didn't have the answers. Why had she gone to him? She didn't need him to search for Jade. She didn't need him for anything. "I appreciate you coming up here, but I'm sorry I interrupted your day. I don't need your help. I've gotten this far on my own and can take it from here."

Oscar sat for a few seconds, his hands on the steering wheel. Then, without looking up, he started the car, backed up with a screech and drove off, spitting gravel and leaving a plume of dust in his wake.

His departure sucked the air out of her lungs, and she struggled to breathe normally. She'd just shoved away one of her closest friends.

What's wrong with me?

THIRTEEN

Jade

BROOKLYN'S DOG could do lots of tricks. Jade had never had any pets, unless she counted the mice she'd fed in her closet in San Leandro. Which hadn't ended well. They weren't tame mice, and when they left the closet to explore other areas of the house, Jade's dad laid traps and exterminated them all despite tears and pleading.

But Brooklyn's dog, some sort of spaniel, could dance and beg and play dead. And it liked Jade. It cozied up to her on the couch, and she liked its warmth on her hip.

"Do you want to play a game? Or do a puzzle?" Brooklyn bounced on the couch and couldn't sit still. "We could watch a movie."

Brooklyn wasn't as fun as her dog. She acted much younger than Jade and seemed way too excited about Jade being in her house. She kept asking what they should do next. Jade and her friends in California had known each other since kindergarten. They'd never had to ask each other anything. They simply hung out.

Brooklyn's constant bouncing annoyed Jade, although it beat being in school where all the kids stared at her. *Fuck 'em*, she thought, taking a page from Auntie Lita's limited vocabulary. She didn't give a damn about these kids or this town.

Her first step in going back to California was getting Auntie Lita to realize she was in over her head. And Jade had a few thoughts about how to do go about it.

"Does your dad have any alcohol?" Jade almost couldn't believe she'd asked, but she had to start somewhere.

Brooklyn stopped bouncing and stopped talking, which Jade hadn't known was possible. Her eyes widened, and she studied Jade. "Do you drink alcohol?"

Jade shrugged nonchalantly. Sneaky sips from her parent's glasses counted, didn't they? "Oh, yeah. I've had it a few times."

Brooklyn studied her, then nodded. "He's got some over here." She ran to a small wooden cupboard in the living room with two cabinet doors which she flung open. "I don't know what any of this stuff is," she said cheerily. "My mom used to let me sip her wine, but I never liked it." She began pulling bottles out of the cabinet, reading the labels haltingly.

"Jim Beam... Johnnie Walker... Smirnoff... What do we want?"

Jade didn't know. She looked at the bottles and chose vodka, the only bottle she recognized from her parents' dusty liquor shelf. She opened the bottle and sniffed. Whoa. It might be better to mix it with something else. "Do you have any soda or juice?"

Brooklyn ran to the kitchen and threw open the fridge door. The fridge contained more condiments, margarine, and beer than anything else. Brooklyn pulled out a carton of orange juice from behind a ketchup bottle, opened it, and sniffed. "How about this?" she asked, closing the door and setting the carton on the counter. She gave an excited hop. "Should we use wine glasses?"

Jade kept herself from rolling her eyes. "Any glass will do. Let's use those tall ones." She pointed to a row of mismatched glasses in the cupboard Brooklyn opened. Brooklyn reached in and handed her two glasses, and Jade poured them half full with vodka and up to the top with orange juice. She handed a glass to Brooklyn and raised her glass up for a toast. "To skipping school."

Brooklyn raised her glass with a wide smile and giggled. "To skipping school!" She took a drink and gagged. "Gross, this is awful!"

Jade agreed. Her first taste burned like swallowing a match. She took another and grimaced. "It's always like this with the first sip. It'll get better."

Brooklyn looked doubtful but continued to sip. "Do you want to smoke pot?" she asked suddenly. "My dad has some."

"Pot? How do you know?"

Brooklyn smiled impishly. "He smokes it sometimes after I go to bed. I found a bag of it in his underwear drawer when I was looking for money."

"Have you ever smoked it?"

"No, but I know how, with a pipe."

Jade wasn't sure she wanted to smoke pot, but it wouldn't hurt her mission to get sent back to California. "Okay."

Brooklyn leapt up and ran down the hallway. She returned with a broad smile and a plastic bag full of tight green buds. Retrieving a leather box from a bookshelf, she opened it, pulling out a small pipe with a green dragon outlined on the stem. She tossed the bag and pipe on the coffee table.

"I think we just put the pot in the pipe and light it." She looked up at Jade. "Do you want to do it?"

Jade shook her head. She'd never seen marijuana before. The green buds curled tightly together, like the diagram of a brain in science class. Brooklyn open the bag, and Jade couldn't believe the immediate stink. "Ugh, that's strong."

"Yeah, my dad usually does this part in his room so it doesn't smell up the house."

"He smokes pot in front of you?"

"No, he does it after I've gone to bed. But I'm usually awake.

I can always smell it. Sometimes I sneak into the hallway to watch TV and see him smoking on the back porch." She plucked a bud out of the bag and stuck it in the pipe. "Do you want to try?"

Jade felt slightly dizzy. Maybe this wasn't a good idea. "No, you go first."

Brooklyn went outside to grab a box of matches from the barbecue grill and brought them back. She drew out a match and lit it, held it to the bowl and inhaled deeply. Immediately she began choking and coughing and exhaled a huge cloud of smoke. She continued coughing and gasping for breath, holding the pipe out to Jade.

Jade looked at it doubtfully, but took it, grabbed a match, and lit the pipe. As soon as she inhaled, it felt like a cat were trapped inside her lungs, scratching and clawing to get out. She choked and coughed at the bitterness, and her throat burned.

Jade grimaced at Brooklyn. "Your dad does this for fun?"

A flash of defiance crossed Brooklyn's face, and she frowned at Jade. "You don't have to do it, you know." She wobbled slightly, and Jade realized she and her new friend were both drunk.

"Oh, I'm not done." Jade took another hit off the pipe, which resulted in another explosion of smoke and coughing fit. For some reason she found this extremely funny and started laughing. Brooklyn joined her, and soon they were rolling on the floor, holding their bellies from laughing so hard.

"Here." Jade stopped laughing and handed the pipe to Brooklyn, who tried a second time. It ended with another gagging, coughing fit, which made the girls roll on the floor laughing again.

They were laughing so hard Jade didn't hear the front door open. She didn't see Brooklyn's dad walk through the front door. She laughed straight up until Brooklyn's father grabbed Brooklyn by the shirt and slapped her hard across the face.

FOURTEEN

Evie

THE PERKY BLONDE woman hums and bounces at the wheel of the comfortable boxy silver car and remarks on the significance of buildings and streets. Evie doesn't recognize any of it, nor this woman, bouncy as she may be.

Wherever she is, this town has colorful houses and characters. She sees a small man with a little dog walking three feet in front of him with no leash. A young woman pulls a small wagon laden with ribbons and five or six small children. "Are those all hers?" She asks.

The blonde woman laughs. "No, I think she runs a childcare."

"What about those people?" Evie point to a group of white-haired people getting off a minibus and walking into a building labeled the Copper Kettle.

"Those are seniors from Manzanita Manor."

"Manzanita Manor?"

"An assisted living home. For folks your age who might not be able to live independently."

"My age?" Evie wonders.

The woman's cheery face momentarily turns pensive. "I'm

guessing. You seem quite young at heart." The smile returns. "How old is Lita? She's your youngest?"

"Lita? Oh, she's a little girl. And so quiet." She thinks about her children. "Jake's my oldest. He's been fifty since he was five. So solemn and serious. And there's Laurel. Never a serious day in her life. Always looking for a party."

Evie stops talking. She struggles to think. She's forgotten. A thought's stuck in her head and can't get out.

"So you had three kids? It's quite unique you lived in Mexico with your family. Were they all born there?"

Evie hears the question, but she can't find her way out of the images in her mind.

PHILLIP'S GONE SO MUCH NOW. His trips to the States take him away for weeks at a time.

"It's great money, Evie. We'll save enough to move back and buy a place in California."

"California? What about now? I miss you. The kids miss you. It's been three years. Hadn't we saved enough?" The children's neediness and nonstop movement overwhelm her. "Can't you stop now? I'm going crazy," she complains, pulling closer to him in the dark and leaning her head on his chest. The only time they have alone is after the kids fall asleep.

He takes a deep breath and lets it out in slow sigh. "My employers aren't flexible, Evie. I can't suddenly quit."

"Why not?" Her voice sounds shrill to her. "Phillip, I can't do this alone." Last week the water pump had broken, and she'd spent two days without running water before he'd returned to deal with it.

"Jake can help you."

"He's only eight. He can't fix the water pump. What if there's an emergency? We're all alone here."

"Evie, you have friends. I have friends. They can help."

"But they've got their own problems, Phillip. Why should

they have to respond to mine? I need you. We need you." Her voice rises, then she quiets, not wanting to wake the kids.

He shakes his head. "I can't leave. Business is really picking up now, and I don't think they'd let me go." His blue eyes meet hers, and she wonders if she sees fear in them. He speaks softly and quietly. "It's not up to me, Evie. They've lent us money. I've got a couple of years to work it off and then can start saving."

"Lent us money? For what?"

His eyes cloud over, and he looks away from her. "Truck repairs. Gas. Rent. We weren't actually doing that well until I got this job." He clicks his tongue. "This is good money, Evie. And I've got a plan to get us debt-free and back to the States."

Back to the States.

To what? Her letters remain unanswered. No response to the three birth announcements. She's tried to call home, to make contact with her mom using the phone in the post office. But whoever receives it hangs up rather than accepts the collect call. She's not sure she has a life in the States anymore.

Phillip smooths her hair and kisses her forehead. He shifts to his side so he's facing her. "Tell you what. I'll find someone to help out around the house. We'll pay him. You can call him when I'm gone."

EVIE SHAKES HER HEAD. She's sitting in a small café across the table from a blond woman with a ponytail facing a mural of a neon desert scene: pink saguaro cacti, purple jumping chollas, and an aquamarine owl peering out from the saguaro's branches. The woman stares at her, eyes pinched in concern.

"Evie, are you okay?"

A sickening feeling overcomes Evie. She tries to stand, but her legs feel weak. Where is she? Where is Phillip? Her kids? She begins to tremble, reaches for the water glass and knocks it over. Her kids are gone. Her husband is gone. She is all alone.

"I didn't mean for any of it to happen," she whispers.

FIFTEEN

Jade

"WHAT THE HELL ARE YOU DOING?" Brooklyn's dad's face was a mottled red.

Brooklyn scurried to the edge of the couch, wrapped her arms around her knees, and began to cry. Her dad turned angrily to Jade. "Who the hell are you?"

Jade shrunk into the couch, mute in terror.

A big, burly, bearded man with blazing blue eyes and an angry, blotchy face, Brooklyn's dad towered over her. She couldn't talk.

"She's Jade, my friend." Brooklyn shuddered in a small ball.

"What the fuck are you doing, Brooklyn?" He picked up one of the glasses from the coffee table and sniffed it. "Jesus Christ." He muttered.

Picking up both glasses, he carried them to the kitchen and dumped what was left down the sink. Jade wanted to run away but couldn't make herself get up.

Brooklyn's dad came back and picked up the pipe and bag of pot. "What the hell, Brook? Sneaking through my stuff? Stealing from me? Is it okay to smoke my pot and drink my booze now?"

Brooklyn whimpered again. "No, Dad."

He turned angrily towards her. "Shut up. Don't say a word." He looked at Jade. "What's your name?"

Jade's voice disappeared, and she could only whisper. "Jade."

"Jade what?"

"Jade McGovern." She could barely hear herself. Her mouth felt like it was filled with paste, and she could hear a shrill ringing in her head. She didn't want to look at him, but she couldn't face Brooklyn huddled and sniffling, snot streaming from her nose.

She hung her head. Her parents would be very ashamed of her. She wanted nothing more than to be wrapped up in her mom's arms, her mom whispering that everything would be okay.

"Who's your mom, Jade?"

"I live with my Auntie Lita."

"Give me her number."

Jade gave him Auntie Lita's cell phone number. He walked out the front door, his voice, loud and angry.

He came back in and told her to grab her stuff. "Your aunt's been looking for you. We both got calls from the school." He glanced at Brooklyn, crying and holding herself. "She tells me you're new to town."

Jade nodded dumbly. She got up and searched for her jacket and backpack and couldn't meet his eyes, didn't know where to look. She swallowed, terrified and lost, wanted to go home to California where people loved her, where friends knew her. Brooklyn was a mess with swollen, red, puffy eyes and tangled hair. Jade's hands trembled as she zipped up her backpack. What would it be like having this brute for a father?

"You stay away from Brooklyn," he continued. "If I ever catch you and her drinking or smoking or skipping school again, it won't be pretty."

Jade nodded dumbly. Auntie Lita's rattling truck announced

its arrival with a bang and a pop as it pulled up in front of the house.

She could barely look at the sobbing puddle that was Brooklyn. Shame filled her as she turned to say goodbye. Brooklyn had wanted a friend, and Jade had given her trouble.

"Bye, Brooklyn," she said, hesitating.

Brooklyn gulped. Then the corners of her mouth turned up slightly, and, despite her shuddering shoulders, her eyes flashed mischievously.

"See you tomorrow," she whispered before she dropped her head back to her knees.

Brooklyn's dad marched out the front door ahead of Jade, back tall and rigid, thick arms carried loosely away from his body. He met Auntie Lita as she rounded the front of the truck and lit into her as soon as she stepped onto the sidewalk.

"Keep your fucking niece away from my daughter. They've been drinking and smoking pot. Brooklyn's a good kid. She's never done anything like this."

Auntie Lita grew three sizes in front of Jade's eyes. She squared her shoulders, straightened her back, and stepped squarely into the shadow cast by Brooklyn's dad.

"Watch your fucking language," she said. "And don't blame Jade for your kid's problems." She squinted at Jade. "Get in the truck," she said coldly.

Jade rushed to the truck, head down, eyes full of tears. She jumped onto the passenger seat and started to cry. The day had turned black on her. Her body shook as she slumped against the door of the truck. She didn't want to see Brooklyn's dad ever again.

Auntie Lita's voice shouted. "Your house, your alcohol, your pot. How is it Jade's fault?" Jade peeked out the windshield. The man towered above her aunt. Brooklyn hovered at the door, a tiny figure in the shadow of the frame.

Her dad roared back. "She's eleven years old. She's never done anything like this before." He lowered his face to within inches of Auntie Lita's and dropped his voice so low Jade could barely hear. "I don't give a shit about you or your niece, get it? Let her fuck up her own life but keep her away from Brooklyn."

Her aunt's face twisted in fury. "Back up, meathead. Don't yell at me." Her voice seethed with anger. "Jade," she shouted suddenly, "did you force anyone to do anything?"

Jade stole a glance at Brooklyn hiding in the shadow of the front door with her puffy eyes and tear-streaked cheeks. Their eyes met, and Brooklyn gave her head a quick shake.

"No." She avoided looking at Brooklyn's dad. She felt like shit. The alcohol buzz had been replaced with a heavy sense of dread. Her fault.

Auntie Lita nodded. Her body was coiled tightly, ready to spring. "You like to push small people around? I don't respond well to force."

Her head came up to his chest, but her eyes were locked onto his like lasers. She clenched her jaw and shifted her weight. *Oh god.* Jade feared Auntie Lita might throw a punch at Brooklyn's dad, whose face looked so furious she thought it might explode. He growled—like a beast—and clenched and unclenched his fists.

"Daddy, no!" Brooklyn screamed, and she ran out of the house, slamming herself into him, wrapping both arms around his waist and sobbing. "No, Daddy. It's my fault."

She fell to her knees, crying and clutching his legs. He stood rigidly for a couple of seconds, breathing heavily and glaring at Auntie Lita. Then he leaned over, picked up Brooklyn and set her on her feet. He pushed her into the house ahead of him without a word or a backwards glance and threw the door shut. Auntie Lita walked stiffly around the front of the truck, got into the driver's seat, and slammed the truck door.

Jade had no idea what Brooklyn faced. But whatever happened to Brooklyn, she'd caused it. She felt sick to her stomach.

Auntie Lita's hands shook as she put the key into the ignition. Jade sat silently, head down. Her aunt cruised slowly to the park, pulled up to the curb, and turned the engine off.

"You okay?" she asked, her voice tense.

Jade nodded. She didn't trust herself to talk without bursting into tears again.

Auntie Lita exhaled forcefully. "I don't know what to say, Jade." She tapped the steering wheel with her fingers. "You caused a whole lot of trouble for your friend."

Jade sniffed head down.

"Look at me," her aunt ordered.

Jade met her aunt's gaze. She couldn't get the image of that awful slap out of her head. She'd rather face Auntie Lita than Brooklyn's brute of a father. All the same, she didn't actually want to face her aunt. And though she knew she should apologize, she couldn't form the words.

Her aunt studied her. "Cutting school, getting drunk, getting high…. You know where this ends, right? Did your dad ever tell you about your Auntie Laurel? She started out rebellious and young, too. Is that what you want?"

Jade knew about Auntie Laurel who'd died of a drug overdose years before Jade was born. "No," she whispered.

She dropped her eyes again and sniffed as her emotions churned. Anger, hurt, and confusion swirled inside her head. This was what she wanted, wasn't it? To get her aunt angry enough to send her back to California? But it didn't feel good. It felt awful. She really wanted her mom. Or her dad. She'd wanted them so much in these past weeks it felt unbearable. Their loss shadowed her every thought, her every move. She squeezed her eyes shut, her hands clenched in her lap and began to shake. She didn't want to cry in front of Auntie Lita, but she couldn't keep it back.

Auntie Lita spoke again, softer. "You're twelve, Jade. Your friend looks like she's ten. What the hell were you thinking? Drinking her dad's booze and smoking his pot?"

Jade stiffened, then cried harder. She wanted this to be over.

She wanted to go back to the house and crawl under her covers and stay there forever.

"Your friend—what's her name?" Auntie Lita wasn't going to let this go easily.

"Brooklyn."

"She's not going to have a pleasant evening, Jade. I wouldn't want to be her. Whose idea was it, anyways? Did she invite you to her house?"

Jade nodded.

"To drink? To smoke pot?" Jade shook her head, and her shoulders shook harder. Her aunt's voice rose angrily. "You used her."

Jade sobbed harder. Auntie Lita didn't understand the half of it. Brooklyn's dad's face had been so ugly.

"He hit her." She sucked in air and let it out in a moan. She started openly crying, tears flooding her cheeks, her nose running like a broken gasket. "When he saw us in the house, he hit her."

Her aunt's voice sounded hard. "Did he touch you?"

"No." Jade's crying slowed. She wrapped her arms around her stomach. Her face felt hot and swollen.

"Did your dad or mom ever hit you?"

"No!" Jade lifted her head, surprised by the question.

Auntie Lita's tone changed, became less confrontational. "Well, some parents rule by fear. Like your friend's dad's. But one day, she'll stop being afraid and figure out she has nothing to lose. And then, win or lose, she'll be gone."

Her aunt sighed deeply. She rubbed a hand through her hair. "Your dad kept the nasty side of the world out of your life, Jade. I wish he were still here."

Her words struck Jade like lightning. She covered her face and began to cry again. Auntie Lita couldn't possibly miss him more than Jade. She wanted nothing more than to be wrapped in his big bear hug. It had only been three weeks, but it felt like three years.

Auntie Lita continued. "Your dad and I grew up differently. Your grandmother wasn't as good at parenting as she was at drinking. But your dad wanted you to have a normal life instead of the fucked-up one we had."

A small whine escaped Jade.

"I don't know what a normal life looks like. I've been told nothing about me is normal. But like it or not, Jade, I'm what you've got. My job is to keep you and Jersey and Jupiter healthy and safe. I'm on your side."

Her aunt paused. She rolled her window down and took a deep breath, then let it out in a sigh. "You know, Jade, I moved to Mexico to live with my dad when I was fourteen. It was tough."

Jade didn't know anything about Auntie Lita's other family. Which made sense, because she didn't know much about Auntie Lita at all.

"He'd married Rosa, my stepmom. They had six little kids, and she was pregnant with another when I arrived. A big family. But I was in a bad place, and Rosa wasn't happy to have me there. She complained there wasn't enough room in their small house for another body, especially a moody teenage girl who didn't cook or clean.

"So after a few weeks my dad took me to live with my abuela in the village where I was born. They enrolled me in school, but since my Spanish was so rusty, I got placed in classes with younger kids. I stopped going to school and ended up in the only place where I remembered spending time with my dad— the garage where he worked. Eduardo, the old man who owned the place, let me hang out and help out."

"What does this have to do with me?" Jade didn't want to hear her aunt's sob story, but apparently everything had to be about her.

"Because I don't want you to get lost, Jade. And I don't know what to do. No one knew what to do with me, either. I started partying and driving trucks in the desert with some of the boys from the village. I could barely see over the windshield, but I drove fast and hard, one of the few things I liked to do. Of course, I didn't have any boundaries back then, and my drinking and wild ways shocked Abuela. So after two years with her, she sent me back to Hermosillo to live with my dad, though I knew he didn't want me."

"Like you don't want us." Jade spat the words out bitterly. She understood now. Her aunt's story reinforced what she already knew.

"No," she said sharply. "That's not what I'm saying. Things got better. Things changed. It may feel tough now, but it'll get better."

Jade laughed humorlessly. "It won't get better. Nothing can change what's happened."

"Nothing can change what's happened," her aunt said softly. "Losing your parents won't ever feel easy, Jade. But I understand how you feel."

At this, Jade lifted her head and met her aunt's eyes. "No, you don't."

Lita's eyes flashed with anger, her voice defensive. "Don't tell me what I do or don't know, Jade. My life hasn't been a picnic."

"You don't know anything," Jade hissed. "You still have both of your parents, Auntie Lita. You're not all alone, an orphan. You weren't forced to leave everything you know and love." At this her voice broke, and she began crying again.

"Neither one of them wanted me, Jade." Lita said softly.

"You don't want us either!" Jade's voice rose shrilly. "We're just causing problems in your life!"

"I'm sorry if I gave you that impression, Jade. I care about you and Jupiter and Jersey. I want to keep you safe. But I didn't have the greatest role models, so, yeah, I don't know what I'm doing. I've never been a parent before. But know this: I won't sit by while you screw up your life. I won't get distracted by other things like my mom. Look what happened to our family."

"You hate Nana." Jade spit the words out. "She's part of our family, but you're mean to her. You're going to send her back to California." She pleaded with her aunt. "Send me back with her."

"What? How did you hear that?" She seemed surprised. "I don't hate Nana. She doesn't know who I am. And yeah, I've got her on a waitlist for a care home in California, but she's from there."

Her aunt gazed out the windshield then fixed her eyes on Jade. "This isn't about Nana. This is about you. You getting into shit you know nothing about. Drinking, drugs, cutting school… you're grounded. School, home, school, home. It's all you're allowed to do for the next two weeks. If you don't get off the bus every afternoon, it'll last much longer."

Fine with Jade. She was on her own.

SIXTEEN

Lita

LITA DIDN'T GET BACK to the gym in Tucson until three months after her last fight. She'd struggled to stay in shape. Weights and cardio at the Bisbee gym had helped, but her sparring and technical skills had gone to shit. Between the time crunch in the morning getting the kids and Evie out of the house—thank god for the adult daycare program and for Elise, Jodi's wife who told her about it—working at the shop all day, and the flurry of pickups and meal prep in the evenings, she hadn't been sure she'd ever get back to training.

Kroker gave her no slack. "Your speed is down, Lita," he scolded while she punched a bag during warm up. "I'm trying to line up a fight for you for next summer. You've got a lot of time, but it's gonna be a lot of work with the shape you're in."

"Throw it at me, coach," Lita panted. "I can handle it." She hit the bag and bounced on the balls of her feet. Coming back after this long break, the familiar smell reminded her of the first time she'd entered a gym.

SHE'D BEEN BACK at her dad's in Hermosillo for a month but had barely left the house—another rough transition. The city didn't feel safe like Abuela's little village. Her friends in Perdido had warned her the drug trade had become a major employer in the city. She sensed danger everywhere.

When she went into town with Rosa and the kids, she didn't like the openness of the streets. She focused solely on her little brothers and sisters, avoiding eye contact with anyone. She didn't want attention, didn't like the eyes roaming over her. She tried to shrink, to make herself invisible, but she felt exposed and vulnerable.

One day, Lita trailed behind Rosa in the mercado, herding Gloria, a chubby five-year-old, and Marco, two years younger. They passed through a group of young men who greeted her with whistles and catcalls. Her pulse leapt, and she pushed her siblings blindly forward before the men could follow her, rushing to get out of the crowded market but finding no exit.

"Why are we going so fast?" Gloria complained.

Lita couldn't breathe. She began to shake, wide-eyed and unable to focus. She put her hands on her knees and struggled for air.

"Where's Mama? Where are we going?"

Lita couldn't respond. She froze, saw attackers everywhere. A group of young men laughing behind her. An old man approaching her with a goat on a tether. A young couple strolling through the market, arm in arm. She grabbed Gloria's hand, took Marco's arm, and began weaving through the market, swerving around groups of people and animals, stalls full of fruit and vegetables, clothing and household goods.

"I want Mama." Gloria whined. Beside her, Marco slowed and dragged his feet.

"No running!" he pronounced. "No running!"

She burst through the exit, dragging them into the street where she stopped, gulped for air, and shook. Lita didn't care where Rosa was. She took her siblings home and forced them to stay inside with her, plying them with bread and cheese and a game to keep them distracted while she waited for Rosa to return.

Rosa came home livid. She chewed out Lita for taking off, for leaving her to carry all the groceries home alone, for her overall uselessness.

Lita tried to ignore her. She hadn't asked to come to Hermosillo. She hadn't asked to play child minder for an overwhelmed stepmother. Rosa complained bitterly to Jose when he arrived home, and her dad studied her at dinner. After dinner he told her to skip the dishes.

Rosa frowned. "Now she can't help with the dishes?" Jose kissed Rosa's forehead and made a joke about Lita's poor dishwashing skills. Rosa scowled at her husband and looked at Lita disdainfully. "Useless, Jose. She's useless. I do everything. Cook, clean, take care of the babies. She skips out. Go ahead! Take the useless girl away and bring me back another daughter who doesn't have so much gringa in her."

Her dad placated Rosa in soft tones, and Lita looked at the floor, her eyes burning hot with tears she wiped away angrily. She wanted to go home but didn't know where home was.

By the time her dad finished speaking to her, Rosa was singing along with the radio as she washed the dishes. She didn't say a word at their departure.

Lita hadn't spent much time alone with her dad since she'd been back. He worked at a garage six days a week, taking only Sundays off. With a wife and six young children, he had little time for his strange teenage daughter.

They walked to the city center, empty of crowds. The mercado sat shuttered. The streets, bare of families, had begun to fill up with a sparse night crowd: street-food vendors, performers, and groups of men.

Always groups of men. Her heartbeat quickened, and she stuck close to her father, refusing to glance around her, focusing only on the road ahead. Jose happily greeted passersby, and Lita felt their eyes on her. Though considerably smaller than her dad, she stuck out all the same. Her hair, grown shaggy in the past two years, fell down her neck and shoulders, wildly out of control. Rail thin and gawky, looking more like twelve than sixteen, she jumped and twitched at loud sounds.

"Your mama loved to dance, Lita."

His words pierced Lita's fear. It shocked her to hear him speak of her mom. She'd spoken to her mom only once in the two years since she'd left California.

Her dad had forced her to call. "She needs to know you're safe."

Drunk and hysterical, Evie had been out of her mind. Lita had held the phone helplessly as her mom shrieked and cried until her father took the phone from her, listened quietly, then hung up. They hadn't spoken of her since, and Lita hadn't heard from her again. This mention of her made Lita uncomfortable.

"When I knew her, your mother had passion, mija. A passion for life."

"And alcohol," Lita said bitterly. "And men."

Jose chuckled softly. "Maybe those too." He continued to greet people as the city changed from day to night, the sky a deepening violet. This part of the city had few working streetlights, and Lita stuck close to her father. "But those aren't passions, mija, those are addictions. When you give up yourself or your responsibilities to feed your passions, they become addictions. It starts to hurt you."

"I hate her." Lita felt her chest constrict, and her eyes suddenly welled with tears. Her mom didn't deserve pity.

"No, mija, no. She's your mother. Be mad at her, but don't hate her. Hate won't help you. Or her."

"I don't want to help her. She didn't help me."

Was he going to tell her he'd decided to send her back to her mom? She felt sick. True, she'd chafed at the restrictions of life with Abuela in Perdido and felt more and more boxed in in

Hermosillo. But she felt safer with her dad than she'd felt in a long while.

Had she already blown it? Had Rosa drawn the line?

She stopped walking and watched her father's back as he walked ahead. When he turned around with a question on his face, she couldn't help it. She started to cry.

Jose's face dropped, and he frowned as he walked back to her. "What's happening, Lita?"

"Don't send me back." She couldn't catch her breath and began to take in huge gulps of air. She looked around wildly, seeing threats in the empty market to their right, in the door frame to their left. She wasn't safe anywhere.

Her father stood directly in front of her. "Look at me," he ordered.

Lita wiped her eyes. Her shoulders shook.

Though only six inches taller than Lita, he seemed to tower over her. His eyes fixed on hers, and she felt a deep, burning shame. Unlovable, she knew. Her mother didn't love her. Her abuela couldn't handle her. And her father had never wanted her. He was going to send her back.

"Mira." He told her. "Look." He motioned towards a wall of windows behind him on the street, where a big sign read "El Tigre Kickboxing." Light streamed from the windows and spilled out onto the street. Inside, small figures moved about rapidly on red and blue mats. Heavy bags hung from hooks along the back wall, and bodies moved purposefully around them.

Lita's mind reeled in confusion. "It's a gym. People are fighting." What did he want her to see?

"Sparring, chica. Not fighting."

Lita didn't know the difference.

"You can't be afraid the rest of your life, Lita. You can't drink or run away. You know where that goes. Come, Lita. There's someone I want you to meet."

She followed him into the gym, hot and humid despite the

fans and the late hour. The smell of sweat and rubber assailed her. The activity in the room stopped. Men stared as they walked in, and she followed her pop closely. A broad-shouldered, thickly built man greeted them. Older than her dad by a decade or so, with cropped graying hair and a flat nose broken more than once, he wore black gym shorts with a white tank top. His eyes took them both in and settled on her dad.

"Jose! What's going on, amigo? Haven't seen you in a long time." He slapped one hand on her dad's shoulder and shook his hand with the other. "What brings you to this part of the city?"

"My daughter, Lita."

The man's eyebrows flew up as if aliens had landed in front of him. He looked from Jose to Lita and back. "This is news, Jose. Where have you been hiding her?"

Jose laughed. "She's been in the States with her mom."

The man whistled. "I never imagined." He turned to Lita and held out his hand. "Ramon Ortega."

Lita shook his hand. She looked around the room rather than meet his eyes.

He turned to her papa. "My friend, what can I do for you and Lita?"

Jose smiled and motioned around the gym. "She needs to learn to fight."

Ramon smiled broadly at Lita and held his arms up in a clear gesture of welcome. "You are in the right place, my dear. I can teach you how to fight." He studied Jose. "You'll be coming too?"

Lita was dumbfounded. She'd never asked to learn to fight. And it smelled funny in this gym. She looked at her dad questioningly.

"Yes, I'll be coming, as long as Rosa lets me." He chuckled.

Ramon laughed and clapped Jose on the back. "A good man always knows who's in charge. When will you start?"

• • •

"SWITCH UP YOUR FEET! Move your head!" Kroker's voice brought her back as she pounded the bag. Lita shook off the memories and focused on his voice—*Keep your hands up! Balance!*

The stress from the past month eased, and she was back in her element. No prepubescent grieving niece. No little boy flinging himself onto her without warning. No little girl tantrums or tears. No Evie.

She finished the bag work and put on sparring gear. Despite the cardio and weight workouts, she hadn't sparred in three months. She preferred the striking elements to the wrestling or jiu jitsu. But her speed and agility made her adept at floor techniques, too. The constant movement kept her on her toes, the balance between striking and groundwork, taking what Kroker taught her and applying it to each new session. Escaping from a hold or a mount, submissions.

She relaxed for the first time in months. The gym felt more like home than her house full of kids and Evie. Cap entered the ring, and they circled each other. They'd agreed to take it slowly, but slow didn't mean easy. He threw a jab, and she adjusted. They sparred for two-minute rounds, and it only took two rounds before she was exhausted. She'd have to work hard to get back into fighting shape. Her timing was off, and her combinations were slow.

After she'd showered and changed, Kroker flagged her into his office. She entered and moved a blue gym bag to the floor before sitting on the vinyl chair. The office's white walls were yellowed with age, and it smelled dank, like a closet filled with dirty socks and mildewed towels.

"Whatcha got for me, Coach?"

"We talked about a fight next summer, but I want to make sure you're up for it," he said. "You've got a heavy load right now, and I'll scale back the search for an opponent if you think your priorities might be changing."

"Was I so bad today?" Why was he bringing this up? Not once had she thought about quitting. In fact, getting back to the gym had given her a flash of her old life. "I'm not quitting fighting, Kroker. What are you trying to say?"

Kroker shook his head. "Don't worry, Lita. You can fight as long as you want to. It's just going to be a lot more difficult now."

"No shit. But you know what would make this ten times worse? If someone took fighting away from me." The comfort she'd felt in the gym began to leave her, and the small office started feeling overheated.

"Cool down. No one's taking anything away from you. I'm sorry I brought it up. You're the most dedicated fighter I know, and I'm ready to help if I can." He flipped a pen with one hand and caught it before it hit the desk. "I guess I want you to know I'm going to push you hard as always, Lita. But if you need to step back, it's okay. Life has a way of making our decisions for us."

Lita stood up, uninterested in continuing the conversation. Finally back in the gym, and Kroker was freaking her out. "Okay, I got it. I'll let you know if anything changes. But Kroker?"

He stood and held her gaze.

"Fighting is the only goddamned thing I control in my life right now, and I'm not going anywhere." She picked up her bag, and he nodded at her. "See you next Saturday."

SEVENTEEN

Jade

JADE HEARD the whispers at school after the incident at Brooklyn's, and she caught some of the students casting furtive looks at her. A couple of the boys and girls studied her openly, and one boy asked her, before lunch, if she wanted a drink.

Brooklyn missed school for the next two days but greeted her shyly when she returned. She attempted to draw Jade into games or conversation, but Jade rebuffed her. She kept seeing Brooklyn's head snapping back when her dad slapped her, reliving the way Brooklyn scurried to the couch and huddled in a mass of snot and tears. Jade didn't want to cause more problems.

But Brooklyn didn't get the memo. When her initial attempts were rebuffed, she began slipping Jade notes and waiting for her at lunchtime. She wouldn't give up, and it annoyed Jade. Because Auntie Lita had been right—she'd used Brooklyn.

If she suspected this, Brooklyn didn't seem to care. She continued to follow Jade and talk to her, despite Jade's cold shoulder. "I hope we get to work on the same float for the Founder's Day parade."

Jade didn't understand why Brooklyn was so excited about a school parade. She couldn't care less. But when the groupings were announced, she'd been teamed with Brooklyn and five other students—three boys and two girls—tasked with designing and decorating a float.

"A jailhouse float?" Jade didn't see the connection to Founder's Day. Wasn't Founder's Day about the founders?

Max, the only boy in their group who had ever spoken to her, scrutinized her, hands on hips. He had a round, freckled face and wavy red hair, long enough to wear in a ponytail. Most days he wore Wrangler jeans with boots and a button-up, short-sleeve shirt. Somedays he smelled like horse shit.

"Haven't you heard of the Bisbee Deportation? Obviously a jailhouse isn't one hundred percent accurate, but if we made it look like a rail car, no one could see in." Max studied a diagram in his hands. "The trick is getting everyone to recognize what's going on. I think we'll have to make a sign."

Jade shook her head. He sounded like a geek. "I have no idea what you're talking about. I never knew Bisbee existed until I moved here."

He stared at Jade like she'd told him she'd never eaten at McDonald's. "Really? Guess they don't teach history in California. I did a project on it last year. The copper miners went on strike, and the sheriff of Bisbee formed vigilante groups to round them up. He loaded twelve hundred miners onto boxcars, shipped them to New Mexico and abandoned them in the desert, locked in a rail car in the heat without food or water."

"What?" Max didn't seem like a liar, but Jade found it hard to believe. None of the other kids contradicted him. "No way."

"Yeah, they were stuck there for two days until the army arrived. My dad says it pretty much killed the labor movement here. Two people died, but no one got punished."

"That's not fair."

Max shrugged his shoulders. "That's life."

Jade hadn't heard of this before. Was it common? Did things like this happen in every state? Did California have its own ugly history she hadn't heard about? This seemed like something everyone should know. She wouldn't want to bake to death in a railcar with a thousand people. She knew that much. "Why does the town celebrate this with a parade? You'd think they'd want to leave it alone."

Max smiled mischievously. "They don't celebrate it, but we get to design our float around whatever topic we want. It was my idea."

Max had been selected by the teacher to organize tasks for their float, and Jade could see why. He delegated well and wasn't distracted by what the other kids said or did around him. The other boy in their group, Scotty, detached himself to sit on a bleacher with his headphones. The two girls, Emmy and Jenna, chatted and giggled together but accepted instructions from Max. They smiled at Jade shyly but didn't talk to her.

Max told her she'd be working on the jail itself. "You might know what one looks like."

He flashed a smile, but Jade glared at him. Her mom once told her boys teased girls because they liked them. She didn't care. Max was a loser like the rest.

Brooklyn, of course, ignored the task Max assigned her and stuck close to Jade. She was quite helpful, Jade realized, and more creative than anyone she'd ever met. Some of her ideas were completely irrational, but a lot of them would make their float stand out. She gladly let Brooklyn take the lead.

Emma and Jenna worked in pairs making crepe paper decorations and painting signs. Scotty eventually left the bleacher and teamed up with Max. Every other Friday for the rest of the year, their team was going to work on the float during the last hour of school. Jade began looking forward to those days, often sorry when the bell rang and she had to run to catch the bus.

Max took the same bus as her. He sat in the front and got

off early, at the junction between the highway and a red dirt road stretching east. She searched for a house but could only see a long gravel driveway curving around a bend. Things were so different here from San Leandro.

But kids were the same all over, Jade thought. There were straight-A students, a group Jade had proudly been a part of in California but which she didn't care about now. Then there were the popular students, attractive and confident. The Shades, a dozen or so kids, left school to smoke cigarettes in the shade of the three large oak trees off the south end of campus. And the lone cowboys—Brooklyn and Max fell into this category—didn't hang out in a group.

In California, she'd had the same circle of friends for so long she'd never had to think about it, but now Jade didn't know where she belonged. Following the events at Brooklyn's, she guessed the other students thought she'd be one of the Shades, but Jade wasn't eager to repeat that experience.

After picking up the middle school students, the school bus drove to the high school to pick up the older students before heading up the hill to Bisbee. The high school kids talked loudly and boisterously, pointedly ignoring the junior high students, which Jade appreciated. She didn't want any attention. She sat by the back left window and ignored all activity.

The seat next to her remained unoccupied for the first several weeks until one day a broad-shouldered boy jumped onto the padded bench and slung a pack to the floor in front of him. Jade didn't look at him but stared out the window.

Her new seatmate stood and yelled at a boy who stood in the middle of the bus, blocking the aisle. "Keep moving, Schroeder! You're blocking the line!"

Two boys engaged in a pushing match, and the blockage finally broke. The students who hadn't yet boarded climbed on and sat down, and the bus pulled away from the school. When the boy tapped on her shoulder, she found herself staring into the brown eyes of the boy she'd met downtown with Nana. Logan.

"You might want to plug your nose," he said cryptically.

She flushed at his broad grin. It lightened her mood, despite his second warning.

"I mean it, you'll want to cover your nose for this." He took a Ziploc bag out of his pack. Inside sat six peeled hard-boiled eggs, grey-green and slimy. When Logan unzipped the plastic, a rotten stench radiated.

Oh my god. She choked back a cough and held her breath. Before she could cover her mouth, he took the eggs and rolled them one by one towards the front of the bus. It took only a few seconds before kids started reacting.

"Oh my god, what's that smell?" A high school girl pinched her nose and looked stricken. A boy coughed and covered his mouth. All around the bus kids were looking at each other and covering their faces. Logan laughed until his eyes watered. Jade didn't think it was that funny, but she smiled anyways. She'd rather be in on the joke than the butt of it.

At the first stop—Max's stop—the bus driver parked the bus with a jerk. He stood up and put his hands on his hips, blocking the door. "No one's off until the eggs are cleared out."

The kids gave a collective groan. Max, who stood in the aisle with his backpack, ready to get off the bus, scowled and half-heartedly looked for the source of the horrible smell. He pulled his shirt over his mouth, but the gaps between his button-up collar made it useless as a mask.

Logan continued giggling while the kids looked around the bus for the eggs. The stench floated over everyone.

"I need gloves!" said a girl, looking down at her feet in disgust.

"Use this," said another, holding a wad of paper away from her body. As students found the eggs, they tossed them, one by one, out the window.

The driver glared at them. His sweaty face shone like a cranberry ready to burst. "This bus isn't moving until I know who's responsible for this."

Max stood in front of the driver with hunched shoulders, waiting to get off. When he turned around to look at the students in the seats behind him, a paper airplane hit him in the forehead. He recoiled in surprise; a look of hurt flashed across his face. A few kids laughed, but Jade felt sorry for him. Though shy and geeky, Max was nicer than anyone else she'd met at school.

The bus driver didn't like the paper airplane either. His face turned scarlet, and Jade thought he might collapse. "That's it! Off the bus, all of you."

The bus went silent. Even Logan stopped laughing.

"I need to get home," a voice cried out.

"I have a piano lesson," another said.

"Blame that on whoever brought these eggs aboard." The driver didn't budge.

"How will you know who did it?" Logan yelled out. Jade couldn't believe he was so bold. In spite of herself, she snickered, and he glanced at her with a wicked smirk, then stood up. "I'll search everyone's bags."

The driver frowned at the boy. "Logan, you're my number one suspect. Empty your own bag first."

Logan held his arms up in protest. "I'm innocent, Mr. Murphy."

"Get up here, Logan."

Logan smirked and moved forward, his fist clenching the plastic bag that had held the eggs. He sidled past Max in the narrow aisle, and Jade saw him "stumble" and slip the bag into a pocket on Max's pack before he righted himself. When the driver ordered him to empty his backpack up front, he did so loudly and quickly, dumping it on the floor and looking back at the other students cockily, with a wide, smug look.

"Innocent of all charges." He held his hands together above his head and shook them in victory.

The driver grunted, then motioned for Max to empty his pack. Max held out his pack for inspection instead. Logan peered into it from behind the driver Then he drew back in surprise, his eyebrows shooting upwards in exaggerated astonishment.

"What's that?" He pointed to the egg bag in the side pocket of Max's backpack.

The driver plucked the bag out, sniffed it, and gagged, then regarded Max with narrowed eyes. Max's face dawned with realization, and Jade felt the wrongness of it.

"That's not mine." Max protested.

"It's in your pack."

"It's not mine." Max glared at the Mr. Murphy defiantly.

Mr. Murphy faced the students. Logan stood behind him, mimicking the man's motions with exaggerated movements. "Max says this isn't his. Anyone else want to claim this?"

Some of the students giggled nervously. Others looked out the window. The rest watched.

Did others see Logan plant the bag on Max? Should she say anything? Jade liked Max. He wasn't a braggart or show-off. But she also didn't want to be a snitch, especially not when it involved a popular high school boy like Logan.

Max looked helplessly at the students and then at the driver. No one on the bus spoke, and his shoulders slumped in defeat. "I didn't do it." He scowled and pursed his lips. "Why would I do this?"

"Trying to make a stinking impression!" Logan yelled out.

Some of the students chuckled nervously, but most had their heads down. Jade looked around helplessly. No one else was going to say anything. Should she?

The driver pointed to the door and tossed his head towards it and ordered Max out. "Out. Now. Save your story for the principal. Have your parents call the office, and don't get back on my bus until you're cleared."

Max glowered at the driver and the rest of the students as he left the bus. Logan high-fived his way back to the seat he shared with Jade.

He plopped down with a large sigh and ran a hand through the mop on his head. "A man's work is never done."

He smiled broadly at Jade then winked. Though she hated herself, she smiled.

EIGHTEEN

Evie

"COWABUNGA!" One boy jumps into a pit of balls. Another swings at him with a foam sword, then dives in after the other.

Open and cavernous, filled with gym mats, climbing structures and a ball pit, the room looks like an indoor playground. Little bodies dive and shriek everywhere. At the table, several boxes of pizza lie open and ransacked. Discarded plates and plastic cups roll around the table. In front of her a glass of water sits next to a half-empty pitcher of brown soda. She needs a drink.

"Are you enjoying the party, Evie? Pretty neat little birthday spot we've got here, isn't it?" The curvy woman has a friendly face and a big laugh.

"Who are you?" Evie asks.

The woman smiles. "I'm Karmen, Lita's friend. We've met."

"Which one of these kids is yours?"

"Oh, I don't have any kids. Jupiter invited Felix and me to his party."

"Jupiter?"

"Your grandson. He's wearing the pirate hat and carrying a sword. Over there."

Evie recognizes the boy. He lifts his head and sees her

watching him, then sticks out his tongue and stiffens, grabs his throat, rolls his eyes, and falls into the mass of balls.

Evie turns to the woman. "Where can I get a drink around here?"

Karmen's eyes widen. "Oh, there's no alcohol. Would you like some soda?"

"No," she says irritably. Why would she want brown, bubbly sugar water? She stands up slowly and smooths the back of her skirt. "I'll slip out and find a real drink."

Karmen looks confused. "You're leaving?"

"I'm heading somewhere quieter. This place is hell on the ears."

Karmen stands too. "Let's talk with Lita first. I think we're going to have cake soon. You don't want to miss the cake!"

Evie waves her hand dismissively. "Not for me, thanks. I'm done." She wraps her sweater around her shoulders and heads towards the door.

Karmen keeps pace with her. "Let's check with Lita. Don't you want to be here when Jupiter opens presents?" She gives Evie a hopeful, cheery smile.

"He'll open them whether I'm here or not. Time for a drink."

Evie pushes open the swinging glass doors and exits into the bright sunlight. Despite the cool air, the sun glares at her. She squints and looks right and left down the street. Christmas decorations line the streets and rooftops. A sleigh and plastic reindeer sit on the roof of the building across the street. Paper snowflakes dot the storefront windows. A Christmas tree stands in a display with a flashing Michelob sign. *Bingo!*

She heads towards the flashing sign. Karmen trots alongside her. "Maybe we should go back and see if the party's over."

"No thanks."

"Do you have any money, Evie?"

Evie stops for half a second, then keeps walking. "That's not usually an issue."

Karmen keeps pace alongside her, and they reach a big, black, hardwood door beneath a painted sign with "The Drift" in gold letters. Solid except for a grimy crescent window at its very top, the door feels sticky and heavy when Evie leans into it. It creaks open into a dark, narrow walkway, tunnel-like. The stale, sweet scent of alcohol drifts towards her and she inhales deeply, then walks in.

Evie has never been here. *Strange.* She knows all the local watering holes. The dim walls resemble rock but are actually painted and contoured drywall. Evie emerges in a bar—relief! —and heads straight to the bartender, who smiles as she wipes the bar with a towel.

"How can I help you?" Her brown hair is thick and curly, restrained by a headband.

"A vodka tonic with a water back, please."

"Sure thing. Anything for you?"

The woman with Evie stares longingly back at the tunnel with her hands on her hips.

"Uh, no. Water please."

Evie perches on a bar stool and waits. When had she last had a drink? Too long ago if she can't remember. There's been so much confusing activity recently. Has she been traveling?

The drink arrives quickly, and she gulps at first, the sting of the tonic tickling her nose.

"Six fifty," the bartender says.

Evie shrugs. "I don't have my purse." She waves at Karmen. "Can you pay for this?"

The bartender waits.

"Evie, are you sure this is a good idea?" Karmen looks back at the entrance, then at the bartender. "My purse is in the car. I'll run and get it."

The bartender looks from Karmen to Evie and shrugs her shoulders. "I don't care who pays. I can start a tab if you'll be here a while."

"Yes, a tab!" Evie says brightly.

"No tab. I'll pay." Karmen sighs. "I'll be right back. Evie, I'm going to get my wallet and let Lita know you're here."

The familiar rush of the first sips calm her. Evie takes another large gulp. "I'm not going anywhere."

Karmen leaves, and Evie surveys the bar. A man in dirty coveralls and a filthy ball cap sits in a back corner, his head tilted over his beer. Three young men play pool along the back wall. A striking blonde woman sits alone at a table near the bar, two beer bottles dripping with condensation on the table in front of her.

A dark-haired, good-looking man emerges from the back hallway. His cologne drifts over Evie when he walks by to sit at the table with the blonde woman. He speaks to her, and she replies with a shake of her head. He clamps his lips together and begins picking at the label of his beer. When he looks up, Evie waves. His eyes widen and his mouth forms an *o*. He speaks again to the woman, and her eyes lift to Evie with a slight grimace.

"Evie!" He smiles and scans the bar before getting up with a slight downturn of his mouth. "Are you here alone?"

"Not if you join me."

He coughs and reddens slightly. Evie peers at his face. "Do I know you?"

"Yeah, we've met. I'm Oscar." He looks around the bar again as if searching for someone. "Why don't you sit with us?"

The man's companion watches her closely. Her blonde hair hangs loosely around her shoulders, and her freckled, sunburnt nose wrinkles as she gazes at them. She acts bored.

The man's table looks more stable than the twisty stool she sits on. "If I can get off this stool, sure."

Oscar holds his hand out, and she grabs it with one hand and grips the bar with the other. She slides her legs down and plants them firmly on the ground. Oscar keeps hold of her hand as they walk towards the table. "You smell good," she says.

He smiles and pulls a seat out for her, then returns for her drink, still on the bar. The bartender speaks a few quick words to him, and Oscar glances at Evie, then pulls out his wallet and hands the bartender a few bills.

Evie studies the blonde woman sitting across from her. She doesn't seem happy. Forehead creased, she tilts her bottle and drinks.

Oscar returns and hands Evie her drink. She smiles gratefully and takes another gulp. She'll need another soon.

"Evie, have you met Rikki?

The woman's eyes lift to Evie. "Hi." She says dully. She turns to Oscar. "I wanted to spend some time alone."

Oscar sits back and furrows his brow. He begins to respond, but a storm cloud forms with the appearance of a small tattooed woman at the end of the tunnel entrance. When her eyes land on Oscar, her jaw softens, and her rigid brow relaxes. Then she sees the woman next to him and her eyes harden, her mouth tightens in a thin line. Her eyes meet Evie's and flash with anger.

Oscar chokes his words off as soon as he sees her. The blonde woman looks up and scowls.

"Great," she mutters.

The buzz from the alcohol has gone straight to Evie's head How long since she'd last had a drink?

"You're rude," she tells Rikki.

The blonde's mouth drops open, but Evie switches her attention to the approaching woman. She knows her. From where?

The tattooed woman nears their table. Is she sneering? Evie can't make sense of her expression.

"Evie, you found a drink."

Evie looks at her drink, then back at the woman, who speaks again before she can respond.

"Hi Oscar. Hi Rikki." Her voice, taut with anger. "Glad to see you drinking with my mom."

Mom? Evie stares at the woman. She looks around the bar, suddenly nervous. She catches the bartender's eye and motions for another drink. The bartender nods, but the tattooed woman groans and wags her finger in the air.

"No, Mel, she's good."

"Lita, it's not like that." Oscar sounds impatient.

"Lita?" Evie stares at the woman. "I have a daughter named Lita."

"No shit." Lita glares at all of them, her eyes flashing danger.

"She's a girl," Evie says, though no one at the table appears to hear her. She sits back and watches the tattooed woman shoot daggers at the man with her eyes. Why is everyone here so rude? She really wants another drink. Evie catches the bartender's eyes and holds her empty drink in the air, shaking the ice cubes. The bartender shifts her eyes from Evie to Lita, then shakes her head and walks to the other end of the bar to wipe the counter.

"She didn't take my order!" Evie is flabbergasted.

"You don't need any more drinks, Evie."

"Says who?" Evie feels certain she needs several more, though this one has gone straight to her head. She feels dizzy.

"Listen, Lita, I didn't bring her here." The man sounds defensive.

"No, you saw her here and thought, 'let's share a stiff one.'"

"For Chrissake, Oscar. Do we have to go through this?" Rikki shakes her head, frowns at the table, then turns her displeasure onto the man. "Let's get out of here. I didn't expect to share a table with your ex-girlfriend and her mom."

Oscar's stands up and shakes his head, a faint look of disgust rippling over his face as he takes out a bill and tosses it on the table. He starts to speak but Lita interrupts.

"I'm not his ex-girlfriend, Rikki. You've got a clean title."

"Whatever." Rikki rises and puts on a faded denim jacket. "I'll meet you outside, Oscar. Nice meeting you, Evie."

Was it? Evie watches her storm away from the table, hips swaggering in faded jeans. Oscar grabs his jacket and Evie puts a hand on his arm.

"Thank you for the drink."

He smiles at her, but his eyes aren't smiling. A shame. He has beautiful eyes. "It was nice to see you again, Evie." His lips thin when he glances at Lita. He leaves without another word, shrugging his shoulders into his jacket as he exits through the tunnel.

Lita watches him go, then turns to Evie with an angry scowl. "Why'd you leave the party? And how the hell did you end up with Oscar?" She doesn't wait for Evie to respond but motions for her to stand. "Let's go."

Evie looks down at the empty drink and the money Oscar had thrown on the table. "I don't want to go anywhere. I want another drink." She stands to get the damn bartender's attention and sways slightly with dizziness.

Lita curses and grabs her arm firmly but gently. "No, Evie, we're going back to the party. Jupiter's about to open presents." She leads Evie out the tunnel to the street, and Evie follows without further protest. She'll find a drink later.

NINETEEN

Jade

MAX HAD BEEN SUSPENDED from the bus for two weeks due to the rotten egg incident. The old Jade would have said something, would have immediately told the driver Max wasn't responsible. But that Jade no longer existed. This Jade didn't care about rules or consequences. She had few friends in this new town and wasn't going to start off as a snitch.

Besides, Logan seemed to like her. He continued to sit next to her on the bus, and despite him being a dishonest sneak, his goofy smile made her feel special. He told her jokes, rocking into her with his shoulder and making faces when she looked back at him. They didn't talk, at least not about anything important, and she rarely saw him outside of the bus. But she began to look forward to the bus ride home.

One day Logan plopped down on the seat and rifled through his backpack. He pulled out a box of animal crackers and held it up for Jade. "Do you want these?"

"Uh, why?" she asked. Heat grew in her cheeks.

His grin widened. "I don't like them. They're my sister's favorite, and I picked up a couple of boxes for her. But now that I think about it, my mom's been complaining about her cavities, so I've reconsidered."

"How old is your sister?" Jade wondered if she knew her or had any classes with her.

"She's little, only six. And actually, only my half-sister because I live with my mom and stepdad. My dad lives in New Mexico." He stared at the train-car box in his hand. "Do you want it?"

Why would he offer her a gift? What would it mean if she accepted it? Would they be going together?

"Why?" She asked suspiciously. She wanted to trust him.

Logan shrugged. "You and I sit together all the time, and you seem like you could use some sweetness."

"What does that mean?"

He shrugged again. "You're new. You seem sad. I thought you might like it." He started to put the box back into his pack. "I can always find someone else."

"I'll take it." Jade didn't want him to give it to anyone else.

He beamed at her and tossed the box in the air. "Catch!"

She cupped her hands and caught the box, then stared at it. What did it mean? Should she open it? She would probably keep this box forever.

Logan knocked his shoulder into hers and gave her a goofy smile. Jade averted her eyes and held the box of cookies. In California, boys had been irritating interruptions. She'd never paid attention to them. But in Bisbee she had nothing. No real friends, unless she counted Brooklyn, which she guessed she should, because Brooklyn tailed her all day long. Or maybe Max. She and Brooklyn had started joining him at the far end of the lunch yard, where he ate with a book in his lap.

Logan's friendliness knocked her off balance. She had no idea what this gift meant. He leaned his head towards her, and her heart thumped wildly as his forehead almost touched hers. She caught a faint whiff of sweat and cinnamon.

"A couple of friends of mine are planning a little party tonight. Do you want to go?"

Jade couldn't hide her surprise. "Me? Really?"

Logan laughed, and her heart leapt. "Uh, yeah. I'm not talking to anyone else." He stopped smiling and stared at her. "We're going to meet up around seven p.m."

Ohmygod ohmygod ohmygod. Logan wanted to take her to a party. "What kind of party?"

Logan leaned in conspiratorially and whispered. "A high school party." His breath tickled her ear. It felt intimate somehow, despite the noise and chatter of the students, and Jade's heart raced. "I hear you know how to party. You up for a night with the big dogs?"

Had he heard about her adventure at Brooklyn's? Few secrets in a small town, she guessed. She wanted badly to go with him. But Auntie Lita had kept her eyes on Jade since the incident at Brooklyn's three months ago, and Jade doubted very much her aunt would let her go to a high school party.

"I… I don't think my aunt will let me."

Logan rolled his eyes. "*Avatar*'s playing at the Lion's Club. Tell your aunt you're going to see the movie. It's almost three hours long, so you won't have to be home until after ten."

Jade couldn't believe Logan wanted to hang out with her. Wanted to take her to a party! What would she wear to a high school party? Would she wear black? She certainly couldn't wear pink or baby blue like a toddler. She studied the high school girls on the bus.

"Earth to Jade, earth to Jade." Logan knocked into her shoulder with his. The bus slowed to a stop and Logan stood "It's my stop. You want to hang out tonight, or what?" He gathered his pack on his shoulder, and Jade spoke without thinking.

"Yes! I'll be there once I figure out what to tell my aunt."

Logan flashed a broad smile and leaned over before he left. "I'll meet you at the Lion's Club at seven. Do you have a cell phone?"

Jade shook her head.

"Bummer. I'll wait for you. Wear a warm jacket and bring a flashlight."

A warm jacket and a flashlight? Jade wanted to question him, but Logan flashed her one last smile, then marched towards the door of the bus and climbed down the steps to the road. She lost sight of him and sat back with her heart fluttering. A party. He'd invited her to a party!

What would her friends back home think? Despite keeping in touch regularly, she hadn't told them about the afternoon at Brooklyn's. Something about the slap had taken all the fun out it. If she were honest, they'd be appalled at her drinking alcohol and smoking pot. But she would definitely tell them about this. She'd been invited to a high school party. By a cute boy!

From the bus stop, she slowly walked up the canyon. The evening couldn't come quickly enough. How could she wait that long? She'd have the house to herself for the next hour until Auntie Lita arrived home with Jupiter, Jersey, and Nana. They used to go to Felix and Karmen's for dinner on Fridays, until Auntie Lita and Oscar stopped speaking.

Jade didn't understand why he was no longer around. It's not like they'd been a couple or anything—Auntie Lita barely touched him in public. But Oscar had been a regular visitor to the house for the first few weeks. He'd cooked dinner, a much better cook than Auntie Lita. Then he'd stopped coming over, and Auntie Lita's short fuse blew when Jupiter asked about him.

"He's a grown man with his own life, Jupe. I don't keep tabs on him."

"But he said he'd show me how to shoot a bow and arrow," Jupiter whined, which Jade knew annoyed her aunt.

"Well, he's not here, is he?" Auntie Lita snapped back, frowning at Jupiter who looked defiantly back at her. "You'll have to figure it out yourself. But I could teach you how to fight!"

Jupiter's eyes lit up. "I want to fight!"

Just like that, Oscar was gone.

• • •

WHEN AUNTIE LITA came home with Nana, Jupiter, and Jersey, she carried two frozen pizzas into the living house. "Pizza tonight," she announced.

Jade rolled her eyes. Auntie Lita's go-to meal was frozen pizza, and she couldn't do that right. For some reason, she didn't use the oven timer, so they often ate pizza singed black around the edges. Jade figured maybe Auntie Lita needed to smell the crust burning before she knew it had finished cooking.

Jade broached the movie quickly. "*Avatar*'s playing at the Lion's Club tonight, and some of my friends want to go."

Her aunt looked up curiously. "That's an older movie, isn't it? Could we all go?"

"I want to go to the movie!" Jupiter jumped up and down in the living room, then climbed onto the couch and jumped on it.

Jade hadn't expected this. She stammered her reply. "Uh, I think it's too violent. It's PG-13. Maybe too scary for them."

"Jupiter, stop jumping on the couch," Auntie Lita growled at him before turning her attention back to Jade. "Huh. Who are you going with?"

"Some friends from school." Her aunt frowned. "Brooklyn. And Max, from my float project." Her palms began to sweat, and her pulse sped up.

"What time does it start?" Auntie Lita headed into the kitchen with the pizzas.

Jade followed her. "Seven. It's about three hours, so I'll be home about ten."

"How will you get home? I don't want you to walk up the canyon alone late at night." Auntie Lita turned on the oven.

Shoot. Jade didn't want to walk up the canyon at night, either. "Max's mom can give me a ride." Her forehead felt clammy. She'd never lied like this. There were a lot of details to cover. How *would* she get home?

Her aunt took the pizzas out of their boxes and set them on the countertop while the oven heated up. She faced Jade with her hands on her hips. "How much is it? Do you need money?"

Jade's heart raced triumphantly. *She could go!* She nodded. "Yes." She remembered Logan's parting words. "Can I take a flashlight?"

"A flashlight? What do you need a flashlight for? I don't want you walking home alone."

"I know." Jade said quickly. "But it'll be getting dark when I walk down there. The sun's down by six now."

Her aunt studied her, then shrugged. "Sure. There's one in the glove box in the truck. But don't forget to bring it back." She reached into her pocket, pulling out three five dollar bills. "Will this work?"

Jade nodded and took the money, stuffing the bills in her pocket. She ran to her room to scour her closet for the right outfit.

TWENTY

Lita

LITA ANSWERED the phone from the kitchen. "Hey Karmen," she said.

"I'M PREGNANT!"

She held the phone away from her ear as Karmen shrieked. When the sound died down, she put the phone back against her head. "Holy shit, Karmen, great news! When did you find out?"

Karmen launched into the details, and Lita sat down at the table littered with dirty plates and pizza crusts. Evie, Jupiter, and Jersey were engrossed in a movie on the couch, and Lita listened to her friend's excitement. Karmen had always wanted kids. She'd been a babysitter and had worked at summer camps for years until she'd finished nursing school. And Felix—well, he taught kindergarten. Anyone teaching kindergarten has to love kids. She felt truly happy for them. They'd make great parents.

Unlike her. She felt a growing weariness. The overwhelming responsibility for these three kids smothered her. Jupiter kept getting in trouble at school for swearing. Jersey had to be reminded constantly not to hit kids at day care. And Jade—well, nothing since the incident with Brooklyn three months ago, but Lita worried it was only a matter of time before the other shoe dropped.

She could no longer pop over to the Old Miner for a quick beer after work. She couldn't take off on the Hornet for a quick spin in the desert or go to the gym in Tucson without making five hundred logistical arrangements. She couldn't make any decisions without thinking about how it affected them. Everything in her life now revolved around a role for which she had never prepared and never wanted. *Fuck.*

"Felix is so excited, Lita!"

There must be something wrong with her. She was happy for Karmen. She truly was. But bitterness clung to her. She cleared it away with effort. "That's great, Karmen. It's awesome. When are you due?"

"June! It's still so early, but I'll have time to prepare."

On the couch, Jupiter and Jersey laughed at the movie. Evie stared at the kids laughing and laughed with them.

Lita wondered how much Evie understood. She'd started going to the adult day care program at Manzanita Manor and seemed generally content to go where told. Except for the day when she'd ended up drinking with Oscar and Rikki at the Drift, Lita had managed to keep her mom away from alcohol.

"Will you come with me?" Karmen wanted her to go shopping for baby gear.

"Of course! Where?"

"Tucson! I'm going to wait a few months. No sense in buying anything too early. But it'll be fun to spend a day shopping."

"You don't want to go shopping with Felix?" Lita suspected she had no way out.

"No, he'll get bored before we hit the second store."

"How many stores are we going to hit?" A day shopping in Tucson would be full. But if she could fit in a training session, she'd get something out of it.

"There are at least five baby stores in Tucson, and I've already figured out our itinerary. Solana will come with us, and she and I will eat a late breakfast while you go to your gym. Then we pick you up and make it a day!"

"Sounds like you've got it all planned." Lita sometimes wondered how she and Karmen were so close when they were so different. Karmen organized her life with checklists and schedules and planned for events far in advance. Lita barely knew what she'd be eating for dinner—though it was a good bet it'd be frozen pizza—and she'd never planned for anything. Even her fight training plan, which she followed religiously until she'd gained her new household members, had been developed by Kroker.

"Felix tells me I'll have a rude awakening when the baby arrives. Says all my planning will go out the window once the little one starts making demands." Karmen laughed. "I take that as a challenge. I can't wait!"

Lita smiled. "You'll be the most organized parent ever. And the best. Karmen, I'm so happy for you."

"Thanks, Lita. Do you think Jade will want to babysit?"

"Probably. She likes you and Felix. And I bet she'd be good at it. She's out at a movie right now."

"How's she doing?"

"She seems okay. Bored all the time, always moping around the house. She's doing okay in school, from what her teachers say. At least she's not failing classes." Lita ran a hand through her hair and glanced at Jupiter and Jersey, engrossed in a quiet scene on the TV. "She doesn't really talk to me, Karmen."

"Don't worry, Lita. She's at that age. I hated my mom and dad butting into my business. I didn't want them to find out what I was up to! Don't you remember what it was like?"

Lita stiffened. At that age, the sound of Lita's bedroom door opening in the night had been her biggest fear. "Uh, not really. My mom only butted into my business when I started stealing her liquor."

"Well, it's normal, Lita. And not only is she a typical adolescent, but she's also dealing with losing her parents. Love her and keep steady and consistent."

Which was the problem. Could Lita love her? When she thought of her dad and his family, she felt a strong sense of belonging, of warmth. And security. Was that love? Her dad had brought her back from the edge of fear, had given her fighting, taught her to be strong. She loved Karmen, who for some reason had become Lita's closest friend. But otherwise, Lita fought love. It was a black hole dragging people into destruction.

Did Lita love her mom? She remembered tiring at the beach in Perdido as a little girl and curling up in her mom's lap while her sister and brothers ran wild with other village kids. Her mom's long arms wrapped around her had felt like love. But everything changed with the move to California, and she'd lost any comfort or security. After Lita's first call to her mom from Perdido, she'd waited for her mom to call her back, to tell her how sorry she was, how much she missed her and loved her and wanted her. But Evie never called.

When Lita looked at Evie she felt simmering anger, not love. It spilled onto her nieces and her nephew, totally innocent and vulnerable, but she resented being responsible for these lives. These kids needed exactly what Karmen said: love, consistency, steadiness. Not rage.

She realized she now found herself in the same situation her mom had faced years before. Pulling herself out of the ashes of tragedy and raising three kids alone. Her mom had screwed things up for their family, and she didn't want the same for her nieces and nephew. She wouldn't. She owed it to Jake to make it right, to fix it.

But based on the past few months, she had to do better. She still felt two steps behind. And she'd be lying to herself if she said she knew what she was doing. It all felt so daunting, like fighting an unknown opponent. More reactionary than prepared. Was there a way to learn how to do this better? Did she have time to learn? Her time was not her own anymore.

Maybe this was what Kroker was referring to. Their conversation had confused her, but maybe he had some sense.

"Well, Karmen, you and Felix are cut out to be parents. And I'm working on it, though I'm afraid everything I do is going to break them somehow." She'd never say she couldn't love them. They needed her.

"What about you and Oscar?"

The question felt like a slap. "What? What about Oscar?"

"When are you two going to patch things up?"

"I'd rather not talk about this, Karmen."

"Well, when the hell are we going to talk about it? You guys are tight for ten years and then suddenly you're not talking? What's up?"

Lita didn't want to get into it. Of course it didn't make sense, but that defined her life, didn't it? Who the hell pushes away her best friend when she needs him the most? She did.

She missed Oscar, and not only his cooking. But her anger flared at the thought of him telling her to put the past aside and welcome Evie back into her life. *What did he know?*

"It's been three months, Lita. Time to suck it up and apologize for flying off the handle."

"Flying off the handle? Who told you that? What do you know?"

"Oscar wouldn't have caused this. He's not the fighter here. You are. Which means you're the only one who can stop the fight."

"What fight? Karmen, what are you talking about? We don't have any claim on each other. He's free to date Rikki or whoever he wants. I can care less." Her words didn't match the clenching of her heart.

"Oh no, Lita. I don't believe you. I'll drop the subject for now, but you can't toss aside one of your best friends because he said something you don't agree with."

"Ah, c'mon, Karmen." Lita didn't toss aside anyone. Oscar stepped back. She didn't force him to stay away. "Oscar's obviously not missing me. He's got Rikki keeping him company."

"Sugar, I don't know what to say. I hope you can be friends again."

Karmen could be so frustrating sometimes. "We're still friends. Nothing's changed. But I've got a family to consider, and Oscar's got a girlfriend. Separate lives, that's all." She hung up and ended the call uneasy.

TWENTY-ONE

Evie

EVIE LEAVES the little ones on the couch and enters the kitchen where the woman is staring out the dark window, dishrag in hand, over a soapy sink full of dishes.

The woman lifts a cookie sheet out of the water and rinses it, then leans it over a small dish rack. "What can I do for you, Evie?"

"Oh. I'm not sure." Why has she come in here?

The tattooed woman's eyebrows lift in surprise. "Feel like doing some dishes?"

Evie does not want to do dishes. She frowns at the suggestion and looks back to the other room where the little girl and boy are giggling. She walks to the back door and looks out at the small back porch and the black night. The sound of crickets fills the air, but nothing moves.

"I think it's time for me to go home."

The woman pauses, her hands deep in soapy water, and Evie can't interpret her expression.

"How?" the woman asks.

Evie doesn't know what she means. "I'll drive."

"Okaaay." The woman draws out the word. "But you don't have a car."

Evie is stumped. She is certain she does, but she doesn't know where it is. "I just have to find it."

"Best to do it in the morning," the woman replies.

She makes sense, but Evie feels unsettled, restless. The two children laugh in the other room. The small woman pulls the drain plug out of the sink, and the water begins swirling in a whirlpool. Her movements remind Evie of someone.

"Who are you?" Evie asked.

The woman's eyes flash, and her face darkens. "Lita," she said.

Evie stares at her. "I have a daughter named Lita."

"No shit." The woman wipes her hands on a towel and hangs it from the handle of the oven. She puts her hands on her hips and faces Evie. "Where is she?"

Evie steps back. The question bounces around her head. Where is Lita? She looks around the kitchen and at the dark window, the room feeling somehow smaller than minutes ago. She sniffs but can't pick up the sea air of Perdido. Where is she? The wind whirls suddenly, and a branch smacks into the kitchen window. Evie jumps and cries out.

THE STORM STRIKES when Phillip is away. It surprises the entire village. The wind rages across the sea and slams into the house after dinner, the clouds darkening the sky to the blackest midnight. The sudden onset and its violence terrify her.

Rain pours down, and sheets of water pound the roof. Randy, a toddler who never stops moving, shrieks as thunder crashes overhead. He clutches Evie's legs. Out the window, a flash flood rushes down the street, a plastic bucket bouncing and disappearing in the surging waters. A window shutter slams into the wall, the sound of it like the crack of a rifle. Evie holds back a scream. From the kids' bedroom, Laurel shrieks. Evie rushes in, Randy in her arms. The window's open, and water blows in, soaking the dresser beneath it.

She shuts the window and throws a towel over the dresser, then picks up Laurel with her free arm and carries her two littlest into the main room. Eight-year-old Jake follows, wide-eyed and quiet, clutching her long skirt. She gathers all three onto the couch with her as the tiny house shakes with the wind. Their house is cinder block—strong and sturdy. But the roof... could it fly off?

Something big and metal crashes into the side of the house, and Evie's heart beats wildly. Panic rises like the swells of the black seawater near the little house. Laurel and Randy clutch her fiercely and howl. Jake shakes beside her. Evie is frozen by fear. The kids grip her so tightly she can't see out the window, can barely move.

The wind shakes the house viciously, and a large limb from the massive tree in the front yard suddenly falls onto the porch. With a crash, one if its branches whips into the front window. The window breaks, and glass shatters into the house and rains down on the couch where they sit. Water blows sideways into the exposed room.

Pushed into the hallway by the sudden deluge, Evie huddles with the kids against the wall, away from windows. The lights flicker off. Then back on. Another gust of wind slams into the house, and the house goes black. With the wind pushing and pulling, she worries the house might crack apart. She whimpers and crouches, holding her children close. The tree in the front yard creaks and groans. She pulls the kids closer to her, shuts her eyes, and begins to cry.

She awakes, startled. Rain falls steadily outside in the dark, but the shrieking wind has quieted. Damp air flows into the room through the broken window. How has she fallen asleep in the storm? The kids slumber in a pile next to her, Jake's arm slung over Randy's tiny body, and Laurel flopped over Jake's legs. It's too dark to be morning. She gets up slowly, legs stiff and tingling, eyes burning, and she carries the kids one at a time into her room, putting them all in the big bed.

A knock on the front door makes her jump. She moves into the front room and sees a young man peering through the broken porch window, his eyes narrow and searching.

A cry escapes her. José, the neighbor. Phillip hired the eighteen-year-old to help out with the house. He visits daily but stays only if there's a task to do.

She's no longer alone. Tears streak down her cheeks as she nears the door, and she can't catch her breath. The terror she'd felt the night before returns.

José's face widens in surprise, and he opens the door and lets himself in. "No, señora, no te preocupes. Tranquila, por favor. Todo está bien."

She clutches his arm. Her breath comes in short stuttering gasps. José pats her shoulder as he would a child. "No te preocupes. Está bien, señora, está bien."

She leans her forehead onto his shoulder and begins to cry in deep gulping sobs. She's alone, afraid, unable to protect her children, her home.

José stiffens, then puts his arms around her, patting her back and rubbing it in small circles. Evie cries harder as the night's storm surges in her memory.

"I didn't know where to go, what to do," she sobs. "I'm all alone."

"No, no. Shhh." He murmurs softly. "You're not alone."

His body feels strong and comforting, steady. She becomes aware of its solidness against hers, the taut lines of his shoulders, the strength in his arms, the warmth of his breath. She draws her head back and meets his eyes.

"Gracias," she whispers. She kisses his cheek, then wraps her arms around his waist and lays her head on his shoulder. When she lifts her face again to kiss his other cheek, her lips brush his. She feels a pulse in her belly, and alarm bells ring in her head. She sinks into him, pressing against him in a silent plea. His breathing quickens. His arms tighten around her.

When she lifts her face again, their lips meet, and she moans and pushes into him. She reaches a hand down to touch him. His breath catches. She shudders. Evie sinks to the floor and pulls him with her.

He leaves when the rain slows, and the birds begin their morning serenades. She cries and scrubs herself raw in the bathtub before the kids awake.

"EARTH TO EVIE."

Evie starts. She's in a kitchen with a short, tattooed woman who's leaning against an oven staring at her. She reminds Evie of someone. A warm, friendly face appears in her mind.

"José," she says softly.

Now the short woman jolts. "You remember José?"

Evie turns sharply. "Yes," she says. Her throat aches. "There was a storm."

Evie wants to say something about the storm, how it shook the house, her life. How it changed everything. But the thought remains in the shadows and lurks there, hiding, then disappears.

"Yeah, the storm. I owe my life to a massive storm." The woman leans back into the cupboard and crosses her arms. "Pop always told me I was a gift from God."

"The Lord giveth, and the Lord taketh away," Evie recites. Her eyes pinch with pain. "Your father is blessed. But not me. My father cursed me. My father's God has taken everyone I've ever loved."

"Yeah, I believe that, Evie." The woman stands, arms folded, and stares at Evie intently. "Except Lita's not gone. But maybe you didn't ever love her."

"Lita? No. She's gone. I couldn't get her back."

"Really, Evie? Seems to me if you'd tried to get her back, I might remember. But I heard nothing. Nothing."

Evie's thoughts jumble, twisting and curling together like a nest of snakes. She's tried. Called Lita's father. The police. She's pleaded with them, begged them to do something. Her girl disappeared. Desperately, she asked for help from her own father, who told her she was reaping her just rewards. Yes, she's lost everything and everyone.

Suddenly overwhelmed, Evie sits heavily at the kitchen table. The heavy ache of loss presses on the back of her neck like a weight.

"Do you have any wine?" Evie scans the small countertop and sees a box of granola bars, a toaster oven, a coffee maker, and a bowl with apples, oranges, and bananas.

The woman sighs deeply. "No, Evie. I don't keep liquor in the house."

"Wine is hardly liquor," Evie points out.

"Alcohol is alcohol."

"You don't drink?" Evie can't keep the astonishment out of her voice.

"Not much anymore. I partied lots when I was young, trying to find my way. Pop pointed me in a different direction. Plus I knew where drinking would lead… I had a role model."

Evie doesn't like the look in this woman's eyes. Pointed and sharp. Accusatory. She puffs her chest up. Screw this forced abstinence. "I'll go to the store to get a bottle of wine." She scans the kitchen for keys or her purse, then turns to the woman. "Do you know where my keys are?"

The woman clenches her jaw. "You don't have a car, Evie. You don't drive anymore. It's dark out, and there's nowhere for you to go." She studies Evie. "We'll deal with this tomorrow. Let's go sit with the kids and watch TV." She pushes herself away from the counter and waves to Evie to go ahead of her.

Evie doesn't like being dismissed. She can't find the words to argue. She thrusts her fist towards the tattooed woman and stops it in the air inches short of her face. "POW!" she says, then she walks out of the kitchen.

TWENTY-TWO

Jade

LOGAN MET her at the Lion's Club and led her east up a small street to a dead-end where a dusty trail climbed into the dark. Jade felt happier than she had in months.

"This is where you'll need your flashlight," Logan instructed. She pulled it out, flipped it on, and scanned the trail in front and to the side of her, glad she'd chosen to wear sneakers. Logan moved fast, and Jade scrambled to keep up.

Where the heck were they going? They wound up switchbacks, and despite the chill, she took off her jacket, sweating with the climb. The darkness felt disapproving somehow, made her nervous. With no streetlights, no pavement, no ambient light from cars or houses, a pitch black surrounded them.

She grew tired of climbing. Logan laughed at her huffing and puffing, and she scowled in the dark. He didn't seem to be tired at all. But Jade didn't like sports. She'd never voluntarily climbed a mountain.

"Are we almost there?" She didn't want to whine, but her feet hurt, and her lungs were bursting.

"We're almost there." Logan snorted. "I guess you haven't done a lot of hiking."

His tone irritated her. "Not exactly. We didn't have to climb mountains to get to a party. We had roads and cars. You know, civilization."

She sounded snarky. But what did he expect? Dragging her out here into the wild? If it took a midnight hike in the mountains to get to a high school party, maybe she'd skip the next one. This was ridiculous.

Logan laughed. "I guess we do things a bit differently out here. But we have fun. And," he said slowly, "no adults!"

He climbed a final switchback to a rounded peak, then held his hand out to her. Surprised and grateful, she grabbed it. He pulled her up. His hand felt dry and calloused over her hot and sweaty one. He didn't drop it when she reached his side.

Maybe the hike was worth it. She'd only ever held hands with her parents and siblings. Did this mean they were going together?

They stood shoulder to shoulder and stared. Below them lay the valley with the lights of Bisbee and what would have been an expansive view to the south if not for the blackness.

"Bisbee looks kinda small when you see it from here, doesn't it?" Logan dropped her hand and swept his arm towards the black expanse. "That's Mexico."

Jade thought Bisbee looked small no matter where she stood, but she didn't say anything. She wished he'd grab her hand again.

The smell of smoke drifted over. Beyond Logan's shoulder, a small fire blazed in a gap below a large rock face. Six kids stood around the fire and looked up as they approached. Jade recognized some from the café with Nana.

"Logan!" A cheer erupted from the group, and two boys peeled off from the circle and greeted him with broad grins and shoves. They glanced at Jade curiously. One had short dark hair underneath a black Troy-Bilt knit cap. The other's shaggy blonde mop looked like it hadn't been cut in months. Logan stumbled under the blows and held his hands up.

"Hey! Be nice, and maybe I'll share the bottle I brought."

"We've already started. It sure took you long enough. We've been up here for half an hour." The shaggy-haired blonde boy eyed Jade as he spoke.

"Yeah, well we had to sneak Jade out of her house." Logan cast a sideways glance at Jade and laughed loudly. "Technically, she's watching *Avatar* at the Lion's Club."

"We're all watching *Avatar* at the Lion's Club!" the boy said. Everyone laughed as Jade and Logan neared the group. A remaining boy and three girls stood in a circle around a small fire, watching them. One of the girls wore a short black skirt with thick, holey black tights and leather combat boots. She appeared to be fused to the boy who stood behind her in jeans and a hoody, his arms slumped over her shoulders.

Another girl held a cigarette in one hand and a bottle in the other. She took a swig from the bottle as Jade and Logan approached, and her brown eyes shone as she greeted them.

"Woohoo! Party has started!" She held her hands in the air and danced in a circle.

"You've had a head start." Logan grabbed the bottle from her and drank. She protested as he handed it to Jade with a wink. "We've got some catching up to do."

Whoa. A fast start. Jade took a sip from the bottle and grimaced. As at Brooklyn's, it burned her throat and made her cough.

"Looks like your friend needs some practice, Logan." The girl grabbed the bottle from Jade and held it close to her chest. "Who is she, anyways?"

"This is Jade. She came from California this year."

The girl stepped closer and studied Jade like a zoo animal, circling her, assessing. Jade caught a faint smell of flowers, alcohol, and unwashed hair. The others eyed her curiously but weren't as rude.

"I'm Zoe." She wore purple eyeliner and bright pink hair tucked into a black beanie. Her jeans must have fallen victim to a lawnmower, with multiple slashes across the shins, thighs, and butt, exposing green leggings underneath.

"Do you go to Bisbee High?"

Jade started to reply, but Logan knocked into Zoe with his shoulder and cut her off. "She rides the bus. She got busted in her first week of school at Bisbee Middle for drinking and smoking pot."

Zoe's eyes widened, and she drew her head back to get a better look at Jade.

The second girl, with dark hair and black eyeliner, released herself from the boy and looked Jade over. "A young'un. You're starting early. Your parents drinkers too?" She laughed with a nasty smile and checked an imaginary watch on her wrist. "Oh, it's seven thirty. Time for my parents to begin arguing about who ruined whose life first."

She grabbed Jade's wrist and pulled her towards the fire. "I'm Angel." She laughed at Jade's surprise. "Yeah, they chose the wrong name."

Logan disappeared into the dark with the two boys who had greeted them. Angel introduced Jade to the last girl by the fire, a pale blonde with flat, wispy hair under a black hoody pulled loosely around her face. "This is Taylor." Taylor nodded and raised studded eyebrows when Jade smiled at her, but she didn't smile back.

"And this is Trey. He's mine." Angel gave Jade a sharp look, then circled her arms around his neck. The boy ran his eyes over Jade then wrapped his arms around Angel's waist. They began kissing.

Jade looked away, embarrassed.

"Knock it off." Logan returned with the other two boys and slung his arm loosely around Jade's shoulders. "Jade, this is Javier." The dark-haired boy who had initially greeted them smiled goofily. "And that's Cody." The shaggy blond nodded and smiled. Zoe snuck up behind him and wrapped her arms around his waist. He leaned back into her.

"And this"—Angel extricated herself from Trey's embrace and leaned down to rifle through a backpack on the edge of the circle, pulling out a second bottle—"is vodka!"

Logan cheered, and Jade's heart flipped over a few times. His arm felt foreign on her shoulders but thrilling. He released her and pulled a third bottle out of his backpack. Jade felt cold where his arm had been.

The first bottle was almost empty—no mixed drinks for this crowd—and though it made her eyes water and burned when she swallowed, she helped finish it.

"Gotta catch up, Jade!" Logan grabbed his bottle as she emptied the first one. He cracked open the cap, took a swig, and passed the bottle to her.

She was at a high school party!

Until moving to Bisbee, Jade had never so much as gone into the hall without a pass. What would Ophie and Lily think? Or Annie? Honestly, they'd be horrified. She lifted her eyes to see Logan watching her, his eyes dancing.

"What's your story, Jade?" Zoe asked the question, but the other kids stopped chatting to stare at her.

Jade's heart pounded, and she drew back. Her face flushed hot despite the chill at her back. Few kids knew about her parents, just Brooklyn and Max.

She also desperately wanted these kids to like her. Logan's interest had given her a chance to rise above her geeky new-girl status and become something more. And if she had to live in a dead-end town in the sinkhole of the country, she should at least be someone interesting.

A strange looseness overcame her. Her limbs felt light, and her thoughts ran wild. Maybe they wouldn't stare at her blankly like other kids. Maybe they would understand it didn't make her different.

"My parents died. My brother and sister and I came to live with our angry aunt."

Silence.

"Shit." Angel took a swig of the bottle Trey had passed to her. "That's a downer. Sorry. I didn't mean to make fun of your parents earlier."

Jade felt a hard edge of cold, like ice, throb in the back of her head. None of the kids met her eyes.

Logan squeezed her shoulders, and he leaned into her. "Well, at least you don't have to worry about pissing off your aunt if she's always angry."

She marveled at the warmth of Logan's hand on her shoulders—or maybe it was the vodka—and didn't care so much about any of it. Dead parents, demented grandma, rage-filled aunt. Logan's arm across her shoulders felt like a promise of better things to come.

She leaned into him slightly. His chest felt solid against her shoulder, and again, she marveled at where she found herself. *At a high school party with a boy!* Grabbing the bottle from him, she took another swig. It still felt like drinking gasoline, but she'd learned enough not to cough. She felt a strange dissociation from her body as she handed the bottle to Javier. She giggled. *She was drunk!*

"Let's play a game!" Logan looked around eagerly.

Jade melted when he looked at her. She loved his grin, with his wide mouth and beautiful teeth. His eyes sparkled like fireworks.

"What type of game?" Angel asked mischievously. "Ow!" She winced and burst out of Trey's embrace. He doubled over laughing. She rubbed her backside. "No pinching, Trey. Not funny."

Zoe grabbed the empty bottle and set it on the ground. "Let's play Spin the Bottle."

"How about Truth or Dare?" Javier stood on Jade's right with Taylor on his other side. Angel wrapped herself back into Trey's arms. Jade wondered what it would feel like to be wrapped up in Logan's arms.

"Truth or Dare? What are we, in fourth grade?" Logan

scoffed as Jade laughed nervously. The ground spun slightly, and her eyes struggled to focus. She'd played Truth or Dare at slumber parties but never Spin the Bottle. Though she'd had several middle school crushes, she'd never kissed a boy. Since fifth grade she'd towered over them, and they'd all seemed like little kids. Unlike these boys.

Zoe leaned forward. "One round of Truth or Dare, then a round of Spin the Bottle. Me first." The others backed off, and she studied the group. "Okay, Angel, truth or dare."

Angel didn't hesitate. "Dare."

Zoe sat back. "I dare you to stand on the rock over there and howl like a wolf." She pointed to the rock from where Jade and Logan had admired the lights of Bisbee.

Angel rolled her eyes. "Is that all?" She ran to the rock look-out, lifted her head and howled. "*Aaaarooo! Aaaarooo!*"

Jade watched Angel closely. She couldn't imagine hiking up to this spot in a skirt. Angel returned from howling and held her hand out to Javier who passed her the bottle. "Okay, Logan truth or dare."

"Dare, always dare." Logan's face turned solemn as he faced Angel.

"Okay, take your shirt off and run to the shrine and back."

Shrine? Jade looked around her. *What shrine?*

Logan's eyes sparkled. He stood up and yanked his jacket off, then tugged his shirt over his head and threw it onto Jade. Despite feeling like a coat hook, she appreciated the extra warmth and felt a slight thrill as she held his clothes and inhaled his cinnamon scent. His chest flashed white and bare in the fire-light. He switched on a flashlight, then ran into the dark, beyond the trail they'd hiked up earlier. The light bounced up and around a corner, then vanished before appearing farther away and higher. Logan flashed the light on and off several times as the kids cheered, then he came back panting and shivering. He shook with the cold but flashed Jade a cute, goofy smile as he put his shirt and jacket back on.

"Brrrrr." His teeth chattered. "Jade."

Jade's heart leapt. Of course. Of course, he'd choose her.

"Truth or dare."

The cold pressed in on her, and in no world would Jade leave the warmth of the fire to do anything on a dare. "Truth."

"Oooohhh." The group pressed in to listen. She hoped Logan wouldn't ask anything about kissing boys or partying. She couldn't lie and didn't want to suddenly seem like a dweeb.

"Tell us a family secret."

The other kids murmured, and Jade paused. She really wanted these kids to like her. Logan seemed to be into her, and the others had been treating her like part of their group. They were so different from her friends in California—disdainful of their parents, dismissive of other kids. They probably hated school.

What could she tell them? Was it a secret Auntie Laurel died of a drug overdose? Not really. Jupiter used to parade around the house in gowns pulled from Jade's dress-up box. But she didn't want to label him. It had to be Nana. Yes, Nana.

"My nana used to be a stripper."

Gasps. Wide-eyed faces around the fire. Jade felt suddenly embarrassed. Had she given them truth too big to handle?

Logan hooted and squeezed Jade's shoulder. "I've never heard that one before! Fill us in, Jade."

The other kids laughed. Angel agreed. "Sure tops the list. What's the deal?"

A whisp of guilt wound around her heart like smoke.

"I heard my parents talking about it once when I was supposed to be in bed. I don't know much about it."

Except she did know more. She'd overheard her dad talking to her mom. Nana had loved to drink and dance, and, after they'd come back from Mexico, she'd found a job where she could do both. Jade remembered her dad's voice and his anger. "At first, Laurel and I didn't realize what she was doing, and heck, Mom had always been a dancer. I figured it out in high school. I confronted her, but the money was good, and she enjoyed the dancing, for god's sake."

Logan was leaning into her and looking at her face. "Who are you choosing?"

Jade turned to Zoe. "Zoe. Truth or dare."

Zoe chose dare. Jade didn't quite know what to dare out in the wilderness. "I dare you to do ten pushups on the flat rock over there."

"Really?" Zoe grimaced but got up and lay down on the rock. She attempted a pushup and then another but didn't know how to do them, apparently. Jade's dad used to do pushups every morning in the living room, and he'd steam through them, muscles straining rigidly, counting through his breath. Zoe looked like a dog stretching after a nap, butt in the air and nose to the ground.

"Weak!" Logan yelled.

Zoe managed four or five attempts—Jade couldn't call them pushups—and collapsed on the ground. Cody walked to the rock and stood over her. "C'mon Zoe, four more. Otherwise you drink."

Like an earthworm, Zoe maneuvered up and down. When she finished, she danced a victory dance.

Logan turned to Jade with a high five, and she slapped his hand victoriously. "Successfully played." He passed her the bottle.

She took a large swig, ignoring the burning sensation in her gut. Logan watched her with his big smile, and she didn't think she'd ever seen a cuter boy. He leaned his shoulder into her, and a giggle escaped her. She put her hand over her mouth. Everything suddenly seemed so funny.

Zoe declared it was now time to play Spin the Bottle. She spun the empty vodka bottle around, and it pointed to Logan. Cody hooted, and Zoe rolled her eyes, then leaned across the circle and touched her lips briefly to Logan's. "Your turn now, Logan." She sat back and leaned into Cody.

Logan spun the bottle, and it landed on himself.

"Spin again!" The kids chanted as one.

He spun, and it pointed to Trey.

"No way." Trey waved his hands and shook his head. "Not going to happen."

Jade laughed and hiccoughed again. Her head started to spin, and her stomach flipped sourly. Logan turned the bottle again, and it pointed at her. Her mouth dropped open, and her heart skipped a beat. He leaned over, and she tensed. She'd never kissed a boy. She held her breath as his face neared, and he touched his lips to hers. Like touching a live outlet, a shock ran through her body. A thunderbolt, then a silent tremor ran through her. Kissing a boy! His tongue burst through her lips, and she marveled at the amount of force he used, how he shoved it here and there. She met it with hers tentatively. Before she was ready, he pulled away. She wanted more. But her forehead suddenly broke out into a sweat, and her stomach quietly started to roil. She swayed.

"Your turn, Jade!"

Her heart beat quickly. She spun the bottle, and it twirled rapidly, then slowed and pointed to Angel. Trey shoved his girlfriend playfully. "You gotta kiss Jade!"

"No! If it lands on someone you don't want to kiss, you kiss the next person." Angel shoved Trey back. "I'm not kissing her."

Jade felt relieved. She didn't want to kiss Angel.

"Then she's kissing me." Trey sat up straighter and looked Jade in the eye. "You ready?"

Logan protested. "No, she can go again."

Why did Logan feel he could speak for her? Jade didn't like anyone making decisions for her. A sudden swelling of nausea rose in her stomach. She pushed it back and straightened her head which, for some reason, had begun to flop backwards. "I'll kiss him."

Trey look pleased and Angel surprised. Logan frowned. Jade moved towards Trey. Her limbs felt weighted down. Each movement pulled her slightly off center. She focused on standing straight and reaching her target. When she faced Trey, she giggled. He looked serious. She leaned forward, but suddenly she was falling, falling, falling, a slow motion collapse into Trey who stumbled backwards, then fell to the ground. She landed face down in his lap and couldn't get up. She giggled hysterically and felt a burst of saliva fill her mouth.

Uh-oh.

She knew she should move, but she felt off-balance. She closed her eyes to quell the spinning. Her stomach churned.

"She's going to puke!" Angel shrieked. Trey moved frantically beneath her, pushing and shoving her shoulders to get her off him.

Jade's stomach clenched and twisted. She clutched Trey, hoping he could help her, but it was no use. She couldn't control her body.

He scrambled out from under her, and her stomach coiled, then hurled its contents onto the dirt in front of her. She braced herself on hands and knees. Her hair fell into the pile of vomit. She lifted it as a second wave came pouring out, and she pushed up on her arms to raise herself out of the mess.

She looked up to see seven faces staring at her in horror, but she didn't care. Her head lolled on her shoulders. Her stomach constricted, and she puked again. She closed her eyes and shuddered. She'd stay here, and everything would be alright.

TWENTY-THREE

Lita

I'M curious why you were given custody of the kids when you've had little to no contact with them." The social worker, Lacy Rogers, sat on a plastic chair across from Lita on the back porch, brown hair pulled into a loose bun, writing notes on a clipboard. "I'd like a bit more information about your family. Do you have other siblings who might be able to help?

Lita didn't want her here, couldn't believe Jade had brought this on. A social worker. A fucking mess. "I'm the only option. My siblings are dead, and my sister-in-law Amy didn't have any living family. My mother has dementia."

"Okay, thank you." Ms. Rogers wrote on her clipboard. "Are you married, Ms. Bravo?"

"Lita, please." Her legs bounced up and down, and she focused on calming them.

Breathe deep, she told herself. *This is not a fight. It's about endurance.* "No, I'm not married."

"Any significant others? Jade mentioned you've been involved with an ex-convict, Oscar Torres."

"How the fuck is that relevant? Aren't we focusing on Jade getting drunk?" Lita wanted to change her stance, to switch it up and take control of this situation.

The woman put her pen down and straightened her back. She locked eyes with Lita. "Let's be clear: My responsibility is to make sure your nieces and nephew—and your mother, who's a vulnerable adult—are under the care of someone who can adequately supervise and provide for them. These questions may seem invasive to you, but as I've said, not many twelve-year-olds get dumped anonymously at a police station and hospitalized for alcohol poisoning. I'm required to investigate Jade's home life and provide recommendations based on what I find."

Lita felt a slow boil within. When fighting an unknown opponent, she held her ground and struck when she saw an opening. But this opponent had a nuclear weapon: taking the kids away. Lita had no quick counter to that. Only a long, hard slog through a system she'd run away from years ago. She stopped her jumpy legs and twirled her coffee cup around on the table. She struggled to think of an effective offensive strategy.

She also hated hearing this woman talk about Oscar like a violent criminal. "Oscar is one of the calmest, coolest people I know, despite his record. But we've had a falling out, so he's not around much. And I have no significant other."

She waited for the next volley.

"What do you do for work?" The woman was studying Lita, particularly the tattoos sticking out of her shirtsleeves and rising out of her collar.

"I'm a mechanic. Fully certified. Been doing it for a decade." She stopped twirling her coffee cup. "It's why we came back to Arizona so quickly. I have a job and a life. There was nothing in California."

"Depends on your perspective. I'm guessing Jade feels differently." The woman met Lita's eyes and held them for too long.

Lita grunted. "Of course she does. She's twelve. She doesn't know anything else, and her parents just died."

"More reason to think of the kids, Ms. Bravo. Do you have any experience with kids?"

"As much as the next person, I guess." She felt jittery and picked at a loose thread on her shorts.

"Care to be specific?"

Heat rose inside Lita. Any minute she'd be sweating through her clothes, dammit. She tried to keep her voice level.

"No. I've avoided kids, to be honest. I took care of my younger siblings at times, but I didn't like to babysit. And a lot of people become parents without a background in child care, Ms. Rogers." Her voice shook, and she fought to keep the anger out of it. "These kids are family. I'm the only competent family they have left. Does the state want to split us up because a grieving twelve year-old got drunk?"

Shit. She needed to get away from this woman before she really lost it. She pushed her coffee cup away and stood up. "Do you want a glass of water? My mouth's dry."

"No, thank you."

Lita went into the kitchen and glanced at the kids and Evie on the couch. Jade's eyes met hers but dropped to her lap. She'd brought all this mess into their lives. Police officers, ER visits, social workers. Fuck, she'd gone off the rails quickly.

Lita grabbed a glass from the cupboard and filled it with cool water. She drank half of it, then filled it again before heading back to the porch. The woman was looking at her phone but put it away and spoke as Lita sat down.

"Ms. Bravo…" the woman began.

"Lita."

"Okay, Lita. You and your family"—Ms. Rogers inclined her head towards the inside of the house—"have gone through a tremendous shock."

"No shit," Lita intoned. She kicked herself. *Back off, Lita.*

Ms. Rogers ignored her attitude. "The kids, particularly Jade, are showing signs of anxiety, and your mother has little to no ability to care for herself. While I have concerns, they don't rise to the level of removing the kids or Evie from your care."

Some of the tension left Lita's shoulders, but she remained on edge.

"However…."

Lita braced herself.

"I'm recommending parenting classes for you, and counseling for you and Jade."

What the fuck? Lita frowned and crossed her arms over her chest. Ordered to go to counseling?

The woman rifled through her messenger bag. She drew out a sheet of paper and slid it across the table to Lita. "I've got a list of community providers here, and I'll be checking in with you biweekly to see how you're all doing."

"Wait a second. Back up. Counseling?"

"Yes."

"Okay, Jade, I understand. But I'm not going to any counseling." Lita drew the line. She wasn't talking to anyone about her life. "Parenting classes? Sure. But no counseling."

"Ms. Bravo— Lita—while these are only recommendations, a lack of engagement may prompt additional visits and oversight. No one can force you to go to counseling. But you have all experienced significant trauma."

"Yeah, well…." *Shit.* "How long do we have to do this?"

"I'll be checking in on you for the next six months. If no new issues occur in the meantime, I'll close the file. This isn't to penalize you, Lita. And there's nothing wrong with seeking help."

"To be clear, I didn't seek this out."

"Well, inadvertently, Jade did. This strikes me as a cry for help."

Lita shook her head. "I don't see it that way. Kids party, Ms. Rogers. They make stupid mistakes. Jade's trying to figure out where she fits in."

"She's too young, Ms. Bravo. She's not even a teenager yet. *She's twelve.*"

"And it happened once." Lita sighed and stared at the paper in front of her. She'd begun stealing alcohol from her mom at age eleven, easy enough at night when her mom worked, and it helped Lita sleep through the drunken laughter and loud whispers when Evie returned from the bar with a man in tow. Her stomach lurched as she suddenly realized how young she'd been. "She's a year older than when I started drinking, and I turned out okay."

Ms. Rogers took her glasses off to study Lita. "'Okay' is hardly thriving. You want Jade to thrive, don't you?"

Lita's palms were sweating and her heart thudded. She didn't want Jade to go through what she'd been through. But she didn't want to revisit her life. She'd shut the door behind her, locked it up and thrown away the key. She lifted her eyes to meet Ms. Rogers's and struggled to control her voice.

"What's the benefit of dredging up the past? How will my going to counseling help Jade stay on the straight and narrow?"

"You going to counseling is not to help Jade. It's for you. Many of us have had trauma in our lives. From what little I know of your family, you could all use some support. Counseling is one of those supports."

She has no idea. Lita rubbed her face with her hands, then ran them through her spiky hair. Her body thrummed like a taut wire. Inside the house, Jersey squealed, and Jupiter guffawed. Lita peered in and saw Jade smile. Evie looked from one kid to another, then sat back with a laugh. A picture of family. Her family. She sighed heavily and sat back in the hard plastic chair.

"Tell me what I need to do."

TWENTY-FOUR

Jade

THE SOCIAL WORKER had been a surprise, showing up with her clipboard and her sympathetic smile. Nice enough but a little pushy.

"Jade, I'm very sorry about your parents." Ms. Rogers said. "You're going through a lot and experiencing big changes in your life. It's natural to want to escape. And alcohol is an attractive way to escape."

She asked a lot of questions about the party, but Jade didn't share anything important. She might be a lightweight in the drinking department, but she wouldn't get her new friends in trouble. She tried not to roll her eyes. Ms. Rogers looked so serious, so earnest. The Jade who followed rules would have wanted to please her, but she'd left that Jade in California.

"Were you with friends, Jade? Who left you in front of the police station? How did you get those bruises?"

Jade couldn't remember the end of the night other than vague memories of being carried and dragged down the trail. Her many bruises told her she'd run into rocks on the way down. She shrugged. "I was with some kids. I don't remember their names."

"This is very concerning. Jade, I've talked with your school in California, and this type of behavior is new to you."

"I want to go back."

"Back? To California?"

Jade nodded. "I don't want to live here. I want to go back to California. My friend said I could live with her family."

"Oh Jade, it's not that easy."

"Why not? I'm not from here. This isn't my home. Auntie Lita doesn't want us."

"What makes you say that?"

"Because she's always angry. She swears. She doesn't know how to be a parent. Everything she does is wrong." Jade felt tears building. She blinked. She would not cry.

"Like what, Jade?"

"She can't cook."

Ms. Rogers smiled faintly. "Go on."

"She yells at us. And she hates Nana. How can she hate her mom?" Jade's face felt hot, and she felt the push of tears. "I'd never hate my mom. " She choked back a sob. "I don't care about Auntie Lita, and I don't care about Bisbee. I want to go home."

"Jade," Ms. Rogers spoke softly. Jade squeezed her eyes closed to hold the tears back and shut out this clueless woman. "Your home in California is gone. You'll always have your friends, but your family is here. Your aunt is your family."

"Then how come we never met her until Mom and Dad died?"

There'd been a mistake. Her parents hadn't wanted this to happen. Auntie Lita was a complete mess who couldn't handle having kids. Why couldn't anyone else see it?

"It feels wrong, Jade, but your aunt is family. And I can tell you," Ms. Rogers paused to look Jade in the eye, "she does want you. She may not have much parenting experience, but she made it very clear to me she wants you. While it seems like adults should automatically be able to put on a parenting hat, she's got to build her parenting skills, and nothing's going to happen overnight.

"Life won't be like it was. For any of you." Ms. Rogers put her hand on top of Jade's, lying on the table. She squeezed it. "You're an incredibly strong, brave girl. Your brother and sister look up to you."

Jade wished she were strong. She'd never had to be. Maybe it was true, what Auntie Lita said. Maybe her mom and dad had taken care of all the hard stuff, so she never had to face it. Their loss swirled around her, made her angry. The shiny table surface blurred through teary eyes. Jersey and Jupiter didn't look up to her. They'd adjusted to life with Auntie Lita without a thought. They didn't look to her for anything anymore. They seemed happy, the traitors.

"Jade, it's tempting to find ways to escape life right now. And alcohol—or drugs—can look like an easy escape. But you're hurting yourself, and your own life."

"Are we done?" Jade didn't want lectures. This woman knew nothing of her or her family.

Ms. Rogers leaned back and studied Jade's face, which she kept neutral. She fought the urge to roll her eyes and slump back in her chair. Adults could be so dense. If this woman thought scare tactics would keep her from going back to California, she had a surprise waiting for her. Nothing could scare Jade anymore. The worst had happened.

"Jade, you have a lot of people rooting for you."

"Hooray." Jade spoke with no joy.

Ms. Rogers smiled sadly. "I'll be following up with your aunt for the next few months, and she'll be acting on the recommendations we've talked about. She's also set up an appointment for you to see a counselor. Do you have any questions for me?"

Jade shook her head.

When Ms. Rogers left, Jade went into the kitchen where Auntie Lita sat, her elbows on the table and head in her hands, legs bouncing under the table. She frowned and pushed herself up as soon as Jade entered.

"The social worker said you think I don't want you. Which isn't true, Jade. I may not show it in the right way, but I want you here. You and Jersey and Jupiter."

"You don't want Nana."

"I'm trying my best with Nana, even if it doesn't seem like it."

"It doesn't."

"Fair enough. We're all learning. And I don't expect you to understand everything. You worried me. When you didn't come home, I didn't know what to do. And when I got the call from the ER? Honestly, complete terror, afraid something irreversible had happened. I felt relieved you were alive." Auntie Lita swallowed and took a deep breath. "And then I got angry. I'm sorry."

Jade snorted. Her aunt had blown a gasket, had cursed her out on the drive home as Jade had pressed her cheek against the passenger window and tried to ignore the pain of it all: the emergency room visit, her throbbing head, the loss of her parents. Jade hadn't wanted to cause this much of a problem. She'd wanted to have fun and forget everything for a little while. It wasn't fair to Auntie Lita, even if she wanted to go back to California.

"I'm sorry too," she mumbled.

"Thanks, Jade." Her aunt put her hand on Jade's shoulder and squeezed softly. "I care about you. All of you, even Nana. And I'm a fighter, so all I know is to come on hard. It's what I do. I know more about takedowns and leg kicks than I do about chore lists and homework. But I'm learning. I'll figure this out."

Jade nodded. She couldn't picture her aunt attending school conferences or volunteering for school activities. But then again, she'd never pictured herself in a scene from a TV hospital drama, either.

. . .

THE WHOLE SCHOOL seemed to know about Jade's misadventures. She felt the stares and heard the whispers but ignored them. Aside from Brooklyn and Max, she didn't care about any of them.

Except maybe Logan. She'd missed the first two days of school this week and hoped to see him on the bus.

Brooklyn seemed to read her thoughts while they ate lunch on a bench in front of the library. "Max said he saw Logan yesterday."

Jade's attention had been on a squirrel stealing a Cheeto by the corner of the school, but her head whipped around to Brooklyn. She tried to keep her voice level. "Oh yeah? What did he say?"

"He said he heard Logan bragging about partying at the shrine last weekend. You didn't party at the shrine, did you?"

The shrine.

Jade's stomach soured and flipped. What had started as so much fun had ended in disaster. She couldn't remember anything after Spin the Bottle. She'd woken in the hospital with a pounding head, a sick stomach, and bruises all over her limbs. Not the greatest place to party, she thought. Brooklyn was aware of Jade's trip to the ER and the party. She didn't know any of the details, however.

"There was a shrine up there. I didn't see it, but Logan had to run over to it on a dare."

"You shouldn't party at the shrine, Jade. That's sacrilegious." Brooklyn berated her.

"We weren't at the shrine. I didn't see it. We were near it." Jade had heard enough scolding.

"I'm surprised your aunt didn't chew you out for it."

Jade frowned. "I didn't tell her anything. She doesn't know who I was with. All she knows is where I ended up. And I got chewed out plenty."

"Well, you shouldn't party at the shrine. I can't believe you did." Her scolding tone turned inquisitive. "Max heard Logan say there's going to be a big party at Cody Miller's house. His parents are out of town. Did he say anything?"

Another party! Maybe she'd skip the alcohol this time. It had taken her two full days to feel normal after last weekend, and she really didn't want to see Ms. Rogers from Family Services again.

"Got room for me?" Max stood before them, his long hair tucked into a ponytail. They scooted over, and he sat down.

"You guys doing anything this weekend?" He tossed a rock back and forth between his hands, a green rock the size of a golf ball, marbled with black veins. He often carried interesting rocks and gems in his backpack. Jade wondered if he knew Oscar.

"What a pretty stone!" Brooklyn eyed the rock in Max's hands.

He handed it to her. "It's called malachite."

Brooklyn studied it, then handed it to Jade. About an inch long, the stone was rough and jagged green with black lines like webbing running through it. She'd never seen a stone like this. The green edges looked crystalized, like coral or the stalactites she'd seen during a visit to Carlsbad Caverns with her parents.

Gems and minerals were a big deal in Bisbee. In school last month they'd finished a unit on the Copper Queen Mine, which drove Bisbee's economy for nearly a century then became a tourist site in the seventies. One of the largest open pit mines in the world, it had produced not only copper but a wide range of minerals. People from all over the world traipsed to Bisbee annually for a rock convention, and mineralogists loved to visit the little town.

"I don't have any plans for the weekend yet." Jade wanted to go to the party, but she needed an invite. "What do you do with all these rocks you find?"

Max held the green rock in front of his face, then lowered his hand, holding the rock in the flat of his palm. "I have a collection in my room and keep a list of them. I've never found any rare rock samples, but my parents have, and those get sold to private collectors. Lots of people prefer to buy gems and minerals rather than spend the time looking for them." He tossed the stone gently in his palm. "This is for my mom's birthday. It's not worth much, but green's her favorite color."

With a pang, Jade remembered her mom's love of purple. But she didn't know her dad's favorite color. She suddenly feared she'd forget everything about her parents. She'd never really paid attention to them. They fed her, clothed her, hugged her, and kept her safe. And now they were gone. Her throat clogged up, and a pressure built behind her eyes.

Brooklyn spoke with a mouthful of sandwich. "Jade's going to go to a party at Cody Miller's house."

Her pain disappeared in shock. Jade turned to Brooklyn, her mouth agape. "I haven't been invited."

"Logan likes you. He'll invite you."

Max scowled and clutched the rock in his fist. "He's a bully and a liar. You shouldn't be hanging out with him. He's no good."

"He's cute," Brooklyn proclaimed. "And he's popular."

Max's eyes flashed angrily. "Logan is an empty-headed poster boy for birth control."

Jade narrowed her eyes. "What makes him worse than the other popular boys?"

"They're all bad, but he's the worst." He unzipped the front pocket of his backpack and slid the rock in before grabbing his water bottle and taking a long drink. "I've known Logan all my life, and he doesn't think about anyone except himself."

Jade pondered his words for the rest of the afternoon. She got on the bus at the end of the day and waited eagerly for the high schoolers. As the bus shuddered to a stop at the high school, she searched the small group of students waiting on the curb but didn't see Logan.

The students lined up, and she saw Taylor, dressed in the same black hoody with black jeans she'd worn to the party. Her hair hung lackluster over her face, and she looked tired. While boarding, her eyes passed over Jade. Jade smiled broadly and waved. Taylor's eyes widened, and she nodded imperceptibly but sat down several rows in front of Jade.

Logan didn't get on the bus. Jade wanted to ask Taylor where he was. She hadn't seen anyone else from the party since that night. She got up and walked to Taylor's seat, her heart pounding, ignoring Max in the seat across from them.

"Hi Taylor." She sat down quickly so the driver didn't yell at her.

Taylor winced when Jade sat down. "Hi," she mumbled. She scooted closer to the window and looked out at the parking lot as the bus began to move.

Taylor wasn't being friendly at all. "I haven't seen Logan this week, and he usually sits with me. Do you know where he is?" Jade said.

Across the aisle, Jade could feel Max's eyes on her. His stare bothered her.

"I don't keep tabs on Logan." Taylor gazed out the window. She didn't look at Jade.

"Hah. Yeah, I know." Jade shifted in her seat. "Was he at school today?"

Taylor shifted her eyes from the window to meet Jade's. "I don't track his whereabouts, and I don't remember if I saw him at all."

So rude. Jade tried again. "Are you doing anything this weekend? I hear there's a party."

Taylor's eyebrows lifted in surprise. "I might go. It's supposed to be a small party, but Cody's parties have a way of getting out of control." She looked sideways at Jade with a smirk. "I'm not sure if it's appropriate for you. We don't plan on inviting the cops."

Jade felt like she'd been slapped. Taylor continued. "We've never had to drag anyone down the mountain before, you know. It was a first, thank you Logan. I told him we might want to put an age limit on our circle, you know? Keep it to teenagers only?"

Why was Taylor acting so bitchy? Weren't they friends now? Jade wanted to go back to her original seat. She didn't know what to say.

The bus pulled to a stop, and Max stood up. He threw Jade an amused glance, and she felt her face grow hot as he walked down the aisle.

She turned to Taylor. "Did I do something to you? Why are you so rude?"

Taylor's eyes opened in mock surprise. "Rude? You sound like my mom. But no, you haven't done anything. It's who I am. You're still a little kid, and I don't take on Logan's pet projects."

Pet projects? Little kid? Taylor couldn't be more than fifteen, just three years older than Jade. She stammered. "I…. What…." She felt like a fool sitting next to Taylor.

The bus started again, and Taylor looked out the window. Jade leaned back on the seat, defeated, wanting to return to her old seat but not wanting to give Taylor the satisfaction. She clenched her fists so her fingernails dug into her palms and wondered if she'd ever be happy again.

TWENTY-FIVE

Evie

"WE'RE GOING to Manzanita Manor. They're having a music night." The woman opens the passenger door of an old yellow truck and holds a hand out to Evie. "Climb in."

Evie grabs the hand and scoots herself up to the bench seat. The truck is old, but the interior is clean and tidy. Her body tilts on the seat as the driver gets in, and she steadies herself with the door's armrest. "This isn't my truck," she pronounces.

"You never had a truck."

Evie remembers the color. "Blue," she says. "I drove it with the kids."

"I don't remember a truck."

Evie spins her head and narrows her eyes. "I wasn't with you."

"Well, if you're talking about your kids, I was there." The woman starts the truck and backs up and out of the lot.

Evie huffs in frustration. This woman wasn't with Evie. She'd remember those tattoos. "I have four children."

"Yeah, and I'm Lita."

Evie pauses, off-balance, uneasy.

Lita. Phillip's holding the baby, dark-haired and tinier than any of her others. Something about the baby has made Phillip angry with Evie. She doesn't like the way he's looking at her, the way his blue eyes have hardened towards her, like her father's.

"What did you do, Evie?" His voice is rigid until it breaks, then it's sorrow she hears. "How could you?"

Evie shakes her head and leans into the door as the truck turns a corner and drives past a school and a cemetery. She recognizes the dry, red-brown hills. "Are we in Mexico?" she asks.

The woman shakes her head, her mouth a thin line. "Nope. Arizona."

"Are you from Mexico?"

"Yeah, you could say that. I have two families; one is from Mexico."

"Two families? Lucky for you." Evie chuckles, then stops laughing abruptly as an image of her father's angry face appears before her. "Unless they don't want you."

"No one wanted me," the woman says, her voice flat. "My pop was too young, and my mom—well, you were busy with other things."

Evie doesn't like this conversation. "It's not personal," she says. "Mothers and fathers love differently. My Daddy's love depends on living a godly life. I'm not so good at that part."

"You and me both," the woman agrees. "Pop moved to Hermosillo shortly after I was born, so I saw more of my abuela than him. Phillip treated me differently, but I was too young to know why."

"Phillip?" Shadows drift over Evie, invisible but thick. She opens her mouth to speak but can't find the words. "I...."

Like the whitewashed wall in Perdido, her mind is blank. Fear suddenly fills the emptiness. She looks around but doesn't recognize the street or the buildings around them. She clutches her purse to her stomach. "Where are we going?"

The truck pulls up to the curb in front of a well-lit, single-story L-shaped building. People stream in and out, but Evie doesn't move as the driver parks and unbuckles her seat belt. *Where am I?*

"Let's go check this out, Evie. They've got a musical show tonight, a family mixer. I thought you might want to come, but I didn't think the kids would be so keen, so Karmen picked them up. We'll meet them for dinner."

Evie hears music and feels the tension slip away. Her shoulders begin to sway with the faint beat. She climbs down and follows the music into the building. She recognizes the horseshoe entry, familiar in an institutional way. A short, curly-haired brunette with a happy face greets her.

"Evie, you made it! And Lita, this is great! What a surprise."

Behind her a bright room overflows with chaos and movement. Music playing, people talking and dancing, and lots of laughter.

"I never miss a party!" Evie says brightly.

"Hah! Understatement of the year." The tattooed woman growls. "Nice to see you Elise. I figured it was time to check out Family Night."

Evie doesn't hesitate but steps into a large rectangular room with peach walls. A four-person band plays near the back bank of windows overlooking a large patio. One wall is lined with tables filled with punch, coffee and snacks. Rows of chairs face the band, and a couple dozen white-haired people fill the seats. Other adults mill about the room talking, holding plates of food. A couple dances past her in a box-step shuffle, and she laughs. The music doesn't fit the box step, but they don't notice or care, and neither does Evie.

So young, these musicians. She approaches them, three boys and a girl who barely look up as she begins to move in time with the music. When it finishes, she speaks to the dark-haired girl holding a saxophone.

"Why are you here?"

The girl looks at Evie with a big smile. "We're practicing for the state high school jazz competition next month. My mom works here, and they're letting us practice. Do you like it?"

Evie nods vigorously. "Oh, yes, I love music. And especially dancing. I used to be a professional dancer."

The girl's eyes widen. "Really? What type of dance? Ballet?"

"All of it." Evie waves dismissively, then notices a box of instruments—triangles, tambourines, maracas. She picks up a tambourine as the band launches into a new song.

A woman claps her hand on Evie's shoulder and leans in with a smile. "How do you like the music, Evie?"

Evie nods and sways her hips. She holds the tambourine over her head and taps it against her hand. Evie can't remember the woman's name. In one ear and out the other these days.

"What's your name?" She smiles at the woman and shifts her hips side to side.

"Elise, your neighbor. It's fun, isn't it?"

Evie doesn't reply but nods, spins, and shakes her tambourine. Her movements grow as the music picks up tempo. She whirls and twirls, her long skirt flowing outward. Evie prefers classical music to jazz but has never turned her back on a band. Dancing brings light into the world. How can anyone be unhappy when they dance?

A man and woman waltz by. Evie snorts. A waltz! Then she laughs because it doesn't matter. People should dance how they please.

She pauses. Only a small fraction of people are dancing. Many sit in chairs smiling vacantly and nodding their heads with the music.

They need lessons. She drops the tambourine, approaches the first line of seats, and takes a deep breath. Placing her feet in first position with her back straight and her arms curved into a half circle below her waist, she smiles at the faces staring at her.

"I can't see." A woman grumbles and cranes her head to peer at the band behind Evie.

Evie frowns. "Eyes on me," she commands. "Let's work on the arm movements first."

The eyes shift to Evie, and she smiles at her students. "Yes, alright. Necks straight. Arms lightly curved. Out from the body. Above the waist." Eight sets of arms stick out awkwardly from eight bodies. She frowns. They look like cacti or crooked tree branches. Not dancers' arms.

"Round your arms, add a curve."

"My arms are tired." A big man in the center of the row drops his arms. Two others look down the row at him and follow suit. The others round their arms.

"When's dinner?" The man stands. Another student drops her arms.

"It's not time to eat," Evie spits out irritably. She raises her voice. "Now draw your arms up and out, like so." Evie demonstrates a graceful arc with her arms and watches several of her students lift their arms.

"No, no, no." She shakes her head and tries to regain eye contact with the row facing her. The hungry man remains standing in front of Evie, lost in action. He stares at his seat in confusion as Evie demonstrates a few pliés with her arm movements.

He turns to walk away and bumps Evie out of position. She stumbles and glares at him. "Sit back down. You're interrupting the lesson."

The man opens his mouth to speak, but Evie doesn't let him. "Do you hear the music?" She points behind her to the quartet jamming by the window. He nods.

"They're playing beautiful music for us, and you're sitting like a bump on a log."

"What's she saying?" a woman's voice cries from the end of the row.

Evie raises her voice. "Now let's try again."

The man taps Evie's shoulder and sticks his face close to hers. "You're standing in my way."

His sour breath forces Evie to take a step back. She puts her hands on her hips and faces him. "You're rude."

"Who put you in charge?" He points to the quartet and the few dancers in front of them. "They don't have their arms out."

Evie backs up a step, then picks up the tambourine she dropped. She hands it to the man, who takes it with confusion. "Play this. I can't help you."

The man grumbles as the music picks up tempo. His gaze switches back and forth between the band and Evie until he grunts and sits back down, banging the tambourine against his leg in time. Evie nods, satisfied, and begins her lessons again.

She's lost her students' attention, however. She tells them to watch her and twirls to face the band as she gyrates. The music makes her spirits soar.

A meaty hand falls on her shoulder, and she finds the big man, red-faced, holding the tambourine out. He smacks his lips a few times and gazes at her.

"Take this back. I'm no good at it." His bushy white eyebrows narrow in a frown. "I need a drink."

Evie stares at the man, the music forgotten, the dance unfinished. She takes the tambourine from him and tosses it on a chair, then loops her arm under his and leans into his side conspiratorially. "I like the sound of that."

He grunts, and she begins leading him towards the door before realizing she's left her students. She turns back to the group, many of whom are watching her. "We're going to get a drink," she announces. "Follow us."

The man beside her smacks his lips

"Hold up there, Evie. Where are you going?"

The tattooed woman stands in front of her, coffee cup in hand, blocking the doorway. She scans Evie and her companion and the line of seniors behind them. "Is this a breakout?"

Evie doesn't have patience for this red-striped, inked-up woman. "We're going for a drink," she states.

"There's coffee and punch on the table over there." The woman casts her arm to the tables against the wall.

Evie scowls and drops her hand from the broad man's arm. She gazes around the room but doesn't see a single wine glass or tumbler. "We want wine."

The man beside her grumbles and shifts, his upper lip wet with a thin sheen of sweat. A middle-aged man approaches him. "There you are, Dad." He smiles at Evie and the tattooed woman, then speaks to him in an apologetic tone. "I got stuck in a conversation with a very interesting man who used to raise emus in Utah."

"Hah!" says the tattooed woman. "I met him, too."

The two laugh, but Evie isn't in on the joke. Neither is the man beside her. She loops her arm through his again and tries to walk around the tattooed woman.

"We're heading for a drink," she announces.

"Hang on, Evie. How are you going to get there?" The tattooed woman glances at the man. "I'm Lita, by the way. This is my mom, Evie."

"Nice to meet you Lita and Evie. I'm Wayne. This is my father Errol." The man sticks his hand out like a crossing guard.

Evie smiles like her mother taught her, gracious and accommodating, and shakes with her free hand. Then she tugs on Errol's arm and smiles an apology to the man and woman. "Nice to meet you. Let's go," she says to Errol.

Wayne's eyebrows shoot up in surprise. "Where are you going, Dad?"

Errol's lips press together and his cheeks fill with air before they empty in a sigh. He scans the room and the people in front of him, then turns to Evie and rears his head back in surprise. He loosens his arm from hers and steps away, his eyes darting around the room. "What am I doing here?" he asks roughly. "Where's Bev?"

"We're at a party, Dad. Mom's not here." The man's voice is soft and kind.

Errol's confusion frustrates Evie. She too doesn't know where she is or why, but he should know. It's a man's world, after all. "What good are you?" she asks him. She scans the room. For what, she isn't sure.

"Evie, let's go dance." The tattooed woman inclines her head towards the small dance floor and holds her hand out.

This surprises Evie. "You dance?"

A big sigh. "You taught me."

Evie stands tall. She smooths her skirt with her hands. "I'd rather dance with him." She points to Errol who's watching people return from the food table and examining their plates as they walk by.

"Dad." Errol's attention turns towards the man. "Evie would like to dance with you."

"No." Errol says flatly.

Evie's shocked. She rarely gets turned down. She isn't sure what to do, and she suddenly doesn't want this man's fat face near her. Evie throws her arm straight out, a fist at the end like a superhero punch.

"POW!" She proclaims, her arm about eighteen inches from Errol's face.

"What the fuck, Evie? That's rude." The tattooed woman puts her hand on Evie's arm and pushes it down.

Errol tilts his head at Evie and the tattooed woman. His nostrils flare, and he throws his hand up and turns his back on them, moving towards the exit.

Wayne smiles broadly. "Guess we're done! Nice to meet you both."

"He's not nice." Evie says.

"He doesn't want to dance. Not everyone wants to dance."

"Don't be silly." The music shifts to a quicker tune, and Evie feels herself drawn to the dance floor. But she lacks a partner. She searches the room for single men.

The tattooed woman follows Evie to the dance floor and begins to dance by herself. Evie's mouth falls open, and she scans the room to see if anyone else is surprised to see a woman dancing alone. No one seems to care.

Evie joins her. They twirl together and apart, and Evie marvels at the ease of her tattooed companion's turns and twists. Though lacking polish, she moves fluidly, her hips and arms naturally flowing with the beat and the rhythm. Her eyes take on a happy shine, and her mouth loosens into a smile. Her tattooed body no longer looks hard and unyielding.

Evie loosens up too and loses herself in the dance, occasionally clasping hands and twirling with her tiny but strong partner. She loses track of the number of songs until eventually she tires and plops down on a chair near the dance floor. The tattooed woman sits down hard in the chair beside her.

"I always loved dancing with you," she says. "You were always happiest dancing."

"Who are you?" Evie whispers.

"I'm Lita." The woman voice is defiant, but her eyes are calm. "Your daughter."

Evie feels a sharp pain in her chest. The woman's eyes remind her of her Lita. But nothing makes sense.

She stammers a reply. "Lita's gone. I can't get her back." Her mind closes on those words. Lita's gone. Lita's gone.

"She went to her dad's," the woman says. "She wanted you to come for her."

"No. She's disappeared." Evie insists.

"Okay, well, this Lita is ready for some dinner. Snacks don't cut it. You ready to pick up the kids?"

Evie wonders which kids this woman wants to pick up, but she's game. The music has stopped, and the musicians are packing up their instruments. She sees no reason to stay.

"I'm always ready," she says. "Let's go."

TWENTY-SIX

Lita

FRIDAYS WERE NOW DOUBLE-WHAMMY DAYS, with parenting classes and counseling back to back in the afternoon. She didn't want to go, and she had plenty of work at the shop, but Ronaldo had been too happy to give her time off.

"Parenting classes, Lita? Yes, go. I wish someone had told me there was such a thing. Do you know how long I looked for an off switch for our screaming little baby Karmen? Marieta and I could have used some lessons."

Without work as an excuse, Lita found herself on a hard plastic chair in a circle facing seven other adults: three singles and two couples. She sat between two women in the windowless room, one whose thin brown hair lay flat and dull, the other whose bleached-blonde locks were perfectly curled and shellacked, like a shiny helmet. One of the couples looked young, possibly teenage. Hunched over their phones without acknowledging anyone, she guessed they wanted to be anywhere else. The other couple was older but didn't look any more comfortable. The woman looked like she'd lost the energy to wash her clothes or brush her hair; the man looked similarly run down and fidgeted in his seat, turning to look at the doorway several times while the group waited. Another woman sat glowering, her arms folded across her chest and a scowl on her face.

Lita felt boxed in. Her leg bounced, and she eyed the door impatiently.

When the instructor appeared, she greeted the students with a smile and began handing out workbooks. She wore a black beret over curly auburn hair with fitted khaki pants and a pink button-up blouse with white paisley swirls. She looked to be in her thirties and smiled at each student as she handed them a book. Lita flipped through hers.

Parenting Principles*: Building positive parenting skills and supporting your child through all ages.*

Boring. Too long. Why couldn't they use snappy names, like "Parent Patrol: Enforcing positivity across the ages," or "Family Fuck-ups: Don't do this." More realistic, for sure.

The instructor introduced herself. "I'm Janelle. I've been with Family Support for five years now, and I've been teaching these classes for the past three. I love teaching and working with parents. And I want to thank you for being here. Not everyone recognizes how challenging parenting can be, and not everyone has a support system in place."

Lita hadn't recognized anything; she'd been forced to attend. She doubted anyone there had come voluntarily.

"The workbook is a compilation of information, strategies, and exercises, and we'll work through it over the next eight weeks. Each of you have children at various ages, and this work-book is designed to address all stages of childhood." Janelle's eyes shone with the fervor of the converted.

"Now before we introduce ourselves and get started, let's go over a few ground rules. First, this is a safe place, and everything said in this room is completely confidential. Details about our children and events in our lives don't leave this room. Second, we don't criticize each other. This is a group for learning and for supporting other parents in our community. We've all had moments we wish we'd handled differently, and we're here to learn. Third, whether you believe it or not, participating in this group will help you build confidence in your parenting. You'll learn new strategies and gain tools to strengthen your role in your children's lives. But"—Janelle paused and looked around the circle—"you won't learn if you don't participate. Sometimes the biggest hurdle in this class is a reluctance to share. But sharing is a way to build community and resources. We need both. And we all have something to contribute."

Well, fuck. Lita didn't want to share anything, certainly not with complete strangers.

They began introductions, and Lita forced herself to pay attention. She'd always had a hard time sitting still. When it came time to introduce herself, she swallowed and looked at the others. "I'm Lita. I actually never thought I'd be a parent, but my brother and his wife died in an accident last summer, and I'm guardian to their three kids. They're twelve, seven, and four, and I have no idea what the fuck I'm doing. I'm here because I don't want to screw them up. I owe it to them and my brother."

There. She admitted it. No one stood up and told her she'd already failed.

The rest of the students introduced themselves, a mix of unprepared and super-stressed out parents with kids of all ages. None of them appeared happy to be there, except the instructor.

"I'm glad you're all here," Janelle said. "Your parenting experiences share a common thread of overwhelm and frustration, which are big challenges for all parents. Suddenly your life isn't your own anymore, and no matter how much you've planned, and especially"—, she nodded at Lita—"if you haven't planned. Now let's open our workbooks and take a look at chapter one."

As the class continued, Lita shared occasionally but mostly flipped through the workbook and listened to the instructor and the other participants. Unlike most of her fellow students, she had a solid support system. She had Karmen and Felix to help with the kids. She'd had Oscar, but she pushed those thoughts away. And Ronaldo was always willing to give her time to deal with situations that pulled her from work.

Lita thought of Evie, moving to California alone with three kids after Phillip and Randy died. At least Lita wasn't alone like her mom or these others in the class.

When the class ended, Lita had thirty minutes to get to her counseling session—double whammy Fridays—and arrived ten minutes early after a quick drive. She killed time by jogging around the block six times. The only way she'd be able to sit for another hour would be to move now.

The counselor's office was in a small bungalow with bedrooms converted into offices. Lita entered a living room-turned-waiting room, its neutral walls covered in photos of colorful desert flowers and cacti and a sign asking clients to sit until a counselor came out to greet them. The room was empty.

Lita didn't want to wait, wanted to get this all done and over. She ignored the comfy armchair and paced. After the hourlong parenting class, she thought another hour of sitting might kill her. How did people sit at desks all day? She'd hated school for all the sitting and couldn't ever have worked a desk job. She picked a magazine—*Psychology Today*—and thumbed through the pages, then threw it down again.

The counselor came through one of the closed doors and greeted Lita warmly. Older than Lita by at least twenty years— perhaps mid-fifties—she had neatly trimmed silver hair with purple highlights. She wore glasses and a light burgundy sweater over a silky blouse and offered her hand with an introduction.

"Lita?" At Lita's nod, she continued. "I'm Diane Gibbons. It's nice to meet you."

Lita shook her hand. "Lita Bravo." The woman's hand was firm, her smile genuine.

"Well, Lita, I'm glad you're here. Let's move into my office so we can get to know each other."

She ushered Lita into an office decorated with colorful

abstract paintings and a tabletop water fountain lending a soothing backdrop of sound to the little room. Lita sank into a soft blue loveseat across from Diane, who sat in an armchair with a notebook in her lap.

"So, Lita, tell me a bit about yourself and why you're here." She opened her notebook and gave Lita an expectant smile.

Lita took a deep breath and blew it out with a sigh before speaking. She ran her hand through her hair and tried to keep her leg from bouncing. No luck. It went up and down like a jackhammer.

"Basically I've been mandated to attend counseling because of my niece Jade," she said. "I got custody of her and her brother and sister when my brother and his wife, their parents, died last summer. So last weekend, Jade went out partying and ended up in the ER. She's having a hard time adjusting to all the changes. We all are, I guess." Honesty was probably the best way to go here.

Diane murmured condolences. "I'm sorry to hear about your brother. It must have been quite a shock."

"Yeah, understatement of the year." Lita's temple started to throb, her palms became clammy. She wiped them on her jeans. "Jade's twelve, Jupiter's seven, and Jersey's four. But what's worse is I didn't know them at all. I'd never met them, hadn't seen my brother in twelve years. I have a fucked-up family. I never wanted kids. Figured they'd get fucked up too. So I wasn't prepared for this. But now I've got them. And I don't want to fuck up my brother's kids."

"That's a lot to handle." Diane spoke slowly, her eyes fixed on Lita's. "And you're carrying a lot of assumptions. What makes you think you'll 'fuck up' the children? It's interesting you didn't meet them earlier. Were you estranged? How were you given custody if you had no previous contact?"

Lita's leg bounced, and she scratched her fingernail along the loveseat's soft fabric. She didn't know where to start. Maybe from the beginning.

"I'm the child of an affair, if you can call a one-night stand an affair. So I wasn't exactly welcomed by my stepfather. He wasn't ever mean to me but didn't love me. I could feel it, even though I was little. My real dad was young, like eighteen, and he wasn't ready to be a father. Plus we lived in a very small village in Mexico, and pretty soon after I was born, he went to work in Hermosillo, about an hour south of the village. I think my abuela sent him away. I don't remember much time with him when I was little, but I do remember a lot of time at Abuela's."

Lita paused. That might have been the most she'd said about her family in one sitting. She felt parched. A pitcher of water sat on a small end table next to the loveseat. Lita eyed it longingly. "Can I have some water?"

"Of course, help yourself." Diane waited for Lita to pour a glass of water and chug half of it before speaking again. "So you were born in Mexico. How many siblings do you have?"

"I have two families. I'm the youngest of four in my mom's family, and I've got seven younger siblings on my dad's side. But everyone in my mom's family is gone. My stepdad and my brother Randy died when I was four. My sister Laurel overdosed when I was fifteen. Jake died last summer."

"A lot of loss for one family." Diane's face softened. "What about your mom?"

Lita growled. "She's still alive. She's got dementia, and my brother had power of attorney over her, which has now been transferred to me. But she's out of it. She doesn't know who I am and doesn't understand where she is. I've got her on a waitlist for a care home."

"So you've also got custody, if you will, of your mother?"

"Yeah. Which has been challenging too." *Fuck.* Lita didn't want to go into all of this. Digging all this up made her feel raw inside, made her want to punch something.

"I bet it has." Diane nodded, her eyes creased in sympathy. "You've had quite a disruption in your life."

Lita breathed slowly and deeply, her lips clamped together. This woman didn't know the half of it.

"And you'd never met your brother's children?"

"No. He moved to California before Jade was born. I last saw him before he left Arizona, thirteen years ago. I don't like California—dirty skies, too much traffic, cement all around, people and cars everywhere. Bad memories. My mom was born there, took us there after my stepdad and brother died. But she'd never had a job before and didn't do so well. Our family kinda broke down.

"To make a long story short, Jake joined the army when I was nine. Laurel ran away at about the same time, so I lived with my mom for a few years. But, like I said, she didn't do so well, especially after Jake left. He'd always been the most responsible of us—more so than Evie."

"Evie?" Diane tilted her head and lifted her eyebrows in a question.

"Yeah, my mom."

"Okay." She jotted something down in her notebook and nodded thoughtfully. "But I'm still not clear on why you didn't feel compelled to visit your brother and his children. I've always enjoyed my nieces and nephews. Was it a distance issue? Or money?"

Lita shook her head. "No. I didn't visit because California holds bad memories. And I assumed Evie would be there. I skipped Jake's wedding in Sierra Vista because I didn't want to see her."

"Hold on." Diane set the pen down on the notebook and looked Lita in the eyes. "Why didn't you want to see your mom?"

"Ugh. How is this going to help Jade?" Lita's voice felt raw like sandpaper, and she resented the fact she had to speak to this woman about things she'd rather forget.

"Lita, this isn't solely about helping Jade. You've suffered multiple tragedies. You've told me you're having a hard time adjusting. It's understandably difficult now, given it's only been a few months. And we'll talk about Jade. But right now, I'm trying to understand you and your situation. You've shared your mom wasn't a great mother, and you want to do better. Why wasn't she good enough?"

Suddenly Lita felt cold, the helplessness and fear she'd felt as a child rushing over her like a wave. She spoke in a voice as frigid as she felt. "My mom started dancing as a stripper. She worked late nights, brought men home, then drank with them until nearly dawn. When Jake and Laurel left, I wasn't safe and ran away. She never looked for me, and I only heard from her once. I never saw her again. Not until Jake died." Her fingers dug into the soft arm of the loveseat, and she fought the urge to storm out of the room.

Diane's eyes remained fixed on Lita. "And Jake stayed in touch with your mother." Diane stated this as a fact, but her eyes questioned.

"Yes. But we didn't talk about her." She closed her eyes and took a deep breath, then opened them and blew the air out audibly. "I don't like talking about my mother."

"But you live with her now."

"Yeah," she said miserably. "It's hard enough with the three kids. I'm already on my back foot trying to parent. But now I've got my mom mucking around in my life, and I hate it. I hate seeing her, I hate hearing her voice, I hate having to take care of her when she never did the same for me."

"Do you hate her?"

Lita paused before answering. Though she wanted to say yes, she wasn't one hundred percent sure she hated Evie. "I don't know," she said honestly. "It's complicated. Before Jake died, I thought I did. She failed us. Left us kids to fend for ourselves when we needed a mom. I needed her. But she suffered too."

By the end of the meeting, Lita felt a slight release, like after a sparring session. She got into the truck and started it, thinking about Evie's father, her grandfather.

What she knew about her mom's dad would barely fill a piece of paper. When Lita was nineteen, Jake contacted her from Fort Huachuca, an army post near the US-Mexico border six hours from her home in Hermosillo.

"Our grandfather's dead," he announced.

"He's not already dead?" Lita had assumed Evie's parents had long been deceased. They'd never made an appearance during her years in California.

"No. Estranged from Mom for thirty years, but not dead. Apparently our grandmother sent Mom money to bring us home from Perdido after the accident, but our grandfather didn't know. And she visited us once or twice, alone, when we'd settled in the Bay Area, but she died suddenly a few months after we moved there. I'm not surprised you don't remember. You were only four. She was timid, and I don't think our grandfather knew she visited us or sent us money. He sounded like a hard man who never forgave Mom for getting pregnant and leaving with Dad."

"So, what do I care?" Lita felt no sadness, no connection to this grandfather.

"He had a lot of money. He left most of it to charity, but he set up a trust for his grandchildren: you, Laurel, and me. Of course it's just you and me now. We're each getting thirty thousand dollars."

Lita was speechless. Though content working alongside her father, she'd begun to wonder what life had to offer other than kickboxing and working in a garage. Her only friends were fellow gym rats, but they weren't close friends. And while she loved her dad, she'd begun feeling trapped in a life that fit someone else. She'd rarely thought about her mom's family. This dead grandfather, however, had put a different future on a plate and set it down in front of her.

"What do you mean?" She wasn't sure how this worked.

"You've got to contact the lawyer who's overseeing the estate and give him the info he needs to transfer the money. Apparently Mom got a trust too, except ours is in a lump sum payment, and hers is distributed monthly as a stipend. Crazy how her dad's willing to support her in death but wouldn't see her when he was alive."

Lita couldn't care less about her mom. She thought for a moment. "Do I have to come back to the States?" She hadn't been back since she'd left California five years earlier. She wasn't sure where she'd go if she did return but knew it wouldn't be to California, where Evie lived and Laurel had died.

"I'm sure you could have the funds deposited into an account in Hermosillo. But Lita, I'm right across the border, only five or six hours from you. Why don't you come for a visit, then we'll talk to the lawyer together and get it set up?"

She'd said goodbye to her dad and his family without knowing when she'd see them again. She'd struggled with the threat of tears as her dad had rattled off nonstop advice. "Don't disrespect the border guards. Don't trust anyone you meet in a bar. Stay with your brother, chica, and listen to him." She'd hugged him long and hard, then said goodbye to her siblings. Rosa sniffed and ducked her head, and Lita embraced her quickly. They'd found a peace of sorts.

She'd driven her bike to Arizona, a backpack and duffel bag strapped on the back. Her first stop had been Bisbee, right across the Naco border crossing. She arrived on a Friday night, landing at the Old Miner Restaurant for dinner where she sat in a booth by herself. Across from her, a curvy woman with dark wavy hair, about her age, wore a plastic tiara and a big smile, celebrating her birthday. People young and old surrounded her with sparkling eyes and laughter. Family, Lita thought. She smiled at the woman as their eyes met, and the woman got up and approached her.

"You look like you could use company. I'm Karmen."

TWENTY-SEVEN

Jade

THE DEEP EMERALD liquid swirled into the drain like a whirlpool. She hoped the sink wouldn't stay permanently green, though Brooklyn didn't seem to care.

"I've done mine before." She shrugged her shoulders and dismissed Jade's concern. "It always comes off."

Jade eyed the sink and the countertop dubiously. Green dye splattered across the mirror. Emerald streaks ran across the faded blue laminate. Two beige towels lay flung over the side of the tub, streaked with various shades of green.

"Your dad's not going to get mad?"

Four months after the incident at his house, Brooklyn's dad had finally allowed Jade to visit again. Auntie Lita had supervised her apology with a warning beforehand. "Don't kid yourself he's forgotten it, Jade. It's up to him to move on. But you apologize and watch your step."

She'd been so embarrassed. Auntie Lita had stood behind Jade as she'd stammered her apology to Brooklyn's dad, his arms folded and face unreadable. Brooklyn hovered behind him, big eyes watching her.

"I'm sorry, Mr. Willis. What I did was wrong. It won't happen again."

He dropped a meaty hand on her shoulder, and she flinched. Brooklyn gave her a thumbs-up and a smile. Jade's lips twitched to smile, but she held the smile back and shifted her eyes up to his. They bored into her, and her face flamed.

"I'm not a fool, Jade. I don't like people taking advantage of me. Brook has been begging to have you over, but not if you're drinking and smoking. Or stealing from me."

"No, Mr. Willis." Jade dropped her eyes. "I won't do it again."

"This isn't about me. I don't want Brook mixed up in alcohol or drugs. Do you understand? I need to hear you promise me you won't be doing any drinking or drugs at my house. Or with Brook anywhere."

Jade's face flushed, and she nodded her head. "Yes," she said softly. "I promise." She wanted this to be over.

Brooklyn's dad studied her. "Brook tells me you're a good friend, and your aunt tells me you're going through some rough times."

Jade swallowed and nodded.

"Well, we're square. Thank you for the apology."

Auntie Lita clamped a hand on Jade's shoulder and squeezed it. Her face was thoughtful. "Okay Jade, well done, kid." She looked at Brooklyn's dad and nodded "Thanks, Dave," she said, then left.

Jade rubbed her head down with a third towel, then shook her hair and looked in the mirror. Green hair. She'd never dyed her hair before. Hadn't seen her mom do it. But she needed a break from the past, wanted to switch things up. Maybe Zoe's pink hair inspired her.

Brooklyn cut Jade's hair—"I do my dad's all the time"—and she had to admit, it looked good. Instead of her boring, straight, long, brown hair, a short green bob framed her face, with a side part so her hair swung over her eyes when she moved.

Brooklyn fussed at a few long strands as Jade stared at herself. "Hair shrinks when it dries, you know."

Jade pursed her lips in a kiss towards in the mirror. Her cheeks and lips looked full. She felt older. "Got any makeup?"

Brooklyn's eyes brightened and she squealed. "Oh, yeah! I've got a makeup box in my room. Should we do purple eyeliner? Check this out!"

Jade followed as Brooklyn ran into her room and excitedly pulled a book out of her closet. She flashed the cover at Jade. "*Vogue Looks Makeup Guide*! My dad got it for me, but I haven't had a chance to practice. Do you like purple? Purple and green go together."

Jade had come to appreciate Brooklyn's bubbly positivity. Though she had initially thought Brooklyn incredibly immature, she'd reconsidered. Brooklyn didn't care if someone else told her what to do or where to go. She simply wanted to be included. Jade, on the other hand, wanted to control her own life. She didn't want anyone telling her anything.

They went into the kitchen where Brooklyn sat Jade on a stool. "Lift your chin," she instructed. Brooklyn took out an eye pencil and began sketching a line on Jade's eyebrow.

Jade lifted her chin, and Brooklyn clamped her lips together in concentration as she leaned over Jade's face, sweet breath hot on Jade's forehead. "What are you going to do for your birthday? You should do something unique."

Jade's birthday was in two weeks. She hadn't thought about it.

"Like what?"

Brooklyn bit her lip as she held a palette of eye shadow and peered at Jade's face. She used light pink to swab Jade's eyelid, then frowned and grabbed a tissue, wet it with her tongue, and wiped the spot to start over.

"Your aunt could give us fighting lessons."

Jade's eyebrows flew up.

"Don't move." Brooklyn admonished. "Your aunt is small, but no one would ever pick on her because she's so tough. I'm small, and I want to be tough, so no one can push me around anymore."

Jade thought about this. She'd never been pushed around, but she'd always been tall. Right now, she was taller than most boys in her class and taller than some of her teachers. Was Brooklyn bullied because she was small or because she was different? It didn't matter. She couldn't argue with Brooklyn's logic.

"She'd probably love to teach us how to fight. It's one of the only things she knows how to do."

"Oh, your aunt knows how to do lots of things. She fixes cars! She drives a motorcycle! I bet she's a lot of fun."

Jade rolled her eyes.

"Hang on!" Brooklyn frowned. "Don't move your eyes. I'm almost done."

Brooklyn made a final few touches to Jade's face, then stepped back to gaze at her. "Looks good!" she squealed. "You look like you're seventeen, at least."

Jade ran into the bathroom. The face looking back at her had transformed. It wasn't garish as Jade feared, but rather like a runway model. Her cheeks appeared hollow and contoured. Indigo eyeliner made her eyes pop out in a startling shade of blue. And the rest of the eye makeup blended together into shades of violet and amber, giving her eyes depth rather than making them clownish. She hadn't expected to see this. She actually looked good.

"Wow, Brooklyn, where'd you learn to do this?"

Brooklyn smiled shyly, uncharacteristically subdued. "My mom used to do makeup with me all the time. I was little, but it was one of my favorite things."

Jade hadn't heard Brooklyn talk about her mom much. "How old were you when she died?" They'd been friends for several months now, and Jade hadn't ever asked.

A shadow passed over her friend's face. "Eight." She took a

compact mirror out of her bag and then pulled out a ruby lipstick and began to apply it to her pursed lips. "We lived in Tucson, my mom and me. One morning she didn't wake up."

Jade felt the loss of her own parents slam into her chest, like Jupiter jumping on her from the back of the couch. Loss shouldn't happen so suddenly. Ophie, who attended church every Sunday with her family in San Leandro, assured her it was God's will. Jade didn't think so. If there were a god and it wanted Jade's parents or Brooklyn's mom dead, then it was a sick god, and she wanted nothing to do with it.

"I tried to wake her up, but I knew she wouldn't wake. She looked like marble." Brooklyn's jaw trembled and she turned to face Jade. "I'd seen her do drugs before. And she had the kit in front of her. I knew she was dead, but I couldn't do anything about it."

"Drugs?" Jade felt ignorant. She tried to imagine her friends' parents doing drugs—drugs that could kill. She couldn't.

Brooklyn kept talking. "I came to live with my dad in Bisbee, but I didn't make any friends here. Until you came." She put the lipstick back into her bag and peered intently at Jade's face. "Do you want cat-eyes? I can try to swoop the eyeliner at the outside edges."

Jade imagined Brooklyn alone at school, motherless and outcast. Suddenly she felt an immense gratitude to Brooklyn for making the transition to Bisbee so much easier.

"How about Max? Was he friendly?"

Brooklyn stopped rifling through her makeup bag and glanced at Jade thoughtfully. "He never teased me." She sighed and looked down to search the bag, then came up with a smile and eyeliner pencil in hand. "But he didn't talk to me, either. That started when you came around."

For some reason, her words made Jade both happy and sad.

. . .

THE NEXT DAY Jade could barely contain her excitement. Auntie Lita had forced her to remove the makeup before bed, so she had no runway look to cap off her new hair color, but she could tell the other students were impressed. No one else in her school had green hair.

"Is that for St. Patrick's Day?" Max asked with a furrowed brow.

They were working on the float. With a few months to go, they seemed to have done little. Hopefully it would pull together before June.

"Of course not." Brooklyn replied in a prickly voice. "It's not March yet."

Jade had chosen green because it had been on sale. St. Paddy's Day hadn't been in her mind at all.

"Is it permanent?" Max studied Jade's hair. His own hair blazed naturally, and she realized, with Brooklyn in-between them, they looked like the Mexican flag hanging in the room she shared with Nana. Green, white, red.

"It'll wash off in a few weeks," Brooklyn jumped in. "My mom used to dye hers, and the colors will fade and wash out. If we wanted the colors to stay longer, we would've had to do it at the salon. But it's a lot more expensive than a box from the store."

"What did your aunt say about it?" Max asked Jade as he twisted crepe paper to make a flower and glued it on the base of the float.

"Have you seen my aunt? She's got a red skunk stripe down her head."

"Her aunt's going to teach us how to fight," Brooklyn squealed.

"Really?" Max lifted his eyebrows. "When?"

"At Jade's birthday party. In two weeks. Do you want to come?"

Jade hadn't been sure she'd wanted a birthday party; she

didn't feel much like celebrating a new year. But apparently Brooklyn was taking care of it for her.

"I still have to ask my aunt," she protested weakly.

"She'll do it! She's got awesome moves. My dad watches MMA fighting, and if your aunt fights anything like the ones on TV, we'll fight like pros!"

"Who else is coming?" Max narrowed his eyes at Jade. "I'm not going to a party with Logan."

Jade felt a momentary thrill at Logan's name, but it fizzled at Max's tone.

"You can't tell Jade who to invite to her party." Brooklyn's voice rose with indignation. "It's her birthday. She can invite who she wants."

Would Logan come if she invited him? She didn't know. "It'll probably just be you and Brooklyn." Did she have any other friends? She hadn't made the effort to get to know anyone else.

AFTER SCHOOL LOGAN jumped onto the bus with his usual broad smile and swung his backpack off his shoulder fluidly as he plopped down next to her.

"How's it going, Jade? Long time no see." Logan acted like she'd been hiding from him when it felt like the other way around. She'd been wondering why he hadn't been on the bus lately.

"You haven't been on the bus," she replied.

"It's basketball season, so I've got practice after school," he said. "Except today, because we've got a game tonight. Are you coming?"

It had never occurred to Jade to attend a high school basketball game. "Uh, no, I don't think so."

"Ah, shame. The gang will be there, and we'll probably go party afterwards. You still in trouble with your aunt?"

Jade shook her head. She wasn't in trouble with Auntie Lita, but Taylor had been so rude to her she wasn't sure she wanted to hang out in any group with her in it. "I've got plans with Brooklyn."

"That little blonde girl with the gap between her teeth? Isn't she, like, ten or something?' Logan threw a wadded up ball of paper at a high schooler three rows ahead then ducked as the other boy turned around. He sat back up. "She looks like she's a little kid."

Jade didn't like his tone. "You don't know her. She's my friend. And she may look like a little kid, but she's not. She's just small." Logan had no idea what Brooklyn had been through.

"Oh, yeah? If she walks like a little girl and talks like a little girl, then she's a little girl. But you're right. I don't know her. Give me the scoop."

Jade hesitated. How could she get Logan to see Brooklyn differently? True, she dressed in little kid clothes and hardly brushed her hair. And sure, she may act immature, but she'd seen things Jade could only imagine.

"Brooklyn's had some rough times," she said finally. "She lives with her dad because her mom died. And I don't think her dad pays attention to how she dresses or if her hair's combed."

"Whoa, dead mother. Sad. How'd she die?"

Jade told him before she thought about it. "Brooklyn found her overdosed one morning."

"Really?! Wow, crazy. No wonder she's so weird."

"She's not weird." She shouldn't have told him. Everything seemed to be a joke to Logan, and Brooklyn wasn't a joke. "She's my friend."

"Hey, no offense. Everyone knows she's different. But I wonder," he said, his eyes bright, "if everyone knows about her mom. That's real news."

"What are you talking about? It's not news. It's Brooklyn's life." Jade shouldn't have told him. It wasn't anyone else's business.

"Yeah, but if people knew, maybe they'd treat her better."

Treat her better? What was he talking about? Jade didn't think so. People were mean. "It's no one's business."

Logan stared at her for a few seconds then pursed his lips and nodded his head. "Oh, but I think it is," he said.

Jade wondered what she'd done.

TWENTY-EIGHT

Lita

LITA SCANNED the booths for open seats as they walked into Pietro's, a pizzeria on Main Street. The restaurant was packed with teenagers; the air reeked of their angst and body odor. Teens milled about the video games, the salad bar, the booths—everywhere.

"Are we going to find a seat?" Evie looked around the restaurant doubtfully.

Lita spotted a couple leaving a booth and pushed Jade towards it. "Jade, go snag that booth. Jupiter, Jersey, follow Jade. Evie and I will order."

Jade grabbed Jersey's hand but stopped and faced Lita. "Can you get something other than pepperoni? I'm sick of all the grease."

Watching them move towards the booth, Lita couldn't understand it—as soon as they'd arrived at the pizza place, Jade had turned sullen and stone-faced.

"I'd like red wine." Lita turned to find Evie speaking to the pimply teen behind the register.

"A glass or a carafe?" The teen punched a few buttons on the register.

"A carafe." Evie looked pleased.

"Uh, make it a glass." Lita cut in. Evie frowned. "We're not getting a carafe. You're the only one drinking."

"So?" Evie stared at Lita belligerently, hands on hips.

"So, I'll be picking you up off the floor if you drink a carafe." Lita ignored Evie's glare and ordered two pizzas—one pointedly *not* pepperoni. Two pizzas was a lot, but it made for great leftovers.

"Here you are." A chirpy young woman slid a glass of wine over to the edge of the bar. Evie licked her lips as she reached for it.

Lita beat her to the glass. "I'll carry it, Evie. I don't want you to spill."

"Oh." Worry lines creased around Evie's eyes, locked on the wineglass. She followed Lita obediently and sat down without a sound as they reached the round booth. When Lita set the glass down, she grabbed it with both hands and took a large gulp. Her shoulders relaxed, and she sank into the booth with a satisfied smile.

Lita handed Jupiter and Jersey two coloring pages and a box of crayons, and they immediately began coloring and arguing. She went back to the register and returned with a pitcher of soda and five glasses. Jade slumped, her spine suddenly gone missing, unwilling to interact with her siblings or meet Lita's eyes. Evie hummed happily, eyes flitting across the room as she twirled the stem of her wine glass.

Suddenly two boys tumbled into Lita's shoulder. Her soda splashed, and she nearly upset Evie's wine glass.

"What the fuck?" she yelled at the boys who stopped and turned guiltily. Their eyes widened as she scowled at them, and they held their hands up in a protestation of innocence. One of them, a tall boy, looked around the table.

"Jade!" he exclaimed.

Jade blushed and smiled at the boy.

Lita's eyes shifted from Jade to the tall boy. *How does she know him?* "Watch your roughhousing in here, guys. You nearly knocked over our drinks."

The boy ignored her and flashed a broad goofy grin that took up half his face. *He's trouble.* He put his hands down and leaned over the table.

"Where you been hiding, Jade? I haven't seen you."

Lita looked from the boy to her niece. Jade's eyes shone, and she sat straighter, spine recovered. Jupiter and Jersey stared at him, crayons paused above their coloring pages.

"Hi Logan."

"Who are you?" Lita stepped in between Jade and this Logan kid. "I didn't hear your apology, did I?"

Logan's glance shifted to Lita, and he smiled again, less broadly. Lita didn't like his eyes. Shifty.

"Oh, sorry. It was an accident. My buddy"—Logan looked around, but his friend had deserted him as soon as Lita had stood up—"Heh, my buddy knocked me into the table." He straightened and backed up so he could see Jade again. His eyes swung from to her to Lita. "I'm Logan."

"We ride the bus together." Jade spoke without the note of disgust she usually had when talking with Lita. Her voice sounded breathless, airy and light.

Lita faced Logan. "We're in a restaurant, so act like it. No one wants an elbow in their eye during dinner."

Logan nodded. "Yeah, my buddy knocked into me. I didn't mean to hit your table."

Lita didn't like this kid. She started to speak, but Jade cut in first.

"Was that Cody?"

"Yeah. You can sit with us if you want." He looked from Jade to Lita and then noticed Evie. "Ah, this is your grandma."

Jade's eyes widened, and she nodded with a smile.

How did this boy know Jade? Or Evie? Logan told Evie he'd heard a lot about her. Jade looked slightly uncomfortable.

What the heck was going on?

Evie sat up straighter and tilted her head at the boy.

Jesus Christ.

Lita put her hand down heavily on his shoulder, and Logan turned to face her. "I'm Lita. Jade's aunt."

Logan nodded enthusiastically. "Yeah, she's told me about you, too." He glanced at a table filled with teens a few booths away. Lita didn't recognize any of them.

Jade was smiling at Logan shyly. Before Lita could figure it out, Logan stuck his hand out to Jade. "C'mon."

She took his hand and stood up "I'm going to sit with my friends, Auntie Lita."

Lita stared at her niece who, in five minutes, had suddenly leapt from twelve to sixteen. She didn't know what to say. "We'll call you when the pizza's ready," she said finally.

Jade shrugged. "I'm not very hungry."

"We've got pizza left at our table," Logan said. "Unless you don't like pepperoni."

"I love pepperoni." Jade smiled radiantly and left the table without a glance back.

Lita watched, dumbfounded. Jupiter picked up Jade's soda and chugged it.

"Whoa, Jupe, slow down buddy." Lita grabbed Jade's soda out of Jupiter's hands. "You've got your own."

"Mine's empty," he complained.

"Then ask for a refill. Don't just grab someone else's glass."

"Can I have a refill?" He held up his empty plastic cup as Evie jiggled her wine glass.

"Me too," Evie said in a happy, singsong voice.

Jersey gulped her soda noisily.

Fuck. Evie shouldn't have two glasses of wine. And Jade shouldn't be hanging out with high schoolers. Lita suddenly wanted to get the pizzas to go, throw her family in the truck, and avoid this scene entirely. Why did she always feel two steps behind? She'd learned about the ages and stages of development in the parenting class hours earlier. *Jade's moodiness isn't because she hates me or because I'm a terrible parent. It's normal, like her focus on herself and her peers.*

Lita took a deep breath and relaxed her shoulders. She needed to give herself a break. Like Oscar had said. She poured Jupiter more soda and picked up Evie's glass.

"Last one, Evie. You won't be able to walk straight if you have any more."

Evie looked indignant, but her eyes shone happily. "I know my limits."

Lita barked a laugh. "I've never heard anything less true." She carried the glass to the register and ordered a second wine for Evie. She hadn't intended to let Evie drink at all, but she'd felt sorry for her—a moment of sympathy leading to a loss of control. Did she need to be in control? Someone did. Wasn't that parenting?

"Hi Lita."

Lita froze. She turned slowly to find Oscar in line behind her. Dressed in a navy flannel shirt and jeans, hair falling over his eyes, he smiled at her tentatively. He smelled of cologne and looked fresh out of the shower.

Lita's pulse ratcheted and beat wildly. It felt like years since she'd seen him, though it had been only months. He smiled awkwardly, and she grimaced. "Hi Oscar." She looked behind him. "No Rikki?"

She wanted to kick herself. She didn't give a shit about Rikki or her blonde hair or her sun-kissed nose or her spaghetti-string tops.

His face clouded slightly. "Nope, picking up a pizza." He lifted his chin and glanced around the restaurant. "The kids here?"

A flash of guilt ran through Lita. The kids missed Oscar. Jersey hadn't stopped begging for him to come over. Jupiter adored him.

But still… Lita's anger swelled as she remembered how he'd dismissed her struggle. *What did he know?* She inclined her head towards the table where the kids sat with their coloring pages and Evie tapped her fingers on the table.

Jersey glanced up. When she saw Oscar, she elbowed Jupiter, whose face broke into a wide smile. He jumped up and climbed over Jersey, ran over and slammed his little body into Oscar's in a hug.

"Super Juper!" Oscar greeted him happily.

"Are you coming to sit with us?" Jupiter looked at Oscar who shook his head.

"Nah, Jupe. I'm here to pick up dinner."

Lita felt burning arrows in her chest that flamed out at the happy look on Jupiter's face. Seeing Oscar made her confused and sad. She missed him.

"You can sit with us if you'd like." Evie and the kids would be happy. She paid for the wine and slid it off the bar. "Join us while you wait, Oscar. C'mon, Jupe."

Jupiter tugged Oscar's hand towards the table while Lita carried the wine. Three booths down, Jade's green hair stood out among the crush of high school bodies. Easy to spot, at least. Had any of these kids been with Jade the night she'd ended up in the ER? She'd bet money that Logan kid had been there.

Jupiter climbed over Jersey, and Oscar slid into the booth next to her. She scooted over happily and showed him her coloring page.

"Nice work, Jersey." He pointed to a particular section. "I like the way you shaded in the cloud."

Lita marveled at how naturally he interacted with them. She struggled to talk to them without shouting.

Jersey beamed. "I like pink clouds, like cotton candy."

"I like orange skies, personally."

Jersey looked up at him, eyes wide, and nodded. "Me too." She grabbed orange and began streaking the color liberally on the top of the page.

"You smell nice," Evie said to him, twirling her wine glass.

Oscar beamed. "Thanks, Evie. It's nice to see you again."

Evie stared at him. "Where have you been hiding all my life?"

Oscar's smile grew wider. "I keep myself busy," he told her.

Jupiter chatted to him nonstop, and Oscar nodded and tossed in a word here and there. Jersey held her coloring page up again, and Oscar praised her artistry. Evie sat happily with her wine.

Lita felt off balance, riding a seesaw of emotions: Happiness to see Oscar again. Sadness because it had been so long. Anger at his long absence, the longest she'd gone without seeing him.

What had happened? She couldn't understand it, except she'd reacted quickly and aggressively, as always. Oscar had doubted her, and she needed someone who believed in her.

The waitress arrived with the pizzas and set them down on the rack on the table. Oscar tried to scoot out of the booth, and Jupiter clung to his arm. Jersey blocked his exit.

"NO!" Jupiter bounced with his hands on Oscar's shoulders. "It's time to eat!"

Lita scolded the boy. "Jupiter, let him leave. He's got his own pizza."

"No, he doesn't!" Jersey stuck her tongue out at Lita. "He doesn't have any pizza."

Oscar smiled ruefully, and he shrugged his shoulders. "Not yet, but it'll be done soon."

"You wait here." Jupiter commanded.

Oscar looked at Lita helplessly. She wanted him to stay, too. "I'll get Jade." She slid out of the booth and scanned the teenage bodies for green hair. A flash of emerald in the corner drew her to a booth filled with twice the bodies it typically held. A girl with pink hair and a nose ring sat on the lap of a shaggy-haired blond boy. She stared as Lita approached, then leaned her head down to whisper in the boy's ear. His eyes flicked to Lita, and his eyebrows lifted quickly before he replied and made the girl laugh.

Jade sat next to Logan—at least she wasn't on his lap—looking intently at something in his hands. Lita watched as he placed it into Jade's hands, and she wondered again what to make of this boy.

"Jade!" Lita called out across the table. Jade scowled at Lita. "Pizza. Come eat."

Lita didn't wait. She turned back to the booth where Oscar had begun to extricate himself, Jersey draped over his left arm, and Jupiter clinging to his leg. The kids liked him so goddamned much.

"What's Oscar doing here?" Jade stood behind her.

Lita turned. Jade's face looked flushed and happy. "He came to pick up dinner and got hijacked by Jupiter."

Jade pushed past her to greet Oscar.

"How are you doing, Jade? Green hair! You staying out of trouble?"

Lita barked a laugh. "Hardly! She's hanging out with high schoolers." She looked back at the table where Jade had been sitting and frowned as a couple of boys fell to the carpeted floor, wrestling beneath the corner booth. "Starting early."

Oscar's eyes twinkled as Jade's flashed angrily. "You gotta pace yourself, Jade. Not even in high school yet."

Jade looked like she'd tasted something sour. "Auntie Lita worries too much about the wrong things."

Lita didn't like her niece giving parenting lessons. "I don't think you're in a position to talk."

Jade smiled smugly. "I'm doing normal kid things. You should worry about learning to cook."

Oscar's laugh felt like an old coat, warm and comforting. Lita shook it off. "Uh, no, Jade. You're twelve, hanging out and drinking with a bunch of high schoolers."

Jade's smug smile slipped into a snarl. "Can we drop this?"

Oscar snuck a glance at Lita who shifted her eyes away. "Whatcha got, Jade?" He pointed to a small stone in Jade's hands, and Lita saw a flash of green in between her fingers. "Is that malachite?"

Jade looked down, then glanced back at the table where she'd been sitting. She smiled uncertainly. "Yeah, a friend gave it to me."

"Can I have a look at it?"

Jade handed the stone to Oscar. Jupiter and Jersey, still clinging to Oscar, peered at it.

Evie slapped her hand on the table. "When can I have some pizza?"

Lita dished out the pizza on three separate plates and set them around the table. "Here you go, Evie. Jupiter, Jersey, let Oscar leave now. Time to eat. Jade, here's a veggie piece for you."

Oscar slid out from the table as the kids and Evie dove into their food. He turned the rock over in his hands. "This is a nice piece, Jade. There's a boy your age who comes into the shop with his parents. They've got a nice collection, and I buy from them sometimes. I think his name's Max. Did you get it from him?"

Jade shook her head and glanced back at the table where she'd been earlier. "No."

Lita wondered why Jade looked like she'd swallowed something disagreeable. Her mouth twisted in a slight grimace, and the flush of happiness had faded.

Oscar's eyes followed Jade's to the table, then to the stone. He handed it back to Jade. "Well, I'd put this piece in a pendant. Or a bolo tie. It's got beautiful marbling. Your friend's got an eye for the good stuff."

Jade flushed and stuck the stone in her pocket. She slid into the booth next to Jupiter, grabbed a plate and a slice of non-pepperoni pizza, and took a bite.

Lita met Oscar's eyes. She wanted to tell him she'd fucked up. She missed him, wanted him back in her life. But the words, prickly and awkward, never left her tongue.

Oscar shrugged. "I think my pizza's ready."

He didn't move, and Lita felt a rush of emotion. She'd clear this all up. Why was she so angry with him? He hadn't done anything to hurt her. She'd flown off the handle. Fight first, ask questions later.

She began to speak but saw Oscar's eyes flit to the door and widen up in surprise. Rikki stood on the threshold of the restaurant. Her blue eyes scanned the room and frowned at Lita. Her mouth dropped open in an *o*, eyes blazing, then she turned around and walked out. Lita's anger flickered anew, and she bit back her apology.

Oscar cast an indecipherable look at Lita and hesitated, almost as if waiting for her to say something. But anything Lita had wanted to say had died at Rikki's appearance. Oscar took a deep breath and said goodbye to the kids and Evie, then turned to her.

"Bye Lita. Nice to see you again."

Lita's anger spun like a tornado. She nodded as he picked up his pizza and walked out the door.

TWENTY-NINE

Jade

"DON'T TRY to out-muscle someone who's bigger than you."
Auntie Lita stood in front of Jade and her friends. Felix was on
her right. Against the wall, Nana and Karmen sat at a folding
table covered by a plastic blue tablecloth. A second table next to
them was laden with a cake, a few presents and discarded jack-
ets. "Use momentum and torque to give yourself more power.
And get to the ground if you can. It's a lot easier to pound
someone bigger than you if you've got a ground advantage."

"How do you get someone to the ground if you're smaller
than they are?" Brooklyn wore purple leggings. Her blonde hair
hung limply over her ears. "I'm smaller than everyone."

"So was I. Still am. But smaller also means quicker. Use it to
your advantage. If you're facing someone bigger, use one of the
takedowns we practiced. The double leg is a good one, because
you don't have to have any leverage from the top." She
motioned to Felix to move towards her. "Come in and try to
take me down."

Felix smiled goofily, then wrinkled his face into a snarl. Jade
and the others laughed.

"Go get her, Tiger!" Karmen yelled as Felix approached
Auntie Lita in a half crouch with his arms out.

Jade had never seen someone who less resembled an attacker. Felix couldn't wipe the broad smile off his face. Karmen's heckling didn't help.

"Whoop! Big man!" She yelled across the gym. "Take her out!"

Auntie Lita ignored Karmen. "Felix has a height advantage, so when he's reaching for me, I drop my weight, pop his elbows up, take a big step into his core and hit him with my shoulder." She approached him in a crouch, and as his hands moved to her shoulders, she popped his elbows with her forearms, charged her shoulder into his midsection, then stopped. "When you reach for the takedown, grab the back of your opponent's legs, right here."

She tapped on Felix's hamstrings. "Once you've got your shoulder in his gut and have his legs, move forward, and get him off balance. Then you can turn him to the ground." She demonstrated by throwing her weight and Felix's body to the right. "Or push him against a wall and take him out." She pushed Felix into a wall and lifted his legs to flip him to the ground. Felix sprawled on his back, his smile never fading.

"Ooh, baby, you gonna take that?" Karmen shouted.

Felix nodded happily and raised his voice without lifting his head. "If I stand up, she'll take me out again!"

Auntie Lita instructed them to pair up. Jade and Brooklyn stuck together. Brooklyn's idea for fighting lessons had been a great birthday party activity. Jade had invited only a few kids—Max and Brooklyn, of course; and Scotty, Emmy, and Jenna from their float team. Surprisingly, they'd all come.

"Okay, you come towards me and reach for my shoulders." Brooklyn stood in a crouch, shifting back and forth on her toes and wiggling her fingers. "And watch out, cause I'm taking you down."

Jade smiled at her friend's cockiness. To her left Max dropped his head into Scotty's stomach. Auntie Lita jumped over and stopped Max's forward movement.

"Don't use your head. It'll compromise your neck and won't give you the power you need. Use your shoulder." She repositioned Max so his shoulder connected to Scotty's gut. "And remember to force his arms up before you go in."

"Ready, Jade?" Brooklyn faced her, crouching, and Jade nodded as she focused on her friend's shoulders. She stepped forward and reached for Brooklyn but found a cyclone of trouble instead. Brooklyn whirled into her, her forearms thrusting Jade's arms upwards as she slammed into Jade's body with her shoulder. She twisted sideways, and Jade found herself landing hard on her right side with Brooklyn on top of her, bony hip poking into Jade's thigh.

"It worked!" Brooklyn's eyes shone, and her face lit up happily. Beneath her, Jade marveled at the move. Though she'd known what Brooklyn was going to do, she'd been taken out quickly.

"Great takedown, Brooklyn!" The pride in her aunt's voice surprised Jade. "Now, if this were self-defense and you needed to disable your opponent, you'd follow with a groin punch. Even the pros have a hard time getting slammed in the nuts."

Emmy and Jenna giggled, and Max and Scotty looked wide-eyed at each other.

Felix, who'd risen and taken a seat near Karmen and Nana, groaned loudly. "Please don't tell me you need to demonstrate."

Everyone laughed. They continued to practice, and when it was time to quit for cake and presents, Jade realized she was having fun. The others, too. Maybe Scotty, Emmy, and Jenna could be more than float friends.

She'd waffled on whether to invite Logan. He'd surprised her when he'd given her the malachite at Pietro's last month.

"Hold your hand out." He'd placed something warm and heavy in her hand and folded her fingers around it. She'd opened them to find malachite, the same type of gem Max had shown her and Brooklyn at lunch.

She looked up in surprise, and he smiled crookedly.

"Where'd you get this?" Rough and jagged, it looked coral-like, with divots and holes throughout. She inspected the green, golf-ball sized nugget in her hand and twisted it in the dim light.

"I like to wander around in the bush and collect rocks. I just find things." He shrugged and tossed his head to one side. "The desert holds a lot of surprises."

She'd never heard him talk about collecting rocks. Max, on the other hand, could fill an entire lunch period with his latest finds. Bisbee Blue, a world-class turquoise found nowhere else. And rocks streaked with copper—soothes the pain of arthritis, he'd told them.

She wanted to believe Logan and his claim he'd found the rock during a ramble in the desert. Was malachite a common gem? Easy to find? Logan seemed too social to take a solo ramble in the mountains. She'd put the malachite inside the box of animal crackers he'd given her, tucked in the nightstand.

When they sat down for cake and presents, the group was tired but talked excitedly about their favorite moves. Karmen's parents showed up with Jersey and Jupiter for cake, which Jade had begrudgingly allowed. She hadn't wanted them at her party. *Fair enough,* Auntie Lita had said. But she'd allowed them to come for cake, which Auntie Lita now carried, alight with candles. Jade almost felt happy.

TWO WEEKS LATER, she felt nothing but terror. Invited to Max's house for a horse ride on his birthday, she gripped Sugar's saddle with both legs and clutched the horn with both hands. Being so high on the horse freaked her out. The reins had fallen out of her hands and lay on the right side of Sugar's neck, out of reach. She stretched out her hand towards them, but Sugar's hoof skipped on a rock, and the horse stumbled slightly. Jade squeezed her legs in alarm and grabbed the saddle horn for dear life. Once stabilized, she patted Sugar's warm coat and decided she didn't need the reins. She couldn't steer the horse anyways.

Side to side, she tilted with each step forward and each shift of Sugar's hips. Her fear of falling gradually subsided, and her body began to relax as they proceeded through a dry wash. Max's dad led from the front, and Max followed him on his horse Midnight like a true cowboy—at least what she thought a true cowboy would look like—his body loose and easy as he turned the horse to chat with the girls.

"We're going up Dixie Canyon to Potter Mountain." Max pointed to a high peak. It seemed way too far away to reach in one day. "There's a large a vein of minerals up there we discovered at the end of our last trip, and we've been meaning to go back."

"Is it copper? Silver? Gold?" Brooklyn's voice rose into an excited squeal, and Max's horse shifted his ears back and shook his head up and down. Max led Midnight away and turned the horse around in a few circles before returning.

"Nah, probably worthless. Otherwise, it'd be gone. There've been miners and geologists in these mountains for over a century. They'd have stripped it all long ago."

Brooklyn adjusted the chin strap to her pink cowboy hat and smiled broadly. "I'm going to find some gold!" She kicked her heels into the sides of her horse, and her horse, Honey, took two rapid steps, then slowed again. Sugar quickened her pace at the same time, and Jade bounced and held onto the saddle horn with both hands until the trot slowed.

Max's horse sidestepped next to them and pranced energetically. Jade, clinging to the saddle horn for dear life, watched Max hold the reins loosely and guide his horse easily one way or the other, occasionally spurring Midnight forward and sprinting up to his dad's horse Chewie where he'd chat a bit, then circle back. Though worried her horse would want to trot, Jade relaxed as Sugar maintained a plodding pace behind Honey. Neither horse seemed to want to go fast. Thank god.

Max's dad led them up a wide dusty road winding along the bottom of a dry creek where tall palo verde trees shaded the canyon floor, then he turned them onto a narrow canyon trail and began a slow climb. As their elevation rose, the vegetation became scrubbier and held little shade. Jade appreciated her ball cap as the sun beat down on them.

Brooklyn's body swayed as Honey lurched up a rock step. Jade clutched the horn as Sugar did the same. Her heart leapt when she slipped sideways in the saddle, and she held on for dear life, biting back a squeal. How was Brooklyn so calm? She'd be happy when the horses stopped so she could feel solid ground under her feet.

Max amazed her. At school he acted reserved, aloof, a bit stiff. But riding Midnight, he looked graceful, coordinated, and happier than she'd ever seen him. He narrated a steady stream of information about the area, and she tried to keep up with his chatter.

"Do you remember seeing the red veins in the walls of the Queen Mine?" He whirled around on Midnight in a close circle on the trail.

Brooklyn nodded her head vigorously. Jade shook hers. Their class had toured the mine two months ago, but she didn't remember much of the tour at all except she'd wished she'd worn a warmer jacket. It had been cold underground.

"Most of this began during the Precambrian period."

"The what?"

Jade was glad Brooklyn asked.

Max didn't explain but began to point out layers in the rocks, using a lot of terms that went straight over Jade's head. He pointed to a large rock outcropping at the top of a peak. "We're going up there, to a long, flat rock, great for picnics, with amazing mineral and metal veins."

The outcropping looked far away, and Jade's heart sank. "How much longer do you think it'll take to get there?" Her butt ached, and her thighs quaked from clenching the sides of the saddle.

"Maybe another hour? I'll ask my dad." He quickly turned Midnight and trotted to his father. After a brief conversation, he returned. "He says we'll be there in less than an hour. We'll have lunch and explore the top of the mountain."

Jade didn't know if her butt would survive another hour. She stopped Sugar and looked back down the steep canyon to distract herself, struck by the distance they'd covered—and the beauty. Bisbee lay hidden behind a line of lower peaks, the canyon highway barely visible. The Lavender Pit, the open-pit copper mine that had made Bisbee Blue turquoise famous, lay like a gash on the valley floor. Ribbons of ochre, violet, and slate undulated over and through the land below them.

Jade begrudgingly admitted this land held drama. Striking, like a layer cake, or the dreaded Neapolitan ice cream with the pink strawberry stripe remaining in the carton long after the chocolate and vanilla had disappeared. She'd thought Bisbee a dry, dull-brown town, but at this height it looked more like an earth-toned rainbow.

She breathed deeply and closed her eyes. At a thrumming sound in front of her, she opened them to find a hummingbird hovering ten feet away. She let out a tiny squeak—her mom's favorite bird. The tiny body fluttered left, then right, swooping up and down in front of her. She wondered where it was heading, with so few trees up here. Tears filled her eyes.

"Hi, Mom," she said softly. The bird flitted back and forth, then suddenly darted away. She wanted it to reappear.

When it didn't, she turned back to the trail and found Max watching her. He turned Midnight without smiling and spurred the horse away from her. Brooklyn's voice was rising and falling ahead, followed occasionally by Max's dad's low reply.

Around noon they arrived at the top of Potter Mountain, a rounded peak with a large, flat shelf of limestone. Jade stopped Sugar but had no idea how to get down. Her legs and hips quivered when she straightened them in the stirrups. Max and his dad easily dismounted and looped the reins of their horses around a small, scraggly pine. Max approached Sugar with a soft whisper.

"Hey Sugar. How'd you like some oats?"

Sugar tossed her head up and down and snorted. Jade clung to the horn, but Sugar didn't move as Max fed her. Max's dad approached from the left and offered a hand to Jade.

"Ready for a break?" She took hold of his calloused hand and tilted sideways, practically falling into his arms and grabbing his shoulders as he lifted her away from the horse and set her down safely. Her feet rejoiced with the ground below them as her legs trembled. Max's dad removed the blanket roll from the back of her saddle and held it out to her. "We'll set up a picnic on the limestone ledge there. Can you take this blanket and spread it out over the rock?"

She took the blanket and backed away from the large horse. Brooklyn met her on the flat rock with the picnic roll and helped Jade lay out the blanket while Max and his dad tended to the horses. The pink hat lay askance on Brooklyn's head, the drawstring hung loosely below her chin.

"My legs are wobbly!" She walked goofily towards Jade before she plopped down on the blanket and lay on her back with her arms wide open to the sky. "I'm going to have a horse like Honey when I get older, and I'm going to take kids on trail rides for a living!"

"I thought you wanted to be a Hollywood makeup artist." Max approached with three water bottles in hand, delivered one to each girl, and sat down on the blanket and opened the third.

Jade gulped the water. She was surrounded by mountains rolling west to Bisbee and descending into the arid desert in every other direction. She'd never have imagined living in such a place a year ago. She'd known nothing but the Bay Area where her family had moved, from one house to another, with little change other than street names. San Leandro, Hayward,

Oakland, Union City, Fremont… the cities blurred together. Her dad had often complained about a lack of community, but Jade hadn't understood what he meant until now. Bisbee wasn't one of many. It was one of a kind.

"I can do both." Brooklyn sat up, irritated, and threw a pebble at Max. "Or maybe I'll make a lot of money in Hollywood and give trail rides to poor city kids for free."

Max's dad walked to the edge of the limestone slab, peering at the layers of rock exposed along the bluff where it had crumbled. He took a thin hammer out of his pocket and tapped lightly along the rock. He caught a handful of the shavings, inspected them, then held his hand up for them to see.

"See this pyrite? Fools' gold." He pointed to gold flakes amidst the pale yellow-white shavings. "This limestone is riddled with pyrite, but it hides the real prize." He tapped again, and this time a large chunk of rock with layers of red, gray, and white fell into his palm. "See these veins? Copper. And this is zinc."

Jade and Brooklyn leaned in as he pointed to the dark color. "We live in a land of riches, girls."

Jade agreed. She lay back on the warm rock and enjoyed the sun on her face. March didn't hit with the lashing heat of summer but felt like a warm caress. They spent an hour or so on the mountain, dozing in the sun, tapping away at rocks with small hammers, and arguing as they tried to identify places on the broad valley below them. Brooklyn squealed when she found a small snail fossil embedded in the rock, and Max's dad reacted like she'd won the lottery.

"Good eye, Brooklyn! That's an ammonite fossil. Deposited during the Cretaceous period. We have a few of those, but this one is a beauty." He turned to Max who peered at the fossil in Brooklyn's hands. "Max, have you seen one with so many spirals intact?"

Max shook his head. "I don't think so. Nice find, Brooklyn."

Brooklyn beamed.

"Last time we were up here, Max found a beautiful piece of malachite."

Jade bolted upright. The rock he'd shown them at school. Like the one Logan had given her.

"He showed it to us," Brooklyn informed Max's dad. "He said it was a birthday present for his mom."

Max's dad looked surprised. "Did you give it to her, Max?"

Max shook his head and looked down at the ground. He picked up a rock and tossed it. "I don't know what happened to it. I took it to school one day but couldn't find it when I got home." He looked at Jade and Brooklyn and frowned. "I ended up making her a new flower press."

"Is it easy to find?" she asked.

Max's dad replied. "Malachite's fairly common, especially anywhere you find copper. But a rock with that size and type of marbling is unusual. It might have been the best specimen we've ever found." He put his hand on Max's shoulder and squeezed it as he headed towards the horses. "Let's head down now. If you guys pack up the lunch and blanket, I'll get the horses ready."

Jade stood but couldn't look at Max. She had a sinking feeling Logan had stolen—stolen? Could he have found it?—Max's rock. And it was in her nightstand.

Thinking of Logan brought a rush of confused thoughts. He might not be completely honest, but she didn't have proof it was the same rock. She shouldn't jump to conclusions. She folded the remaining lunch items into the canvas bag, and Brooklyn wrapped it up and tied it, humming pleasantly.

"I'm going to make one of these," she mused.

Jade couldn't reply. She thought miserably about the malachite and wondered what to do. She wanted desperately to talk to her mom. But she couldn't. She also couldn't imagine talking to Auntie Lita. Would she ever be able to?

THIRTY

Lita

LITA WAS WAITING for Diane to call her in for her counseling session when her phone rang. Though her due date wasn't for another two months, Karmen had been calling Lita frequently with pregnancy updates. She wanted Lita to be at the birth and to be the baby's godmother. Lita would do anything for Karmen, but she had no idea what being a godmother entailed. She certainly didn't know how to sew a ball gown or craft glass slippers.

Caller ID showed Hermosillo. Her pop.

"Hola, Papá."

Rosa sobbed and struggled to talk. Lita's pulse quickened. "¿Rosa, cómo estás?"

Her stepmother's words tumbled out so quickly Lita couldn't understand. "¿Rosa, qué pasa?" Her stomach clenched.

"He's very sick," Rosa said in Spanish. "Cancer, Lita. It's bad. It's grown quickly, from his lungs to his lymph nodes." Her voice fell as she sobbed into the phone. "He didn't want you to know."

"Rosa, how long has he been sick? Why didn't he tell me?" The world around Lita shrunk to the tiny couch on which she sat. Sweat broke out on her forehead despite the air conditioning.

Rosa's shuddering breaths filled her ear. "Months ago, when you went to California. He said you have too much with your new family. With your mother. He thought he would get better." She moaned softly. "Lita, he collapsed at the table this morning. We're at the hospital now. The doctors don't think he'll come home." Her voice broke again, and she cried into the phone.

Lita felt herself detach, the waiting room dropping away from her as she spun into a void. She saw her dad's dancing eyes and winced at a sharp pain in her temple.

"Come home, Lita. He wants to see you." Her stepmother's voice sounded far away. Lita blinked and shook her head. She shuddered as Rosa finished talking. "Come say goodbye."

Diane opened the door to her counseling office with a smile. Lita looked away and whispered into the phone. "We'll leave today, Rosa. Which hospital is he at?"

She ended the call and sat still, ignoring Diane at the open door. She wanted to drive home immediately but couldn't bring herself to move and simply stared at her phone, her mind a blank.

"Lita, are you okay?" Diane spoke from the doorway.

"No," she said without emotion. "My pop's dying. I gotta get home so I can go see him."

"I'm so sorry, Lita. Where's your father at?"

Diane's voice sounded far away. Lita tried to bring herself back to the present, but she couldn't think of anything but her father.

"He saved my life." Her voice cracked. "He introduced me to fighting."

She had no words to explain what his introduction to fighting had done for her. It had felt like a superpower, something of her own. An anomaly in the male-dominated world of Mexican kickboxing, she'd followed Ramon's training program religiously, taking each workout—cardio, speedbag, heavy bag, punching combos, foot jabs—seriously. The difference in her body had been staggering.

"Fighting made me strong, and I didn't feel vulnerable anymore." Though still tiny, her body grew taut. "It was the first time in my life I felt powerful. And it was addictive. I stopped being afraid; I no longer saw everything and everyone as a threat." Like her body, fighting made her mind tougher, too. Pushing herself to throw another punch when her arms felt like rubber. Stretching out another five minutes on the bag when she felt like dropping.

Diane made a noise to indicate she was listening. Lita kept talking.

"Not all the men in the gym welcomed me, you know? But my pop told them off. When men got in my way or snatched equipment out from under me, he stuck up for me. And I began to stick up for myself. He taught me to fight harder if men held their punches while sparring or took it easy on me during groundwork. I'd go on the offensive like a tornado, whirling and lashing out and flooding him with blows and kicks until he finally broke and fought back or quit in disgust at the girl who didn't know when to stop. Ramon—my coach—dubbed me El Gato Montés—Wildcat. And it was because of my pop.

"But I didn't thrive at home. Rosa was an unbearable nag. Babysitting, cleaning, cooking, she badgered me to help around the house, and I had no desire to spend my time doing domestic chores. So I avoided her as much as possible—not easy in a small house with nine people. We fought more and more. Ramon had waived the membership for me in exchange for cleaning the place every night. So I'd go there to clean and avoid home. I usually had the place to myself, and while I hated wiping the equipment down and mopping the floors and mats, I loved the independence. I stayed longer and longer each night after I finished cleaning.

"Then one night, my pop showed up, banging on the door. 'Quiet here, this time of night,' he said, and I got really nervous.

I knew he should have been home helping Rosa put my sisters and brothers to bed, but when I asked him why he was there, he didn't give me a straight answer. He sat on a weight bench next to the stack of mats where I'd been sitting, and I kept wondering why he'd come.

"Then he said, 'Mija, it's hard work raising kids. Rosa works hard.' I dreaded what he'd come to tell me. 'You and I,' he said. 'We're a lot alike.' He said when he was my age, he became my father."

Lita stopped talking and remembered how worried she'd been. She'd thought her pop was going to tell her she had to help Rosa with chores and the kids. But it didn't happen. He'd surprised her, again.

Diane's eyes softened when Lita looked up. "Lita," she said. "I know you need to go. But if you have the time, we can talk about this now in my office where there will be privacy." She indicated the doorway and raised her eyebrows in a question.

Lita hesitated, worried about time, but realized she wanted to talk, wanted to tell Diane about her dad. She moved into the office and sat in the love seat while Diane took the armchair across from her.

"Your dad told you he'd been close to your age when you were born." Diane prompted.

Lita continued with a wry laugh. "Yeah, he'd been hard for my abuela to handle. She didn't know what to do with him. He drank lots and listened little. He told me how hard it had been living next door to my mom and my stepdad, who had good reason to hate him. Then Abuela sent him away to work in Hermosillo in her brother's garage. He was angry because he couldn't easily see me anymore." She pictured her dad's face as he'd told her this, sad and tired.

"PAPÁ, I KNOW ALL THIS." She'd said, with no interest in the story of her pop's redemption. "Why are you telling me this now?"

"Because there is no longer peace in my house, mija," he said. "When you and Rosa argue, it's like a thunderstorm inside my house, inside my head. I can't think. The kids can't relax. The babies can't sleep." He stopped and took a deep breath. "When you were born, Lita, I was angry you weren't mine alone. I had to share you with another man, another father."

Lita began to speak, but he held up a hand. "Phillip, he was a good father to you, and I had no place raising a child. When your abuela sent me to Hermosillo, I vowed to make myself into a man who could support his own daughter. Which I did. But by then, your mama had packed you up and taken you back to California."

He raised his eyes to Lita sadly. "I didn't see you for ten years. I worked hard and met Rosa. We started a family, and I found peace with my wife and our babies."

Lita shifted nervously. She stared out the big plate-glass windows to the street. Though mostly empty, under the dim street lights she could see a lone figure disappearing into the shadows. None of what he was saying was new. She already knew her dad loved his wife and children. *What is he working himself up to?* She wanted him to get it over with.

"So what? Why are you telling me this now?"

"Because our house is like a war zone. The kids love you. I love you. Rosa loves you, in her way. But none of us love this war. This constant conflict."

Lita lashed out. "I can't help it. She treats me like a child, ordering me to do this, do that. I'm sick of being ordered around."

"Ah, well, this is the job of a mother. But while you don't see Rosa as a mother, she is. She's mother to my children. I take care of her, she takes care of my babies."

Who takes care of me? Lita wanted to ask. Pressure built behind her eyes. Her throat ached. "What are you telling me?"

"I've spoken to Ramon. He's willing to rent you the little apartment above us, above this gym. But you will have to pay rent. And"—he held up a hand again to keep Lita from interrupting— "you will need to get a job. And my uncle, Bernardo, who owns the garage where I work, has agreed to hire you, to try you out, chica. You know your way around a garage, yes? Your abuela told me you'd been spending time at the garage in Perdido with Eduardo."

Lita nodded. This turn of events surprised her. He wanted her to leave him, which hurt, but he was offering a way forward without babysitting her little brothers and sisters or scrubbing baby clothes and dishes. She'd still see her dad at work and at the gym. She'd be independent.

"I don't know how to cook," she said practically. "How will I eat?"

Her father laughed. "No one will let you starve, Lita. You can eat with our family. However, then you must help Rosa clean up afterwards, so maybe you don't like that so much. But there are other options. Ramon and his wife, Estelle, have the large apartment next to yours. She's willing to make sure you have dinner each night, but you must pay her. And," he said, his eyes twinkling, "you can always learn to cook."

LITA LIFTED her eyes from her hands to Diane, who sat across from her. "My pop arranged for me to move into the studio apartment above the gym. I didn't have much, but it was furnished with a single bed, a table with two chairs, and a small, hard couch. It had a kitchenette with a microwave and a hot plate, and the only other room was a bathroom with a shower almost too small even for me. It still looked empty after I'd moved in.

"The first night alone terrified me. I locked the door and windows and checked and rechecked them constantly. I jumped at noises on the street and at one point put the couch in front of the apartment door. I finally fell asleep in the early morning hours and, though I didn't want to, I got up with my alarm and headed to the garage to start my first shift.

"I acted as shop gofer the first year, working alongside the five mechanics and fetching parts or tools and watching and learning. Bernardo gave me a set of coveralls so large I had to fold the sleeves and legs to keep them from dragging, and they were layered with grease and the scent of gasoline. The smell of tires and motor oil infused my hair and skin, but I loved it. I loved the work, and I loved fixing things."

"Did you enjoy working with your dad?" Diane asked.

"Yeah, you know, it was something I didn't have to share with his family. It gave us something, the two of us. I felt more connected to him. By my second year, I moved into oil changes and tune-ups—small hands make it easier to reach spark plugs and wires on some of the Japanese imports—and the next year I graduated into brakes and suspensions and other repairs.

"For the first time in my life, I had money. Not a lot, but after rent and food, I had enough to fund my first professional tattoo: a small wildcat for my left shoulder. I'd given myself several tattoos: the date of my sister's death on the inside of one wrist above my brother's and stepfather's, the sun on the other wrist, a row of mountains on my thigh—and though they looked shaky, with thin lines and no artistry, I wanted more."

Lita chuckled. "My pop didn't understand the tattoos at all. He called me crazy. 'Loca! Why do you want to mark up your beautiful skin?' he asked me.

"I told him they're my stories. I wanted to tell my stories. 'Tell them with words, chica,' he said. 'Don't mark yourself up like a criminal.'"

Lita met Diane's eyes. "He never understood. He told me to at least keep them inside my clothes. Obviously, I ignored him. He may not have understood me, but he never tried to change me. He's always been in my corner, rooting for me, coaching me, cheering me."

Lita stopped talking and felt a wave of emotion crash over her. She choked back a sob. "He let me choose my own path, even though it led me away from him. He let me make my own decisions, didn't try to change me."

It struck her, not for the first time, the example he'd set. "Is this where I'm at now? What I need to do with the kids and Evie? Let go of what I think they should be and embrace them for who they are?"

Diane's voice was soft. "Your dad's love gave you the opportunity to grow, Lita. Love is expansive. It builds with us."

"Yeah, without him, I don't know where I'd be." Lita felt raw.

He's dying. An overwhelming sense of helplessness and grief whirled around her, and suddenly she wanted to get on the road. She needed to see her pop. She stood. "I gotta go."

Diane rose and walked her out of the office to the door. "I'm sorry about your father, Lita. I'll wait to hear from you. If you need to call, you've got my number."

Lita thanked her then started for the truck, feeling an urge to pick up the kids and give each of them a big hug.

THIRTY-ONE

Jade

JADE LAY on the hotel bed and tried to block out the sound of Jupiter teasing Jersey in the other room, happy to finally stretch out her legs after an unbearable five hours sandwiched between her brother's and sister's car seats in the back of the truck cab. She'd refuse to sit in the middle on the way back. Auntie Lita couldn't force her to sit in the middle, could she?

The highway—can it be called a highway if there are no shoulders and only two potholed lanes?—had been narrow and rough. Auntie Lita had driven fast, barreling through lifeless roadside towns. At times Jade thought the truck would careen off the road when skirting a pothole or another vehicle, but it stuck to the pavement, and Jade developed a begrudging admiration for her aunt's driving.

Tiny cinder block houses with metal roofs sat amidst the barren land, hardly a quick mart or gas station in hundreds of miles. No malls or parks, only a wide landscape of flat land surrounded by the rolling mountains and hills of the high desert.

As the only vehicle on the road for much of the trip, she was surprised when the two-lane highway abruptly transitioned into four lanes of semis, buses, and cars. Amidst the crush of traffic, men pushed large carts laden with goods. People rushed across the lanes of traffic, women holding children firmly, men hefting bags over their shoulders. As the road entered the city, the pedestrian traffic increased, and the stop-and-go of traffic depended not on streetlights or stop signs but breaks in the groups of people dashing across the lanes.

Jade's stomach rumbled. They'd arrived late and hadn't eaten dinner. Auntie Lita hadn't spoken much since she'd announced, hollow-eyed and rough-voiced, that they were heading to Mexico.

Would Auntie Lita change when her father died? Jade had toughened up since her parents had been gone. Could Auntie Lita get any tougher? Maybe it would be different for her.

The trip had given her time to think about what to do about the malachite, but she still had no answers. Logan's little gifts and his big smile confused her. He acted like she was special, but he hadn't invited her to Cody's party. And Taylor called her one of his 'pet projects.' What did she mean? She felt one hundred percent confident Logan had given her the same piece of malachite Max had originally shown her and Brooklyn. She'd asked him about it on the bus last week, and his response hadn't been convincing.

"MY AUNT'S friend is a jeweler, and he said the malachite you gave me is really unique," Jade said. "Do you think we could look for more? Where did you find it?"

"Oh," he shrugged his shoulders and lifted his hands in the air. "Around my house."

"My friend Max showed me and Brooklyn a piece like it at lunch a month ago, but he lost it. Do you think you found the same one?"

Logan gave her a dark look. "I don't know anything about your friend Freckles."

Freckles? Is he talking about Max?

"Freckles?"

"Yeah, he's got 'em."

"What do you have against Max?"

"I don't spend time thinking about your friend Max. It's not my fault if he lost his rock. I told you," he said. "I come across things. I found that piece near my house somewhere."

"Will you take me there to look for more? I'd like to get a piece for my sister."

"Nah, I've scoured the place. I've already found anything worth saving." He shifted in his seat and put his hands on Jade's shoulders, leaning his forehead onto hers. She flushed with warmth. "But it sounds like you want to be alone with me in the mountains."

She drew her head back as if dashed by cold water. "What? No!"

Days ago, she would have loved to go anywhere with him, alone or with others. But his attitude bothered her, and she kept pushing. "It just looks like the same piece of malachite Max had, that's all."

An ugly look crossed his face. "I already told you I don't know anything about your friend or what he does to get his rocks off."

He laughed at his own joke, but Jade frowned.

"I've never heard you talk about rocks before. So it surprised me. I didn't realize you'd get so defensive."

Logan sighed and stood up as the bus neared his stop. "Jade, you're acting like my little sister when she won't stop badgering me. I thought you'd like the gemstone, so I gave it to you. I don't know why it bothers you so much." He shouldered his backpack. "My friends think you're too young, and I'm beginning to think they may be right. I've never had to explain to a girl why I gave her a gift. Usually they say, 'thank you.'"

His eyebrows rose, and he pursed his lips. Jade felt ashamed of herself. Logan had given her a gift, and she had turned it into something uncomfortable.

"Thank you," she said quietly.

Logan nodded once, sauntered down the aisle to the front of the bus, then jumped off. Jade watched him go with a sinking heart.

AUNTIE LITA TOOK them to a restaurant where a dozen square tables with plastic, blue-checked tablecloths and metal chairs filled the dining room. Behind a long wooden counter, a flaming grill took up most of the back wall of the restaurant. Meat sizzled, and smoke billowed up and out of the room through a large fan above the grill. Photos featuring the menu's top items were fastened to the counter.

Her aunt ordered several dishes without asking anyone else, and the food arrived after a short wait. Rather than setting one dish in front of each diner, the aproned woman set platters in the center of the table and placed empty bowls and plates in front of them.

Jupiter scowled. "What's that?" His nose crinkled as he pointed to a steaming cauldron of something thick and bubbly.

"Caldo de queso." Auntie Lita grabbed a bowl and ladled out a small serving. She set it aside and prepared another. "Cheesy soup, Jupiter. One of my favorites."

"I want one of those." Jersey moved from Nana's lap to the chair with a booster seat and pointed to a basket of large tortillas.

"Sobaqueras? Best tortillas ever." She reached into the basket and grabbed one of the steaming tortillas then added some grilled beef, thinly sliced with whole green onions tossed on top. She added a scoop of beans topped with a crumbly white cheese and set the plate in front of Jersey. "Try some carne asada, too. Sonoran beef is the best in Mexico."

Jersey looked doubtfully at the toppings but picked up the tortilla and began to eat.

"Jupiter, hand me your plate."

"Gimme one of those." Jupiter pointed to a platter of thin, tightly rolled burritos as he handed her the plate.

"Ask, Jupe. No demands."

"Can I have one of those?" Jupiter yelled.

"Cool it, kid." Auntie Lita slid a burrito on his plate and handed it to him. "These are burritos de machaca con papas – tender beef and potatoes. You'll love it."

Jade liked the food, aside from a bit of spiciness in one of the dishes. It tasted different and much better than Taco Bell.

Auntie Lita paid and led them out the door and down the street. Instead of turning right, towards the hotel, she guided them to the left.

"Where are we going?" Jade asked her. "Can't we go back to the hotel?"

"We're going to say hi to someone," her aunt replied. "A few blocks from here." Jersey skipped, and Jupiter stomped as they made their way down the block. Nana looked confused but not at all cowed by the foreign surroundings or the occasional callout from men on the street. Sometimes, Nana replied to the men, causing a roar of laughter and much back slapping. Jade wished she knew Spanish.

They stopped in front of a brightly lit building with a wall of windows. A dozen bodies moved around the room on red and blue mats. Heavy punching bags hung along the walls.

The gym fell silent as they entered. All eyes swung their way as a wave of sweat, body odor and old rubber assailed her. Faces, mostly men and boys, studied them. From an office in the back of the gym, a stocky, muscular man emerged and worked his way across the mats to the door. Solid and intimidating, with salt and pepper hair and a weathered face, he had a bulbous nose and two bushy eyebrows which gave him a slightly angry appearance. His face lit up in a broad smile when he saw Auntie Lita.

"El Gato Montés!" He embraced Auntie Lita in a bear hug, patting her on the back and rocking her body with his. The gym jumped back into action as he greeted her, and Jade forgot about the other people as she watched the man and her aunt. He placed his hands on her shoulders and drew back to study her before embracing her again. "Has venido a ver a tu padre."

Auntie Lita drew herself out of the hug and nodded, eyes wet with tears.

The man looked at Lita gravely. "Una cosa horrible, el cáncer. Lo siento."

Auntie Lita nodded again but couldn't seem to find her voice. Her lips remained a thin line. The gym whirred with the clank of weights and the scuffle of feet upon rubber mats. After a few deep breaths, Auntie Lita spoke in English.

"Ramon, these are my nieces and nephew. Jade, Jupiter, and Jersey."

"A pleasure to meet you, Jade," he said in thick, halting English.

Jade smiled hesitantly. She wasn't sure why they had come here.

"Jupiter," the man said, leaning over to greet him, "Are you the big man of the family? How old are you?"

Jupiter looked shyly at the man and nodded. He held up seven fingers.

"And you, señorita, you are Jersey?" Jersey held Nana's hand and nodded. Her bright blue eyes stared back at the man.

"Who are you?" Jupiter asked.

"I'm Ramon, an old friend of your aunt's, also a friend of her father. I've known your aunt since she was a scrawny little girl."

"He taught me to fight," Auntie Lita told Jupiter. "Turned my life around."

"Oh, an exaggeration." Ramon clapped his broad hand on Lita's shoulder. "Your aunt, she was a tough nut. So angry, and so hard. And scared. This little one was scared of her shadow."

Jade got the hard and angry part but couldn't imagine Auntie Lita scared of anything.

Ramon turned to face Nana. "And this beautiful woman, Lita. Who is this?"

"Ramon, this is my mother, Evie."

"A pleasure to meet you, Evie." Ramon held his hand out, and Nana shook hands with him. She said something quickly in Spanish.

Ramon laughed raucously. "A firecracker!"

Auntie Lita spoke rapidly in Spanish and gestured at Jade and her sister and brother. Ramon stopped laughing and listened. He studied them and nodded thoughtfully. When she finished, he smiled sadly and looked at Jade and her siblings closely.

"I am sorry about your mama and papa," he told them. Jersey frowned and buried her face in Nana's thigh. Jupiter furrowed his brow and clenched his fists.

Tears threatened, and Jade quickly looked away. She wouldn't cry here.

A boy, slightly older than her, waited for his turn at a punching bag. He stared at Auntie Lita. Thin, all wiry muscle and bone, he wore a pair of long black basketball shorts and a Cleveland Cavaliers tank top. His face was round, with soft brown eyes and brown wavy hair, and Jade thought he might be the cutest boy she'd ever seen, cuter than Logan. He continued to stare at Auntie Lita then seemed to make up his mind about something. He straightened, left the bag, and walked towards them.

At his approach, Ramon brightened and looked at Auntie Lita with dancing eyes. "Wildcat," he said to Lita. "Did you know your brother Gabriel has joined us in the gym?"

Auntie Lita snapped her head towards Gabriel, then sprang forward and grabbed him into a hug. They spoke softly in Spanish and she turned towards the children

"This is my youngest brother," she explained.

Whoa. A brother? She seemed so solitary. Though she knew about them, Jade hadn't really thought of Auntie Lita's other family. Gabriel was slightly taller than her, and maybe fourteen or fifteen. He looked shy but smiled at Jade and her siblings. He addressed Nana.

"Buenos noches, señora." He turned to Jade and her siblings with a bashful smile and spoke in halting English. "Welcome to Hermosillo. My name is Gabriel." His face lost its happy shine for a moment, then he smiled again, softer. "I'm sorry we meet under poor conditions. It is not good."

Jade wondered how he could be so calm and friendly, when his dad was dying. He seemed so mature. And he looked like Auntie Lita. His eyes and his hair were brown and soft like hers. Jade was glad to meet a kid close to her age, and happy he could speak some English.

"Hi," she said, admiring the dimples in his cheeks. "I'm Jade. This is Jupiter and Jersey."

Jersey leaned into Nana's leg, smiling shyly.

Jupiter said belligerently. "Do you fight too?"

"Oh, yes!" Gabriel's smile grew, and he cast his eyes around the gym. "I don't fight like Lita, but I will one day."

Ramon clapped his hand on Gabriel's shoulder and spoke to Auntie Lita in Spanish. She replied and the three of them reached some type of conclusion.

"Okay. We'll see you at the hospital in the morning," Auntie Lita said.

Gabriel nodded. "Yes, I'll see you all there." He tapped Jupiter on the head with his knuckle and told him to take care of his grandma. Jupiter nodded solemnly and looked at Nana with a serious expression.

Jade's eyes followed Gabriel to the punching bag where he began to bounce on his toes and throw punches. His bones held not an ounce of fat. His shorts hung off his hips limp and baggy, held up by a drawstring. But his punches looked strong.

Jade followed Auntie Lita out the door and cast a final glance at the boy, who stopped punching long enough to wave good-bye. She left with a smile on her face.

THIRTY-TWO

Evie

EVIE SMOOTHS her blouse and adjusts the waistband of her skirt. A dark-haired couple walks past her to the double-door entrance. The signs are in Spanish, as are the words on the vehicle in the circular drive: AMBULANCIA.

Why am I here?

"I want to go up to the room alone." The tattooed woman says to the older girl as they walk towards the double door entrance. "Can you keep Nana and Jersey and Jupiter in the lobby?"

The girl nods.

"I don't want to go in there," Evie says, stopping outside the entrance.

The woman grimaces. "Evie, please stay with Jade and the kids. I need your help here."

Evie doesn't like hospitals, but when the doors whisk open, she enters a lobby with rows of padded aluminum chairs. A young man sits in one corner with his arm around a crying woman holding a baby. An old woman with a young girl watches them solemnly. Three young men are playing cards. They glance at them then back to their hands. A boy springs up to greet them.

"Buenos días, Gabriel," the tattooed woman says.

"Buenos días." He hugs the tattooed woman. "Papá's waiting for you."

Evie tries to follow the tattooed woman.

"No, Evie. You stay here." The woman pushes through a set of doors and out of sight. Evie paces.

"Why are we here?" The little boy whines.

"Auntie Lita's visiting her dad." The green-haired girl sounds tired.

Evie paces along the side wall, staring out the glass double-door entrance into the busy parking lot.

"I don't want to stay here." The boy whimpers softly.

"We have to wait for Auntie Lita."

"I'm tired of waiting," Evie says. The sunshine beckons. She loves the sun.

"We can go to the park down the block." Gabriel suggests.

The little boy jumps up from his seat and runs to the double-door entrance. "Let's go!"

Evie joins the boy. "Good idea."

She holds the little boy's hand outside the hospital. An ambulance pulls up, lights flashing, and a pair of men in blue dart around and open the back doors of the vehicle. They slide out an occupied gurney and whisk it inside. A man in a white coat rushes past, and Evie suddenly freezes, afraid.

What am I doing here? Where am I?

A hand touches her shoulder, and she nearly cries out. A boy with brown hair holds the hand of a familiar little girl. He inclines his head sideways. "It's this way," he says. Evie follows him, casting furtive glances back at the ambulance.

They reach a playground with a large swing set, a tall castle with a twisty slide, and a blue-and-red three-car train of sorts with tiny seats and an engine resembling a tiger. The little boy and girl race to get up the slide first. The older boy helps the little girl up to the top. Evie sits with the older girl on a bench beneath a tree in the shade and plucks her blouse away from her body. Sweat gathers beneath her breasts.

"He looks like a boy I know," Evie tells the girl, who's watching the older boy on the playground. "Cute, don't you think?"

The girl glances at Evie uncertainly, then her eyes return to the boy. "Yes," she admits finally.

"Like caramel," Evie says.

The girl's eyes dart back to Evie's and pinch in confusion. "Caramel?"

"Soft and sweet and a beautiful golden-brown."

"Nana!" The girl quickly glances away.

"Quite the looker." He reminds Evie of someone. "Like my Carmelita, a little caramel. Soft, caramel-colored skin and beautiful deep-brown eyes." Evie's thoughts become jumbled. She sees a brown-eyed young man. A baby. A house by the edge of the sea.

Uncertainty floods her. Despite the heat, iciness seeps through her. *Where is Lita?*

"Lita...." She stammers. "Where's Lita?"

"She's at the hospital."

Evie's alarmed. "At the hospital?" She stands. "I need to be with her."

The little boy runs from the slide to the swings, and the older boy moves side to side, pushing one and then the other.

"No, Nana. She's visiting her dad. She's not sick." The girl stands too. "I'm going to help push them. You stay here."

The girl takes a position behind the little boy and pushes his swing. The older boy pushes the little girl.

Deeper into the park in a large grassy area surrounded by cement walking paths and tall trees, a wooden gazebo shelters a table laden with crisply wrapped packages. Children blow bubbles and laugh. A party. It's Lita's birthday!

Relieved, Evie walks to the gazebo to see if the cake and balloons have arrived. The heat presses on her, makes her feel heavy and sluggish. She sees a little girl running across the grass to the gazebo. Is it Lita? Her pace quickens.

"Nana!"

Evie pauses at the familiar voice but then continues to the gazebo. A group of women watch her approach. She keeps her eyes on the little girl.

"Lita!" She calls out.

The women look confused as she nears, but they smile at her. She doesn't recognize them. A girl is suddenly blocking her way, hands on hips.

"Nana, where are you going?"

Evie blinks. The women under the gazebo watch her. She searches for a familiar face *Who are they? Where is Lita?*

The park is filling with women and children and older couples strolling through the trees or sitting on benches. An ancient, tiny man walks by with a little dog on a leash. Evie chuckles as the dog meets another and the two begin sniffing each other's rear ends. She's glad she's not a dog.

"Nana, let's go back." The girl taps her shoulder and points to the hospital. "Auntie Lita's there."

"At the hospital?" She turns abruptly away and walks towards the hospital.

"Nana, wait."

Evie isn't waiting. She marches out of the park and through the busy parking lot. Near the wide double doors where people stream in and out of the building, visitors and patients smoke and talk at the entrance. Others rest in the shade cast by the trees lining the hospital entranceway.

The boy behind her calls to a group of people walking into the lobby. Two men and three women turn, their faces lined with worry. The oldest woman waves at them.

"Perdona, señora." The boy pushes gently past Evie and greets the group of people who have stopped short of the double doors.

The old woman—does Evie know her? White hair frames a

round, weathered face with deep brown eyes and a rather large round nose. She gazes tenderly at the boy, but when her eyes shift to Evie they harden into a narrow stare.

Evie stops abruptly.

The woman questions the boy, and he speaks to her rapidly. One of the other women chimes in, and all eyes swing back to Evie.

"Who is she?" Evie asks the girl beside her, pointing to the older woman.

"I don't know," she replies. "But it's hot out here. Let's go inside where it's air-conditioned and find out."

A good idea. Sweat runs down Evie's forehead.

The older woman looks back at Evie, then enters the hospital and sinks heavily into an empty chair. The other men and women don't stop but proceed through the swinging doors.

Evie isn't sure where to sit, or if she wants to. "Why are we here?" she asks. "The party is in the park. And where's Lita?"

No one responds.

Evie's mind is whirling. She can't start Lita's party without Phillip and Randy. She walks to the glass doors and peers out into the sunshine hoping for something to help her make sense of all of this.

THIRTY-THREE

Lita

SHE'D TRIED to prepare herself. But she couldn't have imagined how tiny he'd look, the little big man. Sleeping and shrunken in a hospital gown, his arms stick thin, pale and bruised on top of the covers, a blanket covered his legs. An IV ran from one hand into a mess of tubes behind the bed. Two other patients behind curtains shared the room, which smelled of pain and sickness. She sat down next to her papa's bed and grasped his hand. His shallow, ragged breathing hurt her heart, and the hiss and whir of machines filled her with despair.

Rosa entered and gave a little cry at seeing Lita, who stood, eyes filled with tears and embraced her stepmother by the foot of the bed. She clutched Rosa and fought back grief and a surge of anger. It wasn't right to lose her dad. Of all the people in Lita's world, her dad meant the most. He'd taught her how to live, how to fight. But the biggest gift he gave her was the right to forge her own path. To cast off the events and people who defined her childhood, and to create a new future. The freedom to find who she was, regardless of whether or not she fit neatly into his world or anyone else's.

Rosa relaxed her embrace and stepped back, her face weary. Lita kissed her on both cheeks, then wiped her own eyes. The antagonism from her teen years was long gone, and they'd arrived at a place of mutual respect. Lita had watched Rosa raise seven children, most adults now and living on their own. Her stepmother wasn't the ogre of her teenage years. She'd been her dad's partner, given him a family, a second chance after Evie derailed his life.

"I'm sorry, Rosa." Lita choked on the words.

"Lita, I'm sorry I didn't call you earlier. He fell ill months ago, but we kept thinking it was a stomach bug. He didn't want me to worry you." She dropped her head and shook it softly, then lifted her stricken eyes to Lita's. "The doctor says it's only a matter of days now. What am I going to do?"

Lita's found it hard to breathe. She felt Rosa's despair as her own. "You have Jose Jr. and Rafael. And Gabriel. All of your children, Rosa. They're part of Pop's love for you and the beautiful family you created." Her voice broke, and she and Rosa hugged each other again.

"That's what I like to see."

Her pop's voice, hoarse and raw, ripped Lita away from her grief. He smiled weakly, eyes shining. Rosa cried out and went to him, pulling a chair to the bedside and clasping his hand. Lita sat on his other side close to his shoulder.

"I always dreamed of seeing you two together like this. I never thought it would happen because of me." He closed his eyes and struggled to breathe. Each intake of breath seemed to sap his energy. Lita put her hand on his arm. Rosa stroked his forehead. He winced and opened his eyes.

"Lita, I need to apologize."

Lita looked at her father in surprise.

"Why? There's no reason." She lifted her eyes to meet Rosa's, then dropped them quickly when the grief in her stepmother's eyes threatened to push her over the edge.

"I was so young when you were born." He paused again, closed his eyes, and took a few shallow breaths. "I didn't know how to be a father until Rosa taught me."

Rosa stifled a sob, and Lita shook her head.

"No, Pop, no."

"I loved you from first sight, mija. Though I didn't know how to be your papa, I was so in love with you." The machine rasped, and her father's voice sounded weak and hollow. "I wanted to be with you, chica, but it was so complicated."

Lita felt pressure building behind her eyes. She couldn't speak. She looked at Rosa helplessly. Rosa shook her head, tears rolling slowly down her cheeks.

"When you came back to me as a teenager, Rosa and I had our children and our little house. You filled it with your anger, and I didn't know what to do."

"Pop, please," Lita pleaded with him. She didn't need any apologies. "I know this."

"Your mother called. She wanted you back."

Lita stopped breathing, stilled. Rosa's muffled sobs filled her ears. The oxygen machine clicked and whirred. Her mom had called?

"I didn't tell you, Lita. I thought your mama had hurt you enough. She tried for years to contact you."

Lita's breath caught. *She'd wanted me?*

"You were so hurt, Lita. I kept you here. I never gave you a chance to love her again." He closed his eyes, his breath ragged and shallow.

Lita felt as if she were in the closing minutes of a five-round fight and had taken an uppercut on the jaw. Her head rang. *Her mom had wanted her*. She had tried to get Lita back.

He continued, eyes closed.

"Rosa and I fought so much about it. She said no child should be without a mother. I didn't want to lose you again, mija. I loved you too much."

Across the bed, Rosa's shoulders shook, her face puffy and wet with tears.

"I kept you from your mama. I never gave you a chance to forgive her."

Lita felt lost. The ground had shifted beneath her, and she no longer knew up or down. She shook her head. Did this change anything? Her mother hadn't loved Lita enough to pull herself out of her grief and addiction. She hadn't sobered up and come looking for Lita. She'd still given up her child for a bottle.

"Mama was a drunk. She didn't care for anyone, even herself. I wouldn't have gone back."

Her pop's voice was soft, and Lita leaned over to hear him.

"She called me distraught many times. She called your abuela. She wanted you back. But we never told you."

His eyes were dull with pain. A tear rolled slowly towards the pillow beneath his head.

"Forgive me."

Lita shook her head and clasped her father's hand.

"No, Papá. There's nothing to forgive. You and Abuela gave me everything. You were my lifeline." Her voice shook. She clutched his hand.

"Mija," he whispered, and Lita leaned in again. "Forgive her."

Lita stared into his eyes. Forgive who? Rosa? Evie? A dull ache throbbed behind her eyes.

"I don't understand."

"Your mama, Lita. She hurt you, but she hurt too. Losing a child is the worst thing to happen to a mother. And she's lost them all. Forgive her."

Rosa wouldn't look at her. Lita had spent so many years hating her mother and the hurt and sorrow she'd caused.

"Promise me, Lita. Promise me you will work to love your mama again. Forgive her. Do this for me."

She wanted to scream. Instead she leaned over and kissed her pop's forehead. Her voice broke like her heart.

"I can't promise anything, Papá. But I want you to be at peace. I'll try." She choked back a sob.

His face eased, and he closed his eyes, then opened them again.

"Lita, you made me so happy the day you were born. I'm sorry I wasn't always a good father." He drew as deep a breath as his rotten lungs allowed. "I am so proud of you."

Tears rolled down her cheeks as he closed his eyes again. Behind the curtain, a patient groaned. The machines whisked and whirred. Lita felt her world shrink to this moment alone. To this man in the bed before her. To her stepmother sobbing across from her.

She wasn't ready to forgive Evie. But for the first time, she felt uneasy about her anger. She'd never thought about her mother's losses. Randy and Phillip, drowned. Laurel, dead. Jake, dead. She had run away.

Did it matter? Evie's mind was gone. She didn't know who Lita was. What would it help to forgive her now?

A movement at the doorway brought her back into the room. Her brother Jose Jr. stood with her sister Julieta. Behind Julieta, Juan Carlos and Gloria peered into the room. Lita got up and hugged Jose Jr. first.

"Hey brother," she murmured into his neck as they embraced. "I wish I didn't have to see you like this."

"I know, Lita. I know. He's glad you're here. We all are."

Lita hugged Julieta, and they clung to each other for a long moment. Both Jose Jr. and Julieta were married with children: Jose with two little boys, and Julieta and her husband with a little girl. Lita slid past them into the hall to hug Juan Carlos, only sixteen. He'd grown taller than Lita since she'd last seen him, and he hugged her shyly. She clasped Gloria, her youngest sister, surprised at her short hair and business suit. She'd last seen her brothers and sisters two years ago, and they'd changed.

"Gloria, you're so grown up."

Gloria's mouth twisted sideways, and her expression told Lita she'd stated the obvious.

"It's my business attire. I'm assistant to the manager at a bank, so I can't wear jeans."

"Wait 'til you see Marco," Juan Carlos said. "He started working as a teller at the same bank. He wears a suit!"

"That punk in a suit?" Lita asked. Everyone laughed. Marco had been a troublemaker in his teens but apparently had settled down. "I'll have to see it to believe it."

Before leaving to make space for her siblings in the tiny, curtained room, she kissed her pop's forehead, cool and dry under her lips. He was sleeping again.

"I'm leaving now, but I'll be back. I love you, Pop."

His breathing rasped quietly, and he didn't reply. Despite knowing she had to relieve poor Gabriel and Jade from Nana- and child-minding duties in the lobby, she didn't want to move her feet. Losing her dad, her cornerman, her training partner, her biggest fan… the very thought ripped her open.

Powerless. She felt powerless.

She forced herself to step back from his bed. Her voice came out as a whimper. "Find your peace, Pop. I'll try to find mine."

She couldn't manage a smile, couldn't look at anyone except her pop. She motioned for her siblings to take her place, and with a final glance at her father, left them alone.

THIRTY-FOUR

Jade

IN THE HOSPITAL LOBBY, the older woman spoke softly to Gabriel, and he turned to Jade. "This is my abuela, my grandmother, Doña Luisa. She thanks you for coming."

Doña Luisa spoke rapidly again, nodding at Jade and her siblings.

"She is sorry for the loss of your parents."

Jade nodded numbly. She suddenly felt very tired. Tired of condolences. Tired of watching her siblings and Nana. Tired of feeling sad all the time. She leaned back against the chair, wishing she could forget it all for a while.

"Abuela tells me God takes good men, and it's not for us to understand why. She lost her husband, my abuelo, many years before I was born. And your abuelo, your papa's father. He was also taken long ago. Now your papa and my papa. It is their time." He listened as Doña Luisa spoke, then he translated.

"She wants you to know you are welcome here. If you are part of Lita's family, you're part of ours."

Doña Luisa became animated, waving her hands at Jersey and Jupiter

"Abuela is happy to have you. She says every woman needs a husband and children. She has long worried about Lita because

247

she does not get married and have children. Now she no longer has to worry."

Rather simplistic, Jade thought. She wasn't convinced having a family would make Auntie Lita happy.

"Tell her I'm sorry about your dad." Jade wanted to turn the conversation away from her grief and her troubled aunt.

Gabriel's eyes lost their focus momentarily. He paused then spoke to his grandmother. Doña Luisa's eyes filled with tears as she leaned past Gabriel to touch Jade on the cheek. She drew Jade's head towards her and kissed her forehead. Jade teared up at the tenderness and fought her sadness. She was so tired of grief.

Doña Luisa stroked Jade's hair and whispered in Spanish. Jade took a deep breath and smelled the faint scent of roses and mothballs. As the older woman drew away, Jade wanted to throw herself into this woman's arms, to curl up and hand over all her sorrow.

Gabriel translated. "You are our family now and will always have a home here."

Jade could barely swallow. She wanted to go home but didn't know where home was anymore. She nodded at Gabriel's words, then withdrew from the old woman's embrace and leaned back against the chair, staring straight ahead at the rows of chairs in front of her.

Doña Louisa spoke again, a much louder voice. "A dónde vas, Evie?"

Jade looked up quickly. Nana looked uncertain, hesitant, almost frightened, standing midway through the double doors, blocking traffic, the glare of sunshine behind her, waves of heat rolling in from the asphalt parking lot.

Jade went to her. "Nana, come sit by me." She held her hand out, and Nana's eyes narrowed.

"I want to go home." Nana said. She sounded like a child.

Jade understood. She wanted to go home too. "Me too, Nana. But we're here with Auntie Lita. Her dad's dying."

"No!" Nana turned to look out the double doors at the parking lot. People streamed in and out around her. She turned and scanned the room, her eyes worried. "I need to get things ready for the party."

Jade couldn't begin to guess what was in her grandma's head. "Yeah, but we've got to wait for Auntie Lita."

Nana whipped her head back. "It's Lita's birthday." She looked at Jade, then Doña Louisa and Gabriel. "But we can't start until they're back." Soft and insistent.

"Nana, we'll wait here. It's too hot outside." She offered her hand again, and Nana ignored it. She looked over her shoulder at the busy parking lot.

"I don't know anyone here." Nana's voice trembled.

Why did Nana seem so old and frail suddenly? Jade hated seeing her like this, so confused, her eyes darting back and forth. Jade's parents would have known what to do.

"Tú me conoces." A soothing, solid voice spoke, and Jade felt the warmth of Doña Louisa behind her left shoulder.

Nana's eyes widened at the woman's appearance. "Who are you?"

"Doña Louisa, your neighbor. Now come," the older woman said in English. She held out her hand, and Nana started to speak, but halted. She stared at the hand, then looked around the room, her eyes darting from one person to the next.

Doña Louisa spoke to Nana in Spanish. Jade heard names—Phillip and Randy and Lita—but couldn't understand anything else. Nana's voice rose and fell in what sounded like an argument, but Doña Louisa's voice remained steady. Finally Nana took Doña Louisa's hand, and though the fear never left her eyes, she slowly returned to the line of seats and sat down. Gabriel's grandmother patted her hand like they were old friends.

Auntie Lita appeared and greeted her grandmother with a long hug. She wiped her eyes as she pulled away. They murmured in Spanish, and Nana butted in with questions which made Auntie Lita pause and frown.

Gabriel joined the conversation, and after more talking and nodding, Auntie Lita broke away, beckoning Jade and her siblings, her eyes swollen and puffy. "Okay, kiddos, let's go. We'll get some lunch and relax at the motel for a bit, and I'll come back this afternoon."

Jade felt relieved to be leaving the hospital. It felt like a pressure cooker in this lobby, especially with Nana pacing and fretting about a nonexistent party. But she wilted as they walked into the blazing-hot parking lot. Between the hospital, Nana's confusion, and the heat, Jade felt weighed down by layers of grief and worries about Nana, her friends in Bisbee, and, if she admitted it, Auntie Lita.

THIRTY-FIVE

Evie

A FAMILIAR DRY, brown landscape faces her, topped with scrubby plants and small trees and an occasional saguaro standing sentinel over the flat lands, its arms raised in a salute to the faded blue sky above them.

Finally home. They'd been in the car for over an hour, following a line of electrical towers across the desert, through the occasional town to a small village on the edge of a coastline on a flat, large, open body of water. The tattooed woman parked the truck in front of a small, whitewashed church, bright against the blue waters behind it. Broad, short stairs lead up to the front doors, which are open wide.

Evie is grateful to be out of the truck after the bumpy ride. Fine sand shifts beneath her feet as she stretches her back, then straightens. Phillip will be looking for her. He hates the time away from her and the kids.

Speaking of the kids, she's lost track of them, as usual. She turns to thank the driver for the ride but sees her embracing an older woman with a round face and sad eyes. She looks familiar. A neighbor?

The little girl from the truck grabs hold of her hand, her tiny palm hot and sweaty. The boy holds the hand of an older girl with green hair, and the four of them watch the tattooed woman greeting and hugging more and more people who emerge from the church or the rows of cars to swallow her up.

The older woman approaches them. *Do I know her?*

"Buenos días. You must be tired after the drive." Her voice is husky and low. She looks exhausted herself. "You've come a long way with your Tía Lita."

"What's a Tia?" The little boy frowns. "I don't speak Spanish."

"Lita? Have you seen Lita?" Evie peers at the woman. "Do you know where Lita is?" She can't remember where Lita went. Always running off. She can't see any of her kids.

The woman's eyes soften, and her mouth turns down slightly. She points to the tattooed woman. "Lita's over there. I'm Doña Luisa. Jose was my son."

The name hits Evie like a slap, and she recoils. *Jose.* She's done something wrong. A sour taste fills her mouth. Phillip's angry. He's so angry with her. She scans the flat land and twists her hands together, watching as people gather at the church. Phillip must be at home. She doesn't know what to say, doesn't know what this woman wants. She opens her mouth to speak then closes it. Behind the church, the water twinkles an invitation.

"Come inside for some water. The service will start soon." Doña Luisa waves them inside the church.

"What is she saying?" The little boy is whining now.

The little girl tugs on Evie's arm. "I need to pee!"

Evie ignores them. "Have you seen Phillip? My husband. Have you seen him? I don't see the kids. Did he take them fishing?"

Doña Luisa's puts her hand on top of the little girl's head and strokes it softly. "I have not seen your husband." She turns and points to the tattooed woman who is shaking hands with an old man. "But Lita is there."

"No. I'm looking for my little girl."

A girl speaks behind her. "Nana, let's go into the shade. I'm too hot."

Evie whirls around. "Who are you?" she demands of the girl. Something's happening, but Evie doesn't understand what. The girl is familiar, and she recognizes this church, this land, and the sea behind it.

"Nana, it's me, Jade. Let's go inside. It's hot." The girl's face is damp with sweat. She looks tired and unhappy.

Evie wants to be somewhere else. Why is she with these people? Where is Phillip? Where are her kids?

"Come with me." The old woman takes Evie's arm to lead her up the steps of the church.

Evie fights the urge to yank her arm away. She climbs the stairs slowly, surrounded by mournful faces. Evie doesn't want the sadness. She needs to find her kids. Something is wrong.

The woman leads Evie inside the church to a short folding table filled with water bottles and envelopes. She grabs several bottles of water and hands them to Evie and the kids.

A boy appears. Unsmiling, he speaks to the woman softly. She nods and touches the side of his face. "Gabriel will show you where to sit. He'll make sure you're comfortable."

Evie stares at the boy. Familiar, but she doesn't want to follow him, doesn't want to sit. Why is she here? The older woman walks away, and Evie feels very alone. She wants to apologize, but she doesn't know why.

Evie doesn't sit when the boy points to a wooden pew in the church. The heat is less intense here, though sweat trickles down the back of her neck under her braid. A large photo of a man, brown eyes bright like his smile, sits on a table in front of an empty altar. Evie approaches the table, ignoring the pleas of the green-haired girl to sit back down. She sees more photos spread out on the white tablecloth and lifts them to look. He's with a woman in many of the photos. And children. Lots of children. He's always smiling, the man.

Evie gives a little cry as her hand stops over a single photo.

She reaches down and picks it up. *Lita.* Her little girl is in the man's arms, a tiny figure, the fingers from one of her little hands splayed out in a wide greeting to the camera, her mouth open in laughter. His grin is broad.

Jose. Lita's father. This is Lita's father.

Evie looks up. Is he here? Phillip won't like it. He doesn't want her to see him. But Jose went away. He's gone now, isn't he?

The woman from the photos, the one with all the kids in the photos with Jose, watches her from the first pew. She looks awful, her face swollen and puffy, her eyes weepy. Evie recognizes the devastation in the woman's face and looks away.

She glances again at the photo in her hand, but instead of Lita, she sees Phillip's face flash in front of her, rage-filled and ugly. His hand raises to strike her.

Evie drops the photo and backs away. She's done something terrible. Everything's changed. Her friends have stopped coming around. Her husband is angry. Her little home by the sea is full of pain.

"Because of me," she whispers.

The birthday party. She'll get the party ready. She heads to the exit, and a tattooed woman steps into her path, her wiry body blocking Evie's escape.

"Evie, sit with the kids." She points to the pew where a girl watches her, pain covering her face like a veil. A little boy is arguing with a little girl who's kicking the seat in front of her. Evie knows them. They must be here for the party.

"I'll take them with me," Evie announces.

The tattooed woman's eyebrows lift in a question. "Where are you going?"

"The park. I've planned a party for Lita's birthday."

The eyebrows pinch into a scowl. "Oh, for fuck's sake. Not today, Evie. There's no party today."

"What do you know?" Evie looks longingly out the open

doors to the glaring sunlight. This church is filling her heart with heaviness. She doesn't want to be here.

Far down the highway, an approaching vehicle casts a large dust plume behind it like a fog bank over the sea. Evie lifts her head above the tattooed woman to peer outside. Is it Phillip? The dust plume floats at a distance, taking forever to draw near.

"Who's that?" she asks.

THIRTY-SIX

Lita

JULIETA HAD CALLED her three nights ago. "He's gone." Her sister choked out the words.

Grief took her breath away; Lita gulped for air. She'd missed it. She hadn't been with him, hadn't trusted Evie enough to leave her alone in the motel. Now he was gone.

"We're going to take him home," Julieta continued. "We'll have the service in three days in Perdido."

"Okay." Lita barely heard her. She ended the call and sat numbly in front of the TV. She'd never envisioned this moment, had never wanted to.

A small man, he'd been big in the important ways. His love had been big enough for her and for Rosa and all their children. No matter her tattoos or her anger, he'd loved her. Now she felt abandoned, as she had when he'd left Perdido and moved to Hermosillo. But this time he wasn't an hour away. He was a life-time away. He was gone.

She stifled a moan and allowed herself a few minutes of numbness. Then she grabbed her phone, left the motel room, and called Karmen.

"He's gone, Karmen. He's gone." She fought despair as she paced outside the motel. "Can you come to Perdido for the funeral? I don't know if I can do this." She reconsidered. "I can't do this."

"Oh, Lita. I'm sorry. I can't. I told you I've been showing signs of pre-term labor, and the doctor's ordered me to stay close to home. And before you ask, I'm not letting Felix out of my sight. You've got this, sugar. This is your family."

Karmen was right, though it didn't erase the new, gaping hole in her life.

She drove with Evie and the kids to her father's house where she helped Rosa and her sisters wash and dress his body. They laid him out in the main room surrounded by photos and candles, and she couldn't take her eyes off a photo of her pop holding her as a toddler, his face alight with joy and her head thrown back in laughter, her hand splayed like a wave to the camera. Father and daughter. For two days, visitors streamed in and out of the house, sharing their grief and stories about her pop.

They traveled in a convoy to Perdido, the funeral car leading a long procession. The small village hadn't changed much since her last visit a decade ago, though a cell tower now stood on its eastern edge. Family she hadn't seen in years greeted her warmly. Her father's friends, some of whom still lived in Perdido and others who had driven from Hermosillo, offered their condolences.

And now, facing her mom on the front steps of the church, Lita wished Evie would just fuck off and stop causing problems. It wasn't fair to have to deal with Evie right now.

When Evie's eyes lit up at an approaching vehicle, Lita recognized Felix's truck. Her heart leapt with hope but then crashed down. It couldn't be Karmen. Or Felix. He wouldn't leave Karmen.

The truck parked at the end of a long line of vehicles across from the church, and a man stepped out. *Oscar.* Lita's fought back a surge of emotion. *Goddamned Oscar.*

He wore black jeans and a black button-up shirt and

scanned the village as he stepped out of the truck, the dust swirling around him, his eyes hidden behind dark sunglasses. He took the glasses off and threw them onto the driver's seat then turned to the church, his eyes searching the crowded stairs.

"Who's that?" Evie asked.

A noise came out of Lita, a sound she didn't recognize. Oscar barely made it to the bottom of the stairs before she wrapped her arms around him, buried her head in his chest, and clutched him like a life preserver. Her tension eased as she sunk into him.

She gulped, her voice choked up. "You came."

She missed him. The kids missed him. She hated the distance between them these past months. And she hated seeing him with Rikki. Lita had so much to say to him, but there were too many eyes watching them. Too many ears listening. She managed an apology. "I'm sorry. I'm sorry I've been so awful."

"Shh. Lita. It's okay." He stepped back, and his hands rubbed her arms. "And I'm sorry, too. About your dad, And for your family. For you."

Lita shuddered as a wave of emotion washed over her. Losing her pop brought grief and sorrow, but seeing Oscar— and touching him—soothed her and dulled the sharp pain. Her pop's death proved life was too short… the only guarantee in life was death. But his life had been full of family and friends. Had been full.

Guilt and shame washed over her as she thought about the distance she'd put between her and Oscar these past months. Why? Because she'd been scared? Proud? How could Oscar be so calm with her when she'd told him to fuck off?

"I don't deserve you," she told him.

He drew his forehead back, locked eyes with her, and frowned. "Stop."

She needed to say it. She wanted to say it.

"I get so angry sometimes, Oscar. I lose control."

He squeezed her shoulders. "Tell me something I don't know."

Maybe if she kept talking, she could explain how hard these past few months without him had been. How none of her plans had seemed to work right. How she didn't seem to know what to do anymore. "I never wanted any of this: the kids, Evie, a family…. It's turned my life upside down."

He shook his head. "Hush, Lita, we'll talk later." He looked towards the church and gave a short quiet laugh. "We're attracting attention."

Doña Luisa was walking down the stairs. A crowd of family and friends stood at the door of the church watching them.

"I missed you," she told him.

He kissed the top of her head. "I know." He drew away and wiped the tears from her cheek with his finger with a soft smile. "We're good now, Lita."

She felt a flush of warmth, then hugged him again, only letting go when Abuela reached them.

"Buenos," she greeted Oscar. "I'm Doña Luisa, Lita's abuela."

Oscar stuck his hand out and spoke haltingly in Spanish. "Oscar Torres, a friend of Lita's from Bisbee. I'm sorry about your son."

Lita hadn't ever heard him speak Spanish. His pronunciation was slow and awkward. Doña Luisa studied the two of them, then ignored his hand and embraced him. "Gracias. Come, it's time to start."

"I don't want to sit down." Evie's voice was sharp and accusatory, arguing with Gabriel who was pleading with her to sit next to her grandchildren. "Stop ordering me around."

Relief flooded Gabriel's eyes as they approached. Evie scowled at Lita, but her face lit up when she saw Oscar.

"You're here?" she asked incredulously. "No one told me you were coming."

Oscar flashed a smile. "Everyone likes surprises. How are you doing, Evie?"

Evie's face relaxed. "I want to leave. This boy won't let me." She points at Gabriel and his worried frown.

Doña Luisa touched Gabriel's shoulder and led him away. Lita felt a stab of guilt. Gabriel shouldn't be minding Evie and the kids at his father's funeral.

Jupiter protested as Gabriel left. "I want to go with him."

"Me too." Jersey nodded emphatically.

"You don't want me?" Oscar held his arms out with a look of mock surprise. "I thought you'd be happy to see me, Super Juper."

"I'm happy to see you!" Jersey proclaimed.

Jupiter's eyes followed Gabriel, then flashed angrily at Oscar. "I don't want to be here." He folded his arms across his chest and stuck his lower lip out.

Oscar held his hands out to them both and raised his eyebrows at Evie. "Who wants to go for a walk?"

"I do." Evie turned towards the church entrance. The kids got up eagerly and grabbed Oscar's hands. Lita looked at him gratefully.

"I want to stay with you." A soft voice spoke on Lita's right. Lita looked down to see Jade's face. The naked grief on it shocked her. Jade looked lost, younger than her thirteen years, not the sulky teen who contradicted and argued. Not the good girl turned bad who drank and skipped school. She looked like the girl who'd lost her home and her friends. Who'd lost almost everything. Lita held her hand out to Jade and was surprised at how tiny Jade's hand felt when she clutched it.

THIRTY-SEVEN

Jade

THE SERVICE WAS IN SPANISH, and Jade didn't understand a word. But funerals weren't difficult to follow. The only other one she'd attended had been for her parents, and it hung like a dark spectre in her memory. She'd sat in a state of disbelief throughout the service, nodding at talking heads and stiffly letting herself be hugged by people she didn't know.

Emotion clogged her throat so thick she could barely swallow. Her chest ached like she'd been doing timed miles in PE. She wanted her parents so badly. More than anything. She missed her dad's crazy, embarrassing hyena-like laughter, her mother's smell, and the delight her mother took in going places as a family. She missed going to the city once a month, to the Steinhart Aquarium in Golden Gate Park, or to the Exploratorium, or the theater. Sometimes they'd go to Pier 39 to watch the sea lions on the wharf. They'd pick up sourdough bread and fresh crab and head back to the house to watch movies. That old life didn't exist anymore.

Auntie Lita stood with the rest of the congregation, but Jade remained sitting. Her heart twisting, she mangled a tissue in her hands and fought the huge fireball of grief exploding inside her.

Beside her, Gabriel shook silently. Rosa reached over to rub his back.

This display of motherly tenderness pushed her over the edge and a cry escaped from her lips. Her mother would never again stroke her back or caress her hair. She'd never again make ice cream sundaes for Jade's birthday. Jade would never again hear her dad's hysterical laughter. Grief rose like a wave, rushing up on her like the time she'd turned her back on the ocean and got stuck breathless and churning in the surf. She couldn't breathe.

Life wasn't fair. She wanted her mom and dad. She wanted someone to love her again.

Her grief crested, and an overwhelming sense of loss filled her chest, pouring out of her in a moan. Jade bent over her lap, folded her arms on her knees and gulped for air. She felt more alone than ever. Too much. Tears she'd fought for months surged out. She had no energy left to hold herself together, and her body was wracked by sobs.

Only a fool would think she could maintain order in this life of hers. She had no control. Nobody had any control. She'd never in her wildest dreams imagined the loss of her parents, yet they were gone forever. Her heart had broken so badly she doubted it could ever heal. In a room full of grief, she felt alone.

Sorrow pressed on her, so heavy and smothering she didn't notice the pressure at first. But gradually, through her tears, she felt Auntie Lita's hand rubbing her back. Jade turned blindly towards her aunt and crumpled, her head on Auntie Lita's lap. She clung to her aunt's legs and cried, not caring what Gabriel or anyone thought, not caring if she looked a mess.

Auntie Lita's hand stroked her, moving from her hair to her back to the sides of her arms. All the while, Jade cried and gulped air with shuddering breaths.

THIRTY-EIGHT

Evie

NOTHING IS RIGHT. The park. The party should be in the park. But it's empty. Where is everybody? Phillip and Randy are fishing. *They should be home by now. Where are they?*

Evie stares at the sea. Does she see a boat on the horizon? She stands on the threshold of the tienda, holding her ice cream cone like a torch, sticky streaks of vanilla dripping down her wrist.

"I'm going," she announces and drops the cone into a rubbish bin. Evie's tired of this man following her, insisting she have ice cream or water. His children are too rowdy, too loud. Where are her children? It's Lita's birthday. But she can't find the cake or the party favors. She can't find her kids. She leaves the man and children.

"Evie, wait," the man says.

Evie's done waiting. She walks towards the water until it touches her toes, and gazes at the boat. Is it Phillip and Randy? Randy adores his dad, won't leave his side.

Where are my kids?

Church bells ring, and Evie glances across the park to the whitewashed church. *Lita's at church with her abuela.* She relaxes.

Lita's abuela is still friendly to her even if the other women in the village aren't.

Lita's birth has brought many changes. Phillip's ready to move back.

"We're going back to California, Evie. It's time for us to go back home. As soon as we save up the money, we'll leave. Maybe six months, tops."

A small group of people walk across the park. A deep sense of foreboding builds inside her.

A crowd at the park.

A birthday party interrupted.

Something isn't right.

She doesn't want those people to come closer. They're bringing bad news. She knows it, as surely as she knows her name. Evie glances desperately at the water, willing the boat to come closer so she can know Phillip and Randy are safe inside. But a voice tells her they're not coming back. They're not in the boat at all. They're dead.

She cries out then plunges into the sea, waving her hands at the boat. "Phillip! Randy!"

A man yells her name. She pushes forward. She must. Because she remembers now. A chubasco. A vicious thunderstorm. Lightning, violent winds. Churning waters. A boat struck. A boat sinking. Her boy and her husband, lost to the sea.

"No!" she cries.

Her mind churns like the water in which her legs struggle to move forward. Surprisingly cold, the water tugs at her long skirt. She waves her arms and splashes farther in. Up to her thighs now, she throws each leg forward. The soaked skirt wraps around them, growing heavier and tangling around her legs with each step. She stumbles and falls and swallows a mouthful of salty water. Her wet clothing tugs her this way and that, and a sense of peace washes over her. She closes her eyes and thinks about Phillip. She wants to see him again.

Two hands grasp her shoulders and lift her out of the water.

A man's face, eyes wide with fear, looks into hers. *He knows. He knows about Phillip and Randy.*

She clutches his arms. Everything she's ever understood about life dissolves into the waters swirling around her. Phillip is dead, Randy gone with him. She's lost her children. Her parents have turned their backs on her. Everyone she's loved is gone.

Evie throws her head back and screams at the sky.

THIRTY-NINE

Lita

LITA SAT NUMBLY, stroking Jade's back as her niece's shuddering breaths began to slow. She smoothed the back of Jade's hair. Her own grief hung thick like smoke, while Jade's burned hot like wildfire, all-consuming. Though Lita's losses were many—her brothers, her sister, her stepfather—she hadn't considered how much Jade had lost. If her pop's death had opened a hole in her life, then Jade's parents' deaths left a gaping chasm. Not only her parents but also her home, her friends, her entire life. Lita, who'd spent so much of her life fighting, had racked up the losses too, but she'd brought herself out of it.

Or had she? Her dad had introduced her to fighting, supported her on a path to her own life. Fighting had saved her. But maybe fighting, which had given her control, wasn't the most important factor. Maybe it was her dad.

Lita's breath hitched. She hadn't been ready for her nieces and nephew. She hadn't known how to handle their anger or their grief. Their everyday activities were foreign to her. As she'd been to her father. How had he known what to do with her? Lita felt his loss intensely. It was too late to ask him.

Jade's breathing steadied, and Lita's attention shifted. She'd been waiting for Jade to stiffen up, to become hardened, to use her anger and defiance to push herself out of her grief. But Lita's counselor had said each person had a unique way of coping, and finding one's way through grief and transition looked different for everyone.

It struck her she'd never given the kids any reassurances. She'd never told Jade or Jupiter or Jersey she'd stick with them through thick and thin—the hard stuff and the fun stuff. She'd taken them on like a distasteful job.

Like Philip, had. She remembered displeasure in his eyes when he looked at her. As an adult, she could understand his resentment towards her and how tough it must have been to see her every day. But she also knew the pain it caused her, the uncertainty she felt about her place in the family. She wouldn't do that to her nieces and nephew. Her kids.

Jade began to move, her weight shifting off Lita's thighs as she pushed up and wiped her eyes with the backs of her hands. Her raw, swollen eyes met Lita's, then dropped down to her hands. The pews were emptying, and people stood and talked quietly around them.

"You okay, kiddo?" she asked.

Jade nodded, and Lita hugged her. The scent of vanilla-cream hair conditioner flooded her nose, and she whispered into Jade's ear. "I'm sorry, Jade. I'm sorry about your mom and dad. I'm sorry about everything." Jade stiffened, but Lita tightened her hold. "You're such a smart kid. Smarter than me. You deserve better than me. I'm learning, Jade. And I'm trying. I'm proud of you and the way you take care of Jersey and Jupiter, your loyalty to Nana, how you've adjusted to your new school."

Jade stopped pulling away. Her shoulders softened slightly, and she squeezed Lita's ribcage. "I'm sorry about your dad, Auntie Lita." Jade's voice choked off at the end.

"We've had so much sadness in our lives, haven't we?" Karmen's family flashed through her head, fully intact, alive, all the siblings and their parents healthy and happy and connected.

"I don't know why things happen the way they do. But Jade, I'm here. I'm not the greatest at showing you guys, but don't ever doubt it. I'm in your corner."

Jade nodded, then squeezed Lita's hand. "You're getting better," she said. "And I'm sorry too. I haven't been trying to make anything easy."

"You mean it won't always be this difficult?" Lita laughed, her laugh loud in the quiet of the church. Heads turned towards her, and she cut the laugh off. Leave it to her to disrupt the sanctity of the church. Her dad would have laughed too, would have tried to hide it, smirking, then shaking with laughter.

"You shouldn't have to make anything easy. You're a kid. Don't worry about any of this. Focus on yourself and your own way forward. My pop gave me the gift to be true to myself. He didn't pigeonhole me or force me to fit into life his way. I can never replace your parents, but I want to do the same for you. I may not know how, and I certainly haven't started off well, but I won't quit on you."

Jade looked exhausted. Lita felt the same. She'd rushed to Hermosillo from Bisbee and had been moving nonstop between the hospital, her dad's home, and the motel every day since. Now it was over. The service finished, her dad gone.

"Let's get up and see if we can find the rest of our family." Lita stood and offered her hand to Jade. Jade took it and followed Lita out of the pew.

They exited the church, eyes blinking in the bright sunlight. Bells tolled, announcing the end of the service—not that they needed to announce anything in this village. Everyone was already here.

Jade released her hand from Lita's and pointed past the park to a little tienda near the sea. "What are Nana and Oscar doing?" Lita followed Jade's finger and saw Evie and Oscar talking and gesticulating wildly. Were they arguing?

"Ah, fuck." She trotted down the stairs in their direction, Jade and Gabriel behind her. Doña Luisa followed slowly.

Evie marched away from Oscar and headed into the water. *What's she doing?* Lita started to trot as Evie moved deeper and deeper into the dark water, pushing forward into the current. Lita broke into a run, pumping her arms and legs to cross the park. Oscar sped away from the kids and sprinted towards the water. Evie slipped and fell.

"No!" Lita raced through the park.

Oscar reached Evie and pulled her out of the water. Evie clutched him, then let out a scream. Oscar lifted Evie under both arms, and Lita took her legs. Together, they carried her out of the sea. Jade and Gabriel watched wide-eyed, and Jersey and Jupiter cried at the top of the steps to the tienda, ice cream forgotten, melting and dripping over the edge of the table.

Evie's face twisted raw with grief. "They're gone," she whispered, shivering and wet on the beach. She closed her eyes.

Lita fell to her knees, lifted her mom's shoulders and wrapped her mother in her arms as Evie moaned. Lita rocked their bodies together slowly.

"I know, Mom. I know." She hugged her mom and kept rocking her, hot tears streaking down her own face. "It's just us."

FORTY

Jade

JERSEY SLAMMED into Jade and clung to her, crying, inconsolably. Jupiter paced and hopped and talked to himself while Oscar and Auntie Lita carried Nana out of the water.

"Why did she do that, Jade?" Jersey cried. "Why did Nana go swimming in her clothes?" Her sister's voice broke with gasping sobs, and she clung to Jade.

"I don't know, Jersey. Maybe she felt hot." She saw panic in her sister's face. It mirrored the panic she felt in her gut.

Nana's face was ashen and drawn, and her head lolled as they laid her in the sand. She stared at Auntie Lita and Oscar with no recognition, her eyes dull and vacant, a house with no one home. Her clothing, soaked and dripping, lay in heavy layers over her body. Her eyes focused on Lita, then narrowed, and she spoke. Auntie Lita dropped to her knees in the sand, held Nana's shoulders, and hugged her.

Jade walked towards Nana, but Jersey tugged her hand backwards. "No. I don't want to."

Jade looked at Jersey in surprise. "Why not?"

Jersey wouldn't look at Nana or Jade. She stared at the ground and refused to budge. She whispered in a low voice between gulping breaths. Jade couldn't hear her.

"What?"

Jersey sobbed. "Because she's going to die." She turned away from Nana and pushed her hot face into Jade's belly. "Everyone's dying," she cried. She clung to Jade desperately, like the time at the doctor's when she didn't want to get her shots.

Jade caressed her hair. "She's old, Jersey, but she's not dying. Not now. Nana's living in her head, that's all. She's mixing up who's here and who's not."

Doña Louisa appeared behind them followed by a small group of mourners. She placed her palm on Jade's head. "No se preocupan. Estará bien."

Jade wanted to throw herself into the woman's arms. Instead, she squeezed Jersey, then pushed her gently toward the old woman. "Jersey, stay with Doña Louisa."

She walked hesitantly to where Auntie Lita was holding Nana, still rocking back and forth, murmuring softly. Jade didn't like Nana's vacant look, her dull eyes staring blankly in front of her.

"Nana, are you okay?"

Nana didn't smile or look up.

Auntie Lita's eyes looked wounded when she glanced at Jade. She leaned down and whispered to Nana. "Let's get up, Mom. Let's get out of the sun and out of these wet clothes."

Nana stared at Lita dully, her face slack and empty of expression.

Was Jersey right? Was Nana dying?

Doña Louisa's voice rang out from behind Jade. Auntie Lita glanced at her grandmother then nodded at Oscar, who sprang forward and helped Nana up. Nana stood shakily, supported on either side, her hair and clothes dripping, the vacant look never leaving her eyes. Auntie Lita and Oscar slowly led her away from the sea and across the park.

· · ·

JADE SAT with Jersey and Jupiter at the end of a long folding table in Perdido's community hall. A large neon BINGO sign sat, dark and dull, over the stage. Doña Luisa had insisted Nana be taken to her house. Jade and her siblings were to stay with Gabriel, who'd gone in search of food.

During the service the open emotions—wails, crying, and loud displays of sorrow—had surprised Jade, so unlike her parents' funeral of silent sobs and sniffles. Now people filled the hall with soft conversations, tears, hugs, and laughter. Outside the hall, a group of men stood in a circle and passed a bottle around, laughing and telling stories.

Her parents' funeral had been nothing like this one. After the short service at a funeral home, everyone had gone their separate ways. This reception, though heavy and sad, felt more like a celebration than a funeral. Funny how families and cultures are different. She wondered if Mexican funerals were all like this, or if they could be short and impersonal, too.

Jade started at a hand on her shoulder. Gabriel held out a plate laden with tamales and casseroles, rellenos, pan dulce and one dish that appeared to be boiled guts. Despite the guts, her stomach growled loudly. She hadn't eaten in hours. She took the plate gratefully, and Gabriel set his next to hers. Jersey and Jupiter were already eating, without their usual complaints.

"Thanks." She picked up a piece of bread. Why had Nana thrown herself into the sea?

"Your abuela, she will be fine after a long rest." Gabriel smiled confidently as she sat back down next to him.

Jade didn't agree. Nana lost it. Finally, truly lost it. Would she ever be fine? She imagined herself an astronaut on a space-walk watching her lifeline to the ship severed. A link to her old life had snapped when Oscar and Auntie Lita carried Nana out of the water. Jade now floated in an entirely new space surrounded by the foreign bodies of Auntie Lita's orbit. Karmen and her boisterous family. Fighting. Cars. Oscar. Felix. Mexico. Her world had transformed since eight months ago. She'd lost her parents and her California friends but had gained a new family and new friends.

She missed her parents so much. Her eyes welled with tears, and she wondered how that could be possible. She'd cried so much today already. Wasn't there a physical limit on how many tears could be shed? Would she ever be able to think about her parents without this hot, aching grief?

Doña Luisa and Auntie Lita entered the hall. Her aunt's face was puffy, and her swollen eyes softened when they landed on Jade and her siblings. She spoke to her grandmother, whose head turned towards Jade and nodded.

The relief Jade felt as Auntie Lita approached surprised her. Like her tenderness during the service. So unlike the tattoos, the swearing, the attitude… not giving a fuck.

Gabriel stood up when Auntie Lita arrived at their table. He offered her his chair, and she declined. "If I sit down, I might not get back up."

"Where's Nana?" Jersey asked.

"Resting." Auntie Lita ran a hand through the short spikes of her hair. Her eyes darted over Jersey and Jupiter.

"Where's Oscar?" Jupiter asked.

Lita's face softened. "He wanted to sit with Nana. He'll be here later."

"Are we staying here tonight?" Jade wondered how they'd fit all these people overnight in this small village.

"Yeah. You guys are sleeping in Doña Luisa's house, with Nana. I'll be in the camper outside."

"I want to sleep in the camper!" Jupiter bounced in his seat.

Jade thought it might be fun to sleep in the camper, but not with Jupiter and Jersey. They'd never settle down.

Auntie Lita shook her head. "No, Jupe. Too hot and too cramped."

Would Oscar spend the night in the camper too? Jade thought Oscar loved her aunt. When they were in the same room, his eyes followed her. When she needed anything, he offered to help. When she talked, he listened. What would it be like to have someone always in your corner, someone not forced by blood or profession to care?

Ramon, the man from the gym in Hermosillo approached their table and spoke softly with Gabriel and Auntie Lita. He placed his hands on her aunt's shoulders and murmured while she nodded. Gabriel's face tensed as he listened. He bit his lip and nodded too.

Tears filled her aunt's eyes, another new development. Jade hadn't seen Auntie Lita cry until they'd come to Mexico. She'd sat, hard and stone-faced, at Jade's parents' funeral and had been nothing but a prickly ball of anger since they'd arrived in Bisbee. Suddenly there was a new, softer version of Auntie Lita. What happened?

Jade stood suddenly. Everything felt so loosey-goosy and unmoored, the bits and pieces of her life tossed around like a salad. She needed to feel connected again. "I want to see Nana," she said.

Jersey and Jupiter stopped eating and stared at her. Auntie Lita and Gabriel paused in their conversation with Ramon.

"Me too," Jersey said.

"No," Jade replied. She didn't want her sister or brother to hang on her any longer. "I don't want anyone with me."

"She's probably sleeping." Her aunt sounded surprised but held out her hand. "But I'll take you to her."

Jade barely waited until they were away from the hall before firing off questions to Auntie Lita. "Why did Nana do that, Auntie Lita? What's going to happen to her? Will she be okay?"

Auntie Lita took a deep breath and let it all out in one big sigh. "You know Nana's mind is failing. You've been around it longer than me. She's not able to take care of herself."

"I know," Jade interrupted. "But why would she throw herself into the sea?"

Auntie Lita paused. When she turned to Jade, her eyes

looked wounded, uncertain. "How much did your dad tell you about our family?"

Jade thought. She'd heard a few stories about Perdido—kids happily running loose in the small village. But not much about life after Perdido, in California. Jade shook her head. "Not a whole lot."

Auntie Lita paused, seeming to weigh her words. She stared at the ground as they walked. "I don't remember a lot about my early years in Perdido. Flashes of happiness. Some confusion. I knew I was different. I looked different than my brothers and sister, and I had a second family—my pop's family, my abuela. I spent lots of time at Abuela's house, sometimes with your dad and Laurel and Randy, but most of the time with my cousins. When I turned four, Nana planned a big party for me in the park. She used to throw great parties. There were streamers and garlands, a piñata, cake, cookies, ice cream in a cooler. Your Grandpa Phillip and your Uncle Randy were out fishing and supposed to come off the water for the party. But they never made it back. Nana was getting antsy about it and had decided to cut the cake when a group of men arrived. They told Nana there'd been a freak storm and Phillip and Randy had drowned. On my birthday."

Her birthday? Her dad hadn't talked about this. Auntie Lita's upper lip trembled.

"The screams, the panic, those are my first birthday memories. I'd never heard the sound coming out of your Nana. A low, wailing cry… it wouldn't stop. Like a wounded animal.

"She tried to throw herself into the sea, but friends took her back to the house with your dad and Auntie Laurel. I went home with Abuela." She took a deep breath and clenched her jaw.

"Nana never came to get me. I was four and wanted to be with my family. I needed my mom. I waited and waited. Jake and Laurel visited me. They spent lots of time at Abuela's house, but I didn't see Nana. Later, Abuela told me Nana's grief for the dead was so deep she neglected the living.

"Then one morning, I woke up to shouting, and Nana burst into the room with Abuela arguing and following behind. Nana picked me up out of bed. We left Perdido that morning for California. I didn't get to say goodbye to my dad, and I left Abuela's with nothing but the clothes I was wearing."

Auntie Lita's eyebrows pinched together. "California wasn't easy. Nana started dancing, working nights. She drank too much after work and slept days. Though your dad was only fourteen, he kept us together while Nana fell apart."

Jade's head hurt. She hadn't heard any of this.. "Dad said he left home when you were young."

"Yep, I was nine. We had a stepdad by then—Chuck. Nice enough sober but violent when drunk. He and Jake fought a lot, and Jake joined the army as soon as he turned eighteen. Laurel took off a few months later and hooked up with a rough crowd. Your nana, Chuck, and I lasted another year until one night Chuck beat Nana so hard our neighbors called the cops. He ended up in jail and only came back to the house with the police to get his stuff."

Auntie Lita shook her head and looked off to the sea. "I wanted Nana to get better. But she never liked being alone. She couldn't be happy with the two of us. I never understood why I wasn't enough.

"Kids need to be protected, Jade. Your Nana didn't protect me. She pickled herself in grief and alcohol, and I got hurt. When I was two years older than you, I ran away and went to live with my pop. He made me call her when I arrived, but she was drunk and screamed into the phone. I never spoke to her again and always thought she didn't want me. The next time I saw her was last summer, when I arrived in California."

Jade's mind swam. She'd seen photos of Auntie Lita as a child, a tiny fierce face glaring at the camera, daring the photographer to step closer. "She'll never back down," her dad had told her once. "Not when outsized. Not when outnumbered. I'd pull her out of a fight with older kids, and she'd turn on me for breaking it up then jump back into the fight."

Jade understood her family history better, but none of it reassured her about the future. In fact, she worried Auntie Lita didn't want Nana around because it hurt to be around her.

"Dad said families need to stick together, especially when things are hard. He would never turn Nana away." Auntie Lita needed to understand. "Nana's part of all our family, not only yours. She needs family."

"Yeah, I'm beginning to get that." Auntie Lita sighed. "Nana wasn't the ideal parent. And I'm a questionable guardian. But you're right about family. We all need family. Even, like Nana, when they don't know who we are.

"Our family broke, Jade. But your dad didn't." At this, her voice caught. She closed her eyes and paused for so long Jade wondered if she were going to continue. Then she opened her eyes, and they met Jade's.

"I loved your dad. I looked up to him. I didn't listen to him —I haven't listened to anyone since I was a kid—but he took the shit life gave him, and he created good things. A wife, a home. You, Jupiter, Jersey. Love, safety, security. Everything important. Everything that matters. Your dad took care of your Nana, after she barely took care of us."

Auntie Lita paused and took a slow, steady breath. "I don't want to screw any of this up—you, your sister and brother—the beautiful life your dad and mom started for you. I've already fucked things up. I always do. You can fill a book with everything I need to learn about parenting. Or being normal."

Jade snorted. Her aunt was anything but normal. But she understood her a bit better now. They neared the house where Oscar smoked a cigarette in a swing on the front porch. He tamped it out on the ground, smiling. He and Auntie Lita exchanged a glance that Jade couldn't interpret.

"She's been sleeping a lot," he said. "I've been in and out, but she's out cold."

Jade followed Auntie Lita into the house and the large bedroom off the kitchen. Nana lay still, her face like wax. The skin of her cheeks sagged into the pillow.

"She looks so empty." Jade wanted Nana to wake up and give Auntie Lita a *POW*. Or tell Oscar he smelled good. Or try to sneak a glass of wine.

"Old people look empty when they sleep." Auntie Lita's voice changed, losing its edge of sorrow. "I'm going to speak to Elise, our neighbor in Bisbee. She's the administrator at Manzanita Manor who got Nana into the day program. Maybe she can find an opening for Evie there."

Jade glanced up sharply. Did this mean what she thought? Was Nana going to stay in Arizona? The crushing sensation in Jade's chest eased. She studied her aunt suspiciously.

"But you have Nana on a list in California."

"She's helpless, Jade. And as much as she failed me as a mom, she's your grandmother. You guys have lost so much; I can't take her away from you too."

Jade took Nana's hand gratefully. Maybe she wouldn't live with them anymore, but she'd still be part of their lives. Nana wasn't going anywhere.

Jade felt a release when her aunt spoke, like turning in a final assignment before summer break. But she still worried. "Is she going to be okay?"

Auntie Lita nodded. "I hope so." She stared at Jade for a long time. "I don't have any answers there."

Jade leaned over and kissed Nana's forehead. She released Nana's hand and slid hers into Auntie Lita's, and they left together.

FORTY-ONE

Lita

LITA SAT ALONE in the shadows on the edge of Abuela's back porch, elbows on thighs, head in hands. After the last of the funeral guests had left the community hall about an hour ago, she and the sober family members had cleaned up most of the mess and would finish up tomorrow. Evie slept inside, and with luck, she'd sleep until morning. Jersey and Jupiter had fallen asleep in Abuela's guest room, and Jade had curled up on the couch to watch a movie with Gabriel. A Spanish-language movie, but she didn't seem to mind.

"I'll figure it out," she'd said.

Lita didn't have the energy to lift her head. She felt wrung out by the day. Her pop's funeral. Evie's disintegration. Grief all around her. Grief.

Her aunts and uncles, her pop's siblings, had mostly gone home or gone to bed. Now, as the night grew deeper and darker, the lights strung along the tent canopy in Abuela's backyard cast a glow on Abuela and Rosa sitting in silence on plastic chairs under the canopy, Rosa exhausted, her face pinched and eyes puffy, and Abuela, straight-backed and solemn, her left hand folded over Rosa's right. Lita felt a pang of sadness for them.

Gloria pulled up a chair on Rosa's left, leaned into her mom, and put her chin on her shoulder. Rosa smiled wanly and kissed Gloria's forehead, eyes glistening. Marco and Juan Carlos, who'd helped Lita clean up the community hall, arrived together and sat down in the empty chairs under the tent. Marco stood out in his suit, as the rest of the family had dressed in casual, though somberly appropriate, wear. Juan Carlos, at sixteen, sported black jeans with a grey button-up shirt, and a black leather belt featuring a massive silver belt buckle shaped like a horse's head.

Her oldest brothers Jose Jr. and Rafael had gotten pretty drunk at the community hall and hadn't yet made it to the backyard. Julieta and her husband appeared, and he said goodnight while Julieta took a seat next to Marco. Lita watched her siblings, her family, from the porch.

After the mess of her childhood, she'd always believed Karmen's family a better substitute than her own. But here with Abuela and her sisters and brothers, and Rosa, she felt the power of her own family. Her father's family. Was it too late for her mother's?

It was too late for Jake. He'd tried to bring her back to her family. But she'd been young and angry.

Her mom had loved her, had wanted her back.

Still, Evie could have come for her and didn't. She hadn't been able to quit alcohol or men. Lita had suffered for it. Sure, she'd survived and made her own way, thanks to her pop. But she'd seethed at her mother all her adult life.

Until tonight.

The anguish in Evie's eyes had wrenched Lita's heart. Her mom's desperation to find Phillip and Randy, chasing their ghosts into the black waters, nearly drowning. Lita knew pain. She'd embraced it and built her life around anger. But the cruelty of dementia—reliving memories again and again—made her ache for her mom.

Lita didn't want to recreate the landscape of her childhood. She needed to forgive her mom in order to make things right for her brother's kids. And herself.

Her father was right. *Fuck the old man*, she thought. *He saved my life again.* She began to cry. She cried for her pop, for Abuela and for Rosa, and for her brothers and sisters. They'd all lost him. He hadn't been perfect, but he'd loved his family proudly. Including her. She cried for Evie, her mess of a mother, lost in jumbled memories and toppling into an abyss of no return. She cried for her nieces and nephew, orphans stuck with an aunt who had no idea what she was doing. And she cried for herself —the little girl who'd lost her family. The teenager who'd run away. The fucked-up woman who'd inherited three kids and lost control of her life.

The tears slowed, and she wiped her eyes. She'd felt alone for so much of her life. She'd set herself apart. Too damaged to share her life with anyone, she'd wanted to be alone. But her pop's death had shifted something inside her, had broken the barriers she'd built.

She found Oscar drinking a beer on the front porch swing and smoking a cigarette with Jose Jr. and Rafael. Her brothers were drunk and laughing as she walked up the steps. Oscar sported a big smile.

"Hey firecracker." His words slurred slightly, and his face was red. He'd hit the beers pretty hard after the reception had broken up. He'd certainly gotten more than he bargained for on this trip.

Lita could define her own life with those words. *More than I bargained for*.

She'd had so much more of everything. Booze, death, disconnection.

"Have a seat." Jose Jr. offered her his seat on the bench, but she shook her head and walked past him.

She sat on Oscar's lap. Her brothers whistled and snapped their fingers. Oscar smiled like the Cheshire Cat, wrapped his arm around her waist, buried his face in her shirt and took a deep breath.

"You smell good," he said finally.

"You sound like Evie." She smirked. "And I smell like sweat and seawater."

"You smell like you." The arm around her waist shifted, and his hand moved to her thigh where it rested lightly. "I can't get enough of it."

"When are you guys going to get married?"

Oscar's hand squeezed her thigh. "We're not even a couple," he said. "I keep chasing her, but she's too quick. She won't let me catch her."

Rafael eyed them suspiciously, then looked at Lita with a frown. "Don't let this good man go, sister." Lita began to speak, but he held his hand up to stop her. He swayed a bit before he spoke again. "It's too short, Lita. Life's too short to push good people away. This man"—he closed his eyes, and his head wobbled slightly—"this man is good people. Everyone can see he loves you."

Lita again tried to speak, but this time Jose Jr. stopped her. "Lita, give yourself a break. All those tattoos, your butch hair, and your angry face. Despite all your weird shit, he loves you. Don't turn your back on that."

Lita's face flamed. Jose Jr. held up his hands in surrender. He closed his eyes, listed sideways and leaned into the porch column for balance.

"Don't shoot the messenger. But goddamn, Lita, you've got walls all around you." He opened his eyes, pointed at Oscar, and looked straight at Lita. "This man knows you. He loves you. If you can't see that, then you're as blind as one of the three mice. The blind one."

He burped loudly and pounded his chest with one hand. "Shit, I gotta go lie down. Goodnight, Oscar. Goodnight Lita. I love you, sis."

"I'm with you, brother." Rafael stood shakily. "Goodnight, all." He followed his brother down the steps, and they staggered into the dark of the village.

Lita tried to put her thoughts together in the silence left by their absence. She'd been miserable without Oscar. She'd taken him for granted, and goddamn she'd missed him. But marriage? A bit extreme, wasn't it?

Oscar's forehead pressed into her spine. He chuckled without mirth. "They're not wrong, Lita. I'd do anything for you." He took a breath and spoke into the space between them. "I can't force you to love me. But Lita, I love you. I can't stop loving you. I've tried."

She felt like someone had landed a jab between her eyes. She blinked away tears. "You've never said that before," she said carefully. Her heart pounded. Her pulse raced. She felt the urge to start a fight for some goddamn reason.

Fear, she suddenly realized. She was afraid.

"You never wanted to hear it." He rubbed her thigh. "It's not walls you've got, Lita. It's a box. Your heart is locked in a box, and I can't find the key." His voice broke.

Lita's world was splitting in two. On one side, she was alone. On the other, Oscar and her family waited. She had to choose.

"What about Rikki?"

"Chrissake, Lita. She's not you. I tried to move on, but she told me she felt like a placeholder. We broke up."

"I thought I was unlovable." Lita whispered the words. She sniffed. "My own mother couldn't love me. How could anyone else?" She wiped her eyes, but tears rolled down her cheeks.

"All I've ever remembered was the bad stuff," she continued. "The bad stuff that happened to me, the bad stuff I've done. The bad shit I've seen people do. I've spent my entire adult life trying to forget bad stuff."

He tightened his arm around her waist, then relaxed and lifted his face. He smiled sadly at her. "Focus on the good, Lita. I'm good for you, and you're good for me."

"How can I be good for you?" Lita didn't know what she'd ever done for Oscar. "Oscar, I'm a train wreck. Look at my family. Look at my mom. I can't cook. I don't give a shit about home décor. I like to fight in a cage, for god's sake."

He shook his head and slumped his shoulders. When he spoke his head hung low, and she had to lean down to hear him.

"All I know is when I look at you, my heart melts. Every. Single. Time." He lifted his chin to look at her, his brown eyes locked onto hers. She felt a surprising warmth come over her, like being struck by a ray of sunshine. "I don't care if you're a train wreck. I don't need you to cook. I know you. Good or bad, I love you. And I'm stronger with you. We're stronger together." A ripple of uncertainty passed over his face. "But you need to give us a chance."

Lita's heart cracked open. A sliver. She'd never ever in her life quit a fight, but suddenly she understood what it felt like to give up. At this moment, with Oscar's eyes locked on hers, she didn't know why she was fighting.

Oscar had always been in her corner. No one else but Karmen, had stuck by her side as he had. The past few months without him had been a physical ache like a hole in her chest. Was that love? She'd thought love a weakness. But maybe, it made people stronger.

Tears blurred her vision. "I'm broken, Oscar. All my life I've tried to figure out why my mom didn't love me. Why Abuela sent me to my pop's. Pop didn't understand me, but he gave me second chances. He understood me better than anyone. Except, maybe, you." She met his eyes and shuddered at the nakedness of his gaze. "Oscar, I don't know how to love anyone. I'm afraid I'll ruin us forever."

It all felt too much. She'd treated him so poorly. She'd wanted him to leave, and he hadn't. "I'm sorry, Oscar." She whispered. "I'm sorry I hurt you. I hurt everyone."

"Shh, shh, Lita. Love hurts, that's all. It plain hurts sometimes."

She looked into his half-lidded eyes, but they weren't smiling. They were locked onto hers, dead serious. She took a deep breath before she spoke.

"I've spent so much time in these past few months trying to

forget you. Trying to let you live your life without me. And it sucked. But I'm afraid. I'm afraid I'll hurt you if I love you." She gulped and leaned her forehead onto his, the warmth of his skin seeping onto her own. She slid off his lap and onto the bench beside him, burying her face in her knees. Oscar rubbed her back and stroked her hair.

She lifted her eyes to meet his. "I don't want a world without you in it," she whispered. "If that's not love, I guess I don't know what is."

FORTY-TWO

Evie

SHE LIES STILL in the darkness, eyes open. A strange room. She can smell the sea. Where is she?

She pulls the covers up to her chin. The room is hot, but she wants to hide.

Her body hurts all over. Her shoulders ache, and her legs feel loose and wriggly like rubber bands. A strange pressure, like a weight on her chest, holds her down on this strange bed.

Footpads scuff on cement outside the room, and a window scrapes open. The clatter of a spoon hits metal; chair legs slide across a floor. Soft voices murmur behind walls.

"Mom?" she calls softly, tentatively.

She hopes her mom hears her. She hopes her daddy doesn't. He's been so harsh with her. Her mom hasn't been able to make him back down. What did he say?

No daughter of his.

"Mom?" she calls again, louder.

The murmuring in the kitchen stops, and an older woman, not her mom, opens the door. Evie lays still and waits. The woman approaches the bed, bringing with her a scent of fresh coffee, cinnamon and bread. She sits on the edge of the bed and faces Evie. Her thick dark eyebrows lift with her smile. Her face is round and rosy, and she has flour on her chest.

"Good morning, Evie. How are you feeling?"

The woman looks familiar.

"I'm not sure," Evie says. "Do I know you?"

The woman's eyes crinkle upwards. "We are old friends, Evie. From long ago." She holds her hand out to Evie, and Evie takes it. A friend?

"Where am I?" Evie isn't sure whose bed she's in. Or whose house.

"You're in my house, in Perdido. Your daughter Lita is here, and your grandchildren." She pats Evie's hand like a child.

She's speechless. Lita? Grandchildren?

A flash of panic shoots through her. "The others. The children?" Her pulse begins to race, and she struggles to get up from the bed.

"Shh, shh, shh. No te preocupes." The woman strokes Evie's hand. "You will see them again. But for now, you rest up and recover your strength. You went for a swim in the sea yesterday. You made your family very worried."

Evie stops struggling and lays back. The woman's hand feels dry and rough but comforting, like a sweater against the chill. "Oh, Mom always worries. But Daddy never does. He's got everything under control. Except me." She giggles and catches herself. Something isn't funny.

"Where am I?"

The woman sighs. "You are in Perdido, Evie. You and your family will be heading back home soon." She stands up and squeezes Evie's hand. "You rest here. I'll bring you some coffee and bread."

Evie nods. "Thank you."

The woman disappears and closes the door behind her.

Evie doesn't understand. Maybe it's better to stay in bed than venture out of the room. Besides, her body doesn't want to move. It aches all over. Her eyes feel heavy, and she closes them, for a little while longer.

When she opens them again, she sees the kids. Not her kids, but a boy and two girls.

"Nana!" the littlest girl jumps on the bed, and Evie's body rocks sideways. The boy joins her, and Evie laughs at the sudden commotion. The older girl gives her a little wave from the doorway. She waves back.

"What are you doing here?" she asks the little girl.

"We're waiting for you to get up so we can go home." The child frowns. "You slept a long time, and you missed the food."

"Food? A party?"

"Not a party," says the older girl. She walks to the edge of the bed and leans down to kiss Evie's forehead. "It was a funeral for Auntie Lita's dad."

"My Lita?" Evie questions.

The girl's mouth twists sideways, and she nods. "Yes, Lita, your daughter."

"Where is she? Is she here?" Evie hasn't seen Lita in so long.

"I'm here." A short, tattooed woman walks into the bedroom, which is suddenly very crowded.

"Lita?" Evie is confused. This woman looks almost chiseled, her face and body so muscular. She's Lita? Where's her daughter? Her little girl?

"Yeah, me."

Evie looks away, out the window, and sees the black sea. She doesn't know where she is or why. She doesn't know if this is her Lita standing in front of her or not.

Everyone's looking at her. She makes a fist and thrusts it towards the tattooed woman.

"POW!"

FORTY-THREE

Jade

"LET'S GO SWIMMING!" Gabriel was wearing his swimsuit and held two towels. He pointed to the bathroom. "Get in your suit."

Jade had agreed to go for an early morning swim before the drive back to Bisbee. Gabriel had warned her it would be cold, and she'd scoffed. "You've never been to Santa Cruz!" she'd said. Entering the water at her family's favorite beach required a pep talk and a dare, and she'd always envied the surfers wearing wetsuits.

She'd fallen asleep before the end of the movie and spent the night on the couch in the living room at Doña Louisa's. Gabriel had slept on the floor next to Marco, still cocooned in a sleeping bag, unmoving. When Gabriel tapped her shoulder, she rubbed her eyes and reconsidered going swimming, thinking how nice it would be to go back to sleep.

The front door opened, and Juan Carlos stuck his head in. Two years older than Gabriel, he had the same dark, wavy hair, brown eyes, and cute dimples. Jade hadn't spoken with him much. His eyebrows raised, he held a finger to his lips for silence.

As if she'd be talking this early. She could barely think. She yanked her swimsuit and shorts out of her suitcase and went into the bathroom to change.

Daylight hadn't officially broken, and as they left the house, the air felt warm. Jade's eyes burned and scratched from lack of sleep. Why had she agreed to this?

"You come back again?" Juan Carlos didn't speak English as well as Gabriel but was friendly, with an easy, goofy smile. He sported cowboy boots with his swimsuit as they walked to the water.

"I hope so." Jade didn't know. With Auntie Lita's dad gone, would they come back here?

"You are happy to go back home?"

Jade thought about this. Home conjured different images now. "I'm still trying to figure out where my home is."

"Home is with family," Gabriel insisted. "When I come to Perdido to stay with Abuela, I'm home. When I am with my family in Hermosillo, I'm home."

"Then I guess Bisbee's my home now."

"You have lots of friends." Juan Carlos stated it as fact, but Jade wondered if he meant it as a question. He looked at her expectantly.

"No, I don't, actually." Thinking about Logan, Max and Brooklyn dampened her mood. Logan's attention had felt good, helped her forget her grief. She'd been dazzled by his smile and swayed by his swagger. But it was all fake. He was petty and mean. He'd targeted her friends and lied about it. He'd gotten Max kicked off the bus. He'd stolen the malachite and given it to her. "I moved to a new school, so I only have a few. And I think one of them is actually a big jerk."

Juan Carlos looked puzzled and spoke to Gabriel in Spanish. Gabriel replied and chattered with his brother back and forth before he spoke again.

"A boy?" Gabriel asked. At Jade's nod, he added, "Juan Carlos says boys who are jerks are no good. And you are our cousin. We say don't waste your time with boys who are no good."

She'd never had cousins before. She felt like she'd won a prize without a competition, though the feeling subsided a bit when she reached the water's edge and thought about diving in. "I'm glad I have cousins, because I've made a mess of things with my friends."

The three of them stood a few paces from where Nana had thrown herself in the day before. Jade touched the water with her toes. The boys stripped off their T-shirts, and Jade, slower, took off her shorts and top. Juan Carlos ran into the shallow waters, then dove all the way under. He popped up with a shout and a holler.

"No chicken! Swim!"

Gabriel gave Jade a thumb's up and followed his brother. Jade inched into the water and wondered how badly she'd get teased if she didn't go in. The water wasn't cold like the ocean in Santa Cruz, but it felt much colder than it had yesterday under the beating sun.

Gabriel emerged and whipped his hair into a pompadour. "The only way is to dive in, no stopping." His eyes sparkled. He beckoned her to come deeper into the water. "It's the same thing with friends. Dive into your mess and fix it."

Was it so easy? Dive in and fix things?

Jade took a deep breath and ran into the water squealing, lunging forward into a dive when the waters reached her thighs. She surged upwards, gulped in a lungful of air, and stood next to Gabriel while Juan Carlos swam like a dolphin in circles around them. The shallow water didn't reach higher than Jade's waist. The water wasn't cold exactly. But not warm, either.

How could she fix the friend mess she'd left behind? Max was kind and patient. Brooklyn was wholeheartedly devoted to their friendship. And yet she'd been willing to drop her only true friends for a boy who thought rotten eggs and fart jokes were entertaining.

"Have you ever had a friend who wasn't always nice to you?" She looked at Gabriel who spit a mouthful of water into the air like a fountain.

He frowned. "No. Sometimes we have arguments. But people who aren't nice to us are not our friends. Friends help us and listen to us. And are on our side."

That described Brooklyn to a T. She'd allied herself with Jade from day one. And Max had given her no drama and no doubts about his character. He'd been nothing but a friend.

But Logan? What had he given her? Little gifts, like the animal crackers and the malachite—which he'd stolen from Max. His attention flattered her for sure, took her mind off her parents and everything she missed from her old life. But he'd lied to her when she'd confronted him about the malachite. She'd seen it in his face, as clear as Max's hair was red.

Juan Carlos swam underwater and grabbed Gabriel's legs. Gabriel thrashed wildly before getting pulled under. Cousins. She had cousins. Juan Carlos was the same age as Logan, Gabriel a couple of years younger. And they weren't jerks. They didn't mock Nana; they spoke to her respectfully, even when she was mixed up. Would Logan change? She didn't know what to do.

SAYING goodbye to Auntie Lita's family was hard. They felt like family now, which surprised her. Did Jersey and Jupiter feel it too? She'd taken them to the park after her early morning swim to run off energy before the long drive, and they'd been full of it, racing around the playground, bickering over swings, and pushing each other off slides. Still normal at least.

But Nana wasn't.

Nana waited in the truck, shrunken in the passenger seat. The tall dancer who'd walked regally and poised throughout her life looked tiny in the cab, her face hollow and confused. Jade hurt to see her.

A crowd of family surrounded Auntie Lita. Oscar stood by Felix's truck, a faint, happy smile on his face, eyes dancing. He winked at Jade. She smiled back. Jupiter and Jersey wanted to ride with him, but Auntie Lita stopped the discussion in its tracks.

"He needs adult time, guys. You'll see plenty of him in Bisbee." Oscar surprised Jade by wrapping his arms around Auntie Lita and kissing her forehead. Auntie Lita frowned, then smirked and pushed him away quickly. But not before kissing him back. Huh.

Tears sprang to Jade's eyes as she hugged Doña Luisa. She'd cried a lot in the past day and wanted to be done with it. But at least she didn't feel sad anymore.

"Eres familia." Doña Luisa's voice was strong and soothing. "You are family now," she said in English.

For the first time since her parents' deaths, she didn't feel alone. Nothing could remove the pain of their loss; she'd never, ever forget that. But her heart felt lighter than it had since they'd died. She'd discovered a new family. A bigger family than she'd had before.

She smiled as she hugged Gabriel who'd lost his father but wasn't full of rage.

"I'll see you next time," she said.

FORTY-FOUR

Evie

TRAPPED IN THE SLING CHAIR, canvas squeezing her legs rigidly together, Evie can't move. The little girl squirming on her lap isn't helping either as she tries to stand up on Evie's thighs.

"Jersey, stop moving or I'll take you off of Nana's lap." The tattooed woman grabs the little girl's hand, but she yanks it away and sinks into Evie's lap.

"No! I'm still."

Evie takes a deep breath of the girl's hair. It smells like syrup. "What are we doing?"

"We're waiting for the parade," the woman says. She picks up the little girl and sets her on the curb, holds her hand.

A parade? Evie likes parades. She's danced in many of them. She peers up and down the empty street lined with people. "Where are the dancers?"

"Dancers? If there are dancers, they'll come with the floats. And the floats are starting at the top of the canyon right about now. They'll make it here soon. Jade's on one of them."

Gobbledy-gook. Evie doesn't understand her. "The dancers…." She begins to reply, but a police car with flashing lights approaches, and she blinks and stays silent as the car cruises by slowly.

"The band's coming!" a child hollers.

The music reaches Evie first. Then, from around the curve, a banner—Bisbee Community Marching Band—followed by people swaying as they play instruments and march down the highway. Evie bounces in her chair. It's catchy, happy. The crowd lining the street presses in on itself, tightening shoulder to shoulder.

"Which one is Jade's?" The man yells to be heard over the band. Evie likes his eyes.

"It's got a jail," the woman shouts back, laughing.

Evie stares at her intently. Can't take her eyes off her face. Never mind the tattoos, her face attracts Evie like a magnet.

"Sounds right." The man chuckles.

Evie continues to stare. Familiar. But she can't place her. Or this location. None of it has meaning for her. She thinks the answer is in this woman, but how? Fear flutters, and she pushes it away. She closes her eyes, and music moves her again.

The music recedes as the band marches away, but new music takes its place. Evie opens her eyes to see the floats approach. They're colorfully decorated with crepe paper flowers and streamers, cardboard cutouts and large signs. Men and women in military caps and leather vests wave at her from a float labeled "American Legion #16." Another float, "Mr. Barry's Woodworking Shop," features a trailer full of acne-riddled boys in jeans with trucker caps. She wonders if there's a dancers' float. A float with ballet. She loves to dance.

Around her, everyone smiles. The crowd chatters excitedly. Parades make people happy. Something tugs at her, compels her to stand.

"It's Jade!" The little girl shrieks in a high pitch. "She's with Brooklyn and Max!"

A black float with a cardboard jail approaches. "Remember the Bisbee Deportation" reads the sign. Ominous. Beneath the sign, a black cardboard jail contains two girls. Evie recognizes the tall one.

Her mouth drops open. She points. "I… I… That's… that's…." She can't place her, but she *knows* her. "Why is she up there?"

She feels a mixture of pride and confusion as she stares. The girl smiles broadly and waves at Evie.

Evie waves back. Her heart swells with happiness. She waves and claps her hands. "Bravo!" she shouts. The music from the parade has a catchy beat, and Evie's shoulders bounce and sway.

Nothing makes sense anymore. These faces puzzle her, and she has no idea where she is. But music? She knows music. She steps into the street and begins to twirl.

FORTY-FIVE

Jade

OH MY GOD *Nana is dancing.* She'd waved at Jade, then stood up and begun to dance. Twirling and shaking her shoulders, she sashayed into the street. Max's dad had had already been driving slowly, and the tug of the brakes slowed the float even more as Nana stepped in front and began pirouetting.

Jade and Brooklyn stood behind the bars of the jail and watched Nana dip and glide deliberately, if not gracefully. "What's your grandma doing?"

"Ballet," Jade said matter-of-factly. "She loves to dance."

"I'll say."

Jade saw Auntie Lita and Oscar watching Nana—Auntie Lita with a crooked smile, and Oscar's eyes wide with surprise. Jersey, perched on his shoulders was trying to get down. He swung her down lightly, and she dashed out into the road to join Nana, twirling and gyrating her hips. The two moved in front of the float and down the highway, and excitement rippled out of the crowd as they approached.

"Is that your sister?" Max sat on a milk crate next to the jail in a cowboy hat, a sheriff's star pinned to his shirt.

Jade nodded. They had passed her family, but Auntie Lita was trotting in the gutter parallel to the float, keeping her eyes on Nana and Jersey as they danced along the parade route. Oscar watched them go, holding firmly to Jupiter, who pointed and tugged at his hand.

Jersey's blonde curls shook, and she shimmied her hips arrhythmically without an ounce of self-consciousness. A month ago, Jade would have been mortified by the both of them, but for some reason, she felt proud. Nana could really dance. Despite the lack of practice and stiffness of age, she moved beautifully and gracefully, beaming as she twirled and spun. Jade couldn't resist cheering.

"Go, Nana!" Nana didn't respond, but Jersey heard Jade and increased the pace of her movements, her face crimson and sweaty. People pointed and cheered the two dancers as the float neared the post office where the city council had set up a large grill in the parking lot. The crowd surrounding the grill laughed as the float and dancers neared. Others stood on the curb with hot dogs or hamburgers in their hands, smiling and bobbing their heads.

Jade saw Logan with a group of his friends, and her heart sank. Their eyes met, and he smiled a wicked smile and winked at her. He ran alongside the float on the opposite side of the road from Auntie Lita and trotted alongside Nana in front.

"What's *he* doing?" Max hissed angrily.

Logan smirked at Jade, then shouted at Nana. "Take it off!"

His buddy Javier barked a sharp laugh and echoed him. "Yeah, take it off!"

Jade whipped her head around, looking for Auntie Lita, who she spotted elbowing her way past the crowd at the post office. *Take it off?* Was Logan for real? What a jerk.

Nana beamed and rose onto her toes with her arms arced above her head. Jersey ran in looping circles around Nana, throwing her arms up in the air every few seconds. Logan kept pace with her float.

"Take it off!" he yelled again.

As she danced, Nana unwound her long braid, and a silvery

cascade of hair tumbled down her back. She shook her head and stretched her arms up to the sky.

Oh no.

Nana started unbuttoning her blouse. Jade stared aghast as she coquettishly tilted one shoulder forward, then the next and began to work her way through the buttons. Jersey began to lift her own shirt over her head.

Oh god.

"Jersey, no!"

Jersey's shirt fell to the road as Nana finished unbuttoning her own. She peeled it off, leaving only a thin beige camisole over a white bra. She continued to shimmy and sway as she twirled her shirt above her head, then let it loose to fly into the crowd. The crowd hooted and shouted.

Jade had to stop this.

"More!" Logan egged Nana on from the curb, and his friends joined him.

Nana put her hands on her hips and moved suggestively.

Oh shit.

Jade had strict instructions not to leave the float *under any circumstance*, under pain of banishment from future floats. But what else could she do? She couldn't let Nana and Jersey strip in front of the whole town. And she couldn't see Auntie Lita anywhere.

"I gotta get off, Max." she told him. "Nana's going to strip if I don't stop her."

"Will she really?" Max looked dubious.

Jade sighed. "You don't know my nana. I gotta stop her."

In the street, Nana was running her hands down her body and gyrating slowly. Jersey seemed to be flagging, walking in circles and panting. Nana's hands stopped on the waistband of her skirt.

Jade swore and jumped off the float, leaving Brooklyn and Max alone. She stumbled as she landed on the pavement and ran to Nana who looked surprised but happy to see her. Jade clasped her hands around her grandma's bony fingers. "It's a duet, Nana!"

Nana's eyes shone with pleasure. She twirled with Jade. Jersey joined in, and Jade led them to the curb. Max and Brooklyn stared at her as they moved away. She mouthed "I'm sorry" as the float disappeared down the road. Their float wouldn't win any awards now.

Jersey's hand felt wet with sweat, and Jade let go and wiped her hand on her shorts. Nana beamed as she looked around at the cheering crowd.

Logan sidled up to Jade and knocked into her sideways. She nearly toppled into Jersey and caught herself so that they didn't both fall to the pavement. He grinned. "Your grandma's a crowd pleaser."

Jade turned on him angrily. "Why'd you do that?"

He took a step back and frowned, hands in the air and eyes wide. "How was I to know she'd start a striptease in front of everyone?"

Jade recognized the look, the same one he'd given her the day he released the eggs on the bus. The identical look he had when she'd confronted him about stealing Max's malachite. She glared at him. *How did I ever have a crush on him?* Logan was a bully.

Auntie Lita ran up with Nana's blouse and Jersey's shirt. "There you go, Mom. Get that arm in there. Jersey, put your shirt on, girl."

Jersey sat down on the curb to put on her top. Her face glistened. Their neighbor, Jodi, walked up, wearing a broad sun hat. She smiled. "I've never seen audience participation in a parade before. Your family knows how to liven things up."

Jade smiled but brooded inside. She saw Logan for what he was now, a bully and a creep. How could she have liked him? How could she have confided in him? It made her sick to think about it.

Logan knocked into her shoulder again and this time she

braced herself. "Let's blow this joint and find a place less crowded." He smiled again, and her stomach flipped sourly.

"No thanks."

He looked offended. "Come on, Jade. Trey's got some brewskies. We're heading to the shrine."

"Great, drinking at a shrine. Real respectful." Her tone dripped with derision.

Logan drew back. "Suit yourself, Jade. You're done trying to be cool then? Going back to little girl life?"

Jade couldn't believe she'd liked a boy who ridiculed old people and partied in sacred spaces. A roaring anger filled her head and pushed out every thought. She sucked in her breath and blew it out with a hard laugh.

"Why are you still here?" She narrowed her eyes. "Oh, yeah. You're so mature. Go suck your beers down and pretend you're a grown-up, Logan. Because pretending is as close as you'll get. Real men don't make fun of old ladies. Real men don't use secrets someone told them in confidence to make themselves feel better. Real men don't steal things and give them as gifts. You're a pretender, Logan."

He sneered at her. "I only tried to be friendly because you were obviously a loser. I felt sorry for you. But you're hopeless. And your entire family is crazy."

Sometimes Jade hated her family. Sometimes they embarrassed her. But her demented grandmother always had a hug for her. Her tattooed aunt fought for her, even when she shouldn't. Her hyperactive brother and whiny sister depended on her. She loved them. No one else was allowed to call them crazy.

Rage exploded inside Jade, and she did the first thing that popped into her head. She barreled into Logan's stomach headfirst, wrapped her arms around his thighs, grabbed the backs of his knees, and leaned her weight into his midsection while lifting him off balance. Logan crashed to the ground beneath her, and Jade ended up on top, throwing a perfect double-leg takedown.

FORTY-SIX

Lita

LITA BUTTONED up Evie's blouse and checked Jersey to be sure she was again fully clothed. A strip-tease in the biggest event in town. Wow.

A flash of movement caught her eye. Jade threw a proficient double leg takedown of the Logan kid. *Good technique.* The boy's face twisted angrily as he hit the ground. He tried to push Jade off him as she flailed her arms and screamed at him, using language Lita had only heard come out of her own mouth.

Whoa.

She ran to Jade and pulled her off Logan. The boy scrambled to his feet and backed away with an ugly sneer on his face.

"You'll be sorry for that, Jade." Spit flew out of his mouth, and he stumbled, almost falling. "You're fucked up. Your whole family are losers."

Jade struggled in Lita's arms. "Takes one to know one!"

She stopped struggling and leaned back into Lita. Lita tightened her arms in a firm embrace. Her niece breathed heavily and trembled, her body sweaty and hot.

Logan stomped off without looking back, though his friends kept glancing at Lita and Jade until they turned the corner. Lita gave Jade a last squeeze, then let her go.

"You okay?"

Jade nodded and began to cry. Lita folded her back into her arms. She knew the feeling. Physical street fights, outside of a sanctioned match, left her shaky and queasy.

"A classic takedown, Jade," she whispered. "Badass."

Jade laughed through her tears. She wiped her eyes. "I'm sorry, Auntie Lita."

Surprised, Lita drew back to look at her niece. "For what?"

"I told him about Nana. This wouldn't have happened if I hadn't told him."

Lita blew out a puff of air. "Nana does what she wants. She doesn't need encouragement. Besides," she held up a hand to stop Jade from responding. "She and Jersey gave the crowd a good show, didn't they?"

Jade wiped her face again and chuckled, then snorted, then laughed harder. She leaned on Lita who laughed at Jade's snort. Lita's own laugh sounded like a coyote, and Jade snorted again. Lita laughed and laughed, until she doubled over, hands on knees. Jade, leaning on Lita, stumbled sideways but kept hold of Lita's shoulder for balance.

Oscar walked up with Jupiter. "What'd I miss?"

Jupiter eyed them suspiciously. "What's so funny?"

Lita wiped her eyes and stood, still smiling. "Jade slapped a bug on the windshield of life."

Jade's eyes streamed tears as she laughed louder.

Jupiter rolled his eyes and looked at them doubtfully. "Sheesh, they're crazy."

"We sure are crazy, Jupe." Lita picked him up and swung him around. "And so are you. It's a family trait! Don't let anyone ever tell you to stop being crazy."

"Never," the little boy nodded solemnly and crossed his heart. "Never."

Jade turned to Lita. "I want to go find my float. I don't know if they'll let me back on, but I feel bad I left them."

"Go for it, girl, but catch them before they go past the mine.

Once they start heading down the hill, they won't stop until they get to the school."

Jade hugged Jersey and Nana, then gave Lita a quick hug and ran after the parade float. Lita watched her go with an unexpected warmth. The heaviness she'd felt for months had dissipated. She felt lighter, happy. Was this what it meant to have family?

She turned at a hand on her shoulder. Jodi stood with Elise, her broad sunhat big enough to shade half of her wife's face. "Evie wants to come with us for coffee at the Lucky Bean." Jodi pointed down the alley to a street running parallel to Main. "I'll bring her home. Is that okay?"

Evie's hair hung loose and wild, like the old crone in Snow White. Standing tall between the two women, her blouse buttoned back up, she panted slightly. She looked at Lita expectantly.

Lita's heart skipped rapidly, and her pulse shot up. She had gotten the call from California yesterday and had officially cancelled Evie's name on the care home waitlist.

"Mom, do you want to get some coffee with Jodi?"

Mom. It felt strange to use the word, but she was trying it out.

Evie looked surprised. "Yes, I'd enjoy that."

Lita spoke to Jodi. "Oscar, Jupiter, Jersey and I are heading to Ronaldo Ramos's house. It's one of the last places up Wood Canyon. We'll be there all afternoon."

Jodi smiled and put a hand on Evie's arm. "Great. We'll take our time, and we'll bring her later. Come, Evie. Let's get a cup of coffee."

It was now or never. "Hey Elise, are there any beds opening up at Manzanita Manor?"

Elise tilted her head in thought for a quick moment. "I'll have to check our waitlist Monday morning. But if there's nothing now, spots are always opening up."

"Can you put Evie on the list?"

"Sure thing. Drop by Monday, and we'll get the ball rolling."

"Awesome, Elise. Thank you. You've made my day."

As they walked away, Evie turned to glance at Lita and the kids several times. Before they were out of earshot, Evie asked about a glass of wine. Lita shook her head but smiled.

Lita and Oscar led the kids to the curb to pick up Evie's chair. With the parade over, the crowd had begun to scatter. A police car cruised slowly down the road as a work crew wearing high-vis vests took down the barricades.

Lita drove to Karmen's parent's house and parked among a long line of cars on the street. Felix whooped as they walked into the yard, and Jupiter dropped Oscar's hand and ran to him, getting swept up in a hug.

"How's it going, Super Juper? How was the parade?"

"Nana and Jersey danced in front of the float and took their tops off. And Jade tackled a big boy who was teasing her."

"Oh?" Felix's eyes widened into a question aimed at Lita and Oscar. "Sorry I missed it!" He touched foreheads with the little boy. "Do you want to see who else is here? You might know my nephew, Rico."

Jupiter nodded and scrambled down. He and Felix went into the backyard, and soon Jersey was tugging at Lita's hand. "Can I go find Solana, Auntie Lita?" Jersey loved Karmen's youngest sister.

"Go for it, kiddo." Jersey ran off, leaving Lita and Oscar on the edge of the party.

Oscar draped his arm over Lita's shoulder and squeezed, sending shockwaves through her body. She felt wound up, though she didn't know why. She leaned into him and tried to loosen up. Since they'd returned from Mexico, Oscar had been over every night, helping with meals and Evie and kid logistics before returning to his own place. She hadn't asked him to stay over. Lita never wanted to be dependent, like Evie, on a man to tell her where to go or what to do.

And yet. Oscar's arms felt custom-fit around her shoulders, and she felt a strange desire bubbling up inside her, an impulse.

"Hey Oscar," Lita's heart thumped wildly, and her pulse raced, like before a fight. She faced him, her hands on his waist, her eyes on his. "How would you feel about making us official?"

Surprise flashed across his face, and he squeezed her hands. "Official like how? You ready to get married? Because I am."

Lita's heart spiked. *Was* that what she meant? "Uh, married?" Her voice squeaked. "I, uh, thought maybe we could live together."

Oscar gazed at her steadily. "How long do we do that for? We've known each other for nearly a decade, Lita. Do we need to take this slow, or can we get to the commitment part?"

"Holy shit, Oscar. I didn't expect you to go fully conventional on me. Marriage? Why not move in with us?"

"You sleep on a couch bed," he reminded her. "And I've got my own place with a king-sized bed. But I'm not averse to the idea. To be honest, I'd sleep on a bed of pallets if I could wake up with you every day. But think, Lita. What are you looking for? A boyfriend? Or a partner? I want to be your partner."

Heat rose in her, and she focused on steadying her breath. What the hell was she doing? Giving up her independence and aligning her life with someone else's? A man's?

Was she ready to give up everything for Oscar?

She'd never expected to share her life with anyone, but Oscar wasn't just anyone. He knew her, understood her. She knew him and trusted him. The kids loved him.

Besides, hadn't she lost any independence when the kids and Evie had moved in? And what would she truly be giving up? Lonely nights on an ancient, smelly couch-bed? Being out-maneuvered by the tag team of Jupiter and Jersey? Making tough decisions about the multiple lives that had abruptly become her responsibility?

She'd be losing nothing. She'd be gaining an ally, a partner, a permanent cornerman.

"Okay." She wrapped her arms around him and sank into his chest. His arms circled her, fit her like a glove. "Let's give it a trial run. No marriage, not yet. But a home together."

Oscar's breath smelled faintly of cigarettes. His lips touched hers softly and awoke a full-on, raging desire in her. What the fuck was happening?

He pulled away, then leaned his forehead onto hers, their eyes inches apart "You sure about this?"

Lita gazed into his brown eyes and felt weepy, goddammit. "Yes." She nodded. "I love you, Oscar. Let's do this."

They kissed again, and like a roundhouse kick followed by a hook and jab combo, it nearly dropped her. "Oh god, Oscar," she moaned. "Let's stop this or else get out of this damned party." She released herself from his embrace and stood back shakily. Her body thrummed like a live wire.

Felix interrupted, throwing his arms around both of them.

"Break it up, lovebirds." He rocked them side to side. Lita broke free and laughed. Oscar smirked. "I need Oscar's throwing arm, Lita. Ronaldo thinks he's king of Horseshoe Mountain, and I'm on a mission to humble him."

Lita watched them go, then grabbed a bottle of water and found Karmen on the back porch swing. She plopped down, sipped some water, and admired her best friend. At eight months, pregnancy looked great on Karmen. Her hair was lush and thick, and she glowed with happiness despite swapping skinny jeans and a low-cut sweater for maternity pants and an extra-large T-shirt.

"You and Oscar looked pretty intimate there," Karmen said, lifting her eyebrows and giving Lita a 'no BS' look. "You guys certainly made up. What happened in Mexico? God, it's been forever since we've talked."

Lita watched Jupiter run around the jungle gym with a crowd of little boys. Jersey held a fistful of cookies and followed Solana from the food table to a sun tent where guests sat on plastic chairs. Lita leaned her head on her friend's shoulder.

Thinking about Mexico brought back pain, but also the moments she'd had with Jade and Oscar. "It was hard saying good-bye to my pop, Karmen. I wouldn't wish that on anyone. He was so sick. I hated seeing him in the hospital. He could barely talk, but he told me to forgive my mom."

"Did you say, 'your mom'? What about 'Evie'? Wow. A lot can happen in a few weeks." Karmen suddenly sucked in her breath and held her belly with both hands. She breathed in and out deeply then relaxed. "Ooh, that was a big one. I've been getting pre-labor pains. And I'm sorry about your dad, Lita. I'm sorry I couldn't be there. The timing was so bad. Did your dad tell you to make up with Oscar, too?"

Karmen bit her lip, and Lita laughed, then filled her in on the events in Perdido after the funeral. "So, my mom's out of her mind, nearly drowned, the kids are all shook up, and who was right beside me the whole time? Oscar. And I realized how much he gave me. How much I missed him. Other than you, he's been my best friend since I came to Bisbee. And maybe when I got the kids I felt like I was out of my league and got a little defensive."

"Ya think?" Karmen tsk-tsked.

"Yeah, yeah. Well, you know me. Fight first, ask questions later."

"And? So?"

"So, uh yeah, we're going to move in together."

"What?!"

Lita nearly dropped her water at Karmen's screech.

"When is this happening? And where are you going to live?"

"I don't know yet. This is all new. We can't stay at my place; we've been maxed out for months. Maybe we'll move to Oscar's. He's got one more bedroom in his place than I do. But I don't really know. I'm a bit shell-shocked, honestly. A lot has happened in the past weeks."

"What about your mom? And where is she?

"Jodi and Elise saw us at the parade, and they took Evie for coffee. They'll drop her off here."

"Have you heard from the care home in California?" Karmen didn't approve of her plan to take Evie to California.

"Yeah, that's the other thing. I'm not taking her to California."

"You're not?!" Karmen's voice rose again. She resumed in a hushed voice. "What are you going to do? She's only going to get tougher, Lita."

"Oh, I know. Elise said she'd put her on a list for a bed in Manzanita Manor. I'm not keeping her at home longer than I need to."

"So, she's on the list? Wow, Lita, so much has happened." Karmen stood and stretched, putting both hands on the small of her back and grimacing. "What about your fight? Still going ahead with it?"

"Why wouldn't I? I'm not in peak shape, but I've never cancelled a match. To be honest, I have been thinking about how this ends, though. Like maybe I quit fighting and start teaching. I had a great time with the kids, and I wonder if maybe more kids want to learn to fight. I'm not sure how many actual fights I have left in me—maybe I'll be done after this one —but I can't give up the sport entirely. What do you think?"

Karmen beamed. "That's one of the bravest things I've heard you say. Considering how much fighting means to you. And yes, I think not only kids will want to learn, but adults, too. You've got some serious skills, Lita. There's no one else in town who knows fighting like you do."

"Well, I'm not a hundred percent sure. I've got to quit some-time, but I can't just drop it all. I'd go crazy." Lita stood and watched Jupiter race another boy to a swing set. "I need to grab more water. Do you want anything?

Karmen shook her head. "I'll come with you. My mom's empanadas are the best, and I'm eating for two!"

Lita wouldn't be able to eat real food until after her fight in two weeks, but maybe the strict training diet would soon be a thing of the past. What a change from this time last year. She felt relaxed and happier than she had in a long time.

FORTY-SEVEN

Jade

JADE CAUGHT up with the float before they started down the hill towards the school. Max's dad stopped the float, allowing her to climb on. Brooklyn and Max welcomed her back to the jail cell, and she sat next to Brooklyn to wave at the crowd, her heart pounding.

"What happened?" Brooklyn asked.

"I took out Logan the turd." Jade told her.

"What?!" Brooklyn screeched. Max leaned in through the jail bars to listen.

Jade told them about the double-leg takedown. "He turned into a dick pretty quickly afterwards."

"He's always been a dick." Max's eyes grew distant, and he scowled.

Jade swallowed. She pulled the malachite from her pocket. "I think this is yours, Max."

His eyes widened as he took the rock from her and examined it. "Where'd you get this?"

Jade flushed. "Logan gave it to me."

Max eyed her rigidly.

"He said he'd found it."

"You believed him?"

Her face flamed. "I didn't know him back then. Now I know he's a creep. And a liar."

"You've had this for two months?"

She nodded without speaking.

"You knew I was looking for this." He shook his head. "I thought you were different, Jade. But you're like all the other girls, aren't you? Blind and dumb to the charms of the walking, talking jockstrap."

"C'mon, Max. She didn't know." Brooklyn looked back and forth between them. Her eyes narrowed with worry.

Jade swallowed. She fought back the anger she felt rising. Blind? Dumb? Max hadn't lost his parents, hadn't been forced to move out of the only home he'd known, to leave behind everything and everyone he'd loved. Tossed into a churning river, she'd grabbed hold of the largest branch—Logan—she could find to pull her out. Tears stung her eyes. Was Max right? She'd known Logan hadn't found the rock. And she'd known Max had lost his.

She'd chosen the wrong side. But didn't it matter if she came clean now?

"Look at her face." Max nodded his head in Jade's direction. "She knew alright."

Brooklyn's eyes creased with worry. "Jade, tell him you didn't know."

Jade felt a slow whirlpool of dread swirling in her stomach. She wanted to deny it. But her lies so far had led nowhere but trouble. "I did know," she whispered. "And Brooklyn, I told him about your mom. I don't know why. I'm sorry."

Brooklyn's face crumpled. "You what? Why?"

Jade didn't want to see the hurt in her eyes. "I'm sorry."

The confusion on Brooklyn's face made Jade look away. Max shook his head with an angry scowl and turned his back on her.

Jade stared at the brown mountains as the float entered Warren and headed towards the finish at the high school parking lot. Before it stopped completely, she jumped off. They'd planned to get ice cream after the parade, but she knew it wouldn't happen now. Brooklyn called her name, but Jade didn't look back. She'd learned how to be alone in these past few months and knew when she wasn't wanted.

Walking towards the highway, she hadn't gotten out of the parking lot when something soft slapped between her shoulder blades. A wet splash cascaded down her back. Another splash land on the pavement, a shred of blue rubber shuddering next to the puddle. Water balloons! A projectile screamed past her head, and she turned to see Max winding up for another throw. Before she could move out of the way, a green balloon hit her in the chest.

Max crouched next to a five-gallon bucket filled with water balloons. Jade sprinted towards it, zig zagging to avoid his next throw. He picked up the bucket and tried to run with it, but she closed the gap too quickly. He dropped the bucket and scooped water balloons into his shirt, then ran away from her in a lumbering jog. Jade reached the bucket, grabbed a balloon and chucked it at him as hard as she could. He threw one at the same time, and their balloons met in midair and splashed on the concrete. She grabbed more and stuffed them in her shirt.

Brooklyn swiveled her head back and forth between the two of them, and Jade threw a balloon at her. It hit her chest and sprayed her face. Brooklyn darted to the bucket to scoop up her own supply. A balloon exploded on her neck.

Jade turned to throw at Max but stopped smiling when she saw his face, taut with anger, eyes filled with tears. She dropped her arms, so they hung loosely at her sides, and stood still. A perfect target.

"This is for choosing a bully over your friends." He threw a balloon at her head, and she resisted the urge to duck. It splashed on her left ear.

He threw another one. "That's for my mom's missing birthday gift." The water cascaded down her shoulder.

His last throw sunk towards her hip. "That's for lying to me and Brooklyn." It sprayed her leg as it broke.

Jade dripped. Max glared at her and panted.

She deserved this.

She started to apologize, but a balloon slammed into her right thigh. Brooklyn stared defiantly at her. "That's for talking about me behind my back." She aimed another at Jade, and it broke on Jade's stomach. "That's for walking away when I was calling you."

Brooklyn turned and slammed one onto Max's head. "And that's for calling Jade blind and dumb."

Max's mouth dropped opened, and he backed away from Brooklyn. Jade slammed his shoulder with a red balloon. The three of them hurled balloons at each other until the bucket was empty, and they stood around it panting, their clothes dripping wet.

"I'm sorry," Jade said.

"Me too." Max replied.

"Finally!" Brooklyn stood hands on hips.

The sun broke through the clouds, and the worry she'd carried since Perdido dropped away. Jade felt lighter and happy. "Thanks for being my friends, guys. I wouldn't have any without you."

Brooklyn scoffed. "Tell me about it."

Max looked smug and nodded, lifting one eyebrow and folding his arms across his wet t-shirt with a sagging sheriff star.

Jade pulled her friends together in her arms and squeezed until Brooklyn yelped. She laughed, then let go. "Anyone else want ice cream?"

FORTY-EIGHT

Lita

LITA PRACTICED a few combinations and jogged in place in front of the mirror. Third on the fight ticket. The second fight had started, so she could be called into the cage anytime. She paced in a choir room filled with shelves of sheet music and a closet of white robes. A gold cross sat atop a blue framed mirror with "Rejoice In His Glory" embossed in script along the frame. A bumper sticker affixed to a wooden desk stated *God is My Sparring Partner.*

Lita didn't normally fight in a church hall, but the pastor was a fighting fan who'd convinced some of the Arizona gyms to broaden their appeal and cut out the drunken fan base. She'd met him when she'd arrived, a clean-cut man with auburn hair, a trim, brown beard and clear blue eyes with a shiny eagerness to please. The back of his shirt had an image of large white boxing gloves at the foot of a cross with: "Jesus Knocks Me Out" written below.

Cap went out to watch the fight's progress, but Kroker stayed with her. They'd be in her corner throughout the fight, coaching and giving her water and ice between rounds. One of Kroker's fighters had lost by submission in the third round of the first fight. Lita had never been submitted. She preferred to fight on her feet, and if she got thrown to the ground, she scrambled like a spider to stay on top and attack her opponent's limbs or trunk.

The crowd roared and applauded in the other room. Her pulse quickened. Had the fight ended? She threw another combo set and did some squat jumps around the room on her toes. Her whole family had come. Heck, half of Bisbee had made it to Tucson.

Karmen, who had watched one fight years ago and had sworn never to attend another—*I've never seen so many white men, thick necks and trucker caps, like NASCAR on steroids*—had promised she'd go to this fight, lured by the G-rated Christian family version of MMA. But her water had broken that afternoon, and she and Felix had gone to the hospital. Lita's fight mattered little compared to the birth of a child, but right here, right now, she had to focus. She boxer-shuffled around the room, swinging her arms, trying to stay loose.

The crowd cheered wildly. Cap came back into the room. "We're on." He nodded at Lita whose heart surged into her throat. Kroker called her over and took both of her gloved hands. Sweat broke out on her forehead.

"You know what you got, Wildcat. Calm your nerves in the first round and don't rush in. Get a feel for her. Take your time. Look for an opening, and don't hesitate when you see it." He shook her hands, loosening up her arms as she trotted in place. "You've got one of the best right hooks I've ever seen, and your cross is a devastating follow-up. Work to your strengths." He dropped her hands and squeezed her shoulders then led her into the hall. Lita took a deep breath and trotted out the door. Cap and Kroker followed with a bucket of ice and water for the corner.

As she walked into the hall, applause and shouts greeted her. She kept her eyes focused laser-like on the ring but heard the voices of friends and family. The referee frisked her. The cut man applied Vaseline to her face.

JoJo "The Terminator" Ames was already in the cage. The nickname came from her opponent's strong submission record, so Lita would have to watch her ground game. She studied JoJo as she swung her arms and stretched. Taller, a bit thicker, blonde hair tightly braided against her scalp, she looked younger than Lita, maybe late twenties.

The fight bell sounded, and The Terminator came in fast and hard. Lita met every takedown attempt with a jab or a hook and connected enough to make her opponent wary of rushing in. They clinched, a meeting of sweat and muscle and panting bodies, then Lita twisted her shoulders to free herself and back away, throwing a left hook as they separated.

Lita attacked with a flurry of combinations to push her foe across the mat and pin her to the cage. Her opponent grabbed her in a clinch and held her close. Lita shifted her hips, leaning into The Terminator while fighting to gain control and avoid her opponent's arms. The Terminator strained to take it to the mat, but Lita wanted to fight on her feet. She threw a few body shots then pushed back from her opponent, landing a cross as she pulled away. The Terminator's head rocked back, and she stumbled into the cage. Lita jumped to strike but got caught by a wild left hook and knocked off-balance. She lurched sideways and got hit with a jab before she recovered her feet. The Terminator grabbed her left leg and took her down.

Fuck. This was not where she wanted to be. Her opponent fought for side control, and Lita defended. If she could wrap her legs around the Terminator, she could effectively defend her guard and look for a submission.

In nine years of fighting, she'd won only by strikes or decision. She'd never submitted an opponent. As she countered the Terminator's mount attempt, she kept her arms tight near her face to create space but with enough pressure to separate her from her foe. The Terminator transitioned to strengthen her hold, and Lita pushed against her, shifting her hips to the side. Her opponent overcommitted, driving into her with too much force, and Lita used the fighter's momentum to push her body over and re-guard. Her arms and legs felt like rubber. She didn't know if she could get back to her feet.

The best defense is a strong offense. Her pop's words rang in her head. She'd attack from her back.

Keeping her legs wrapped around the Terminator, she grabbed her opponent's right arm, trapping the elbow on Lita's belly. She crossed her right arm over her opponent's trapped arm and pushed the Terminator's face away with her left. Her adversary reared up, giving Lita enough space to swing her right leg in front of her face while her other leg wrapped around the Terminator's back. She slapped her left arm over her opponent's wrist and glued herself to the woman above her so when she moved, Lita hung off her.

"Keep the angle!" Kroker's voice broke through the roaring in her head. "Release your right! Get the arm, Lita! Go for the arm!"

His voice echoed in her head. She felt frozen in place – spent, exhausted, and barely able to hold on. Her opponent leaned heavily on Lita's chest, her arm trapped between Lita's legs and body. Lita pushed her hips up into her opponent as she retracted her right arm from the space and joined it to her left at The Terminator's wrist. She squeezed her knees together to lock out The Terminator's movement then lifted her hips off the ground and pulled her heels downward, towards the floor. Her opponent's arm straightened then grew taut as Lita pushed her body up and pulled the arm down.

The crowd cheered. Kroker yelled. Lita's body lifted as her opponent tried to shake her off, but she held fast and pulled back hard.

"Hold!" Kroker shouted.

Lita held. The ref leaned over them, and the Terminator tapped her shoulder. The ref called it, and Lita released her opponent and collapsed on the mat to catch her breath. The Terminator sprawled next to her.

Lita had won her first fight by submission. She'd tapped out The Terminator. Kroker pulled her to her feet, and the women exchanged a hug and a handshake. As the ref called them into the center of the cage to announce the winner, a little body slammed into her hip and grabbed her by the waist. She stumbled sideways then righted herself.

Jupiter held onto her so tightly Lita couldn't move. She tried to pry herself free, but he clung to her like a baby monkey. He was crying, and she felt a surge of emotion bubbling up inside her. She'd never had so many people cheering for her. She'd never known how good it would feel to have a family in her camp.

She wrapped her free hand around his shoulders. "It's okay, Jupe. I won." He sobbed into her waist, and she rubbed his back with her gloved hand while the ref held up the other and declared her the victor.

FORTY-NINE

Jade

AUNTIE LITA PULLED off the highway at the hospital in Warren. She opened the back seat for Jade and her siblings. Oscar, who'd arrived in his own vehicle, scooped up Jersey in one arm and Jupiter jumped in the other. Auntie Lita opened the passenger door and held it open while Nana looked around in confusion.

"We're heading inside to see the baby," Auntie Lita told her. "It's a baby boy."

"A boy." Nana's face lit up for the first time since they'd started the drive. "I love boys."

Auntie Lita smiled wryly. "I know, Mom."

The word still startled Jade. No more wisecracks? No angry sighs or proclamations about Nana's ignorance?

Auntie Lita took Nana's hand and helped her out of the truck. She marched them all into the hospital, a one-story building with two rectangular wings stretching out in a V from the entrance. Oscar spoke to the woman at the front desk, and they proceeded down a quiet wing that grew louder as they neared a room at the end of the hall. A small crowd overflowed out the doorway. Jade recognized Karmen's parents and several of Karmen's brothers and sisters. Oscar set down Jersey and Jupiter and stuck his head into the room.

Felix gave a shout and whooped before he plowed through Karmen's family to grip Oscar in a tight hug.

"She did it!" He threw his arms back at the room, where Karmen sat amidst a pile of pillows holding a tiny bundle. Her hair was wild and tangled, her face tired and puffy, but she glowed with happiness. "Look at that Mama. And my son!" Felix beamed, thick chest broader than usual. He went to Karmen and kissed the top of her head before gently taking the baby from her arms and turning towards the doorway proudly. "Look at our boy."

The knot of Karmen's family loosened to let the new arrivals in, and three of Karmen's siblings exited to make room. Oscar clapped Ronaldo on the back and shook his hand as Auntie Lita worked her way towards Karmen. Nana stopped at the door, confusion written all over her face, so Auntie Lita went back, grabbed her hand, and pulled her towards Karmen. Felix paused to give them a close look at the baby, then carried the boy to Oscar.

"Oscar, my man, meet Victor." Jade circled around Oscar to get a look at the baby. She'd seen her brother and sister as newborns but didn't remember them looking like raisins. Victor was plump and wrinkled, with thin spidery veins running below his pale skin. His eyes were closed, but as Felix handed him to Oscar, they opened. He gazed at Oscar, opened his mouth, then turned his head rooting for milk.

Oscar looked nervous. "Uh-oh man. I think he needs his mama." He held the baby out.

Felix took him back eagerly and carried the boy to Karmen. "He's already a pro at latching on. Such a quick learner!" Felix stroked Karmen's head as the boy nursed, and he beamed at the little boy with such tenderness that tears welled up in Jade's eyes.

Auntie Lita reached for Karmen's hand and squeezed it.

"He's beautiful. Congratulations, you two. Good work!"

Auntie Lita touched Victor's tiny forehead then turned to Nana. "Mom, look at him. He's just hours old."

Nana hesitated then touched the baby's cheek with a thin, shaky hand.

"So handsome. I forget how tiny." She stroked the baby's cheek, then stopped, her hand hovering in the air. "Like Carmelita. My little girl." Her eyes lost their focus, and her outstretched hand moved to her chest.

Auntie Lita took Nana's hand and held it. Nana's eyes refocused on Auntie Lita, and she stared, her eyes moving across her face and tattoos. "Like Lita," she murmured.

They visited until Jersey and Jupiter, bored and ignored, began stomping up and down the vinyl-floored corridor. The next stop would be tougher, and Jade left the hospital dreading it. At the parking lot, Jupiter and Jersey climbed into Oscar's car while Nana and Jade followed Auntie Lita to her truck. Oscar drove up the hill towards downtown Bisbee and home while Auntie Lita turned in the opposite direction.

She drove one block and parked the truck in a circular drive in front of a large sign indicating they'd arrived at Manzanita Manor. Auntie Lita parked, blew out a large gust of air and sat stiffly with her hands on the steering wheel.

Auntie Lita spoke. "Mom, you're moving into a new home today." Her voice cracked, and Jade dropped a blurry gaze to her hands. She couldn't look at either one of them. She should have gone with Oscar.

"A new home? With you?"

"Not anymore." Auntie Lita's voice faltered. "But you can visit us. We'll visit you. This place is safer. You can do things. Hang out with people your age."

Nana, who'd been reaching for the car door handle, stopped. "My age? What fun is that?"

"Manzanita Manor. You'll like it," Auntie Lita persisted. "You've already got friends in the day program. Remember Errol?"

Jade knew this was the right thing to do, so why did it feel so bad?

Auntie Lita got out of the truck and opened the door for Nana. Jade offered her hand, and Nana held it as they walked in together. Nana didn't acknowledge anyone greeting her as they proceeded into the facility.

Elise met them. "Hi Evie, welcome! Hi Lita. Hi Jade."

"Who are you?" Nana narrowed her eyes at Elise.

"I'm Elise! I got you a room with a south facing window, and it's all set up. Let's go take a look. Bring your family!" Elise led her to a room with a large photo of Nana on the door. "Here we are."

Jade and Auntie Lita had come here yesterday to decorate the room with photos and hang Nana's clothes. They'd even brought Auntie Lita's throw rug from Mexico that Nana loved so much. Nana peered inside then entered. Jade followed her, leaving Auntie Lita and Elise speaking softly in the corridor. The room was simple: a single bed with a nightstand and dresser, a small bathroom with a shower.

Evie examined the photos that Jade had hung on the walls. "I know those people!"

She reached a tiny nightstand and examined a photo on it, one Jade had never seen until Auntie Lita put it there yesterday. It showed Evie standing with Grandpa Phillip, her arms holding a tiny baby Lita. Uncle Randy sat beaming on Phillip's shoulders. Jade's dad was next to his dad, and Laurel stood next to Nana. Sunburned and windswept, the kids looked wild and happy. Nana picked it up and examined it, her hand shaking. She looked up, her eyes brimming with tears.

"My family," she whispered.

Auntie Lita had finished speaking to Elise and moved into the room after them. She swallowed. "Yeah, I've had that for a while."

"Thank you," Nana said. She clutched the photo and gazed around the small room.

"You're welcome." Auntie Lita took a deep breath then lifted her eyebrows at Jade and tilted her head towards the door. "Ready to do this?"

Jade wasn't, but there was nothing else left to do. "Nana, we're going home now."

"Okay." Nana glanced around the room, her eyes touching on the photos and her clothes, but she followed Lita and Jade out of the room and into the corridor, still holding the photo from the nightstand. When they reached the double-locked entrance with a sign warning that the alarm would sound if opened without authorization, Auntie Lita and Jade stopped.

"Alrighty, Mom," said Auntie Lita. "We're going to leave."

"We'll come back tomorrow," Jade said.

"What?" Nana swung her head from Jade to Auntie Lita, her eyes wide. "I'm coming with you."

Jade's heart broke. "Nana, this is your home now," she said thickly. "You're going to live here now."

Nana shook her head, eyes wide, from Jade to Auntie Lita. "No." Her voice shook. "This isn't my home."

"It is now, Mom." Auntie Lita's voice sounded strangled.

Elise appeared behind Nana. "Evie," she said, coming alongside Nana's shoulder. "It's nearly lunchtime, and we've got live music today. Come join us."

Nana swung her gaze between Jade and Auntie Lita. "I want to go with you," she murmured.

Tears slipped down Jade's cheeks. She sniffed and looked down at the floor. She'd been sharing her room with Nana for the past three years. Leaving her here felt wrong, even though she knew it was right.

"Give us a hug, Mom, and we'll see you later." Auntie Lita's voice hitched. She cleared her throat. She hugged Nana tightly then stepped away.

Jade embraced Nana and wiped her eyes.

Nana touched her hair as they separated. "You're a beautiful girl," she said. "You look like Jake."

Jade choked back a sob, and when Elise pressed the button that released the door lock, Auntie Lita herded her out. She cast one look back at Nana, who seemed shrunken despite her height.

Auntie Lita wrapped an arm over her shoulders and guided her away. As soon as they made it out the second door and onto the sidewalk, Jade clung to Auntie Lita and cried. Auntie Lita didn't say anything, just rubbed circles on her back and took deep breaths. Jade felt as if she had just closed another chapter in her old life. It hurt, but this time felt different. She wasn't losing Nana for good. And Nana would be safer. Somehow she knew it would be okay.

FIFTY

Lita

LITA LOOKED at her phone and tried not to panic. Thirty minutes to go.

Scared. Shitless.

Had she taken care of everything? She hoped so, thanks to Karmen and Solana who'd pointed out little details she would have overlooked. Decorations. Flowers. Bottled water.

Felix had taken Jersey and Jupiter with him to Sierra Vista to pick up the karaoke machine, and Jade had gone to Brooklyn's an hour ago. It was weird to be alone.

Shit.

Lita paced and drummed her fingers against her thigh. The colors in the room popped out at her—silver, ivory and purple. Balloons and crepe paper streamers hung from the ceiling. Rows of chairs faced two tall balloon sculptures joined in an arch. Behind the arch, windows looked out on the mountains and houses of Bisbee.

She wanted to throw up.

Beads of sweat gathered on her forehead. She felt light-headed and plopped down on one of the vacant chairs. Another year, another birthday. But, for the first time in her adult life, she wasn't getting trashed.

Fuck the past. She'd take control of this day. No longer a day for mourning and getting shitfaced. It was time to break tradition. She'd have to survive first, though.

Fuck.

Her hands trembled as she wiped her forehead. Thank god she hadn't let Karmen convince her to wear a dress.

Karmen bustled into the room with Victor in her arms. "God, Lita. You look awful. What's wrong?"

Karmen's sister Solana entered, and her eyes widened at Lita.

"I'm either going to pass out or run away." Lita swayed. God, it was hot.

"No, no, no! Lita, come with me." Karmen motioned for Lita to follow her, then turned to her sister. "Solana, do you have the playlist? People will be arriving soon. Get some happy background music going!"

Solana smiled brightly. "Got it, chief!" She held her arms out to Victor and wiggled her fingers. "I think Victor wants to help me. Hand him over."

Victor practically jumped into Solana's arms, kicking his legs and smiling broadly as she set him on her hip.

Karmen took Lita's hand to lead her out of the room. "Oh my god, Lita, so sweaty!" She dropped Lita's hand and shook her own. "Let's get you out of this room."

Lita followed gratefully and entered the long, sterile hallway of the long-term care home. They ran into Elise, who smiled and congratulated her. "I don't think we've ever had a wedding here before."

Lita groaned, and Elise's eyebrows raised in surprised.

"Don't mind her. A few jitters," Karmen said, grabbing Lita's hand again and rushing out a side door.

The sunlight blinded her. She squinted. Her sunglasses were in the truck.

"I need my sunglasses."

"No, Lita." Karmen led her to a picnic table under the

shade of a tree. "You need to sit down with me and tell me why you're freaking out."

Lita moaned. "I don't know, Karmen. Is it normal to freak out before your wedding?" She sat down on the bench and put her arms on her thighs, hanging her head over her knees. "Oh god, is it me? I feel like I'm going to pass out. What if it's all a mistake? What if it ruins everything?"

"Lita, what the hell's going on? You know Oscar. Oscar loves you. And he knows you as well as I do. Or better!" She rubbed Lita's back. "Do you think I'd let you ruin everything? Sugar, look at how far you've come in the past year. Think about everything you've done. Has it been perfect? No. Are you perfect? Hell no! But who knows you, and who's been by your side? Oscar."

Karmen threw an arm over Lita's shoulders and leaned into her. "You get less nervous before a fight."

Lita stared at the ground and struggled to regain control of her breathing.

"Lita, look at me."

Lita looked up to see Karmen's eyes shining with tears. "Lita, you know better than anyone life is tough. And I'm not kidding you, marriage is hard. You remember when Felix and I hit a rough patch just after we got married?"

Lita nodded. She'd been shocked. Karmen and Felix had been together for seven years, and within three months of the wedding, Karmen was on the couch at Lita's.

"It took me by surprise how difficult it was to live with that man. But it didn't take long for me to realize I didn't want to live without him, toilet seats and dirty socks on the floor be damned." She paused. "You've been living together. So you've already crossed that bridge. And sweetie, Oscar's been your man since you met him. I've never seen anyone so doggedly in love. Despite your best attempts to get him to quit you."

Lita inhaled deeply. A warm breeze blew in from the south,

drying the sweat on her forehead. Her jittery legs were still bouncing. She stilled them.

Focus. She told herself. She closed her eyes and pictured Oscar.

"You're right, Karmen."

"Of course, I'm right."

"But Karmen, what if he realizes he's made a mistake? What if he leaves?" The next thought rushed in on her like an opponent going for a takedown. "What if he dies?" Her voice caught, and her shoulders sagged.

Karmen leaned her head on Lita's shoulder. "Everyone dies," she said softly. "It's about life. It's about how you live your life, Lita. You're the strongest person I know. Don't let fear keep you from living your life with Oscar. And the kids. I've never known you to be afraid of anything. Why now?"

Lita's breathing started to slow, and the fog in her mind began to clear. She didn't want to imagine a life without Oscar. He made her a better person. His humor, his patience, and his unrepentant love filled holes in her life she hadn't known existed.

"Fuck, Karmen, why am I freaking out?" She slapped her palm down on her knee and sat up straight.

Karmen grabbed Lita's hand. "Because you're human. It's okay to be scared."

"You're right, it's okay. But love shouldn't be tied to fear. I love Oscar. He's the best man I've known."

"*One* of the best men. Don't forget Felix."

Lita laughed. Why the fuck had she been freaking out?

"Holy hell, Karmen. I'm gonna get married."

"That's right! No more death and doubt."

Lita pulled Karmen into a hug. "I can't imagine a world without you, Karmen. Thanks."

Karmen squeezed her back. "Anytime, Lita."

Lita broke the embrace. "You don't need anything from me? I want to hunt down Oscar before we start."

"I don't need anything, but you know the groom's not supposed to see the bride before the ceremony."

"Karmen, you know I give zero fucks about tradition."

She found Oscar smoking by himself in the parking lot. He smiled at her, a reflexive smile, not the smile of a happy man.

"Hey, what's up? How come you're out here by yourself?"

Oscar tamped out his cigarette and threw the butt in a designated container. "Not a lot of people smoking these days. I guess it means I should quit." His mouth twisted, and he looked skyward. "And I've been wishing Mom were here."

"Oh, Oscar." Lita murmured. She wrapped her arms around him and squeezed his waist, leaning her head against his chest. "I'm sorry."

"She'd have been so happy to see me getting married. And she'd have been thrilled to know it was to you." His voice cracked.

"I know, Oscar. I wish she could, too. She loved you fiercely."

Oscar looked lost, and she hated to see it. "I love you fiercely, too, Oscar. And I could beat myself up for taking too much time to figure that out, but I'm here now. I'm not going anywhere. We're getting married today, and I'm going to stick by your side like glue until maybe you think it wasn't such a great idea."

"That'll never happen," Oscar said quickly, his voice rough. "This is the best idea I've ever had."

"Then let's do it," Lita said, letting go of his waist and taking his hand. "Let's get married."

FIFTY-ONE

Jade

THE CEREMONY HAD BEEN MERCIFULLY short, presided over efficiently by a tiny round woman with bright purple hair. Jersey started the ceremony by gleefully throwing fistfuls of flowers overhand at the guests as she walked up the aisle into the room. Jade and Jupiter had flanked each side of Auntie Lita. Jupiter had rebelled against wearing a tie, but when Felix loosened it so it hung more like a necklace, he'd relented. He literally bounced into the room with Auntie Lita, flashing a toothy grin at everyone.

Jade recognized lots of smiling faces—their neighbors Jodi and Elise, Karmen's parents, Auntie Lita's fighting coach—but many strangers sat among the guests. Some looked like fighters —taut, thick-necked and muscular, tattooed. Others she'd seen around town. Auntie Lita's brother Rafael had arrived from Hermosillo last night. He winked at Jade as she entered the room, and she smiled shyly.

Nana sat alone. Her face lit up when Jade and her siblings sat down next to her.

"I didn't know you'd be here!" Nana spoke loudly and looked at Jade in astonishment. She pointed to Auntie Lita. "And her. What's she doing up there?"

"Shh, Nana, let's watch."

"I know her." She spoke loudly and stared at Lita.

"She's getting married, Nana."

Nana's mouth dropped open in wonder. She stared at Lita, then furrowed her brow. "Where's her dress?"

"Shh Nana." Jade held her hand.

She looked at Jade and smiled. "You're a sweet girl."

Karmen and Felix bookended Lita and Oscar. Behind Jade, Victor fussed, and Karmen's mom murmured to him. A simple ceremony with no talk of god or obeyance, Auntie Lita and Oscar held hands, gazed into each other's eyes, and repeated their vows in steady-enough voices.

Only when the newly married couple turned to face the guests did Jade see the emotion in her aunt's eyes. She beamed through a sheen of tears, then clutched Oscar's hand and held it over her head as if she'd won a match. Felix whooped, and Oscar lifted her in the air. The entire room burst into applause.

Soon the karaoke machine kicked into full swing, and the doors to the hallway were flung wide open. Manzanita Manor residents walked past, stopping in the room to shimmy their hips, visit, and sample food. Nana carried on like a queen, greeting those who had come to pay their respects.

"So glad you could come," she told a trembly man with a cane. "Do you need a seat?" she asked a short woman with a walker.

Max and Brooklyn piled their plates high with chicken, tacos, and churros at the food table. Jade grabbed a plate and joined them, nudging Max out of the way to reach the enchiladas. These enchiladas were nothing like the soupy, soggy mess they served at Taco Bell, and the dish had become her favorite, one she'd practiced with Oscar a few times. He'd been teaching her to cook, a lesson here and there on the weekends when they had time. She'd learned more from him than Auntie Lita probably ever knew.

Was Oscar now her stepfather? She eyed him at the table

with her aunt. His hair was slicked back with gel, and he laughed at something Felix said. His eyes shone, and he looked handsome in his bright white shirt and black suit.

Next to him, her aunt wore a loose, spaghetti-string lavender top with a draped neck. Tattoos jumped out – a mandala like an unfolding flower sat on her shoulder, a Mexican skull rose out of her chest, a wildcat sat poised on her collar bone with an open mouth full of sharp teeth. She wore flowy ivory slacks Jade had never seen before, and her hair hung loose and curly over her shoulders. She'd stopped cutting her hair since the fight, and amazingly, Auntie Lita had beautiful hair.

"Your aunt has crazy tattoos." Max spoke through a mouthful of churros.

"She told me she doesn't know how many she has," Brooklyn chimed in despite her full mouth. Chili sauce dribbled down her chin.

"She's had tattoos since she was twelve. She did the first few herself."

"My dad would kill me if I got tattoos." Brooklyn hadn't wiped the sauce off her chin, and the bottom half of her mouth reminded Jade of a clown.

"My parents would send me to counseling." Max nodded.

Jade wondered what her dad and mom had thought of Auntie Lita and her tattoos, and what they'd think if she got tattoos. She sighed. It didn't matter. Thinking of her parents brought a familiar stab of sadness. The pain was a dull ache, no longer all-consuming, but she'd never stop missing them.

"Where's the wine?" Nana's voice sounded irritated. She stood by the table with her hands on her hips looking at the punch bowl and the coolers full of bottled water and soda. "Where can I find a drink around here?"

"There's no alcohol, Nana. Do you want punch?"

"I don't want alcohol. I want wine." Nana turned to her with one eyebrow raised. "Do you work here?"

Brooklyn giggled. Nana scowled at her, which made

Brooklyn laugh harder. Nana pointed her finger at the three of them.

"I'm watching all of you. Any funny business, and I'll ask you to leave."

"Sounds good, Nana. We'll watch our step."

Nana tilted her head and eyeballed Jade suspiciously. "Can you get me one of those?" She pointed to a casserole dish filled with chicken mole.

Jade scooped up some rice and topped it with chicken and sauce. "Anything else, Nana?" She turned to find Nana talking to Jodi, their neighbor. "Where do you want me to put this?"

Nana looked at her in surprise. "Put what?"

"Your food, Nana. You wanted some chicken."

Nana pursed her lips and shook her head. "No, I wanted some wine." She turned to Jodi. "Have you found the wine?"

Jodi smiled at Jade, then turned to Nana. "I haven't seen any wine, but there's a delicious punch. I could get you a glass of it."

Nana rolled her eyes. "If you say so."

By the time Jodi returned with the punch, Nana had wandered away, and Jade was standing alone holding Nana's plate. Jodi's eyes met Jade's, then looked around for Nana. She laughed.

"Let's deliver these to her, shall we?"

They delivered the food and drink to Nana. The stereo system squawked loudly, and Jade cringed as Felix tapped the microphone with his finger. "Testing." His voice barked at the guests, and everyone looked up.

"Uh, so I'd like to make a toast." The crowd quieted, and Felix ran his finger along his collar. Solana and a few others began circulating through the crowd, handing out glasses of non-alcoholic sparkling apple cider. "Many of you know I teach kindergarten."

"He's my teacher!" Jupiter exclaimed loudly.

The room laughed, and Felix winked at Jupiter, then continued.

"I love the beginning of each school year. The new students arrive, and boy are they nervous. Kindergarten students have to learn so many things. Where to put their stuff, how to line up, how to sit still, when to eat lunch, how to make friends and get along with other kids who are nothing like them." He looked at Oscar, sitting to his right.

"I met Oscar in kindergarten. He was one of those kids who was nothing like me, but we were seat partners, and he gave me his cookies during our first lunch hour together. His cookies! That's gold to a kindergartener. And during the rest of that year, I learned over and over that Oscar wasn't only generous, but loyal. No matter what was going on, Oscar had my back. We've been best friends since then, and I've never needed any other."

Felix turned to Lita with a broad smile and shook his head. "Now Lita—I met her many years ago. Karmen and I weren't a couple yet, though I was trying, I'll tell you." Karmen beamed and the crowd chuckled. "I was with Karmen's family at the Old Miner, and this tiny woman was sitting by herself. She didn't have half as many tattoos back then, but she was still as striking as she is now."

Auntie Lita grimaced and shook her head. Oscar slung his arm around her shoulders and leaned into her.

"If you know my wife, you know she doesn't have a shy bone in her body. She'll talk to anyone and learn their life story in fifteen minutes. So next thing I know, Karmen brings this stranger to our table, and I learned a few things about Lita, and they're still true today. First, she's a fighter."

The room laughed.

"And I don't mean in the cage. She fights for what she believes, and she fights for what she cares about. I rarely see Lita back down.

"Second, I learned she can't sit still. If she were in my kindergarten class, she'd be the student who bounces out of her seat when she's supposed to be working, or who fidgets so much it disturbs the other kids.

"And third, she loves to dance. Before her, I'd never seen anyone dance on tables at the Old Miner." The room laughed, and Lita smirked. "When Oscar returned to Bisbee and saw Lita at the next gathering at the Old Miner, I could tell my man was lost. I'd never seen him dance voluntarily with anyone, but he never stopped. He couldn't take his eyes off her."

Felix smiled at Lita and Oscar. "Lots of others got up and danced, but Oscar danced the hardest. I watched as Lita captured my best friend's heart."

The room stilled. Felix pinched his fingers on the bridge of his nose and cleared his throat. Oscar wore a slightly embarrassed smile, but his eyes shone. Lita knocked into his shoulder with hers then sat straight again.

"For ten years I've watched Oscar and Lita dance around each other, like fighters in a cage. Karmen and I, and probably lots of you, have wanted to see this day for a long time. We didn't know if we'd ever get here."

Felix raised his glass of sparkling cider in a toast and turned to face Lita and Oscar. "This day makes me happy because I know you two have started down this path together with clear hearts. When I look at you, I see two people who know each other and know what they want. I see the happiness you give each other, and I see the love and strength you'll need to carry you through the rough times. Most of all, I see two people committed to each other and to these three beautiful kids, Jade, Jupiter, and Jersey.

"So I propose a toast to the happy couple. May they continue to love and grow together. May they face their new life and challenges with the strength and loyalty they both share. And may they remember to always dance."

Jade lifted her glass and toasted, sipping her sparkling cider. Next to her, Brooklyn bounced in her seat, her glass already empty. Max sat next to Brooklyn in a blue dress shirt and a bolo tie with a Bisbee Blue gem set in silver. It contrasted well with his hair. He looked way too serious but flashed a peace sign when he saw Jade studying him. She grinned and had an idea.

"Hey, Brooklyn!"

Brooklyn looked up immediately.

"Give me your glass."

Confusion crossed her face, but Brooklyn handed her glass to Jade. Jade poured some of her own cider into the glass and handed it back to her friend.

"I propose our own toast," she said, holding her glass high. Both Brooklyn and Max raised their glasses again. "To the three of us sticking together. All for one, and one for all."

She touched glasses with her friends and drank.

FIFTY-TWO

Evie

EVIE RAISES her glass in the air and sips, then stares at the bubbles rising from its bottom. She sniffs it. Too sweet and no kick. This isn't champagne. She grimaces and looks around the room for wine. People chat and laugh. Evie stares at the bride, somehow familiar, sitting at the front table. *She likes to dance?*

A curvy woman with thick wavy hair stands up next to the bride, her face open and happy. Evie immediately likes her.

"I want to propose a toast to the newlyweds, and their new family," the woman says. She holds up her glass.

"To Lita, Oscar, Evie, Jade, Jupiter, and Jersey. May love unite you. May you love, respect, and encourage each other to be the best together and apart."

The woman lifts her glass and drinks. Evie's glass is empty. She finds a different one and tosses it back, then grimaces. It tastes like apple juice. When the room erupts into cheers, Evie's arm jerks, and she drops the glass. But she doesn't move to pick it up. She's captivated instead by the small woman on stage. The bride. Her eyes, her smile. Something about the woman attracts her.

Evie swivels her head back and forth from the woman holding the microphone to the bride.

The bride.

Lita?

Full, shoulder-length hair, beautiful brown skin, and soft eyes.

Like her dad.

She marches over, interrupting the bride's conversation with the curvy brunette who still holds the microphone.

"Lita?"

The bride stops talking. Both women stare at her. "Are you Lita?"

The bride nods slowly, eyes locked on Evie. Evie points to the buxom woman. "She said you just got married."

The bride nods again.

None of this makes sense. Her daughter throws sand at her brothers and sister and chases them across the beach. She's a little girl.

"Where are your brothers and sister?" She scans the room for familiar faces.

Lita's smiled falters. "It's only me, Mom."

Evie can't understand it. Lita, all grown up. Her daughter. A bride.

"Give me that." She thrusts her hand towards the microphone. The woman looks startled but hands it over.

"Hello?" The microphone squawks, and the room quiets. All eyes turn to Evie. She stares at the microphone in her hand. What does she want to say?

"Mom?"

Evie remembers. "My daughter. She's my daughter." Fifty pairs of eyes watch as Evie speaks. The bride's face opens in surprise.

"It's been a long time since I've seen her." A bubbling, burning ball of emotions roil inside Evie's chest. She feels hot and flushed. "She's my littlest girl. A beautiful bride."

The groom wraps his arms around Lita. Her little girl, Lita, a beautiful woman. Married.

Evie frowns. "I've had shadows on my heart for the longest time," she says softly, pensively. The room falls silent.

Lita's eyes shine with tears. Evie's own face feels hot and damp. "I looked for you and couldn't find you." She stares at her daughter, her beautiful daughter, and lets the microphone fall to her side. "I've missed you so much."

Lita swallows and her voice is tiny, taut. "I've missed you too."

Evie embraces her tattooed daughter whose hard body fits inside her arms. Her heart swells with joy. So many things are unclear, but not this moment. She's found Lita.

Lita pulls back and wipes her cheeks. She wraps her arm around the groom who smiles at Evie.

Evie tilts her head. "You're a handsome man."

Lita laughs. "This is my husband, Oscar."

Evie narrows her eyes and studies the couple. "How long have you been married?"

"About five minutes," Oscar replies.

Evie lifts her eyebrows in appraisal then confides to Lita. "He smells good."

"We're glad you're here, Mom," the bride says.

"Where else would I be?" Evie wonders aloud.

The light in the room softens as the sun streams through the windows and sinks lower in the sky. Evie marvels at the fullness of life in this room—young and old bodies flush with energy and pulsing with happiness.

Music starts playing, and Evie's hips sway in rhythm next to Lita and her husband. Her hand is holding a microphone, but she has no idea why. She taps it, and it squawks. The music continues to play, but she lifts the microphone to speak.

"A word, please." The room quiets, and someone lowers the music. Evie speaks into the mic. "I haven't found a drop of liquor in this place, but if someone's got a flask, let me know. I'll cozy up with you in a corner." She lowers the mic, and the room bursts into laughter. Evie narrows her eyes. She doesn't get the joke.

She sighs. Her heart feels lighter than it has in years. As the music increases in volume again, Evie drops the mic, lifts her arms into a pirouette and dances.

Acknowledgments

This novel has gone through many iterations and many years to reach fruition. It couldn't have happened without the help of my friends, family and fellow writers. Though writing itself is a solo effort, I've leaned on an amazing number of others to help me hone Shadows into the story it is today. If I forget anyone in this long list, forgive me.

Thank you to my beta readers: Sheila Ramsay, Carin Peterson, Margaret Becker, Tami Jimenez, Fiona Claire, Gwen Higgins, and Barbara Mealer. Your input answered questions, filled plot holes and helped me strengthen the story I wanted to tell. Deep thanks to Cheryl Andrichuk, who stepped in, dove deep into Shadows and helped me during a moment of panic.

Much thanks to my writing group, The Scribblers, and especially Cheryl who invited me to give the group a try. Fellow Scribblers, your feedback has been invaluable. Whether strengthening structure, tightening prose or asking for more information, your comments on the initial chapters strengthened the entire novel. Though members have changed a few times as the group has evolved, thank you to Cheryl (again!), Susan, Ric, Fred, Lesley, Coco, Ruth, Lorraine, Lauwo, Isobel, and Charles.

While I felt comfortable blending another culture into my story, I wanted to ensure that I wasn't promoting cultural inaccuracies, representation issues, bias, stereotypes, or problematic language. I worked with Writing Diversely, specifically Alejandra Oliva, who offered suggestions to help avoid problematic approaches.

As a non-fighter who's been around mixed martial arts fighting vicariously via an addicted husband, I researched the fight scenes. Part of that research involved visiting Pride Gym in Trail, BC, which offers Muay Thai, Jiu Jitsu, Kickboxing and mixed martial arts training to kids and adults. Many thanks to owner/trainer Glen Kalesniko and trainer Brandon Krumm who worked their way through twenty pages of fighting and training scenes to point out inaccuracies and improvements. Out of their wheelhouse, both came through with a decisive flying knee finish.

Some tasks I find daunting, and book cover design is one of them. Thanks to all who helped me select the cover design. I would probably still be deciding if not for your feedback. Another challenge is marketing. Thank you to Aryn VanDyke of Book Rockstar for breaking it down into small pieces and helping me get my stories into readers' hands.

Lastly, my family. Loren, MMA is your world, not mine, but without your love for the sport, I wouldn't have written this novel. Thank you for your undying support and never-ending encouragement. To William and Hannah, it's difficult to put into words everything you mean to me. I love you all deeper than a grappler sinks an underhook.

About the Author

Elizabeth Oldham has been writing her entire life. She has lived and worked all over the world but now resides in the Kootenay region of British Columbia with her husband, many chickens and a crazed rescue dog. She has two grown children and spends her time camping, curling, and exploring the mountains on foot and on skis.

Her first novel, Tail of Humanity, was published in 2023, was a finalist for the 2023 Best Book Awards and shortlisted for the 2024 Whistler Independent Book Award. Shadows on the Heart is her second novel.

Find out more about Elizabeth at her website: https://elizabetholdham.com/

Stay informed about Elizabeth's new work: https://elizabetholdham.substack.com/